THE CUR
PO

SE OF

VER

THE CURSE OF POWER

UNDISCOVERED

BOOK ONE

MELINA M. GIVENS

THE *Curse* OF *Power*

"*Two worlds were never meant to collide,
but now there's a daughter born of both
sides.*

*By blood of the sea,
by heart of the land,
she will return and claim it all again.*"

- THE WITCH'S PROPHECY

This is a work of fiction. All characters, places, and events are the products of the author's imagination or are used fictitiously.

THE CURSE OF POWER

Copyright © 2025 by Melina M. Givens

Edited by Eleanor Smith
Cover Design by Melina M. Givens
Cover Art by Melina M. Givens
Interior Design by Melina M. Givens

ISBN 979-8-9924997-0-4 (paperback)
ISBN 979-8-9924997-1-1 (hardback)
ISBN 979-8-3492-0387-9 (e-book)

First Edition May 2025

To my best friend—Addison,

*If I'd never met you, I'd brave a new world
if it meant finding you for the first time*

To my platonic soulmate—this one is for you

. ° .*. ⭐ .*. ° .

CONTENTS

N
NW
NE
W
E
SW
SE
S
Ari'an
Angelik Clan
Rividyun
Geynival
Flychestar
Koifinn
Clan
Beach House
Havielat
Shari
Taelani
Adleian
Kingdom
Kaerious
Rhorvy
Troburn
Lauvik
Morian
THE COVE OF
LOST DREAMS
Ociavian
Kingdom
Yleigh
WYNDE

Aemyric

Adleian
Kingdom

Tallesyn

Jaanerih

★ Royan

Jellean
Kingdom

Zrakan

AN

THE FORGOTTEN

Pularis

No'ryn ★

Orcanihan Kingdom

UNDISCOVERED I PLAYLIST

For all my readers who like their stories told through song or for those who simply want to listen.

° ·*· + **BOOK ONE** ·*· ° ·

A Little Wicked - Valerie Broussard
Castle - Halsey
Hold on to Me - Valerie Broussard
In My Blood - Shawn Mendes
I Wanna Be Yours - Arctic Monkeys
Infinity - Jaymes Young
Morally Grey - April Jai
Nightmare - Halsey
No Mercy - Austin Glorgio
Power Over Me - Dermot Kennedy
Reasons - Beth Crowley
Sweeter Place - SVRCINA
The Heart Wants What It Wants - Selena Gomez
Young Love & Old Money - Elizabeth Gerardi
1-800-273-8255 - Logic

POWER

.*⭐ VERA ⭐*.

The stars are beautiful tonight. I hold out my hand to the perfectly painted sky and connect each of them until a picture is in my mind.

Taurus.

Aquarius.

Scorpio.

The constellations come together effortlessly. Although the rooftop always allows access to this vast open sky, there's something different about tonight.

Perhaps it's the air. It's colder than the average March night.

Or it could be the sky...Something about it feels strange, too. There's this insistent pulling that begs me to keep staring. I search it for a sign of what that tug is, but it all seems normal.

The stars are out, the moon's brightness casts its usual glow across the tops of trees, and there isn't a cloud in the sky. Seeing the sky so clearly here is rare, but I would hardly think that's a reason to feel so odd.

A dull pain shoots through my wrist, and I let out a gasp. The constricting feeling on my nerves dissipates not long after rubbing the area.

Maybe this paranoid searching is just the nerves for my party beginning in…What time is it?

I've been out here for a while, judging by the way my skin has grown as cold as ice.

The clock on the farthest wall reads 8:00 p.m.

I guess that means it starts right now. I climb back through my cracked window and rush downstairs to see the smiling faces of my closest friends.

"Way to keep us waiting, birthday girl," Rosalind says with an adjustment of her circular glasses. Before I can respond, she shoves a large present into my hands while everyone else does the same with their gifts.

"I only have so many hands!" I yell with a laugh. I love their thoughtfulness in always going above and beyond for my birthdays, but a part of me feels wrong accepting them. Frankly, I don't think I deserve it. I mean, I have everything I could ever need, so why should I be the one who gets more?

"You'll make do," Elliot says with a rough slap on my back, throwing me off balance. I nearly drop everything as I try to remain upright.

"Elliot!" I say exasperatedly, with a glare in his direction. He holds up both hands and his hazel-brown eyes widen as he backs away into the kitchen. "If you eat my food, I swear I'll make you sleep outside!" I don't actually mind, but there's something so fun about messing with him.

Somehow, within the span of twenty seconds, he manages to eat half of an extra-large chocolate bar sitting on the countertop.

"Okay, look, Vera, hear me out."

"I'm not hearing you out."

"Vera, Vera, VER—" Before Elliot finishes the word, I drag him outside and lock the door. He tries to give me a sad, guilt-ridden look, but with one glance past my face, he bursts into laughter.

Unsurprisingly, Liam had finished the rest of it. He smiles like I can't see the brown smear across his cheek from where he likely missed his first attempt to shove it in his mouth.

"Liam, out," I command with a terrible attempt at an angry expression. He slowly walks to the patio door and unlocks it, stepping outside with Elliot. "Inaya, please remind me why I still invite those two to my parties?"

"Because who else would make us laugh until our stomachs hurt?" she answers and takes my hand, leading us outside with the others. Rosalind makes her way to her favorite seat next to the pool, motioning for us to join her while the boys play...*a game*? To be quite honest, it looks more like two amateur wrestlers fighting while role-playing as horses, but to each their own.

"Did you bring your mom's chicken biryani she made for us the other day?" Rosalind asks Inaya with a look of childish delight. I think she forgets how often she asks that same question.

"She only makes that when you come over because otherwise we would get tired of eating it," she responds with a laugh. A look in my direction makes it clear she's aware of the same thing I noticed. We usually ignore Rosalind's forgetfulness because anything that can make her day brighter is worth it.

She deserves it more than anyone.

"What? I don't go over there *that* often," Rosalind says while sticking out her tongue.

"Rose, I can count on two hands how many days you haven't come to my house after school this year. That's saying something."

"Okay, well, your mom just cooks the best food. What can I say? *Also...*" Rosalind pauses with a pointed finger. "She told me she loves my company, and I can come over for dinner anytime I want."

Inaya's mom knows how Rosalind is treated at home, and if it was legal, I think she'd kidnap her and never let her parents see her again.

"It just so happens that anytime I want is all the time," she adds with a toothy smile. Sometimes, I wonder if Rosalind realizes how bad her life is or if she's grown numb to it all.

Their conversation becomes a gentle buzz as I stare into the distant sky again. There is something out there—something different. It's wrong, a disruption, but I still can't pinpoint what it could be.

A voice calling my name breaks through the haze.

"Vera? Are you alright, honey?" Mom asks with a look of intense concern. She sits beside me and rubs my leg, waiting for me to respond. I feel her pity and wish I could tell her to stop without hurting her feelings. I hate pity.

"Huh? Oh, yeah, I'm alright," I lie to ease her mind. Although I think she knows how troubled my thoughts usually are, she tries to ignore them. My parents are as perfect as they could be, so she knows it's not her fault.

Still, I try to keep her from what I feel to protect her happiness. It's better only one of us is in pain.

"The rest of your friends got in the pool. I think they tried to invite you to come in, but you were completely zoned out. Join them. Today's a *big day*. Make the most of it." Something about how she said those two words sends a shiver down my spine.

I know I'm overthinking it, but I can't shake the feeling that something is seriously wrong.

Don't think.

Don't think.

I take a deep breath and smile, putting up the mask I'm so used to wearing.

I hop in the pool and grab onto Liam's shoulders since he's the only one of us who can touch the bottom with flat feet. That's when I notice Inaya, angry yet smiling, while Rosalind cries with laughter.

"I have some very choice words I'd like to say to you, Rose." At this, I notice Inaya's hijab, still intact but soaking wet from getting shoved into the pool. I can't hold back the chuckle that escapes at the usually graceful Inaya looking completely disheveled.

Her smile dips slightly and tightens at the edges, and I realize how secretly angry and ashamed she is underneath the act. However funny it might have been in the moment, it isn't right for Rosalind to disrespect her culture, even if we are all friends.

"Liam and I have our eyes closed, don't worry!" Elliot calls out. The group knows how important it is to Inaya to stay modest, and a skin-tight, soaking-wet outfit is far from it.

"We didn't see anything! Tell us when you're okay with us looking," Liam adds. She crawls back out of the pool, but not before shoving Rosalind underwater. Grabbing a towel and roughly drying off, she calls out that the boys are good to open their eyes.

In the proper way of a loving friendship, Liam grabs me by the waist and throws me across the pool with his regained vision. I swim back to the surface, spitting out mouthfuls of water and aggressively rubbing my eyes.

I love this small group. Even when I feel completely alone, I know it's impossible with the four of them by my side, but would I even know if I felt complete if I never had before?

I think they make me feel that way, but how can I know until I'm sure I've felt it?

I shove away the thought. They're my closest friends, and they mean the world to me. That's all that matters.

We go inside to see Mom holding five unique towels for everyone.

Many years ago, I started the tradition of sleepovers on my birthdays with all of us, so she made each of us a towel representing our personalities.

Inaya's towel features flowers of all kinds coming together to make a beautiful bouquet. Rosalind's includes clefs, quavers, and other notes with quotes from her favorite songs. Liam's has horses roaming free on an expansive prairie. Elliot's contains many Hufflepuff symbols and paraphernalia from his favorite book series: *Harry Potter*. Finally, mine is a towel with paint splatters and brushes of every design and color.

Everything blurs together, from opening presents, blowing out candles, eating far too much dessert, and ending on the rooftop where my night began. We all lie together beneath the blanket of stars, huddling close to avoid the chill of this strangely cold evening.

"Vera! Are you seeing this?" Rose asks with a look of amazement plastered across her face. I look up to where she points a shaking hand to a bright, copper-colored moon.

"It's a blood moon. No wonder I felt there was something off about tonight," I mutter, but it *wasn't* a blood moon—not earlier this evening. It was a waning crescent, and the color was normal. The second the thought escapes my mind, my eyes go wide, and I reach to clutch my neck.

I can't breathe.

The realization hits me as the last breath of air leaves my body. I heave for another moment before I regain a sense of stablility.

What is happening to me?

Am I going into shock?

Am I allergic to something I ate?

Even as my breath starts returning, the anxiety lingers. I felt like there was something off about today, but I'm almost certain now.

"What the hell, Vera? What just happened?" Liam asks, placing an arm around my shoulder. I don't know how to answer that because I'm left speechless. Never in my life have I lost my breath so suddenly and without reason.

"That's not just a blood moon. It's a supermoon as well. Look at the size of it," Inaya states, never having moved her gaze from the exceptionally captivating sight.

I take a deep inhale but get cut short as an unfamiliar power floods through my veins. A dark, empty part of my mind explodes, with light flooding all around, but only I can see it. It lights up everything around us, the sky turning so bright I might've mistaken it for daylight.

Energy.

Strength.

Freedom.

My senses are bright. My mind is sharp. My body is strong.

I feel as though individual cells are exploding and expanding inside of me, leaving rhapsodies of bliss in their wake.

I feel so strange, yet I've never been more alive. I feel as if I could jump straight off this roof and fly.

As the hundreds of questions flooding my head slow down, my mind becomes a void of darkness. The world paints darkness as scary, the void of all light, the deepest of one's despair, but they're wrong. Darkness is a cloud of freedom and a blanket of protection.

As my metaphysical body drifts into a more profound state of pure relief, my mind floods with images of an unfamiliar world.

I see a young woman. She's crying—no, wait, she's *angry*. Her eyes glow a bright blue before fading out to be a deep emerald-green I nearly mistake as my own.

Her hair is pale flaxen with curls cascading past her shoulders. She's astonishingly beautiful, but I can see a look of affliction on her face.

She's speaking. Or more like yelling, but I can't understand it. The words are foreign, and the language is nothing I've heard before. This doesn't feel like a dream; it's almost like a memory that's been locked away for my entire life.

I try to turn my head to see the faces of the other yelling voices, but my neck is stuck, and my mind becomes blank once more.

I'm underwater. That's not right—I've been underwater this entire time.

I see the dark ocean all around with new voices speaking in the same peculiar language I heard before. What is happening? *Who am I?*

"VERA!"

I'm forced awake with four arms shaking me rapidly. I look around in confusion, eyes flaring after being ripped from an immersive dream.

"What just happened?" I ask no one in particular, rubbing my eyes to readjust my vision.

"You started shaking and passed out! Are you alright?" Elliot asks with distress, putting the back of his hand on my forehead. I realize I'm no longer on the roof but lying on my bed. I take a long time to respond, sighing loudly.

Sitting up with a wince, I orient my thoughts enough to speak.

"I—I don't know. I think I got lightheaded or something." I've never lied to them, especially not so easily. What's gotten into me? "I think I'm going to go to bed early tonight. I'm sorry we didn't get to do everything we planned."

"That's completely fine. We care more about your health than having fun," Inaya says with a gentle hand on my shoulder before moving to the floor with Rosalind.

"We'll just play some cards and then go to sleep too!" Rosalind announces with her bright, girlish grin. I give her a weak one in return before falling back into a deep, trance-like sleep. Maybe I'll have a chance to reenter that dream—or memory—and find out what the hell is going on.

With the last of my consciousness, I hear a voice from a nearby television.

"This is truly incredible! The last super blood moon was exactly seventeen years ago today. Many astronomers have said that this was a surprising sight, and none of their equipment predicted it until it seemed to change. All records and eye accounts claim the moon was nowhere close to full, but then it seemed to morph from a crescent to a sphere in the blink of an eye. Is there something else go—" I can't make out the final words as I give my mind over to the relief of sleep, my body drifting into a calm, faraway land.

KAILEAH

2

FORGOTTEN HISTORY

.*✮ KAILEAH ✮*.

(SEVENTEEN YEARS PRIOR)

Iscream as the peak of labor hits me with an intense wave. I feel angry tears streaming down my face, washing away in the water that surrounds us all, but not from the pain. Being in a room with the three people you loathe more than anything would bring anyone to such a state.

I scream again, but this time it's not because of the pain rippling through my uterus; it's remembering everything associated with this room—the room where the king had his way with me.

Night. After. Night.

I lay on the royal-blue bed where I would cry myself to sleep after he left. The ceiling still has the same glittering chandelier that should make any young girl smile at its beauty, but not me. All I can see in those perfect crystal shards is the memory of everything he did to me. I watched it on each one of those tiny reflections.

The smell of sweat and fear radiates through the room, only adding to the rage I feel flowing through me.

With each excruciating push, I see a wider smile spread across the king's wretched face. It adds more wrinkles to his already old complexion, showing that his age is far beyond mine: *his child wife*. His dark hair has streaks of gray to prove just how hoary that disgusting being is, and his sunken eyes prove how little light is left inside of him.

If there ever was any to begin with.

No one with a conscience would do what he has done to me. No one with a soul or single grain of humanity.

I turn to see my parents looking anxious and impatient at the time this birth is taking. Gods, I hate them. It's hard to say who I hate more...the king or those two sorry sacks of fish scraps that I must call my parents.

My mother has done nothing more for me than what I am doing now, birthing a child. My father, *oh my father*, he has contributed nothing to my life beyond the sperm used to make me. The only thing I can accredit the two of them for is giving me the worst childhood I could've asked for.

Sorry, Mother and Father, let me speed this up for you. I know you have so many better places to be, I scream out in my mind, wishing I could say it aloud but my voice fails me. The only sounds that come from my mouth are the excruciating screams from the pain.

I roll my eyes, but they never notice. They never notice *anything* about me.

With a last agonizing push, my baby girl is born, healthy and crying. I take deep breath after breath until my nerves and heart are calm once more.

The midwife places her small body against my chest, and I cry, gazing upon my beautiful daughter.

My little Asherah, my perfect princess.

I'm so beyond happy she's okay, and while I'm scared of what my life will become now that she's here, I'm ready to experience it. Somehow, with her close to me, I know I can face anything.

She will not know the life I have had.

She will only know complete and utter love and happiness.

From the first look of pure innocence on my baby's face, I know I will always keep her safe. I don't care how difficult it will be to raise my child. I will forever strive to be the best mother in the world, and she will never know my suffering. All my little Asherah will know is unconditional love and attention at every waking moment as long as I live.

All my life, I thought a happiness this completely consuming would be impossible to find, but as I clutch her small body to my bare skin, I know I was mistaken.

However, my feeling of bliss is cut short by my *husband's* voice.

"Oh my gods, she's beautiful. She'll make an excellent princess," he says, swimming closer. His deep, blood-red tail and matching fin become ever more apparent with each movement toward me. I might have even found a color beautiful once if I didn't know what it meant about his inner soul.

"Don't come any closer, you monster," I yell at him. Perhaps it is after my outburst, but everyone finally notices the entrancing blue glow encapsulating my daughter.

They're going to find out.

They all know I didn't love the king, and he definitely didn't love me.

"That's so cute! She was conceived from pure love!" the clueless midwife states proudly.

Pure love.

How funny.

It's true her father and I were indeed in love when she was conceived, but her father isn't here to appreciate such an honor. "I'm thrilled for Your Majesties," she says with a small bow before swimming out of the room. The king closes the distance between us and eyes me closely, and I see my parents shift even more nervously before containing themselves.

We can't have the king knowing you suspect something, can we?

"Explain yourself, Kaileah. Why is our daughter glowing the color of your *maemōjik?*" Maemōjik, the emotion a witch feels the least, and mine so happens to be love. "You know more than anyone in this room that our daughter was conceived out of nothing close to love." I fight the urge to spit in his face at his taunting words.

"Why don't you use that thick skull of yours to think, *Dorian?* I love my daughter, and she has been developing inside me for the better part of a year. Of course she is going to be born glowing with love," I say in a harsh, sarcastic tone that I hope hides the reality of why she glows such a color. If he finds out...

"Watch your mouth, girl. Now that your parents' deal has been fulfilled, I have no need to keep you alive." I hear a knock at the door, and a young witch pokes her head through.

"Are you ready for the birth certificate, King Argyros?" The king sighs and glares in the girl's direction.

"Yes, make it quick," he growls in a tone that makes the young witch shake. She swims into the room, holding a document with words branding into parchment as she speaks.

The majickal binding of royal birth. Nothing can shatter it, and so long as my daughter's name appears on that sheet, regardless of whether she is only of my blood, she will be heir to this kingdom. The thought pulls my glower into a smile.

"Princess Asherah Dlari Argyros of Adlei, daughter of Queen Kaileah Astorah Dlari and King Dorian Lycidas Argyros. Heir to the Adleian throne." The words finish appearing on the page, so she rolls it neatly and seals it with a strong majickal bond.

The runes flare to life before dulling.

After gathering the rest of her things, she swims out the door, but not before I see the look of near terror on her face, having been in the presence of our kingdom's tyrannical king.

Little does she know she just made the worst mistake of her life.

Not long after, a familiar face comes into view as the king is about to speak. My friend, the kind witch with long black hair and a beautiful icy blue hiding beneath swims through the room with such grace that I become slightly jealous. She's always been so naturally elegant, unlike me.

I try to ignore the envy since she's been teaching me to hold myself as she does. The art of appearing perfectly confident, even if it's all a lie.

It's helped me keep myself together, I admit.

She looks at me for some time, and it causes my heart to sink. *How have I been so clueless?* I realize now that her tail is a pure onyx black, and her face is painted with pure anger toward…me? My head swarms with a plague of thoughts.

What reason have I ever given her to feel an anger so strong I can almost taste it?

She hid her true colors for all these months, and I was blind. All the days she would spend with me, gaining my trust just so I would reveal my deepest secrets. I've told her everything—NO.

She knows about—

I look down to Asherah curled on my chest and try not to let them see my heart shattering. I turn back to the woman before me with shock and complete betrayal for what she has turned out to be.

The one other person in my life I felt I could trust beyond my real love. The one other person I felt happy with. All of it was a lie.

How could she? How could she hide all of this from me for so long? How could I have been so ungodsly stupid to not see it?

"Your Majesty, if I may be so bold, I believe the queen has been unfaithful to you," she states with a disgustingly happy grin and a pointed look in my direction. Her gaze reads what I've suspected but never allowed myself to truly dwell on: *I want your title, and I'll get it no matter what.*

"How dare you suggest such an idea?" the king yells. "Present your evidence, *now!*" he spits out, his eyes like daggers waiting to strike. At least it isn't me on the receiving end, but I know I will be all too soon.

"Happily, Your Majesty," she begins at a low hum, swimming toward my newborn princess. I can't tell if it's an exhausted delusion or reality, but her pupils seem to compress to be two sharp lines like a serpentine creature intent on killing her prey.

"Stay away from my daughter! I'll rip you limb from limb if

you so much as lay a hand on her!" I cry out, clutching Asherah closer. My traitorous friend tilts her head while continuing to hum toward my baby.

"It's just a simple spell to show the child's true parents." She smirks. "If you fight me, then it's clear you have something to hide."

She's right. Gods, I hate that she's right.

Asherah's small lavender tail slowly splits in two, starting from the indention of her fin to the top of her hips. Each scale on her tiny tail reforms and changes color.

She fights back and struggles to swim, having two fins instead of one, but the spell can't be ignored for any longer as it reveals one part is a soft blue identical to my own and the other is a light, kind red, nothing like the king's.

His eyes grow wide with anger as my parents' eyes flood with fear. I sit in terrified silence, as I know there is no denying my daughter is not of the king's blood.

The strong, sarcastic front I've put up falls, and I'm back to who I really am: the scared-out-of-my-mind, eighteen-year-old child who just gave birth to a beautiful little girl—the target of everyone's hatred.

That's what I am, and no one sees it. I am a child. *A child.*

Why me?

I can't protect myself from anything the king wants to do to me, and as he said, nothing is stopping him from killing my baby along with me. He probably will, just out of spite, regardless of the outrage it would cause.

"What is your name, witch?" he asks, failing to hide his increasing rage.

"Daevia Phoenix, Your Majesty," she says with a bow at the

waist, staring up at the king in a way that twists my stomach into knots.

Dorian sits in a silence that threatens to send my heart straight out of my chest. Instead, it slams against the walls that keep it in.

Say something, say something.

"And can you cast a curse?" he asks slowly, turning his piercing gaze from me back to Daevia.

NO.

NO.

NO.

I try to use my majick to escape, but it's useless. *I am useless!* I fight back more, determined to protect both my defenseless child and myself. I'm incredibly weak, and I notice the feeling of a majickal restraint binding me.

There is nothing I can do.

"Yes, of course. What was it you had in mind?" Daevia's eyes glimmer with despicable, evil happiness.

"Do what you think will be the best punishment. Make her suffer."

"Gladly." Daevia closes her eyes, clasping her hands as she hums a sound so deep the room shakes. The chandelier of glass breaks and fills the water with tiny shards ready to cut.

I throw my body around my child, protecting her from the incoming glass daggers. My eyes are shut so tight I can't see what's happening, but I feel it. I *feel* the way her power is washing into me, and I can only assume Asherah, too.

There's no use fighting back.

I can't protect my baby, my sweet Asherah. Still clutching her away from them, I kiss the top of her head where the beginning of black hair sprouts—just like her father.

"I will find a way back to you, my darling," I whisper, tears washing away as the room's stagnant water swirls like a tornado. "No matter what separates us, be it life or death, I will find you."

"By the power of the enlarged crimson moon above and the uncontrolled majick inside the child, I cast a curse so powerful only an identical event on this very day could destroy it." With the power she has shown, I doubt such an event will ever occur again. She would likely all but pull the moon from the sky to keep it that way. "Kaileah, you are hereby cursed never to step outside the castle, and, Asherah, you will never become your true form again." Her voice is not entirely her own, and her laugh is echoed like there's a chasm between us.

She did not need to say the words aloud, as our power comes from the mind, not speech, but how could this new version of my old friend ever pass up an opportunity to state her power? That's all she ever wanted, I realize. She wanted power...*my* power.

When she couldn't get it, she found another way.

I feel her words inside my skin, clawing and attacking as the rest of her body turns just as bestial. Her hands twist and morph into long, animalistic fingers, cutting through the water as she dips deeper into the surrounding energy.

She laughs to taunt me, proving just how much power she has after giving up her sanity to a god without morals. Her hands return to their normal form as she focuses on the curse instead of showing off her talents. The idea of it sends my rage over the edge, but I'm too weak to act on it.

Curse this useless body.

Using the last of my strength, I try to sit upright but fall back. She places an unseen barrier between herself and me. I try with everything I have left to push through it, but it's too late.

With her curse complete, the water calms, but I notice Asherah's tail slowly losing its scales until all that is left are two human legs.

I scream as my baby struggles to breathe without oxygen. Her gills disappear as each second passes, and I hold her as close as possible, hugging her small body until she stops breathing entirely. Not once does she scream or fight, and the thought that it was quick and painless comforts me.

Something inside of me breaks, knowing I let my daughter, *my life*, die in my arms without fighting back.

I should've fought back.

I should've found the strength.

"Your child isn't dead, Kaileah. Open your eyes," Daevia states bluntly.

I do as she says and see a small air bubble encapsulating her head. Asherah is smiling and breathing—I don't understand.

"This is the only kindness I will allow you. The witches will take your child to the nearest humans for them to raise as their own. Although, I will make sure she never knows you exist," she says as an evil grin splits her face.

She knows exactly what she's doing. This 'new' Daevia that has taken over my old friend knows very well this is not kindness.

It's a cruel form of torture meant to hurt me far beyond her death, but she's wrong. However much it would tear apart my heart to think of her never knowing how much I love her, all I can hope is that she will live.

And she will. I can feel it as easily as I can feel the tiny beats of her heart. She will live, and one day, I will find her.

Four witches carry the child to a land far enough away that there is no chance of her ever being found. Once they feel they have traveled long enough, the witches searched for the first piece of inhabited land.

There, they meet a human couple crying together, alone, praying for the gift of fertility. The humans stumble back in fear as the four creatures rise from the water, holding the small, human child in their unearthly arms.

"Wha—what are you?" the man asks with a shaky voice. The witches sneer at his fear, for humans are weak.

"We're the answer to your prayers," the eldest witch begins, gaining a snicker from the woman to her right. "This child has been cursed to never know her true form as long as she may live. Her life is now yours to decide. However, if she, or anyone, ever learns of our existence, we will kill her and anyone she loves. Do you understand?" the eldest of the four witches explains as if it is was a script she memorized.

The man's face flushes a ghostly white as he struggles to find words to respond. He wonders what beings could be so filled with evil to kill a baby, but neither what they are nor the severity of the situation hits the two humans. If it had, they would have run at the first sight of the merfolk before them.

Poor, clueless humans.

The couple look at each other before responding.

"What if we don't take her?" the woman asks curiously. She is significantly less afraid than her partner, willing to taunt the creatures with questions. But instead of taunting them, it gains their respect.

"If you do not take the child, then we will have no choice but to kill her," the witch answers blankly with a shrug. The humans' eyes grow wide, and the woman grabs baby Asherah with only a second delay.

"We will take her! What's her name?" she asks with a panicked look, checking the pulse of a child of mer, now cursed with human flesh.

"Asherah. Change it, or the same rules will apply."

"Okay. We will raise her as our own," the woman states proudly, feeling as though she alone is responsible for the child's safety.

VERA

3

TOES IN THE SAND

.*⭐ VERA ⭐*.

(PRESENT)

As my parents and I make our way to the Eastern Florida coast, I remember their favorite story to tell. Mom was nine months pregnant and just had to go to the coastline, even against Dad's wishes.

But to keep the peace, he agreed, and they made the countless-hour drive to a private beach where no one else would be. They knew about it from an old friend who would sneak through the owner's property and enjoy the peace and quiet and the beautiful waters of the Atlantic.

When they arrived, an old man sitting on the porch greeted them with a smile. He claimed he was nearing the end of his life and had no one to leave his beautiful home to, so he gave it to them. They accepted eagerly, happy to have both been given such a beautiful home and that they no longer needed to sneak into his backyard.

On the second day, Mom went into labor and gave birth to me on the sand with waves crashing in the distance. Dad says I didn't cry when I was born and had the biggest smile on my face instead. That part of the story probably isn't true, but Dad has always leaned toward the dramatics.

Long story short, after the beach house was in their name, we started coming here every summer as an annual family tradition.

They always tell me of a time when they had the beach completely to themselves. However, with the rise of tourism and the fact that we couldn't be here more than a month out of the year, my parents made a deal with the local government that anyone could use the beach from 8:00 a.m. to 6:00 p.m.

Standing outside, I feel the fresh, salty breeze blowing delicately across my face. As much as I love my small town, there is nothing quite like the feeling of bliss you get standing on an open shore. It's comforting in a way I could only describe as feeling like you're finally home.

With each step onto the soft, disheveled sand, I grow more at ease, forgetting about the strangeness of my birthday three months ago. Every night, I find myself drawn back to that moment, be it the memory that came to me or the power exploding from my body.

I still can't quite understand how no one saw the blinding light but me. If I hadn't felt that surge so clearly, I might have convinced myself it didn't happen at all.

I smell sunscreen and saltwater wafting to me as children run about with beach balls and water guns. Worried parents palm their faces, rushing after their wayward children while they laugh, scream, and play.

Nothing in the world could ruin a child's fun.

Parents lie on towels and take out books to relax under the

perfect gleaming sun. Among them are Mom and Dad, acting more like the children than the adults.

They throw shovelfuls of sand and dump bucketfuls of water over each other's heads, and they nearly fall over with laughter. Neither one gives the other a second to catch their breath before hurling anything they can find at the other: beach balls, towels, sand, and buckets. I would change nothing about my parents, but I've never felt I truly belonged with them.

Even with my friends, there has always been a sheer veil between myself and them. My life is the closest thing to perfect it could be, yet I'm stuck feeling like I don't deserve it...like I shouldn't have this.

If anyone ever knew how I felt, they'd call me ungrateful, and maybe I am. Rosalind would give anything for the life I have, Liam too, but I would give anything to feel as if this *was* my life.

But I guess it's just human nature to be disappointed.

I love my friends, or I think I do. I don't love them like I love my parents, but I care about them. They're kind and thoughtful, but I don't think any of them know me at my core. I hardly think *I* truly know who I am, so I can't fault them.

If I'm honest, I think it's always been Liam and Elliot, then Inaya and Rose, but there I was. The fifth or the third, depending on how you look at it.

I've never been treated as an outcast or a forgotten member, but when I zone out, they hardly notice because they have each other.

Sitting where each wave breaks at my feet, I feel at peace. I lean back, falling on the pillow of sand below, and close my eyes with the sun heating my skin.

"I wish I could forget about it all for a day. I wish I could belong somewhere as you do with the sand," I whisper to the ocean. I sit up and stare longingly at the somber, sloshing water. The wave covers my legs like a gentle blanket, and I smile.

I walk to where the water is at my knees before sitting and letting it give me a wonderful salty embrace. The waves are calm, so losing myself in their soft touch is easy as they move in and out of the tide.

I look up to see my exultant parents sitting on either side of me.

"What's got you in such deep thought?" Dad asks as I see him grab a handful of sand out of Mom's sight.

"Yeah, you haven't been our bubbly girl recently," Mom says while jabbing fingers into my sides. I clench and laugh, but while I'm distracted, both parents throw sand at each other, unintentionally hitting me from either side.

I laugh even harder as a wave completely knocks me over.

Quickly standing up and wiping the wet sand covering my eyes, I see their hysterical faces full of such genuine happiness it's hard not to smile back. Bending down and grabbing an armful of sand, I dump it over their heads in retaliation.

"Also, to answer your question..." I splash them both with water before continuing. "I've just felt a little off recently, but nothing to worry about."

I feel a sharp pain, causing me to fall to my knees, legs numb and trembling. I try to hide the intense pain encompassing me. Every nerve ending from my feet to the tops of my legs explodes with a piercing sting, making it hard to keep my balance as I try to stand.

Each step fills my body with even more splintering agony than before, and I collapse into the sand. The pain is unlike anything I have experienced. Far worse than a broken bone, ripped skin, severe burn, or electric shock. The feeling is like someone taking an unmedicated biopsy with a dull scalpel.

Somehow, in the blink of an eye, the worst pain of my life is over, as if it had never begun. With utter confusion, I go back inside to wash up for dinner.

Lying in bed with the moon's beautiful light flooding through my open blinds, I can't sleep. I know what I need to do, but I can't say why.

Go to it. Embrace the pain.

A soft and ethereal voice calls out from inside me. I get out of bed and throw on a swimsuit before running outside, greeted by the cold, swirling wind of a midnight storm. A force pushes me to keep walking, promising me a reward for the torture I'm soon to endure. Each slow step closer to the crashing sea sends new waves of anxiety through me.

Come to me.

I bend down and touch the water, jumping back at its frigid graze. Ignoring my better judgment, I take a step into its piercing depths. The agony is overwhelming and nauseating; I can't stay here.

Before breaking away from its grip, I think about the voice again.

Embrace the pain. *Embrace it.* I think about the shooting needles of torture soon to flood through me if I listen to what the voice is asking, but with a sigh, I take one step closer.

What more do I have to lose?

I take a deep breath and let it have complete control over my senses, allowing the pain—*the power*—to take me. I grit and grind my teeth, trying to hold myself together as my legs are flooded with raw, burning fire. I can hardly hold myself in place, yet I can't imagine trying to run away and escape. As the pain nears my neck, it calms, and my muscles relax.

Closing my eyes, I peacefully drift underwater until I jolt at the light that blazes before me. Nearly blinding in its luminance, the glow flows from my skin into the water around me, a light identical to the one on my birthday but brighter.

Before I can stop myself, I try to suck in a breath of air, but somehow, the water coursing down my throat doesn't choke me.

A hand to my throat reveals nothing, but sliding it behind my ears, I can feel two deep parallel cuts perfectly on top of one another, and the other side is symmetrical. After a quick inspection of my fingers, there is no blood from the incision.

Am I dreaming? What the hell is going on?

Before another thought can form, a burst of energy rips apart the skin from each of my legs, and I watch as scales form in their place. My limbs contort and crack as I lose all control of them in the ever-growing ring of light. Power cascades over me in pulsing surges every second as oxygen grows thinner and thinner, and my consciousness falters.

I try to swim to the surface, but where is the surface? I flail my arms in an attempt to swim, but no part of me moves.

Paralyzed.

Every single one of my limbs is paralyzed in place.

Oxygen fills my lungs, yet I can only faintly see the rays of moonlight on the ocean's crest from my depth.

Swim to the surface, Vera. Please, I beg.

My vision blackens from each peripheral as if my sight were a vintage photograph's edges tarnishing with time. Blinking away the growing darkness does little to stop the inevitable: a quick approaching death.

As my body slowly sinks into the immense abyss, my mind diverges into a dream-like state.

I let the water move me wherever it feels drawn to pull, incapable of doing anything else. Becoming a single entity gliding delicately with the movement of the waves, a comforting relief replaces the distress. The constricting feeling of fear previously grabbing me releases one finger at a time until its grasp of trepidation is broken.

I can no longer feel myself.

The silhouette of a tall figure appears in my trance, and it takes my body and leads me to a place I feel is safe.

Safe. You're safe now.

Unlike the angelic voice in my head, this one is masculine and vehement as it hums a soothing song, calming the last of my nerves and leading me into a deeper state of sleep.

Foreign words fill my head.

Soon, the feeling of the figure's touch fades, and the ocean's embrace is as apparent as it was before.

I open my eyes and find that my consciousness has been restored. I regain my body's voluntary movement and shake my head to readjust my senses.

My skin is brighter and more full of life than ever before, shining with an iridescence inhuman in nature, and my hair is long and black as a pure night sky, elegantly flowing as if I had never cut it, and my legs are gone.

In their place is a large tail like that of a fish but incredibly elegant and divine—the fin drapes and folds like a translucent piece of fine Italian silk. Glimmering scales shining with the moonlight's enhancing reflection create an entrancing hue of soft lavender.

While I look strange and should *feel* strange—all I can see is that I look more beautiful than ever. I can't help but stare at every part of myself that has changed, and I feel like I'm looking at someone else—*something* else.

Despite what I've experienced over the past few hours, I am overcome with tranquility.

How can this be real? How am I okay with this?

My mind and body feel comfortable in the water with the attachment of a tail, and in a way, the change is almost natural.

I gently graze my hand over my scales and feel their tough yet delicate exterior. I move my hips, and the tail flings. It will be incredibly difficult to learn how to use this thing.

In the dead of night, in the middle of the vast Northern Atlantic, I can see no hint of where I ventured from. That's when I notice how lost I am.

Come to me, please.

That same feminine voice calls out to me.

"Who are you? Where am I? Is someone there?" I scream into the void.

No response.

I grab fistfuls of my hair and tug as tears threaten to form. There's nothing more I can do; I'm entirely lost, with no idea how to get home. *Not that I could go home anymore,* I think while looking down upon the tail replacing my former legs.

I close my eyes and try to think of the dark figure in my imagination, beckoning them to save me again, even if it's from my illusions. There's only one thing left I can do: trust the voice inside, follow its trail, and hope it saves me.

I move in the direction I'm drawn to go to no avail. Swimming as an ocean-dweller clearly has its differences.

Twisting my hips and flexing my thighs, I try to find the muscles needed to swim, but I falter repeatedly. Where my ankles used to be, there is now an extra foot of tail and fin with new muscles I've never controlled.

By flexing what used to be my subtalar joint, my tail flies up, flipping me upside down.

This tail is useless.

I attempt to pull myself through the water, stroking as I was taught during swim lessons, but the weight of my bottom half makes it impossible to move more than a few inches.

I twist and turn and try everything I know, but nothing works. I feel like a fish out of water, yet I'm the opposite.

Instincts. Follow your instincts.

Eyes closed, I try to focus on my core. My inner instincts. I pull them from the farthest parts of my mind, and, somehow, I swim as if I have done it every day for years. My tail has a mind of its own, propelling at a speed I've never dreamt of.

My eyes fly open as I gasp, my cheeks burning from smiling so widely.

I have always loved the water. I used to swim every day and imagine being a dolphin or a great white shark. Now that I can fly through the water like a plane in the sky, I feel my stomach filling with butterflies of excitement.

I flow like a wave, diving, then rising, tensing my core, and throwing my hips high to keep the rhythm. I know why this felt so normal to me when I was still in shock—because I yearned to swim through the ocean as I am now. Feeling its soft touch and the tickling of bubbles from my tail flapping behind me is something I think I've longed for without ever realizing it.

I see the true depth of the ocean's beauty. Schools of fish swim past me like I'm a familiar sight in their environment. Reefs glow and erupt with life of all designs.

Looking upon the miraculously colored coral, feeling its roughness, I see small crustaceans crawl upon my outstretched hands before jumping off and drifting away. Although it's far past midnight, and the only light in the sky is the white moon above, I can see clearly. The reef is a deep, glowing blue, and the color stands out in my mind with its neon aura.

A shutter crawls from the base of my fin to the top of my spine. There's someone here. Instinctively, I rush to hide inside the enormous reef. That's when I see *her*. The woman from my dream—*my vision*.

Her golden curls are as glamorous as I had seen them months prior. However, she looks aged, no longer the young girl I had seen, but a woman, yet her face appears to be only a few years beyond mine. She seems anxious as she looks around breathlessly.

What is she looking for?

I hear a faint voice and recognize it as the same one in my head.

"*Beaōn val lausik. Beaōn val lausik!*" she cries out in desperation. Shuddering, she grabs her hair, and the water carries away the tears that fall from her anxiety-stricken face.

I go to her, leaving my hiding space before realizing the potential danger. She looks up, emerald eyes glistening with the moonlight, and moves a pale, delicate hand to touch my face. She pulls back and nearly breaks into a sob.

That's when I notice her tail, the shape identical to my own, but hers is a soft blue that emanates a calm love. Her fin is gloriously beautiful, and the way it drifts and flows is like it has a mind of its own.

I can't bring myself to look away.

Peering behind her, I notice that along the backside of her tail there is a fin, just as thin and graceful, that follows half of the tail's spine like a horse's mane.

"*Kileōa daemōre, mōi ji'aenres. Mōi sikai, mi meyur,*" she says with entrancing happiness and disbelief, hugging me tight as if she will never let go.

"I—I'm sorry, but I can't understand you."

"Oh, my darling. I should have realized you wouldn't have been taught Adleian," she says with a divine, otherworldly accent while pulling away to examine my face again. "Oh gods, how I've longed for this day. To hold you in my arms! It all feels so unreal, like I'll wake up from this idyllic dream at any moment."

"If you don't mind me asking, do I know you?" I ask in the softest tone I can manage. This woman couldn't possibly know me, for I have no clue who she is, yet how did I hear her voice? I back away a hair, remembering it coursing through my head mere minutes ago.

"In truth, you haven't known me for a very long time, my Asherah." She looks away before continuing. "Follow me while I explain. It's not safe for you in the open." In a blink, she darts past, moving so quickly I can only see her trail by the bubbles forming in her wake.

"Excuse me, ma'am, but I can't keep up with you, seeing how inexperienced I am." The woman turns around and notices my immense distance from her. She swims back in another blink and grabs hold of my arm, scaring me slightly at how fast her movements are.

"With my help, you should do just fine," she says with her

glorious accent that brings a certain calmness to me, almost like a mother singing her newborn a lullaby.

As she thought, I can keep her pace with the guidance of someone moving with natural grace. As we swim through the beautiful ocean, she continues.

"I think it's time you know the truth of your past," she says with a tight-lipped smile and breaks her gaze from mine. "My name is Kaileah Dlari." She stops and holds both of my arms, locking eyes with me. "I'm your mother, Asherah." I feel my eyes widen with each second of silence that passes between us.

I can't help but feel a deep sympathy for this poor woman, thinking I am the child she lost.

"I'm sorry, but I'm not your daughter. My name is Vera Caddel, and my family is on land. Hopefully, they are still asleep and unaware that I am gone," I say as I pull away. Before letting me go, she gazes through me in a way that can peel away my edges to reveal the very truth of who I am—a truth even I cannot see.

Her eyes glow like a forest of evergreen leaves and seem to stare straight at my soul. She wipes a tear from her eye, carrying it away with the water as though it never formed. Her gaze is difficult to hold, but something in me refuses to break it—as if some long-forgotten part of myself begs me to listen.

So I do.

"I know you have no reason to believe me, but can you not understand the scope of what has happened?" Kaileah swims again, beckoning me to follow. "I could sense your intellectual awareness from the moment I met you. I know you cannot possibly believe this is a dream."

She's right. Everything happening to me is real, although I can hardly fathom it.

"You had some memories unlocked on your birthday. You saw me, didn't you?" Kaileah asks, and I finally pull away from her and stare in apprehension.

"How did you know about that? How are you in my head? *Who are you?*" I ask, on alert. Did she plant that vision in my head?

"In your head? Whatever do you mean?" Kaileah holds out her hands, and I retreat further. She's lying...She knows exactly what I'm speaking of.

"Your voice was inside of my head! It's been calling to me all day. It told me to embrace the pain, come here, follow my instincts, and learn to swim. You're manipulating me, aren't you?" I end my words with a subtle hint of anger as I gain the courage to defy her. "You've been controlling me this whole time. You made me into *this*," I grit out, gesturing at the large purple tail attached to my hips.

"Asherah, please, I don't know what you're talking about."

"Stop calling me that!" I yell, the water around us growing stagnant and silent beyond the echo of my words. "I'm not your long-lost daughter! I have a mother and a father. I don't even know who you are!" Kaileah stumbles back, holding her hands to her chest. "I'm going *home*," I announce, ready to leave and end this nightmare.

She approaches me, grabbing my arm with a strength unusual for a woman of her stature. I see red, but my instincts again beg me to listen, to hear her out, so I calm my raging heart and let her speak.

"You are my daughter, cursed to live as a human but now free once more. I cannot prove this to you, but you must believe me. Think about what happened on your birthday, Ash—*Vera*. What did you feel?"

I have never felt more alive than that moment on the night of my birthday, and I can't deny that, even to a stranger. While it faded back not long after, it doesn't change that initial wave of everything feeling...right.

"What happened when you entered the water? Why did your body erupt with a power unknown to any creature, even me?" She takes a deep breath, releasing her grip. "You can't deny the connection you feel between the two of us. I know you can feel it, just as I do. Look into my eyes and tell me you don't see yourself staring back." Her lips are in a tight line, and her eyes are so wide and full of silent begging that I shake my head without speaking.

I do see myself in her eyes. I see myself in the way her hair curls and flows in the water. I see myself in her nose, her lips, and her smile. Everything about her screams familiar, family, correct, and I find myself reaching to grab those golden curls like a physical tether to this new reality. I stop short, throwing my hands back at my sides.

"Even if I do feel what you say, that doesn't explain why I saw a vision of you or why your voice was inside my head."

"Follow me, and I will explain everything. I promise you," she pleads.

My logic and reason tell me to turn away and never look back, to go home to Mom and Dad and forget this ever happened. I can pretend it was all an elaborate dream brought on by being in the sun for too long.

I'll go home to my friends and family.

My perfect life.

Some 'perfect' life it was.

A life where I've never felt I belonged. Friends I've never truly connected to. A world I've never felt was the right fit.

Those thoughts are all I need to follow her, hoping I might just find my place.

An intense silence cascades between us until we reach what looks to be an extensive cave system. Her body relaxes as if she has been stressed beyond measure while we waded in the open water with nothing to conceal our location.

Entering the largest of the caves, I see a grand door built into the thick stone. The doors open with a flick of her wrist and a soft hum. The sound of the stones rumbling as they open has my hair standing, but I relax my mind and enter behind her.

"This is Taelani. It's the safest place we can be," she says with a genuine smile, staring up at the space around us that looks like the inside of a mountain has been carved out like a pumpkin. We swim into a large room filled with furniture of different kinds, some broken and worn and others brand new.

Above us are large flowers that open upon her command to reveal a glowing light. To assist them in illuminating the space, tiny lanterns float and almost remind me of stars in a night sky.

Cots are placed in a corner, as well as a bookcase stocked with maps and volumes, foreign words scattering its shelves. With further inspection, I notice a piano, fully intact and almost identical to those on land, with the exception of ten extra notes on either side.

Swimming closer, I sit on the stool placed in front of it, and my body doesn't drift from its seat. I run my fingers along the smooth ivory keys, finding the place where my favorite childhood song begins.

Closing my eyes, I feel the music flow effortlessly through my memory. It's been years since I first wrote the song, and even now, I can feel it in my bones. I don't think I could ever forget.

Each note is grand and majestic with its rich chords. In

perfect sync with my playing, I hear Kaileah's voice singing in her native tongue.

"Haenur ti'deōrin,
saenuir mau'jauilōrn.
Jaenōrjik tekōnah naehiema,
nō'laihmi kenjaei."

I glance behind to see her mimicking my hand movements with closed eyes. How could she—

"Cōur saeraih, tekōnah,
no'friunda yaeurōi."

As she drifts further into the song, she loses her restraint. I can't shake the feeling that there's something odd about her words that makes me pause.

Perhaps the tune seems familiar, but she could be simply adjusting a song in her world to match my melody. As my playing ends, so does her singing, and she looks at me with amazement.

"How do you know that song and to play it note for note? I almost can't believe it," Kaileah states, and I frown in confusion. *"No'friunda yaeurōi,"* she says with a soft laugh. I give her a quick smile, unsure of what she said, yet I recognize it from the last portion of her song.

"What do you mean? I wrote that song myself."

"How exactly did you learn to play it?"

"Well, I guess I just started playing until I found chord combinations that sounded nice together," I answer. She smirks slightly before responding.

"If you knew what I was singing, you'd understand why I said that." She pauses and sings it again, but only now has it been translated into a language I understand.

"No matter the time we go,
my love for you will only grow.
You're safe with me, my dear,
I'll keep you close for all your years.
Come, my princess, to me now.
You'll be safe, oh, don't you frown."

She looks at me intensely, seeing my look of disbelief before explaining.

"I sang that song for you every night when I was pregnant and after you were taken from me. I just can't believe you actually heard me."

I rise from the piano and watch as Kaileah perfectly replicates *my song* with a grace I have yet to master. The chords flow past their previous end into even more glorious notes than before.

The sound, the feeling…it is all familiar, like a hummed tune with words long gone but an unforgettable melody.

"Even after they took you from me, there was never a night when that song wasn't played to your dedication." She looks away from me, moving from the piano to pass her fingers along the stone wall gently. "On the worst nights…" She inhales sharply. "I'd scream it out in the hopes you'd hear me."

Kaileah swims back, grasping my hands in hers.

"There wasn't a single moment when I stopped thinking of you. And to answer your question earlier of how you heard my voice inside your head, I really don't know how that's possible. I suppose majick has a way of bending to its holder's will without our knowledge."

I pause, trying to grasp her words fully.

What does she mean by 'magic' and 'holder's will'? Likely seeing the look on my face, she asks, "What's troubling your mind, my child?"

"There's too much that I don't understand. I want to believe that everything you say is true. That this is who I am, and this whole situation isn't some lucid dream, but—" I begin before she cuts me off.

"Ask me any question you have, please. I want you to believe me more than anything in this world," she says with undeniable truth. I turn away from her, trying to build up the courage to do so.

"Who are you? No. *What* are you?" I ask finally, and she breathes a long sigh without meeting my eyes.

"My title is Queen Kaileah Astorah Dlari, and I am an Adleian witch." She pauses and confidently meets my gaze. "*We* are the descendants of a long line of the most powerful witches the oceans have ever seen. The first of our bloodline was so far beyond the others that they called her a sorceress."

Her face has developed a look of happiness and gratification at describing 'our' family history.

"A bloodline like ours doesn't work the same as others. Only a firstborn female can show the gene, so for the past five hundred years, our family didn't know we were majickal," she adds. Either my look of utter shock causes her to stop talking, or she can sense I am full of questions.

I don't know what to think or what to believe.

"Why would you need to be born a witch to cast spells? Don't they just require ingredients and incantations?" I ask. The amount of information dumped upon me makes my thoughts swirl. I've met Wiccans and pagans before, but none claimed magic was a birthright.

"I like to call the ones you're familiar with *grōpaetōn* witches, better known as witches that cast land majick or use spells. However, majick is not the same for Adleians. You must imagine what you want to happen with intense attention to details. It often changes from witch to witch based on the strength of their imagination and how they view their own power. It's fluid, in a way," she explains with ease as if reciting a speech she's given many times over.

Kaileah picks up a stray piece of stone from the cave's ledge and places it on her palm with concentration painted across her pale face. I watch tiny cracks bloom across the rock's surface.

Within another moment, it shatters into a million tiny shards before disintegrating into dust. She looks at me and smiles before placing a similar-sized stone into my hand. "Try it."

I sigh and look at the rock, imagining it shattering as it did in her grasp.

Nothing happens.

"Think of the individual cracks that will combine to give you the desired result," she explains.

I take the stone and turn it in my hand, trying to create a picture in my mind. Then, I close my eyes and imagine the fractures I wish to appear. I can hear the crack of each tiny abrasion and my eyes open to see countless gashes forming together until all that is left are a few solid fibers holding the stone together.

With a smile, I cause the last break, sending the shards in every direction like Kaileah's. However, my shards stab into every surface, from bookshelves to cots and the stone wall itself.

Kaileah throws a wave of power over herself to keep any rogue piece from stabbing her.

The applause I hear with the hug that follows is short-lived, as I remember what she said. If this woman is truly my mother, then I would be royalty. My eyes harden as I back away.

"No more majick and distractions, Kaileah. Who am I?"

"You are Princess Asherah Dlari, the only heir to the Adleian throne," she says with complete seriousness. No one could ever mistake it as a joke, yet I feel the urge to laugh. A princess? Nothing could be so absurd.

"That's ridiculous. What kingdom would cast out their only heir?"

"A kingdom built on the misery of its queen." She swims closer. "A kingdom that sells prepubescent girls to men older than their fathers, hoping they will be naive enough to obey. A kingdom that sentences a woman to an eternity of solitude for simply loving a man who wasn't her abusive husband!" With her last word, her roughened exterior falls, and I see a defenseless young woman instead.

She sinks to the floor below and cries silently.

"What happened to you?" I ask, bending down to her sunken level. "They did all that to you because of me?" A look of pale fear cools her reddened cheeks.

"NO! You are all that is left of the only man I've ever loved. The day you were born was the happiest of my life. Once I lost you, there wasn't a single form of torture I wouldn't endure to see your face again. And now here you are, right before me in the flesh. I just—"

She breaks down and pulls me into the most loving hug of desperation I have ever felt. I wrap my arms around her for the first time and let myself melt into my mother's embrace.

I can't help the tears that fall without warning. No dam could ever be made powerful enough to hold back the unbreakable waves I feel in my heart, and I can see who I get it from.

As each second passes, I watch her body surround us with a light blue aura. It deepens her hug, love, and words in my mind. A mother's love is unlike anything else—it's almost majickal.

Maybe it's the feeling of meeting a part of myself I never knew existed or a connection shared through our blood, but no matter the reason, I know beyond a shadow of a doubt that this woman is my mother.

I gently pull away and look at her again. Everything about her, from the shape of her eyes to the radiating happiness in her smile, makes me even more certain that she has been truthful about our history.

Our tails curl together, and I realize it must be the way our kind truly connects with one another, as I have never before felt so held and content. The blue and purple combine and collide to make a beautiful combination.

We stay huddled together on the floor of this dark, entrancing cave for what seems like hours until I remember the family I've left behind. Am I a horrible child for caring so strongly for my biological mother, a mother I just met, when she isn't the woman who raised me?

Kaileah didn't send me away or let those witches take me, and from the way she acts, it seems she would've loved more than anything to have been my mother.

I ask myself again, is it really wrong to feel for her...to want to love her and learn more? It doesn't take away from my indescribable love for my parents, but I can't help feeling like I'm betraying them both.

I have to confront Mom and Dad. I need to hear their side of the story, and I need them to understand what I must do.

And if I know them at all, they will.

"I need to tell my parents—*adoptive parents*—about everything that happened today and that I won't be home for a while. I promise I will meet you here as soon as I'm done," I say with an even, unwavering tone, hoping she will not fight the decision I've made.

"I trust you, Vera. All I ask is that you don't choose just yet."

"Choose?" I ask, my brows harshly furrowing.

"There will come a point where you will have to choose between returning to the way everything was on land or living a life you've yet to fully discover." She cups my face in both her hands and says, "I don't see a way for you ever to have both." A single tear falls from her eye in sync with one from my own at the idea of making that impossible choice. "Come back to me soon, my Asherah."

After Kaileah has explained twice how to return to where I came from, I make my way to where this night began. With a smile, I picture every distinction in Kaileah's face, and I only have one thought in mind: my mother was right—*it's just like looking in a mirror.*

4

IS THIS GOODBYE?

.*⭐ VERA ⭐*.

As I throw myself above the waves, I worry how difficult it will be to pull myself from it with the added weight of a tail half my size. But it doesn't take long to realize a certain strength floods my muscles: a newfound ability to exit the water with little resistance. I gasp as I inhale the salty air, so at odds with how it feels to breathe underwater.

Its familiar comfort returns with the fading of my gills.

My tail is still attached even though my body lies on the wet sand. Thinking back to Kaileah's explanations of Adleian majick, I imagine my legs returning with one scale falling off at a time.

I wince as each one is slowly pulled by an invisible hand, leaving trails of blood in their wake. I have to rip off a bit of fabric from my top to bite down on as the pain continues down my tail until not one scale has been spared. Only then does it disappear completely, replaced by my human legs.

There has to be an easier way to transform back and forth, I think, my head still dizzy from the pain.

I wipe the blood from my legs as I run back, hoping to make it home before my parents notice.

I stumble slightly as I regain my balance, but my instincts don't take long to return. I am a child of land and sea...I am a creature raised in a world that is not my own, yet *my* world is foreign. The thoughts swirl around my mind like a tornado waiting to devour everything in its path, but I try calming my breathing and remembering what matters.

The cold rain falls against my skin, and I embrace it, letting it cool down the burning I feel from my raging thoughts. Lightly pushing open the doors, I hold my breath as I quietly return to my room. An incessant beeping signals my parents' 6:00 a.m. alarm, and I shove my head into my pillow, fighting back a scream.

So much for sleeping.

Throwing myself across my bed, I lie above the covers, keenly aware of how my comforter is now soaked from the rain and sea. I close my eyes to gain the smallest amount of rest, but I know it's futile. If I don't start moving, they'll likely check if I'm still asleep.

Maybe I'll get lucky, and they'll ignore their alarm and choose to start later in the day.

I'm not ready for the conversation we're about to have.

Footsteps to and from the kitchen and the sound of a running shower shatter my hope of them sleeping in. Reluctantly, I leave the comfort of my bed and look at myself in the full-length mirror.

Fighting back a yelp, I barely recognize the person before me. My skin is glowing with a radiance I've never seen before, and my eyes are brighter than ever. The divine, unearthly green I noticed when looking into my mother's eyes has become my own. Touching my skin, I can feel its softness unlike any human, and Kaileah's was the same.

If I was not horrified by what stood in my reflection, I'd say I have become devastatingly beautiful. It is as if my human self was a muted, dull version of the real me lurking beneath the surface: a part of me so full of light my body could barely contain it.

Everything has changed in ways I hope only I can see. I turn away from the slightly uncanny version of myself and take deep breaths, preparing myself for what's to come.

This will all make sense soon.

I step into my shower without waiting for the water to warm. Its cold embrace comforts my anxiety and allows me to finally think. My first thought is wondering why I don't feel the urge to change back into my other form. It doesn't seem to be triggered by freshwater.

"What has happened to me?" I whisper to myself as I let the water pour over me. "How can I ever look at Mom and Dad the same again?"

How long have they been lying to me?

Do they even know what I am?

I finish washing my short lilac hair, noticing the stark difference between my two forms. I haven't had long black hair for over five years, and even then, it was never as long as last night.

"Vera, darling, what would you like for breakfast?" Mom calls kindly from the kitchen.

"It doesn't matter, but I'm starving," I respond, making sure my voice sounds rested and sweet.

"Alright, I'm hoping to surf, so we'll need to get out there before all the tourists come!" Mom replies.

I hear Dad's voice joining in. "I was wondering who turned my water ice-cold. I'm eating your bacon for that, kid!"

I leave the shower and poke my head out to respond.

"You wouldn't *dare*," I say with a fake glare.

"Five minutes. Then it's all mine." He laughs heartily and waves me off. I chuckle, momentarily forgetting the conversation that's coming—the conversation that is to change my life as I know it and the decision I fear I've already made. Yet, I can't voice it, even in my thoughts. I fall to the floor, every possibility for my future surging as I grip fistfuls of my hair.

Am I really going to leave everything behind?

Could I possibly leave the only parents I've known, who have cared for me all my life?

Will I abandon my friends?

Will they even notice my absence?

Memories from years upon years flood my mind as I try to decide what's next. I hear Mom and Dad's playful laughs, my friends' crude jokes, my teachers' lessons, my first time swimming, my first trip to the beach, the way I would imagine I could swim free in the ocean, and that's when it hits me. Kaileah's words enter my mind without warning.

"There will come a point where you will have to choose between returning to the way everything was on land or living a life you've yet to fully discover."

As much as I cannot believe what I am to do, there have been so many moments when my subconscious tried to tell me what I was, and I didn't listen. So many times, I looked at my reflections in the waves and saw who I truly was: long, obsidian-black hair and eyes that held an otherworldly glow. I always figured it was my mind playing tricks on me, but now, I realize those moments were the ocean calling its lost princess home.

It's time I listened.

Sitting opposite my parents, I look down and attempt to eat while trying to find the right words to say.

"There's something important that we need to talk about," I say as calmly as I can, yet they look at each other with matching, anxious faces. With a sigh, I continue. "What really happened the day I was born?"

"Vera, what are you talking about?" Dad asks, his voice higher than normal. "We've told you the story a hundred times." I stand up with my hands on the table, unable to control myself.

"I know you know what I *really* am. Tell me." My voice cracks. "What. You. Know!" I finish, my arms and legs growing weak. My parents look at each other, their expressions grave and worried.

"It's time we told you the true story," Dad says, gaining a harsh glare from Mom.

"Nathaniel, don't you dare! You know what they threatened," Mom says, her voice a mix of anger and grief.

"She *knows*, Em. There's no hiding it from her now. She deserves to hear it from us," he explains, and she shakes her head, clearly torn. Dad continues without waiting for her to agree. "The day you were born, your mom and I were sitting on the outside patio at home praying to anything at all that our infertility would be cured. We had done every treatment and taken every medicine imaginable." Dad chokes up before Mom takes over.

"Nothing worked, but I had this feeling to drive. We were on the road within ten minutes without knowing where we were going. Countless hours passed, and I stopped at this beautiful little house. I *knew* it was right where we needed to be. The next part we already told you, and it was the truth. There was a kind old man who gave us the house." A big smile grows across her face. "That night, we sat on the beach and begged and pleaded for a child of our own."

Dad stands up and gently grabs hold of my hands.

"The waves parted, and four creatures rose from the dark sea. They carried a small baby that looked human, nothing like the creatures that held it," he says, releasing my hands as a tear falls from his eye. "They said you were cursed to remain human, and we were to never tell you what you were. We took you into our arms and swore to protect you from *whoever* did this to you." They both pull me into a hug I can't help but return.

"But—" I choke. "Why didn't you tell me? I always knew that there was something off about me, but I could never understand what it was. How could you let me live all these years without knowing something so vital to who I am?" Tears fall, and my speech breaks. I can hardly even see their faces as my vision clouds with tears.

"Vera, they told us if you ever found out, they'd—" She stops. "That they'd...*kill you*." Gently, Mom caresses my cheek with the back of her hand. "I wanted to tell you so many times, anytime you swam and didn't connect with children your age. Each year, I somehow grew to love you more than I thought possible, so I would've taken the secret to my grave to protect you," Mom finishes, staying strong, and I can feel her love through every word.

"Mom, I love you so much." I look to Dad, my father in every way it counts, and my voice shakes. "D-Dad," I stumble. "I should've told you a million more times that I love you too."

Without speaking the words, they both know what I am about to say, so they open the back door, leading me to the place I had transformed for the first time.

The three of us stand on the line between land and sea, the barrier between my life as I know it and the one I am to make for myself. No one speaks, and I doubt any of us even breathe.

The world I know and the people I love are behind me.

The world that was taken from me after a witch cursed my fate stands before me.

We all wait for someone to start the final goodbye.

I take one step into the water, feeling the familiar power surging through me, yet this time being able to control it. I turn back and look at their loving gazes, tears streaming down each of their cheeks, but neither of them tries to stop me. I know they won't. No matter how much it hurts to see me go, they'll let me do it.

And, somehow, it makes everything so much harder.

To stay is to never know what I'm missing, to forever feel that I am not like those around me, to never feel a true connection to a friend, to live a life without majick, to never feel the way I did when I swam, to never truly be myself, and to never indulge in every hidden dream and desire I've ever had.

But to stay is to forever have my parents, to live in a world I understand even though it does not understand me, to live in comfort, to never worry for my safety, to be normal, and to have routine and tradition.

To leave is to experience something new, to learn what it means to be what I am, to meet my birth mother, to find those who understand me at my core, to forever find adventure, for every day to be different, to have purpose, and to have power.

But to leave is to leave behind those I love, to enter a place that I will not understand—somewhere I will be clueless and ignorant about its customs and language, and never feel another day of normalcy.

To stay, to leave, to stay, to leave.

I close my eyes so tight my vision becomes pure black, and I feel my eyes darting from each side in violent movements.

To stay or to leave, to stay or to leave.

I turn around, tears welling from the shock of the bright sun as I open my eyes and from what I am about to say.

I hug my mother like it will be the last time because maybe it will. There is no way to know what dangers the undiscovered depths of the ocean will bring me or how I will ever know who to trust.

"How long will it be?" Mom whispers into my ear in a tone more collected than she seems.

"I don't know. It could be weeks, months, *years*—" My voice fails me as the revelation of those words takes the air from my lungs. How would I feel being in an unknown world, away from the two people I love more than anything for years? "No," I whisper, "not years, not even one. I will return to you before long. I promise. This is not forever...just until I know what I had taken from me."

"Oh Vera," Mom says, pulling me closer and soaking her pajamas in the process. Cupping my face in her hands, she continues. "You are the best daughter I could've ever asked for. We will never forget you or love you any less, no matter how long your journey takes or what you become." After kissing my forehead, she steps back to give me space. Dad places a comforting hand on her shoulder as they watch.

Finally, I take a deep breath and embrace the power I've been holding back. My hair darkens in cascading waves as I transform. The gills carve behind my ears once more, and my legs slowly come together in a beautiful display of opalescent scales appearing one after the next.

I feel so incredibly free, and I know this choice is the one I need to make.

Before submerging beneath the raging waves, I give my parents a final look, not yet ready to leave. *Not forever*, I reminded myself. *For now.*

My parents approach me simultaneously, ignoring the water drenching the rest of their clothes. Mom strokes my hair while Dad traces his hand across my ear. The sensation is different, and I wonder if the anatomy has changed.

"I—I can't believe that this is real, yet I don't think I've ever seen you look more like...you." Dad takes my hands and says, "I'm so proud of you, Vera. I'm so very proud of all that you are." His voice shakes with long pauses between each word. "I love you so much, and don't forget that you will always be my daughter."

"Even if we don't share blood, even if we're from two different worlds, we are family. None of us will ever forget that," Mom says, looking from Dad to me as my father nods.

"I will never go a day without appreciating the sacrifice you took raising me, and you will never stop being my mom and dad," I say, voice shaking, as I take one hand from each of them. My composure breaks, and I give in to a sob that shakes me far more than I thought possible. I'm hardly able to stay above the waves. They smooth my hair and wipe my tears, nodding that it's time to go.

I nod as well, realizing that I can't leave—not without them. I will stay, and I *will* be happy. But my mother looks at me, her expression so very knowing.

"You can do this, Vera. You are stronger than you know. You *can* do this," she says, her voice always so confident and brave. If only I had a fraction of that. "You are brave, you are strong, you are kind, and you will leave because I know with absolute certainty that you will live and thrive and love your world. I couldn't be happy with myself if I knew we were what stopped you from seeing it. You will make it a better place, my Vera, because you made *our* world better by just being in it."

I can hardly breathe as I listen to her words and feel their weight. Dad feels the same because he stands behind her, sobbing almost more than me.

"You are a beacon of light, and I would be happy knowing I got to have seventeen years with you, even if I didn't get a second more. But you will return, and you will share so many stories with us, and when it's safe, you can take us there. We will leave it all behind and stay with you as long as it's possible, but for now, you must go," Mom says, finally shedding more than a few tears and hugging me tightly.

"Thank you...for everything," I somehow manage to say, and I let go of her hand, drifting off into the world to come.

5

CONTRADICTIONS

.*✧ VERA ✧*.

The hour-long swim to Taelani goes by in a blur. Every minute of my parents' goodbye has been replaying over and over in my mind. Memories from my childhood make their way into my head, distracting me from the wonders around me. Thankfully, I find the cave without attracting unwanted attention, remembering Kaileah's detailed descriptions of how to get back. I stand before its large stone gates and curse myself for not knowing the spell she used to open it.

"Kaileah? Could you open the gate?" I call out, hoping she can hear. Not long after, it opens in the same grand way as before, and I find Kaileah standing in the middle. I swim forward, but she stops me before I can pass her.

"For the future, the doors can be opened manually. I only used majick because it's easier," she says, and I give her a nod and tight-lipped smile.

We both enter the small living room as she shuts the gates

with a flick of her wrist. Sitting on the roughly worn couch, she places a loving hand on my shoulder. "How did it go?"

"I've never had to do something so difficult. Leaving them feels like losing a part of myself," I state honestly. She struggles to hide the hurt on her face.

"I know how it feels to lose someone you love in more ways than one," she says, her eyes glazing over as she parts them from mine. "But this isn't forever. Tell your heart that they're not gone. They will wait for you to return to them."

"Thank you," is all I can say before leaning into Kaileah's waiting arms, craving to be comforted. She runs her fingers through my hair and hums the tune of her lullaby until I'm calm once again.

"Is there anything else you still want to ask me?" Kaileah asks softly. "There's so much that you still need to learn." She smiles and pushes her beautiful curly hair behind her ear.

I'm aware of why the sensation of Dad touching my ears felt so different. Her ears are remarkably long and pointed with delicate fins matching the color of her pale blue tail.

I reach to touch my own ears once again, feeling the soft, attenuated anatomy. Kaileah notices my intense concentration on her ears and asks, "Have you not seen them yet?"

"Mine felt different, but I hadn't seen them until you moved your hair. Do ours look the same?"

"I'd say so, although yours are a beautiful lavender," she says, touching them the same way Dad did. The memory of our goodbye knocks the smile from my face and replaces it with a pang of guilt so strong it burns.

How could I ever be happy when I chose to leave them behind?

I try to explain the sudden change, but Kaileah puts a hand

over my mouth and urges me to stay silent with wide, angry eyes.

My breath quickens, and I find it hard not to ask *what the hell* is happening. "Hide. *Now*," she whispers with a glass-cutting hiss. I hide behind the partially broken couch and watch the grand door slowly creak open.

A creature so horrifying it sends the marrow of my bones trembling comes through the door, its demonic eyes sliding to meet Kaileah's. Its skin, pale as ice, and two wide, blackened eyes whose only color is a white feline slit in their center stare in assessment. Its mouth is full of razor-sharp teeth, and its snake-like tongue traces the edges of each point as its smile grows too wide for its face. The monster's nose is flattened against its head with two small slits side by side. Its cheekbones are high, and the rest of its face is hollow and deathly.

It moves toward her, revealing its incredible size compared to a creature of our stature. It has to be a whole foot taller at the very least.

Kaileah cranes her neck to keep eye contact with the creature.

"Looks like your freedom has come to a quick end, *Fae Naejikōn*," the thing growls with a threatening yet extraordinarily rich voice. I'm startled by the ability to understand words I *know* are not English. I look to Kaileah, who quickly averts her gaze from me.

Kaileah stands her ground without the slightest look of worry, but I feel her fear. I sense her translating the creature's words as I recognize the feeling of her thoughts in my head once more. Yet now, I realize they were never *in* my head but instead like a whisper around me.

She throws up her hands and hums before yelling back.

"You know what I'm capable of, little siren," she says, her voice laced with pure authority. The cave's rocks begin cracking away, and the creature gains a look of worry that doesn't last long as it's replaced by a large smirk and flick of its forked tongue.

"It's not like you to speak Common unless..." It pauses. "...there's a stray you're protecting." The evil grin on its wretched face grows as I rise from behind the couch.

"Stop! What are you—" Kaileah yells as the thing locks my gaze. Its control falters, and with it, the monstrous exterior collapses. Then, in the blink of an eye, all that is left is...a man.

His hair is long and black, covering part of one eye, and his skin is still pale, but a soft hue of pink has returned. Scars cover his otherwise smooth face, arms, and exposed chest.

Looking down, I see his defined figure tensing with each breath. I move closer, drawn to whatever this humanoid yet monstrous creature is. My mental haze is broken as Kaileah rips me away.

"What in the gods' names are you thinking? He could kill you in the blink of an eye!" she whispers in another harsh tone.

"I'm not here to fight you, *Kaileah*. You, of all people, know there is no choice in what I need to do," he states, grabbing a trident from his back. "If my orders were for your death, I would've never given you the chance to speak."

The weight of the threat and the power it shows he has doesn't have the effect he was expecting. I *should* be feeling fear, yet I'm not.

"What do you want with my mother?" I ask before realizing what I've done. I turn to Kaileah, who wears a face of pure anger.

"Leave now and do not breathe a word of our whereabouts to the king, and I'll be generous and let you leave here alive,"

Kaileah threatens, moving closer to him. His insanely large frame doesn't move, and he only laughs once at the proposal.

"That's an unreasonable request due to my physical obligation to perform His *Naejikōn's* decrees. The most recent of which is taking back his little queen, and, I suppose, his princess, too," he says, lowering his voice and body to reach eye level with Kaileah. To my surprise, she doesn't relinquish a single inch.

"You disgusting *sōurik*. You've been cursed just as I have to serve that *worthless*—" She loses her breath. "I don't want to stand in the presence of a palace slave any longer. GO!"

His face drops any hint of a smile, real or fake, and I see him swallow deeply. I don't know anything about this man, but how could someone I believed to be loving say such horrible things? I move between the two of them, against the grip of Kaileah, before turning to her and shaking my head in disbelief.

"Curse?" I ask with concern, looking back at him. He eyes me delicately without responding. Kaileah is the first to break the silence.

"It doesn't matter. His people deserve it for the suffering they've caused," she spits out. I look at her with disgust before she continues. "He is a siren, and his kind used to lure sailors to their deaths, torturing innocent men and women on land."

She stares deep into my eyes before the siren cuts in, his voice dark and alluring.

"I am a slave to the king, bound to do *anything* he and his right hand want. *That* is my curse," he says, his grip on his trident tightening. "There is no special spell or majick word that can free me except killing those who own me, but I, of course, cannot lay a hand on them or act in a way that could cause them harm. Your mother may claim we were cursed the same, but you are free, and I will never have such a luxury until they kill me," he finishes, his voice and body betraying nothing but neutrality, but *I* feel the pain that lingers just below the surface.

"*Sōuriks* have no regard for your people, so why would you have any for theirs?" Kaileah continues her hateful rant, the words like a statement I would be a fool to disagree with. I can't help how everything in me screams that she's wrong. There has to be more to his people's story.

He opens his mouth to respond before catching a look of sorrow from me. He turns and glances over his shoulder, and his sinister smirk returns while he resheaths his weapon.

"King Argyros won't be happy she's back. I'm glad I'll be the one to reveal the news," the siren states, staring daggers at Kaileah, whose rage boils over. She sends a wave of majick toward him, and he retaliates with unhesitating speed.

I'm diving between them before I can finish processing what they've done.

Time stops as each blast of their majick crackles to life and crawls to me, Kaileah's taking a visual form of blue lightning, each tendril branching to dig itself into my skin. The siren's is invisible to the eye, but I can *hear* it: the raging death that crawls to me like shadows between trees, whispering its promise for a slow, *painful* end.

They both reach me at the same time, and the pain is so unbearable that I can think of nothing else, can only feel the way my skin is being ripped from my muscles with burning hands. Then, thousands of the sharpest knives drive and dig farther and farther into my being, tearing me apart before putting me back together and doing it again.

I cannot breathe, I cannot think, I cannot even begin to imagine a world where this pain does not exist, and I scream for death, for mercy, for anything that will end the torment raging through my body.

I feel myself weakening, slowly collapsing into oblivion, and I welcome it, crawling to the peaceful afterlife. Before death can claim me, strong arms pull me close, and I can tell it's the siren. All I can hear are the muffled voices of the two of them screaming, but that pain—that unrelenting torture—is gone.

"Get your hands off her! I will rip every scale from your body if you hurt her more than you already have." Kaileah screams the threat, choking back tears.

"The last thing I want to do is kill her. Now, please stop speaking so I can save her," he says, words laced with worry while trying to insult my mother. He places a hand on my chest and whispers soft words in an unknown tongue as I feel my breath returning and my vision clearing to a slight fog. "Might I remind you, *my queen*," he says through clenched teeth, "that this damage was not just my doing. You almost killed your own daughter."

I gasp in pain, my teeth clenched so hard they threaten to shatter when he stops his healing whispers. With a slight strength returning, I pull myself closer to his chest, needing him to continue, the cold daggers of pain spreading further.

He turns my head to look at him, and I see the hair was hiding a large scar spanning across his right eye and nose. A second one goes straight through the same eye from his eyebrow to his lower cheek.

"Th—" My voice falters. "Thank you," I say with a pained voice, waiting for him to take it away again. *Please, take the pain away*, I all but scream in my mind. He pushes the hair over his eye before looking up at Kaileah.

"Your daughter thanks me, *Fae Naejikōn*," he says sarcastically.

"She thanks a *sōurik*. A lesser creature undeserving of respect." The siren gently lays me on the couch and places an ear above my heart, likely hearing its beat raging so fast it burns.

My breath quickens as I feel his warm head pressing against me, and I can't control the heat developing across my cheeks. It takes me away from the pain momentarily, as all I can think about are the parts of him that touch me.

Running a tender hand behind my head, he delicately drags two fingers from my neck to the middle of my chest, stopping just before the fabric of my top while whispering in the same tongues as before. My chest pain fades away as his fingers finish their exploration. My body feels healthier and more lively, but my heartbeat accelerates as I realize how beautiful he is, something so deadly masked with a heavenly face.

I turn to cough as he uprights himself and swims to the doorway, turning partially to look at my mother. "If it weren't for her, you'd be unconscious on your way back to the kingdom by now. One day—that's all I'll give you. Get her and yourself out of here because my courtesy will only extend so far," he calls out with barely controlled anger.

"Wait!" I yell, trying to swim toward him before collapsing to the floor, my breath coming in short bursts. I guess he didn't heal me completely.

"You have done enough, Vera! Let him go," Kaileah commands.

"I'm the only reason you're alive right now. Don't tell me what I should or shouldn't do!" I yell back, swimming after him and frantically searching the dark water for a sign of anyone.

Nothing.

Not even a hint that he traveled through here. I breathe out sharply for a moment before regaining my composure.

"Looking for someone?" he asks with a malevolent stare. Instinctively, I punch him in the throat before realizing my mistake.

"*Hei'jaek!*" he yells as he rubs the area where a small patch of red is developing. "You're stronger than I expected for a human." He winces before softening his gaze. "You can stop looking petrified. You're forgiven." I give him an awkward smile in thanks.

"Sorry, but how did you hide from me? There's nothing but water around us."

"They don't call me *T'eiskaeh* without reason." He pauses before coming close and whispering, "*The shadow.*" His face is only inches from mine, and I feel his warm breath against my lips. "Now...now." He moves closer, his voice a taunt. "What now, *saeraih?*"

I move away from him to gain control of my surroundings. He watches me, analyzing my every movement as I do the same to him.

He's dangerous, and he knows it.

My logic tells me I should be afraid, but my heart tells me he's safe.

I shake my head, trying to battle between the contradictions, and he watches me. Each flick of his eyes tells me he's noting something. Am I that easy to read?

"I just wanted to thank you again and ask for your name," I blurt.

"Sirens aren't given names."

"You think I can't spot a liar?" I ask, willing my tone to become assertive. He raises a single brow, likely noticing my sudden change in body language.

"Maybe I just don't want you to know," he counters. He turns his dark eyes to me, sending my heart rate soaring. "You're too trusting. Just because I saved you once doesn't mean I'll do it again. It also doesn't mean you're safe from my bloodlust." He moves closer again, and for a moment, I see the predator behind his beautiful face.

I see a painting of him drenched in blood, not entirely his own, with a smile of pure malicious hunger for violence, darkness swirling as if he is the father of evil itself. I hear the screams of innocents, masked by that raging dark behind him.

But as quickly as the vision comes, it's replaced by another of a young boy, beaten and covered in scars, using his hair to hide what's been done to him. He curls in on himself, wanting no part seen. The two pictures switch back and forth until they morph into something else entirely.

And for a single second, I see him.

As soon as the realization hits me, his gaze darkens, and he looms over me. With my heartbeat quickening, he commands me. "Go back to your mother, *saeraih*."

In the blink of an eye, he's gone.

"I know you're still here, *T'eiskaeh!*" I yell, hoping he'll hear me. It's the first time I've spoken a word in Adleian, and a smile appears as I whisper it again and again.

Chills run over me, and the presence I believed was his is gone, forever faded into the dark abyss around us. What was I thinking following him out here alone?

After everything Kaileah said—

How could I be so quick to ignore her judgment?

Watching my surroundings, I look for the cave entrance and move inside. Kaileah angrily flips the pages of an old, tattered book. At my arrival, she straightens her posture and waits for me to say something, slamming the worn edges so hard I worry it'll disintegrate.

"I'm sorry I didn't listen to you. I know you're trying to protect me, but I won't stand by and watch you treat another being with so little respect," I say softly, moving closer to where she sits. "You know more about this world than I ever will, but I think I know more than you about the consequences of prejudice."

"What are you implying?" Kaileah asks with a glare, placing her book on the nearby shelf.

"I'm just saying that maybe you're wrong about the sirens." What am I saying? What about that interaction proved he was not exactly as she described? I remember those eyes, so intent on violence and fear, but I also remember how they softened.

She laughs, moving before me with a dead look in her eyes.

"I've watched that siren that you seem so fond of kill families. Why don't you ask him about that? Or, of course, you could always ask him about the guards he slaughtered in cold blood. Three of them, to be exact. I'd understand you justifying the hundreds of men, women, and children he's murdered as him following orders he couldn't deny, but the guards...those weren't orders." She says the words with such anger that I can almost taste it in the water between us.

I think back to the grin on his face when he cornered me and the devilish look in his eyes when he told me not to trust him, but every time I see that version, I see the young boy, covered in scars he could not wash away. That side of him was so clear in my head—it couldn't have been all my imagination.

"He kills for the thrill of it. He yearns for blood, and as for why he saved you, I don't know. All I know is that he has a motive we don't yet understand," she states with conviction.

How could I have been so stupid—to swim after him like he was safe?

My chest feels heavy, and it's hard to breathe.

"We're leaving. I know somewhere we'll be safe from him," Kaileah says, returning to that calming motherly voice. I nod, instantly feeling better, but I watch every corner and every dark space for the shadow that saved me.

6

TRUST

.*✮ VERA ✮*.

There's very little talking between Kaileah and me along the journey. I follow close behind while leaving enough distance to avoid the inevitable argument that is to ensue from my outburst.

I wish I knew who I could trust.

What has Kaileah done for me to go by her word? Although the siren isn't much better. Yet I find I trust them both, likely far more than I should.

I trust too easily. I used to call it a good judge of character, but perhaps I'm just too naive to the horrors of the world to realize when someone means me harm. But I've never been wrong before, even when everyone doubted me. That fact is the only thing that keeps my anxiety at bay as I could very easily be damning myself by following my mother.

I gaze at the water around and look for details to keep me distracted. Fish of all colors, seahorses, and algae shaped like the moon, clouds, and stars float and swim around us. I begin to count them, focusing my overactive thoughts. The farther we move from the cave system, the brighter the world around us becomes with the sun harshly shining above and illuminating everything even more clearly, especially with my mer vision.

Staring at her, I notice how beautiful she really is, and I wonder if what I find so divine about her is something I share. While I try to get a better look at her features, she catches my eye.

"Have you decided to talk?" she asks with a neutral voice.

"I was hoping to learn more about our kingdom."

"Ask me anything you would like to know," she answers with a soft smile. "I may be unable to give you the most up-to-date information as I haven't seen it in nearly two decades."

"What's it like there? Well, before you were locked away," I add with a slight grimace.

"It's beautiful. In the capital, Mōrian, there are hundreds of markets and establishments, and the countryside along the edges of Kaerious is *magnificent*. I used to sneak out and dance with your father by the fountain of gold every night I got the chance." Her happiness is contagious, and I smile, too, curious to know more about my birth father and the places she speaks of.

"The fountain of gold?" I ask.

"It's a winter solstice tradition to throw a golden coin into the fountain while whispering your wishes for the coming year. However, many would do it once a month for our various celebrations to increase their chances. By now, I'm sure the fountain is almost completely full of gold. It spans as far as three average houses, and the carvings along each tier are mesmerizing. An enchantment older than our kingdom allows each coin to follow a path resembling a waterfall on land," she explains, closing her eyes and likely envisioning the sight she hasn't seen in nearly two decades.

"I can still remember all those nights I'd dance around its perimeter with your father. Those few hours were the only times I've ever felt pure happiness. He made me feel alive." She stops short, staring off into the distance as if she could spot him in it. My heart breaks for her in that moment. That pain—I can't imagine.

"It's one of the most beautiful sights in all of Adlei. There would be people from everywhere coming to visit and make their wishes. I made a point to be one of them, returning every year for the tradition," she continues, taking out a golden coin and trailing her finger along its raised edges. "Sadly, only one of those was spent with my Lennon. I never thought it would be me on the *aeyla* people threw in," she says with a sad smile, handing the coin to me.

I see her portrait carved into its center, leaves framing her profile.

"What did you wish for?" I ask, and her smile dims, sorrow passing over her perfect features.

"Lennon and I...we'd always wish that one day I'd grow of age and finally break free from Dorian's grasp. I wanted the world to know how much love I felt for him. No more hiding." She touches a small fish passing by and takes a breath. "It wasn't just the fact that your father was a commoner and I was married that was keeping us apart. He was part human, which is highly frowned upon or often forbidden."

I frown at that—what is so wrong with being part human?

"Why?"

"Mixed races are not allowed, and I don't know why. I never cared enough to ask," she explains with a sad shrug. "Needless to say, our wish never came true. There's never a set time when it will or a guarantee it will at all. I suppose the fountain isn't as miraculous as we grew up to believe."

I can tell she is leaving out a part of her story, likely hiding me from the scope of her trauma. She swims in silence for a while longer, reminiscing on a time long passed.

I catch myself daydreaming about what life could have been like with Kaileah as my mother and Lennon as my father, and the idea sends a wave of grief and guilt through me. How can I possibly grieve the death of someone I never met?

But perhaps it was never meeting my father that sent those horrible aches into my chest—the idea that no matter what I do, I will never meet the man who made me.

I touch my hair, looking into its dark layers, and wonder how closely it resembles his. Does Kaileah see him in me? Do I remind her of who she lost? How much of him am I made of, and what about me was because of him, even though he wasn't there to raise me?

I wonder if it was him who was so trusting of others...who thought of everyone else and all their reasons for being who they were.

"The kingdom was so different back then," she continues after a while. "I wish you could have seen it before Dorian. That disgusting king ruined it. No amount of control would ever satiate him, so he never stopped taking."

I let the silence between us trail for a while before I respond.

"What was my father like?" I ask, and she looks at me as if she can see him in my face. The idea washes away a piece of my grief.

"His hair was long and dark, just like yours, and his eyes were a beautiful golden brown. I see him in your smile. He had those same dimples, and his eyes creased just like yours do. He was the kindest soul, and he would help *anyone* who needed it, regardless of who they were." She pauses, looking down at me. "I suppose you're just like him in that way, as much as I am opposed to helping certain *dangerous* people."

"I see why you loved him so dearly," I say, lightly touching her arm.

"I did. I really did," she says, her hands and voice shaking as she quiets.

I want to tell her that he is with her, listening to her tell his daughter these stories. I want to tell her that he is likely smiling just like she described, knowing his daughter loved him without ever truly knowing him, dimples and all. I want to say it—feel I *need* to—but those words failed me.

"Where are we going?" I ask, thinking about the hour of travel behind us and trying to take her away from the painful memory. I fear being in the open as the kingdom's most wanted fugitives is a recipe for disaster.

"A place known for their hospitality," she says, and I stare at her in confusion before she adds, "The Koifinn Clan. A friend to all nations."

Another place I will be a complete, hopeless stranger to, but if they are kind, as my mother describes, then I cannot be upset.

We travel for what seems like an endless amount of time, occasionally hiding behind rocks, plants, and anything else we can find to obscure our path.

I watch the shadows, searching for the siren, but I can't sense or see him anywhere. I can't tell if relief or disappointment fills me each time I check, and he isn't there.

After what has to be two or more hours, I grab Kaileah's arm and motion for us to take a break. I can hardly focus my eyes because my body is so exhausted. If I move one more inch, I fear I will collapse altogether.

"Is something wrong?" she asks with a gentle voice. *Wrong* would be an understatement.

"I'm not used to this much swimming," I say, out of breath and clenching from the tightness in my abdomen and tail. "I just…" I pause. "Need a break." Kaileah leads us to a large forest of plants, most glowing with a beautiful bioluminescence that looks almost alien.

I move to feel them, the soft and jagged edges of the leaves tickling my skin. At the touch of my hand, the plant moves away and cowers. Tilting my head to gain a better look, the leaves do the same, mimicking all my movements before reaching out a delicate leave to graze my cheek. Horrified, yet intrigued, I look to Kaileah to see her smiling so large her eyes are nearly closed.

"*La'minōlu*," Kaileah states, moving closer. "These plants grow in forests to aid prey from attackers. Mer are usually the predators in these waters, so it's often afraid. I suppose the forest rather likes you, though," she says, gesturing to the leaf now curling around my shoulder.

Kaileah whispers to the tall kelp-like vegetation, which wraps around her, taking her away and blocking the path from view. I look behind me to see the forest, watching my moves, mimicking them like the one around my shoulder, but it cowers when I reach out to touch it.

I frown, trying to show the sentient plants that I mean them no harm, but still, they keep their distance. Patting the leaf, I wiggle out of its grasp and swim to the widest beam, slightly larger in all ways than the rest.

"Can you take me to her? I swear I mean no harm," I plead with the *la'minōlu*, but it only sways with the water's current in response. "I don't know what I'm supposed to say to you. I'm not a predator."

It moves forward like a living creature and eyes me as well as a stalk can. A faint push of water trickles past my ears, and before I can conclude what it means, I'm shoved into the forest by its massive branches and soft leaves.

The *la'minōlu's* stems grow and envelop me with a gentle grasp as they shove me deeper into the forest. Looking around, hundreds of la'minōlu that were not there before come into view, shielding me from the world.

A tap on my shoulder sends a tremor of fear down my spine, chills appearing on every inch of my exposed skin as I somehow know the touch isn't my mother's.

"Don't be so scared, princess," a man's voice whispers into my ear, my hair rising with the heat of his breath. "It's just *me*." I turn around, expecting to see the siren, but I see only Kaileah sporting a happy smile.

Searching the stalks, I see no sign of him, and the forest makes no motion that someone else is in here with us.

I'm losing my mind, too. Just when I think I can't fit in any less.

"It's important that you learn skills independently because I won't always be there to guide you. This is a strange and dangerous world, and sadly, you have the disadvantage of time," Kaileah says with the tone of a teacher, but I barely listen.

"Was there someone else here just now?" I ask, peering into the shadows. The forest watches me and sways as if to say *he's not here.*

"No? It's not likely that you'll find mer hiding inside a la'minolu forest. Many of them don't even understand their complexity."

"What did you whisper to it to get taken away so quickly?" I ask, aware of my lack of knowledge. "I should probably learn how to ask for help in Adleian."

"I simply asked to be hidden, but understandably, it didn't trust you immediately. I've come here before, begged and pleaded, to no avail. There are no language barriers amongst these plants; they understand your heart, not your wor—" She stops mid-sentence and pulls me close, forcing my eyes to look where hers are pointing.

I see two men with tridents through the small space between each *la'minōlu*. They look around and mumble in a language I can only assume to be Adleian as they slash the innocent, glowing plants. As each stalk falls to the ocean floor, the entrancing blue glow fades out and dies, and with each one, I feel my heart break.

Kaileah moves closer and whispers, "I will send their words to you as I did before." As she holds my arm and whispers a hum, the inaudible, muffled grunts turn into words I can understand.

"Where is that stupid woman hidin'?" the older of the two grumbles under his breath. His ragged skin is lined with wrinkles, seemingly having endured many years of harsh sun. His voice speaks of his lack of intelligence or, rather, lack of refinement.

The man wipes a bloodstain from his cheek and cuts another stalk. My heart burns as the plants around me shiver with fear and sorrow. "I ought'a cut all this kelp-lookin' muck to the ground."

"Excuse me, General Draik, but I thought the siren said she went farther south. We're heading east." The general turns to the boy, who can't be older than me, and grabs his neck.

"Question me one mo' time, and I'll cut out yer tongue and

feed it to yer mother. You speak when I say so, ya' hear?" With the release of his tight grip, the boy straightens his posture and becomes a shell of himself, all emotion gone.

White and red marks form in the shape of a hand around his throat, and his tight swallows are all I can see to show how badly it hurts.

"Yes, sir."

"If yer sorry self has ta'know, that *sōurik* lies whenever he gets a chance. I don't trust no sirens one bit." He spits to the side and whispers quietly, "*Not one bit.*" I look at Kaileah, and she relaxes, no longer humming her spell.

"They're on to us. Where do we go now?"

"This is going to be very uncomfortable for you, my dear, but we're going to swim down as far as we can. There, we will be safe from view to continue," she says with a wince.

Why will it be uncomfortable?

It doesn't take long to realize what she meant as we dive farther and farther, the sunlight slowly disappearing as we stray from its range.

The pressure of the near thousand-foot plunge is overwhelming; my lungs struggle to inflate, and I feel my eyes popping from my head as my skull compresses in.

"Ka...Kai." I try to suck in enough oxygen to finish a sentence. "Kaile...ah...too deep. I ca...can't breathe." She turns around with a simple look of concern and covers my eyes.

At first, I'm even more worried than before, but focusing on the angelic sound of my mother's song, I can feel myself relaxing.

"*Haenur ti'deōrin, saenuir mau'jauilōrn,*" she sings with quiet velvet tones. My breath returns, and the throbbing sensation in my head fades to a simple buzz. I pull away and rub my temples to remove the remaining pain. Even so, my breathing is still strained, and my vision struggles to adapt.

"What did you do?"

"Nothing. I just distracted you long enough for your instincts to take over. Mer have evolved to handle sudden pressure changes, but your human fears overshadowed that."

When I've calmed my mind enough, we continue. I follow her through endless turns, bare expanses, and dark caves and passages. Sometimes, I must hold onto Kaileah to continue where even my dark vision cannot help. We push through, knowing that what lies on the other side of this trek will be worth it. I *hope* it will be worth it.

Returning to a level where the sun shines on the ocean's surface is when I see the place we've been looking for.

7

NEW BEGINNINGS

.*⭐ VERA ⭐*.

An elegant stone archway with carved brick walls rises high on either side of us, the rocks so large I wonder what could have moved them into such a position. Rows and rows of crops cover the plowed land, with young merfolk tending to the budding plants. Their conversations, chatter, and commands fill the air with the sounds of children frolicking about the fields.

Citizens swim in and out of the gateless entrance, some moving to help children garden along the adjoining walls while others leave to explore. Kaileah and I drift closer, taking in the sights of happy families and lovers, all free from fear.

Along the city are flowers—thousands of them covering and trickling down from every surface. The Koifinn people hold their hands to the plants as they expand in size and color, the weak ones flourishing and the strong doubling in size.

It is a beautiful sight and one I cannot begin to paint into existence, the charm of each petal and the plants' glowing centers. To do so would forfeit my lifetime.

Looking past the wall, I see two young girls in formal clothing playing near a bell tower. A sharp clang hits my ears as one falls against the large brass bell, the two giggling and clutching their stomachs from laughter.

The smaller one catches my eye and motions the other, likely her sister due to their similar appearance, to look. Within a few moments, the older girl is before us and gives an excited curtsy.

Her hair is a sun-touched, muted red with two braids tied together in the back. Her face is covered in beauty marks and freckles around her large brown eyes, like the helm of a sunken ship. A few strands poke out from the loosely braided hair and drape over her soft facial features.

I see her apple cheeks and perfectly full lips as she smiles softly. Her smile could instantly melt the darkest heart, and I can see now that she is the physical embodiment of kindness and everything good in the world.

"Frōndi, Fae Naejikōn," she says while bowing. Her accent differs from Kaileah's, sounding more like those on land, and her tone is soft and delicate. If I had to compare it to one I've heard before, it would have to be from when I visited England. With her moving closer, a sweet, fruity smell catches my attention.

"Oh, darling, you need not use my language. I'm happy to speak Common or my minimal Kefian. This is your country, after all," Kaileah says, extending the same courtesy.

"Wonderful! I'm Korah Fenton, Governor Sarren's eldest daughter. What brings you to Shari?"

"Lovely to meet you, Miss Fenton. This is my daughter," she says while pulling me closer. "I know it's a lot to ask, but if you would be kind enough to allow us safety for the next week, I would forever be in your debt."

Her face lights up with a contagious happiness showing off the deep dimples kissing her cheeks.

"Oh, my *stars!*" She spins around before taking a steadying breath. "I'm sorry," she says with a pause. "It isn't very often that we get foreign visitors, much less royalty. Of course you can stay! Make yourself at home." Korah stops momentarily, her eyes twitching as if searching the catalog of her mind. "Wait. You're *the* princess? The story—Asherah of Adlei—it's true?"

"While I'm not sure of the 'story,' I am the princess, but you can call me Vera," I say, moving back before Korah grabs my hands and flips them so the palms are facing up.

Tracing her fingers across the creases and healed scars, she studies me while furrowing thick, well-groomed brows. Her dainty hands are softer than satin without any scrapes or callouses.

The sensations of her light touch will likely put me to sleep if she continues for much longer.

She shakes her head, pulls my hands closer, pushes them away, lets go, grabs them once more, sighs, and finally meets my confused expression.

"I have no clue how to read palms. My mother tried to teach me, but I can't remember. Oh well! Follow me, my new friend!" she exclaims, her eyes all but sparkling.

What a strange individual.

Korah does what I would assume to be the mer version of skipping. She swiftly swims forward before twirling clockwise, swimming farther, and spinning in the opposite direction. Frankly, I'm surprised at her coordination skills.

With a short, delicate tail and sheer fin nearly half its length flying in all directions, I can't believe it doesn't knock her off balance.

Looking closer at her tail, I notice its differences from mine beyond the size. It's white with groupings of scales pigmented red and orange, mimicking the coloration of a koi fish precisely —no doubt the origin of their race's name. The way it flicks and swishes through the water creates small bubbles that follow her, occasionally causing her to shiver when they catch up.

Korah drags me through the city while hundreds of eyes follow us, some whispering and others gawking. My mother follows close behind, but the usual feeling of safety I get in her presence is replaced with a familiar feeling of fear.

I've never enjoyed being the center of attention. Not as a human, and *especially* not as whatever I am now. I avoid the harsh stares that burn into my peripherals and try to maintain an excited expression for my guide. I grab Kaileah's arm, shutting my eyes and drowning out the sound of their whispers.

I don't need to understand their words to know exactly what they're saying.

What are they doing here? Is that the Adleian queen? If so, who is that girl with her? Her face bears a striking resemblance...could she be the—

During our short yet draining trip, we pass beautiful taverns and shops with intricate, beaded jewelry and hand-sewn, embroidered gowns, all of which leave my mouth wide with admiration.

"Aaand..." Korah draws out the word as long as possible. "Here we are!"

Before us is the grandest shop I have ever seen. It is three stories high and appears to be packed with every clothing item imaginable. Happy customers enter and exit with armfuls of bags stuffed tightly with clothing and accessories.

Swimming inside, we are immediately greeted by an employee, but I'm too distracted by the spritzing of pungent perfumes and fruity mists flooding my senses.

"*Tei, towandi e halan lu fevun?*" the man asks with a slight bow and high-pitched voice.

"Nothing for me, but some visitors desperately need a gorgeous outfit. No budget, and I'm going to need your top stylist," she states with an assertiveness I didn't expect. "Thank you, good sir."

"I—" the man stutters. "Right away, Miss Fenton. Whose name should I put this under?"

"Mine," she says, ignoring Kaileah's objections to her paying.

While waiting, I glance through each aisle, touching the delicate silk and perfect pearls. Each outfit is far grander than any I have ever owned, and I wish I could understand their pricing. I couldn't possibly accept something outrageous.

"Have I said how much I adore your hair? I've never seen any as long or dark as yours!" Korah says, reaching to touch it before stopping herself.

"Well, you have to have seen hair my length before. Your hair is only about four inches shorter than mine," I respond with a half smile.

"Inches?" she asks with a tilt of her head.

How do I explain human measurements with no basis for their understanding?

"Do you see the distance from the top of your pinky to your first joint? That's roughly an inch. Four pinky tips is how much longer my hair is compared to yours," I say while holding my smallest finger to my hair.

"It is? I never realized!" Her eyes widen with joy. "Kiya! I was hoping you were working today," Korah says, turning to a middle-aged Koifinn woman.

Her hair is styled with large twists falling to her shoulders like bright pink vines contrasting her deep, ebony skin.

"You think I'd miss a chance to style runaway royals? Absolutely not!" She winks at us. "The news is spreading all over town," Kiya says, pulling out a measuring tape.

It looks identical to the rulers back home, but the units are completely foreign, and there is no pattern I can discern between each number.

"Lift your arms for me, honey."

I do as she asks, and Kiya wastes no time measuring my bust, waist, and hips. She remains focused and moves on to my mother, who I can tell is more than used to this treatment. Korah stands back, showing me a large smile and two thumbs up when my eyes wander.

"Check back in thirty, and I'll have two outfits ready," Kiya says with a confident smile. "I think I know just the piece for you both."

We swim out of the shop, and I'm once again met with the beautiful sights of the capital city. While each structure isn't grand, its essence is majickal.

Sunlight descends from above and paints each building with the mesmerizing sight of moving water. Each house has a thatch, stone, or wooden roof and multicolored stained wood and brick walls. Their front doors are decorated with bioluminescence and bizarre plants, and I find myself distracted by the expansive fields in the distance as I catch my breath from today's exhausting travels.

The sights are only a temporary distraction from my lack of

energy, and I catch myself on a nearby bench before collapsing into the soft seagrass below.

"Vera?" I turn to see Kaileah swimming closer. "Are you okay?" she asks with concern.

"Yeah, I'm just a little overwhelmed with all of *this*," I say, gesturing my hands to encircle us. "Not to mention, I don't think I could be more drained."

"The Koifinn people are..." She pauses and sighs, trying to find the words. "Vivacious people. It can get overwhelming, but you'll grow used to it."

Korah swims back after noticing the large distance formed between us. She returns and grabs my arm to lead me away once again.

"Keep up, silly!" she says, and I wonder how she can't see the blatant exhaustion all over my face.

"Look, Korah, you're lovely, but I'm beyond tired. I would love to finish your tour, but could it wait until tomorrow?" I ask, hoping my words don't come off too harshly, but her adorable smile falls into a concerned frown of sympathy nonetheless.

She pulls me into a hug, and the fruity scent from before is even more apparent, with hints of honeysuckle coming from her flowing hair. Did a stranger just hug me?

"I should have realized. You poor thing! Let's take a break here and wait until the clothes are ready. After that, I'll take you home!" she says, leading me to a small crescent-shaped bench with cushions. I sit without another second's delay.

"Oh, look!" She points to a man coming our way. He spots us, waving as he approaches. "Vera, meet my brother, Alec," she says, her voice lowering in pitch as her eyebrows lower in apprehension.

"Alexander Fenton. Pleased to make your acquaintance, Miss

Vera," he says flirtatiously with a bow and a light kiss on my hand. His lips are soft and delicate as they linger for a second longer than I would expect. He turns, seeing Kaileah, and adds, "Queen Kaileah! What a pleasure to have you visiting Shari!"

"The pleasure is mine. Your family has done remarkable things for this city. It looks more beautiful than ever."

"Thank you, *Fae Naejikōn*. My family has worked tirelessly to make it what you see today," Alexander states humbly. He sits and eyes me intently. "What is a beautiful girl like you doing so far from Adlei?" he asks, moving his hand ever so slightly closer to mine. His head follows me in my trail from his flattened hand to his face, and as I reach his lips, I catch an all too confident smirk.

I look at Korah and see her disgusted expression watching her brother, and I can't help but laugh.

"Ouch. Way to let me down softly," Alexander says with a chuckle and stung tone, the corners of his smile turning down.

"Oh, no! No! I didn't mean it like that." I try to stop my laughter but fail. "It's your sister's face."

He looks up and laughs along after catching her gagging.

"Alec! Give the girl some respect! That's the queen's daughter you're talking to," she reprimands. His eyes widen as he looks from Korah, to me, to Kaileah, to me once again.

"*Feina!*" he whispers harshly under his breath. "I am so sorry, Your Highness. Excuse my informality earlier."

"I just found out I had a noble title last night. Trust me when I say I don't mind the normalcy."

"What a relief. Wait, I thought the princess's name was Asherah?" he asks, running a hand through his hair.

"Well, it is, but I didn't know that until yesterday, either," I respond.

He gazes at me, deep in thought. With everyone's silence, I notice his appearance. His hair ripples in soft, reddish-brown waves that fall at his shoulders, and his eyes are a deep green matching the depths of a forest. The subtle stubble on his face and deep-set dimples give him an aged yet youthful expression paired with his slightly unkempt appearance.

I look down to see his tail, the color almost the same as Korah's with more colored scales than white, and it's length is a noticeable amount longer. His fin, unlike hers, is about a quarter the length of his tail but falls in the same flowing layers.

Running a hand through his hair again, he looks to his sister and whispers in their native tongue, likely to avoid Kaileah and I understanding. He speaks with aggravation, and his sister chastises him.

"Korah, finish what you're doing here and take Her *Naejikōn* around the city. I'll take Vera to where they'll be staying."

"I don't take orders from you, brother," she states with a level tone and hardened eyes.

He shoots her a warning glance, and she responds with rolling eyes.

"I'll go grab the outfits! I'm sure they're ready by now," she says, returning to her happy, smiley self. "Be back soon! I promise he doesn't bite." She laughs before swimming off, and I move to speak with my mother.

"What's going on between them?" I ask, making sure Alec isn't listening.

"What do you mean? That's just how siblings are," Kaileah reassures me, but it does little to stop the anxiety their conversation brought.

"No, but their tone...It was more than just banter. Do you think it has to do with me?"

"Vera, sweetheart, you did not do anything wrong, so there is nothing to worry about." As she gives me a reassuring touch and cups my cheek, I allow myself to relax. "There's no one who will hurt you now that I've gotten you back, so take a breath and enjoy the beauty of your new world," she says with a gentle kiss on my forehead. As I look around once more, I see Korah approaching with empty hands.

"Unfortunately Kiya said I wasn't allowed to take the outfits until you two tried them on, so if you wouldn't mind coming with me?" she asks, and we follow her back to the clothing store and into a large dressing room with thick curtains separating each room.

I swim into the first one and notice how much larger it is on the inside. Hooks covering the walls show the amount of clothes merfolk try on and purchase here.

Putting on the outfit, I notice its vast details. The top has two large white shells dotted with diamonds covering my chest. The sleeves, made with a sheer silky fabric fading between a purple identical to my tail and a blue like Kaileah's, hang below my shoulders and hug only my forearm and wrist tightly with the rest flowing to make a shape resembling a jellyfish. The fabric is embroidered with flowers, sea creatures, and plants of all designs in an iridescent thread, making it almost invisible at first glance.

The straps holding it up are thin, clear strings strung with pearls and crystal beads. Matching straps hold the shells together and wrap around my back.

The bottom of the clothing set uses the same blue and lilac fabric as the top, and a tight elastic hugs my hip with flowing silk peeking out above. Two pieces of the long flowing cloth span to the base of my fin. Connecting the two fabric pieces is another shell laden with diamonds, along with a string of rock and jewels wrapping around my waist.

While I should feel beautiful staring into a mirror wearing an outfit made for me, I feel like an imposter who has taken another girl's place. I don't deserve this...the kind treatment, expensive gifts, and respectful adoration.

I peek out of my dressing room and look for my mother, but I can't see her.

"Kaileah?" I ask in a little more than a whisper. There's no response for a moment until I see her poking her head out from behind the curtain.

"Yes?"

"I don't know if I feel comfortable wearing something so extravagant. It's going to attract attention." I hold my arms across myself as my insecurity grows.

"You won't garner much more attention than we already have." She swims out of her dressing room. "And I'm sure you look beautiful. Come out so I can see."

Reluctantly, I move out of the room while covering my stomach to hide how revealing the outfit is. Kaileah's eyes light up as she sees me in clothing from her culture, and she grabs my hands, looking intensely into my eyes.

"You look stunning, but you need to stand tall and proud." She lets go of my hands and spreads her arms out wide, allowing me to see what she's wearing unobstructed.

A herringbone silver necklace wraps twice around her neck before connecting to a large blue stone in between her collarbones. From it hangs a slightly smaller stone, falling to below the center of her chest. The first gem connects two pieces of a midnight-blue fabric with glowing details that mimic the color of her pale-blue tail, curving to show center cleavage and some from the side.

The two cloths connect at her navel and fall to the length of her tail, with the back being longer and wider than the front. The intricate material is lined with silver detailing, and her upper arms are left uncovered with two thick herringbone cuffs stacked on either side.

"A mer's skin is one of our most beautiful features. How it reflects the waves' textures and its natural shine shows what it means to be alive!" she says, and I uncover my stomach, feeling more confident after her words. "It's our culture, and I would love to share it with you." She pulls my head to her and gently kisses my forehead before swimming off.

I stand before the large mirror, alone, and look again at what I see. What she describes is true, as I watch the way my skin almost shimmers as light hits it, and I feel like I might be able to show off every inch.

Exiting the shop, I see Korah and Alexander waiting for us. Her mouth falls open, and her eyes glaze over as we continue to approach.

"Oh, for the love of all things sweet! Vera, you look amazing! Do you like it?" Korah asks with her girlish smile. I return it and do as my mother suggested, holding myself strong and confident.

"I like it very much," I say.

"Since my brother insists and cannot wait to speak to you alone, I will take Her *Naejikōn* on a tour of the rest of Shari." Korah turns to Kaileah. "Is that alright with you, *Fae Naejikōn?*" she asks.

"That is fine by me. Lead the way," my mother agrees softly. As the two of them depart from us, I find myself consumed by the silence between Alec and I. Sneaking glances at his facial expressions, I can't read what he is thinking. With each passing moment, I grow more uneasy, waiting for something to break the tension without having to do it myself.

"Now that they're gone, I have something important I need to tell you. Follow me, Your Highness," he says in an even tone. I don't know what could be so important that my mother shouldn't be with me to hear it.

We enter a tavern and Alexander motions to the bartender. There is an understanding between them, and he leads us into a private room with what looks like an oil lamp to light it. Its blue flame flickers and defies all logic of land. It must be majick.

He takes a deep breath and runs a hand through his thick, silky hair, leaning his head back and exposing the muscles of his neck.

"You're killing me. Please spit it out," I say, attempting to liven the mood, but he barely smiles in response.

"I don't know how to sugarcoat this, Vera, so I'm just going to say it," he begins, and my heartbeat quickens as I wait. "It would be in your best interest to not tell anyone you're the Adleian princess. They may know that she's here, but no one knows who she is." He looks at me with piercing eyes. "For your sake, do not tell anyone."

Even with his point made, I can't help the way my heart is incessantly pounding.

"W—What?" I choke on the word. "Why not? Am I in danger?"

"No, it's nothing like that. Do you not understand what I'm implying with this?" he asks with belittling condescension, taking away some of my anxiety and replacing it with budding anger.

"Sorry, but no, I don't," I say roughly. It doesn't take long for me to regret my snappy response, remembering I'm at the mercy of his family for protection. He sighs again and steadies his tone.

"The people of this clan don't like mixed breeds, and in case you aren't aware, being part human makes you one," he says with raised brows. I stare at him with shock at not only the clan's people, but how he said it. "I'm just trying to prepare you for the looks and comments people will make about you."

"What do you mean I'm a 'mixed breed'? I'm not some animal," I say, removing myself from the table.

"I'm sorry, that came out harshly. I just meant that most of us aren't very accepting of unusual things like mixing races," he continues, the words seemingly forced out and awkward. I continue to move away and eventually reach the door where we entered, but I'm stopped by Alexander pressed against me, holding the door shut.

"Listen to me, Vera. I'm trying to help you," he adds.

"Are you trying to help me, or are you trying to save yourself the embarrassment of being seen with someone like me?" I respond too suddenly, and he sighs again under his breath. Pushing past his grip, I open the door and swim out of the tavern back onto the bustling street.

I don't need your help, I want to say, but I know it's not true. He and his family are our only chance at being hidden until Kaileah finds another plan.

He follows close behind, trying to convince me to go back with him.

"You are one of the most beautiful girls I've laid eyes on, so no, I am far from embarrassed about being seen with you. I don't care about the comments the townspeople will make, but I'm trying to prepare you and protect your feelings in case *you do*."

He places a gentle hand on my shoulder. "Forgive my careless tongue. I wasn't raised to be accepting of differences, but Korah has changed me. I still screw up from time to time as you saw, but I truly mean no offense," he adds with a soft grin, and I can't help but forgive him.

"I understand. Thank you for warning me," I say with a reassuring smile. "I'll do my best to keep who I am a secret, although it shouldn't be very difficult, considering I have always just been Vera."

My response must have meant a great deal to him because his shoulders relax and he sighs in relief.

"Let's get you to where you and your mother will be staying. From my understanding, you've been all over the ocean without a break," he says, nudging me with a half-smile.

"You're right about that," I say, returning the gesture.

"Luckily for us, my home is only a five-minute swim away, but we can stretch it to ten if you'd prefer to go slower."

"That would be great. Thank you, Alexander," I say, thankful for the prospect of rest.

"Call me Alec," he says, glancing down at me with a flirtatious smirk pulling at the corner of his mouth.

"Okay. Lead the way, Alec," I say, meeting his eyes. He looks away and begins swimming toward our destination. I grab his arm and lean my head on him, unable to hold it up for any longer, and I feel his skin grow slightly warmer.

8

A TEMPORARY HOME

.*⭐ VERA ⭐*.

The travel goes by in a blur, and before I know it, we've arrived. Their home is grand compared to the fairly simple buildings and homes surrounding it. The walls are a brilliant gray stone, and the roof is made of bronze-colored shingles. As we get closer, I can see the entrance is through a stone patio and archway that leads to a black metal front door with two large panes of glass and curving metal designs.

Alec opens the door and motions for me to enter before shutting it once again. The interior is far more luxurious than the outside.

It's as if I have entered a small castle.

The ambiance produced by the dim candlelight is comforting and serene, and I find myself unable to hear Alec's words, focusing only on the foreign trinkets, furnishings, decorations, and more.

"And here is where we keep our—"

"What does this say?" I ask and notice that not only have I not listened to what he's been saying, but I have also cut him off. "Oh, I'm sorry. I didn't realize you were talking."

"That whole time? You really heard *nothing* I said?" he asks, his brows raised. I shake my head, and he laughs. "If I wasn't so horrifically angry at the disrespect, I'd say that's a skill," he jests.

"I've never seen a smile so large on someone so 'angry,'" I respond with a smile back at him. "How will I *ever* convince you to forgive me, your greatness?" I say, grabbing his hands and pouting my lips. Alec laughs at an excessive volume and immediately covers his mouth to stop himself. It's contagious because I soon join him.

"Alec, *dei o thalen?*" a little boy asks, swimming closer to us. He looks confused yet not surprised at a random woman in his home.

How many women does Alec bring home?

"This is Vera. She's a visitor from Adlei who will stay with us for a little while," he says while bending down to the little boy's level. "Meet my brother, Cyprus." Alec ruffles his brother's hair and Cyprus frowns. "*Uesi Cengleso*, please?" Alec asks coaxingly.

"I hope you no like him 'cause he mean," Cyprus says with an angry pout after shoving his brother away. "I gonna tell Mom you messed up my...my hair."

"Go for it, kid."

The boy sighs in defeat and swims off, muttering to himself in Kefian.

"How old is he?" I ask.

"Just turned four, and his Common isn't the best. He stubbornly resists our efforts to persuade him to learn," Alec says with a shrug.

"I thought he sounded fine for a child, especially that age," I add.

"Oh, really? Mer children often speak full, coherent sentences by two, but to give Cyprus some credit, he speaks Kefian very well for his age."

"Really? That must be why my parents always said I was a gifted child," I say with a chuckle. "Apparently, I was talking like a six-year-old when I was two."

"I definitely can't relate to that. My parents said I was 'developmentally challenged' because I didn't start mumbling until one and a half, and I didn't talk coherently until almost three." He flexes his muscles and bites his lip dramatically before saying, "I guess you could say I was born to disappoint them."

I playfully slap his arm and hold my mouth to try to keep from laughing again.

"You sorry excuse for a firstborn," I say, sticking my tongue out. He shrugs again with a big smile as if to say: *you're not wrong.*

After we finally stop laughing, Alec leads me to their living room, where I see Cyprus and the young girl from the bell tower. She turns and meets my eyes, motioning for me to join her on the couch.

"Hi! I'm Delilah. I saw you earlier, but you probably didn't notice me," she mumbles, looking away. In the well-lit room, I notice her curly saturated red hair and face covered in freckles. Her large deep blue eyes seem to glow with their intensity. "I told Korah to go talk to you because I recognized Queen Kaileah and thought it was something important. When she didn't call me over or come back, I decided it would be best to just go home."

"I noticed you right away, and I was wondering where you disappeared off to when Korah approached us," I say, lowering myself to her level. Her face lights up and her eyes grow even wider.

"Really? Most people don't notice me, especially when I'm around my sister," she says, her cheeks tinting red as she talks.

"I can't see why! Your hair is some of the prettiest I've seen, and oh my, I can't even tell you how much I love your freckles," I say, and she lights up even more. I can tell Delilah needs to feel special, especially to a stranger who has no obligation to compliment her. She touches her face and runs a hand through her hair.

"My freckles? You like them?" she asks with hope and excitement.

"Of course! They look like an artist hand-painted each one to make you more and more beautiful." I mimic how I would paint them, lightly tapping them on her large cheeks.

She covers her mouth and gasps before pulling me into a hug. After she lets go, she rushes to her brother, and I hear her *attempting* to whisper.

"Alec, I love her. Please ask Mom and Dad if she can stay forever."

"Do you even know her name, little shrimp?" Alec asks.

"Well, yeah, of course I do. It's—" Delilah pauses and thinks. "Huh. I guess I don't know." She rushes back over and sits on the couch once again. "Hi again! What's your name?"

"Vera," I answer with a knowing grin.

"I love that name! What are you doing here, Vera?" I look at Alec for guidance, and he shakes his head in warning.

"I'm one of the queen's assistants. She's still on a tour with Korah, but I wanted to see where Her Majesty and I would be staying."

"So you *are* staying with us? For how long?" Her voice can barely contain her excitement as she sways her fin like a puppy wagging its tail.

"I'm not sure. That's for the queen to decide."

How long are we going to run is the real question.

I look over at Alec and see him entertaining Cyprus as he plays with superhero action figures with tails and scales. I lie my head on my arm to rest, trying not to fall asleep in their living room. Noticing, Alec finishes up with Cyprus and puts his arm around me.

"Shrimp?" Alec asks, and Delilah looks up at him. "Go get freshened up for dinner. The queen and Miss Vera here will join us."

"Ah!" She drops everything and swims to the doorway. "How much time do I have?" she asks, her big eyes growing larger as she waits for his answer.

"About an hour or two."

"There's so little time!" she says swiftly, exiting the room and rushing down the long hallway.

"You too, Cyprus."

"Nuh-uh. I no move," he says, not acknowledging his brother. Alec rolls his eyes and leads me down the hallway into a different wing of their manor.

As he opens a rosewood door, my jaw slackens at the huge room before me. Next to the entrance is a fireplace with plants unknown to me piled in front to fuel it. A blue chaise lounge sits in front with a green carpet underneath.

I swim in and look around further, noticing the walls lined with hundreds of books. The bed, a thick blue comforter on top of a king-sized mattress with fluffy pillows, sits in the center of the room with two wooden nightstands on either side.

In front is a vanity with a mirror, chair, and an assortment of ornate brushes displayed on its countertop.

"This can't be my room. Is it?" I ask, glancing back in ecstatic disbelief.

"Yes, it is, but if it's not to your standards, you can always join me in my room. I don't mind." He winks with a wicked grin.

"Woah, Alec! You're too direct. You *know* I'm not that kind of girl," I reply with a melodramatic smirk.

"Oh, forgive my enthusiastic frankness, my beautiful fair lady. It was not my intent to overstep the boundaries of our newly formed acquaintance," he says with a bow.

Breaking character, he looks up with a big smile and bursts into hysterical laughter. I match his laughter, concluding the theatrical scene until we can hardly contain ourselves.

"No, but seriously, not to my standards! This is one of the largest single-person rooms I've ever seen. It's practically a suite!" I say in between laughs at such a suggestion. "But thanks for being considerate. This is just fine."

"All that matters is you're happy. It's used for both a guest room and library if you were wondering about the books," he says, pointing to the shelves. "I'll let you relax and get ready for dinner. Korah will come down here when she gets back with the queen." He bows and moves out of the room. "See you soon, princess," he says with a wink and shuts the door.

Heat swells to my cheeks and brings a small grin to my face, but I shake the feeling away and lie down to rest.

A knock sounds at the door, and I groan into the pillow, not realizing I fell asleep.

"Vera?" a voice calls from the door.

I toss in bed, pretending the voice is in my head and ready to go back to sleep, but the creaking door and light from the hallway take away that possibility.

"It's Kaileah," she says, easing the door open to sit beside me in bed. I squint and rub my eyes, trying to gain enough energy to wake up.

"How long have I..." I yawn. "...been asleep?" She places a hand on my head and runs her fingers through my hair. Her delicate touch sends tingles down my neck, and I close my eyes again.

Before I know it, sleep threatens to overtake me once more as I lie in my mother's lap while she continues playing with the dark strands.

"It's been roughly an hour and a half since I last saw you. I came in earlier, but you were fast asleep, so I didn't wake you." She runs the back of her hand across my cheek. "I wish I could let you rest longer, but Korah informed me that dinner will be ready in ten minutes."

I lazily force myself to fall out of bed, but unlike on land, I don't crash to the floor. Instead, I drift swiftly into a nearby wall before reaching the floor. A grunt leaves my mouth as Kaileah chuckles for a moment.

"Did you mean to do that?" she asks.

"Yes and no. I meant to get off the bed but not hit the wall," I say, rubbing my head and sitting on the floor. Kaileah comes over and lightly kisses my head.

"I'm going back to my room to freshen up. I'll meet you in here when it's time."

I nod, and once she leaves, I go to the vanity and stare at my reflection.

For a while, I'm stunned by who or *what* stares back. The same things I noticed back in my room on land are still true: my skin and eyes are brighter and foreign in a familiar way.

I push my long black hair behind my ears and examine them

with a greater intensity, moving closer to the mirror. They are long and delicately curve into a point like Kaileah's, and as she said, the fin is a soft lavender, slightly darker than my tail. Running a gentle finger across the fin, I feel its smooth texture, and a shiver runs up my spine at the contact.

As I move and bend it, I can see its strange flexibility.

Turning my head farther to the side, I see the gill indentations behind my ears that terrified me all but a day ago. Now, I find them oddly comforting—confirming my transformation into something new.

For a seemingly endless stretch of time, I stare and examine my face, looking for both familiarities and unknowns. As each minute passes, I'm reminded of the event to come and the part I'll be forced to play.

9

TENSIONS

.*⭐ VERA ⭐*.

Kaileah and I enter the dining room with everyone sitting and staring. Perhaps the two of us took longer than we should've, but why we're the last to arrive makes no difference to my racing heart.

The table set before us is a deep mahogany with gold-crusted designs on the edges and corners. The chairs at the heads of the long rectangular table are large and wooden with a purple cushioned seat, and in them sits the governor and his wife.

Korah is the first to rise from her chair, but soon after, the rest of them do the same and give Kaileah a short, respectful bow of courtesy.

Grabbing my arm, Korah leads me to the chair beside hers, the middle seat of three. In the last empty seat, Kaileah sits down elegantly, folding her tail and placing her hands in her lap.

I try to mimic her behaviors, but I fall short of her refined grace.

Korah's mother watches me intensely, her eyes pinning me to

my seat. Readjusting my tail's position and my posture, I can hear her scoff quietly under her breath, just loud enough for only me to notice.

I look away, ashamed, and try to think of anything else.

Behind me is a wall full of what seems to be recipe books along with cups, glasses, and other decorations. In front, I see a magnificent wall with decorative carvings on each of the four pillars along the wall's edge.

Before I can examine further, Governor Sarren speaks up.

"Queen Kaileah! It is such a pleasure to have you joining us for dinner. I hear from Korah that you got a tour of my great city. What did you think?" He watches closely, awaiting a response.

"It was quite beautiful, and so much has changed since I last visited. As I told your son earlier, your family has done great things for this city," Kaileah responds in the voice of a queen.

"*Dei o lu, rouinala?*" the governor's wife asks while locking eyes with me. I dart my gaze to Korah, and she clenches her jaw.

"*Tuy oi peika cengleso, mota,*" she says while her mother sighs. "*O nedi trenlata?*"

"Yes, *trenlata,*" she snaps, looking me up and down. "I will speak my native tongue in my home. If you cannot understand, then learn or leave." She haughtily turns up her chin and looks at her husband, who pinches between his eyebrows at her crass response.

Kaileah grabs my hand under the table and gives it a light squeeze. Looking up, I see her holding back a million words she wishes she could say.

"She asked who you were, and I told her that the two of you would appreciate us speaking Common. If she wasn't okay with that, I said I would translate," Korah explains with a reassuring smile.

"What did she mean by *rouinala?*" I ask, aware that she is leaving something out of her translation.

"Uh—" Korah throws a quick glance at her mother. "She called you a little girl." She winces and whispers a sorry under her breath, and I look away once more.

Directly in front of me sits Alexander who gives me a sympathetic look, seemingly not surprised by the attitude of his mother.

"This is my daughter, Mrs. Fenton," Kaileah says with a loving smile toward me, which lifts my spirits slightly. "I'm happy to show her your clan and the waters beyond our kingdom."

Before anyone can continue the conversation, a maid enters the room with a large bowl of grilled shrimp salad.

Approaching each person, starting from Sarren, she places an average serving of the dish on each of our first plates. Everyone but Mrs. Fenton thank her in Kefian, and she nods in appreciation each time. After everyone has been served, each person begins eating with the first fork to their left.

I hope it looks like I know what to do.

"Your daughter? I'm delighted you could have another one after that *unfortunate* incident with your first," Mrs. Fenton grumbles with a judgmental sidelong glance while taking another bite of her salad. "Such a waste of a firstborn to be mixed with a *landling.*"

Mrs. Fenton smirks and cuts a shrimp in half. Kaileah's respectful smile falls, and her grip on my hand tightens. Locking eyes with everyone at the table in turn, the water grows still, and my lungs tighten at the tension building with each quiet second.

Alexander's stare hardens, and he clenches his jaw, trying to calm himself. His deep breaths show how badly he wants to say something, anything, to fix the situation, but I can see his conflicting thoughts keep him from speaking.

Delilah looks down at her food, afraid and ashamed to look at Mrs. Fenton or Kaileah.

Finally, Korah looks appalled, staring directly at her mother with an open mouth. She is the only of her children brave enough to go against her.

"For your information, *Dawn*, this *is* my firstborn, and her origins are none of your concern," my mother spits back with budding anger. For the first time, Dawn's arrogant demeanor falls, and I see her worry.

"I—" She chuckles for a moment. "I didn't realize. That's even more unfortunate that you weren't able to have a pureborn heir to replace her." She laughs with a disgusting grin. "So disgraceful to allow a *mixed breed* to one day take the throne."

I look from Dawn to Kaileah and rise from the table when I hear my mother's words.

"I *appreciate...*" She forces the word out through a tightened grimace. "...your hospitality and letting us stay here, but what I do *not* appreciate is you speaking such venomous words about my daughter, whom I love." Kaileah tugs my hand, and I sit back down, but the tension only grows thicker.

The maid from before collects each plate and leaves the room once again.

"*E penkai'n e waun nu penka,*" Dawn sneers with satisfaction. Kaileah's eyes dim, but she backs down from her defensive position nonetheless.

"What did she say?" I ask in a murmur to Korah.

"I think it was, 'I have said all I wanted to say.' I'm *so* sorry about all of this. I promise I will make it up to you and your mother," she says with genuine sympathy.

"Dawn, you are out of line speaking to our guests in such a way. I will have Eliza bring the main course to our room for you. Excuse yourself for the rest of dinner," Sarren states firmly.

"No," she retorts.

"*Now!*" he shouts, rising from the table and pointing to the door. She obeys and exits without another word. As she exits the room, it feels as if the water itself softens, and I finally catch my breath.

The maid, Eliza, enters with an even larger plate decorated with green leaves and a large golden-crusted swordfish. The body is cut into eight large steaks grilled to perfection, with the head and tail placed on either end. She lays the fish on each of our larger plates in the same order but stops when she reaches Dawn's seat.

"Bring her serving to the bedroom, dear. Thank you," Sarren says.

"Yes, sir."

After everyone has been served, I grab the dinner knife on my right-hand side, having seen Kaileah go for the same one, and the second fork on the left. Before tasting the fish, I'm taken aback by the toughness but decide to try it before making judgments.

The thick fish has a tenderness that melts in your mouth, and the marinade and spices are delectable.

"Oh my—" I quickly cover my mouth and pause, chewing the mouthful of food and swallowing before speaking again. "Sorry, but I've never tasted something so delicious! Did you make this?" I ask Eliza.

"Me? Yes, Your Highness, it's my specialty." She smiles bashfully and looks away.

"It might be the best thing I've ever eaten. What's it called?" I ask with eyes full of admiration.

"I—" She pauses. "I've never given the dish a proper name, but I often just say I'm serving *espenadai*." She blushes. "Swordfish."

"Well, your *espenadai* is perfect." The apples of Eliza's cheeks protrude as she smiles, leaving the room with the rest of her dish and a hand to her mouth.

"I'm glad that you are enjoying your first meal in our mighty clan," Sarren boasts with arrogance. "Alexander." Alec looks at his father. "I trust you will be a good host if I excuse myself to deal with your mother?"

"Of course, Father," he responds with a nod.

"Good. I guess this will conclude our evening together, Your Highness and Your Majesty. I'd say it was lovely, but that would be a blatant lie." He rises and exits the room.

The moment he leaves, everyone's breath returns and postures relax.

"I am beyond sorry to you both." Alec pauses and takes a steadying breath. "I am sickened by the way my mother spoke to you and your daughter," he continues, now speaking directly to my mother. "I would like you to know that you and Vera will be treated with nothing but the utmost respect by everyone in this room for as long as you grace us with your company."

With everyone finishing their meals, Eliza takes the plates away and clears the table. I stand with the rest of them and notice the confusion and almost anger on Delilah's face.

"You lied to me? You said you were the queen's assistant." Her disappointment shows, and I can't seem to find the words to make it better.

"Alec warned me not to tell anyone who I was to avoid people like your mom treating me harshly. I'm sorry for lying to you," I attempt to explain, but her disappointment soon turns to sadness.

"You thought I'd treat you like that?" she asks, with her large blue eyes sparkling with budding tears. They look as if I have stabbed a knife through her heart.

"No! Of course not." I wince and look at Alec to help me fix the situation.

"Hey, Shrimp, look at me," Alec says and she obeys. "Vera didn't know if she should tell you when you asked her earlier, so I told her not to. If you want to be upset with someone, let it be me."

She slowly looks at me, sees my apologetic smile, and swims over, pulling me into a light hug.

"I would never say or think such ugly things. Please never think twice about telling me something about you. Human or mer." She pulls away and wipes the tears forming in her eyes. "I shouldn't be the one crying, sorry," she says as her wiping becomes more frantic.

"You don't need to apologize. Come here." I pull her into a tighter hug, and she continues to tear up, wrapping her arms around my neck. "From now on, no more secrets."

Comforting Delilah in my arms, I can't help but realize how much I've longed for a little sibling. Someone I can teach to be confident, compassionate, and positive. Someone I can share my successes with and celebrate theirs. I run my hands through her thick red hair, telling her it's all okay, and imagining what life would have been like if I had a Delilah of my own.

When I drift out of my daydream, I see Korah and Alec profusely apologizing to Kaileah. Focusing back on Delilah, I ease away and cup her face.

"Cheer up, little princess," I say, running my thumb under her eye to wipe the last of her tears. "I need to talk to your sister. Will you be okay if I leave?" A part of me hopes she will say no and ask me to stay, but I know she won't.

"Yeah, I'll be okay." She sniffles.

"I'd like to take a short swim. Would you join me?" I ask Korah.

"Yes, of course. If you're sure," she responds. Kaileah approaches me next, placing two hands around my face and sighing. No words are spoken, but I can hear her thoughts crystal clear. She held her tongue at dinner, worried that we would be uninvited and once again on the run without a safe place to stay.

I nod, and she kisses my forehead.

Exiting the warm interior, I'm shocked at the icy ocean's embrace. Goosebumps spring up along my arms, and the water around us sways in aggressive motions. The seagrass on the sandy ground moves quickly like trees swaying in the wind.

I suppose I need to reacclimate to its chill.

Arm in arm, we make our way through the Fentons' yard and into their large field of crops. I touch the grains as they sway and speak first.

"Alexander told me you're the reason he's more understanding, especially with mixed races. Is that true?" I ask.

"It is. I can assure you Alec was never as bad as my parents, but he wasn't who you met today," she responds neutrally, avoiding meeting my eyes.

"You said 'parents.' Is your dad just as bad?"

"Yes, but fortunately for your sake, he has enough sense to not voice what he thinks." From the corner of my eye, I notice her watching me, but each time I look in her direction, she stares into the distance.

What is troubling her?

Another minute passes, and the field looks endless. The wheat, vegetables, and fruit span miles in all directions. Out in cold, refreshing water, my mind clears to my disadvantage. My stomach drops and threatens to expel the meal I'd been served thinking about the disgusting words spat in my mother's face without remorse.

"If both of your parents are such conservative thinkers, how did you become the way you are?" I ask, and she thinks about the question intently.

"I met a man in his forties. He was a siren seeking refuge in our clan, much like you and your mother. If anyone had seen him, they would have thrown him out immediately." She stops and motions for me to sit in the field and listen to her story.

"There was something about him. I felt like it was my job to help in any way I could, so every day I brought him a meal. After a week, I got brave and stayed for short periods of time, eventually having long conversations while he ate. I found out he was the father of a girl in my class who was more gifted than all of us, and I realized something." She pauses for a while and thinks.

How could the clan cast out a siren without valid reason? I guess it's true that their race's reputation proceeds them among the Koifinn as well.

"I realized you have a gift that pureborns couldn't dream of having. You're special, Vera. So very special. Forget everything my parents—close-minded people as they are—and the world will say and just be proud to be you." I stare at her, speechless, unable to think of what to say that could articulate my appreciation for the kindness she's shown me or the fresh wounds she's begun to heal. "This girl had the majick of two races, and together they created something miraculous, just like you have."

"I don't know what to say. *Thank you*." I take her hands in mine. "You are the real gift, Korah." I turn away and begin the trip back to her home, feeling the chill of the frigid temperatures reminding me of the warmth we'll soon return to.

I wish I had my parents to guide me.

I feel so lost without them. It's only ever been the three of us through all of life's tribulations.

I only hope that the two of them, sitting on the porch listening to the soft waves, are thinking of all the fun adventures I am experiencing—happy not for me being gone, but that I can learn who I am.

I hope they never worry about the dangers surrounding me every second.

I want them to know that I will always think of them, no matter what.

No matter who I meet or what I learn, they will know that I would never give up the time we spent together.

If I wasn't the way I am, I might have just convinced myself those thoughts were reality.

They're sitting on that porch, listening to those waves, thinking about the hundreds of dangers in the sea. They know exactly how unlikely it would be for me to give up this world that should have always been my home.

They can't imagine me being happy, even if they want to.

How could Vera ever be happy without us there? they'll think.

They'll mourn me.

Every week.

Every day.

Every minute.

I'm causing them pain. Problems. Headache.

"You can head in. I'm going to sit out here for a while," I say mundanely, almost forgetting I have someone with me.

"Are you sure?" she asks, touching my shoulder in reassurance.

"Yeah, I just need a little space after today."

"I understand. Goodnight, Vera." She smiles with pity, causing my stomach to turn. *Please don't pity me.*

Once the door shuts, I put my face in my hands, and any wall I have built up breaks. Loud and alone, I cry.

10

A NEW SISTER

.*⭐ VERA ⭐*.

Delilah's luscious ginger curls knot into a ball atop her head, and I take one of the many ornate combs off my vanity to brush them out.

"Ouch!" she screams while grabbing her hair. The clementine coils fall across her face, and she tucks them behind her ears. I never paid much attention to the ears of Korah and Alexander, assuming they were the same as mine, but as I stare at Delilah, I see they have their differences.

Instead of a single curving cartilage coming to a thinner end, their ears have two sharp, elongated points separated by a curved fin. Her ear lobe has another small point, still longer than mine, that connects the secondary fin.

"I told you not to sleep without tying your hair up! This is what happens, Shrimp," I say in a gentle yet scolding tone. Delilah lets out a sharp huff of defeat before releasing the tight grip on her curls. I brush with more careful strokes, and she *seems* to no longer be in pain.

Alec told me the origins behind the nickname, and I loved it too much not to use.

One day, when their family was having dinner, Alec noticed Delilah had a shrimp stuck in her knotted mess of hair and went to grab it, only for it to bury itself back in and hide.

Ever since, he's called her 'shrimp hair,' which shortened to simply 'shrimp.' Now, what he didn't *directly* tell me was that the nickname is also because of her bright reddish-orange hair, which looks like the crustacean.

"Thank you again for brushing it for me. It's so much work when it gets in this rat's nest," she says, giggling at her use of *landling* slang. She doesn't even know what she's referencing. "What even is a rat? Do they make nests? *Landlings* are weird."

One thing I love about Delilah is her constant questions. Seeing her childish wonder is so sweet, but a little quiet could be nice occasionally.

"How do you sleep on land? Do you have beds? Can you fly? What are legs like?" Her questions continue.

"Yes, we have beds and sleep the same as you do. Nope, gravity keeps us on the ground, so we can't fly. And having legs is like two fins that stay on the floor as you move around." I ruffle her hair slightly and continue.

It doesn't take much longer before the mess is completely detangled, and what is left is a cluster of silky curls. She laughs and gasps, looking in the mirror. She looks even more beautiful, with her defined ringlets falling past her shoulders and down her back.

Korah never helps brush her hair because she's busy with school, chores, or civil duties around the town, and Alec doesn't understand why he needs to be gentle. Frankly, I'm surprised he has as much hair as he does with the way Delilah describes his hair-brushing skills. He's usually just as busy as Korah, but he finds time for her when she needs him.

Their maid, Eliza, can sometimes help, but cleaning, cooking, and tending to Cyprus means it's hard to make time.

Her father works from sun up to sun down to keep the community running through bi-weekly addresses, trading with other kingdoms, sorting paperwork, and other governmental responsibilities.

Finally, there's her mother. She has plenty of time to help but doesn't because it's 'tedious,' and she doesn't care enough to be bothered with it—*that lazy, horrible woman.*

Seeing Delilah's bright smile is all the reward I need to do the work. It takes up half her face, and her gums show with the grin's purity. I've helped her with her hair for the last few days, and I'll do it for as many more as she asks.

"It's time for chores, *Princess* Vera," she announces while using her tail to spin in circles. She finds it fascinating to be friends with royalty, so she makes a point of saying it at every opportunity. I find it adorable every time.

"Lead the way, little shrimp."

The vast fields before us are even more expansive and extraordinary than when I toured them at midnight. Delilah informed me that today's chore was picking fruit with her puppy. I highly doubt she has a dog underwater, so I'm curious what she means by that.

Most things seem to have mistranslations when they don't exist in my world.

As we enter a compressed shed, I'm surprised by the size of

its interior. Two doors are on opposite sides, but only one is labeled.

VULPANIS
Tidus

Delilah spins to the door, undoes the latch, and uses a special whistle. She pats the door twice before whistling again. I bend to look at what's inside and see a field of grass with a shallow bucket of fruits, vegetables, and grains. By now, I'm not as shocked when I see a door lead to a bigger inside, but yet it still amazes me.

"How exactly do you make these buildings so much bigger on the inside than out?" I ask.

"I'm not sure, but I know that's one of the trades done with your kingdom. I think Adleian witches can do enchantment majick or something, but you'd have to ask Korah to be *really* sure." She smiles broadly. "I'm happy I got to answer a question for you. You always answer mine!" She blushes.

A creature pokes its head out, sniffing the air before jumping on Delilah and licking her face. Then, it turns its attention to me.

The animal is the size of a Great Dane, maybe larger, with the body of a wolf. The head and ears are foxlike, the ears standing up and moving in all directions as they listen. Four muscular legs stand on the shed's floor, not faltering from their place. The tail is equal in size to the rest of the animal's body and is thickly coated with fur. It sways in quick, precise movements, never hitting one of us or an object on the walls.

"Princess Vera, meet Tidus. Tidus, meet Princess Vera," Delilah says, nudging the creature to approach. As he moves closer, I tense, unsure of the animal's purpose or intentions, but extend a hand for it to sniff nonetheless. "Tidus is a vulpanis. They help us pick crops in the fields." Tidus licks my hand in acceptance. "They're super friendly and really strong."

"You know this isn't a 'puppy,' right?" I ask, laughing from the vulpanis's tickling tongue.

"Yes, *I know*." She rolls her eyes with a smile. "We just started learning about land animals this week in school, and I thought it was close enough since you've probably never heard of a vulpanis."

Delilah hooks a harness from the wall around Tidus's waist, and his body jumps into the correct position. She taps his leg, and he lifts it for her to finish attaching each leather strap. It reminds me of the strapping of a horse-drawn carriage, and I must be partially correct as Delilah hooks a cart to Tidus.

Making our way to the fruit field, the sweet smell of berries, melons, and other exotic fruits fills my nose. The scent is pungent, like stepping into a fragrance store, and I can't get enough. I can hardly focus on following their trail, taken aback by a smell so sweet I can taste it.

All around us are trees with plentiful fruits, vines full of budding berries, and small bushes spring from the ground dotted with bright balls of sugar. I swim down and examine one of the larger bushes. The fruit looks like a blueberry but bigger and more vibrantly blue.

I move to pick one before Delilah beats me to it and grabs one for herself. The thick skin allows for it to pop in my mouth, and the inside is slightly chewier than the average blueberry.

The texture reminds me of candy, and the overwhelming flavors soon follow. The sweetness I smell is nothing compared to how it tastes. I open my eyes wide, cover my mouth, and attempt to communicate how delicious the berry is.

Delilah giggles and takes another, popping a few into her mouth and chewing with her prominent apple cheeks. She wipes her mouth and whispers to Tidus.

"You ready, boy?" The vulpanis wags its tail eagerly. She speaks to it in Kefian, although I can't make out the words as I'm still distracted by the berries' taste. Tidus uses his tail, longer and wider than all the plants surrounding us, to grab the bush. Sliding it off and placing the buds into the cart, I look back to the shrub and notice there's not a single berry left.

I—How did—What? I think to myself.

After watching Tidus repeat the process to another three berry bushes, I notice the tail bends with purpose. He controls the prehensile movements like the fluffy tail is a fifth limb, and it allows the picking to commence with considerable efficiency.

After the berries, we move to the fruit growing from trees. Delilah swims up and picks each one slowly, checking for bugs, bruises, and quality, whereas Tidus swims high, reaches around, and grabs heaping tailfuls.

The stack on the wagon he pulls is teetering, and I worry our efforts will be lost if it expels its contents across the field.

"I think we should head back and then make a second trip. What do you think, Shrimp?" I ask, taking Delilah out of her hyper-focused state.

"Huh? Oh! Yes! Good idea, Princess Vera," she responds, throwing the last yellow pear-shaped fruit with the rest.

We make a second trip, a third, and finally, a fourth until the sun starts to set, and Delilah decides that today was a good day of harvesting. We unhitch Tidus, send him off into his field, put up the equipment, and return home for dinner.

"Do you plan to leave all the fruit in the shed?" I ask.

"Oh, Dad tells me to leave the barrels in the shed, and he or someone else takes them before I go out the next day. I don't think he wants me to deal with the trouble after so much hard work," she responds with accomplishment. While it is tedious, the picking is far from hard, especially with the help of Tidus.

I would guess the chore is simply a way to keep his young daughter busy throughout the day with the benefit of helping the community.

"That makes sense. Do you pick crops every day?" I give her my full attention, so she rambles on.

"Okay, so, Dad tells me to harvest every other day for a week, and then..." She pauses with a brimming, open-mouthed smile. "I get to try out my skills and *grow* crops *myself*!" She stims with giddiness.

"I love growing! It tickles my fingers, and—and—and—" She loses her train of thought. "Oh! I love to feel the plants' little plant heartbeats. *Thump. Beep. Thump.*" She makes sound effects with matching hand motions, mimicking a beating heart. Afterward, she describes how the crops grow in a similar manner. I nod and gasp, showing my engagement, which fuels her fire.

"That sounds beyond exciting, Shrimp." I put a hand on her shoulder as we continue swimming. She looks at me with so much happiness that I wonder how often her family overlooks her. It doesn't take any energy to make her feel special, and I can't help but feel a pang of anger toward those who ignore her. As long as I'm around, this little girl will never go a day without feeling like the most special girl in the world.

11

A BOND IS BORN

.*⭐ VERA ⭐*.

The weather has calmed, and every blade of seagrass glistens with the bright, unobstructed sun. Hundreds of herrings swim back and forth in small schools as the young Koifinn children swim after them, grasping their hands out for a chance to catch one. Inhaling deeply, the salty smell of the ocean and the warm water heated by the sun fill my body with the calmness I've been craving.

A little boy stops pursuing the fish and stares at me in a trance, so I wave.

"*Lu a beutia*," he says with an open mouth.

"What was that?" I ask.

"Oh! Right. You're beautiful," he stammers out before fleeing. A smile appears on my face, causing my cheeks to hurt from a broad grin. The amount of compliments I've received from pure strangers is astonishing.

"Asherah Dlari, the most beautiful, eligible bachelorette on both land and sea," a recognizable *dramatic* man's voice says behind me. "How will I contain myself in the presence of such utter divinity?" I turn around and shove Alec away, holding back the mirth building up in my throat but failing to hide it on my face. "Gods, now that I see her *ravishing* emerald eyes shining brighter than a perfect stone...I—I can hardly breathe," he says mockingly, acting like a teenage thespian in their first production of *Romeo and Juliet*.

"You are actually the worst," I say, rolling my eyes. "Could you tell me why so many people have been complimenting me lately? On land, I got one every once in a while, but here, it's multiple a day. What's that about?"

"Oh, that's easy. Only a handful of Koifinn people have ever traveled to Adlei, so they've never seen someone who looks like you or your mom. But there's *another* reason," he says, looking away suspiciously.

"And that would be?" I ask, one brow raised.

"The fact that you are *extraordinarily gorgeous*, my fair princess," he says while blowing me an obnoxious kiss. My eyes will get stuck behind my head with the time I spend rolling them at Alec's idiocy. "Gotta go, princess," he says, turning away, but I notice his expression drop when he thinks I can no longer see him. He looks uneasy, but why? He's been acting strange the last week, yet only when he doesn't catch me watching.

I hope I haven't said something to upset him.

I go to the nearest market to purchase six carrots from an older gentleman, as requested by Korah.

"*Seisa carzondies, pe'il devor.*" *Six carrots, please.* I hope my pronunciation was understandable. Perhaps I should've practiced a few more times before leaving.

"*Quatre fesos, doucen seils.*" *Four fesos, twelve seils.* The old man's smile could lift the spirits of the darkest heart, if only for a moment. He places the carrots in a small cloth bag and hands them to me.

"*Teinta lu!*" I shout as I leave. Studying the bag's contents, I see an extra apple with the carrots and turn back to correct the mistake. "Uh, no apple, *seisa carzondies*," I say, while handing the fruit back to him.

"Apple for you, miss," he says slowly, trying to find the words and pushing the bright red apple back into my hands. His thick accent tells me he hasn't spoken Common in quite some time.

Korah only helped me practice the few words I'd need for the purchase. Beyond that, I'm lost in trying to understand or communicate. I place the apple back in my bag and take the old man's hands, repeating another thank you and slipping an extra *feso* for his kindness.

"Miss! Miss!" he yells to grab my attention, but I pretend not to hear and continue to the stables. I take a large bite of the fruit and am surprised by the intense sweetness each time I chew. I can't help but take another bite, and another, until all that is left is the pit in the center. I suck out the rest of the juice and place it back in my bag, continuing to meet Korah.

As I arrive, I see a glorious outbuilding with walls made of deep, darkly stained lumber and a bronze shingled roof like the Fentons' home. The gateway must be ten feet tall, with brass handles and a matching lock. Pulling the gate open, I see Korah standing inside, waiting for me with her signature deep-set dimples drawn from her smile.

The interior's ceiling extends to the sky, forming a triangle with four hanging lights glowing with blue bioluminescence. The interior is made of white-painted wood. It's spotless, with no notable sand or dirt, and four stalls span the walls on either side.

"Were you able to get the carrots?" Korah asks, eagerly peeking into my bag.

"I did, and he ended up giving me a free apple. I slipped a *feso* for the gesture."

"Aw, I'm glad you could sneak him extra. He always gives me free fruit with my purchases, but I guess I'm not very subtle when I tip. If I get caught, he *will not* let me leave until I take the money back," she answers warmly.

Korah takes the bag, removes the carrots, and hands it back. I notice a small note left at the bottom.

Teinta lu

Thank you for your purchase :)

It reads in scrawly, shaky handwriting. I look it over twice before gently placing it into the bag. I see I wasn't the only one who snuck something into the other's hand without them knowing.

Korah swims with a carrot to the nearest stall, calling for something.

"Come, girl! I have treats!" she yells while waving the vegetable. I move closer to look and see a horse. No—not a horse. I dash back, startled by the enormous horse-like creature looking down at me. It tilts its head, almost as if it's studying me.

"Korah," I say from the ground, slowly moving backward. "What is that?" Looking behind her, she eyes me strangely.

"I believe your people call them seahorses. Why are you startled?"

"Seahorse?" I ask with agitated apprehension while rising

from the ground. "That's a seashire if we're talking horses. Seahorses are those tiny things with curling tails that hold onto coral. I have no idea what *that* is." Since the creature hasn't made any sudden movements, I swim closer to Korah.

"Oh! You're thinking of a ponyfish. Those are the cutest! Sometimes, I will find one, let it grab my pinky, and take it with me while I do my chores. It will eventually swim off, but it's fun while it lasts!"

Korah grabs the creature's head and places hers against it, the two of them closing their eyes simultaneously. She strokes its head, and it wraps its neck around her in a hug.

It's beautiful. The moment and the animal.

She has the face of a horse with multicolored stripes and translucent fins on her cheeks that change colors based on the angle of light. One eye is a piercing white, and the other is virtually black with a thick healed scar across it. Its ears are what I'd expect of a horse, but additionally two long dorsal fins with spikes rise high in the air. Down her neck, the shark-belly skin texture fades to that of fish scales that match the stripes on her face.

Peering farther into the stall, I see front legs with fins stretching along the side and twice the length of its forelimbs. Where hindquarters would be, a long, thick tail comes together at a point, with thick cartilages extending the length, likely to keep her agile.

As I make eye contact with the creature, she tilts her head as I tilt mine. What is it thinking?

Nothing to worry about. I rub my forehead while furrowing my brows in confusion. I could've sworn it *spoke*, but it is not human or mer and, therefore, cannot speak. Not to mention, its mouth never opened, and Korah didn't acknowledge it.

I suppose it's just another example of how I'm losing my mind. Honestly, I don't know why it even concerns me with the amount of strange voices in my head lately.

I'm going insane.

What if I open my eyes one morning to find myself in a psych ward, having just woken up from psychosis?

You are not insane. You are fine. Thanks, head voice. It's probably me being in tune with my subconscious...I wonder if that's a common trait among merfolk. Besides, my sanity is the last thing I have the time or the energy to worry about.

"You seem to be calming down. Would you like to feed her?" Korah asks while handing me a carrot. "She's what we call a hippocampus."

I take the vegetable and swim closer, extending it to reach her. She eyes me closely before looking down at the treat in my hand. Without another second's delay, she eats it and neighs in delight. The hippocampus nudges and sniffs my empty hand in case I have another.

I giggle at her nose tickling the palm of my hand, and she whinnies once more. Pushing her head closer, I lie against her, and she shoves me into her stall, violently catching me off guard.

I lie in the corner, breathing heavily and barely able to think. Am I in danger?

The creature uses its immense tail to push me closer toward its back. It takes me longer than I'd like to admit to relax and realize she wants me to sit on her. I lean down and hug her, feeling a connection of sorts between this elegant beast and I.

I lean to the side to get a better view of Korah, and to my surprise, she holds herself completely still with a look of both consternation and amazement.

"How did you just gain the trust of Astryx in a matter of five minutes?" she asks loudly. "It took me *months* before she let me touch her, much less *ride* her!" Her smile as she speaks makes me think she is thrilled for me, but I can see the hint of resentment she's hiding.

I didn't ask for this.

While I'm honored a hippocampus with as many scars and likely terrible stories trusts me so greatly, I did nothing to warrant it. Frankly, it should've been wary of me because of my fear and apprehension of going near her.

"I'm just as confused as you, believe me. I know nothing about these creatures, so I thought she was about to attack when she pulled me in here," I say as I look into Astryx's eyes. Staring into the white void, I sense something.

The animal can feel what I feel. It *understood* my fear.

It knew I had no intention of touching, riding, or even going near it until it beckoned me to. She must have known that she was in complete control over how much or little she was touched, which made her trust me.

I think Astryx took power from the ability to choose. Allowing herself to push her boundaries because she knew I would not force her.

Korah calls over another hippocampus in the stall beside Astryx, feeds it a carrot, places her head against it, and moves on to the next. She repeats the process four more times, and I join her shortly after.

"This big guy is the last hippocampus we own," she says while patting the creature, who is proudly eating its treat. "I refill their food twice a day, bring a treat every other day, and ride them once a week. Well, only if they're okay with being ridden," she says remorsefully in Astryx's direction. "It just so happens that today is the day I take each hippocampus out! Would you care to join me?"

"I would love to!" I respond, looking back to Astryx and noticing a slight nod. "Although, I'm not sure I would know how."

Korah opens a cabinet at the end of the barn, and inside of it is a wall full of reins, bridles, and bits made of opalescent materials. The rest is full of every form of riding equipment I could imagine. From saddles to carriage harnesses, they have it all.

Korah hands me a bridle and motions for me to put it on the hippocampus of my choosing. Its straps are aquamarine dyed leather with a metal bit, and red algae decorates the browband and headpiece along with a string of pearls and shells.

I swim to Astryx and hold it up for her to see. She shakes her head and knocks it out of my hand. I swim and grab it once more.

"Can I ride you?" I whisper. She nods her head once, so I move closer with the bridle. The event repeats itself, with her knocking it out of my hands after shaking her head. "So you're okay with me riding you, but I can't use the proper equipment? Why not?" I ask, aware at that moment that she can't explain why.

Bad memories, my subconscious tells me. That would make sense. I mouth an 'oh' to her before giving it to Korah.

"I'll show you how to put it on! Don't worry." She takes the bridle and swims to Astryx before I catch her arm to hold her back.

"She asked me not to use it. Is it safe to ride her without it?" I ask, worried that her answer will be no. Korah hesitates, uncertain.

"You said she...asked?"

"I mean, Astryx didn't *literally* ask me. But each time I showed it to her, she would knock it away. I think she might have some bad memories associated with it."

Why is Korah acting so strange?

Please don't tell me she thinks I'm going mad, too.

"Oh!" Korah says while exhaling with relief. "Yeah, that makes sense. Normally, riding a hippocampus without proper outing attire would be dangerous, but I think you'll be fine seeing how Astryx never trusts anyone enough to allow them on her back."

I unlock her stall, and she swims out, circling me and waiting for a command. Korah takes the last hippocampus she fed out. It wears a full set of riding equipment, including a saddle with a large seat backing and strap to hold a mer's tail in place. Seeing the intricate straps, handles, and precautions, I grow worried that my decision to ride with nothing will be a mistake.

Leaving the stables, passersby wave and greet us. Some question what the two of us plan to do with such large beasts, but Korah assures them we will not disturb anyone or their crops. We lead the gracious animals to the edge of the countryside, and Korah then mounts the hippocampus for the first time.

She elegantly places herself in the saddle and grabs her reins, stopping the animal from running off without warning.

I try to mimic her actions, but I easily slip off without the stability of a seating strap or backing.

Again, I try, but I fail once more.

Again.

Again.

I'm ready to give up until Korah rides closer and holds my hips in place while I find my balance. I have to adjust to sitting slightly farther forward than expected to balance the weight and length of my tail.

I grab hold of Astryx's hair. The texture is soft, like strands of velvet fleece, and when I grasp it firmly, she throws her head back in anticipation.

"You ready?" Korah asks with a grin that shows her gums.

"Yes!" I yell, and the second the words leave my lips, both Astryx and the hippocampus beside us sprint forward. She swims majestically, her front legs running through the water and her enormous tail swaying in powerful bursts, propelling us faster. I scream out, full of complete and overwhelming bliss.

Korah follows suit, and we swim faster and faster.

I needed this. I feel the words, breathe them in. I did. I needed the current flowing faster than ever through my hair, the tiny grains of salt scraping past my face, and the feeling of being worthy to ride an untrusting creature.

I feel Astryx's body relaxing. I never noticed how tense she was before, but now that she's allowed herself to calm, her back curves to fit me perfectly. I could ride for hours and never tire of the power and freedom I feel sprinting through the ocean on such a creature.

"Where to?" Korah screams to be heard over the rushing ripples we create. Where in this wide new world would I like to go? That's a hard question. I'd like to see it all—to see every part of the world that was stripped away from me as a little girl.

I want to wake up and understand everything around me.

To look at the walls of my room and know precisely what ocean plant it was made from. To look at my nightstand and remember picking the flowers myself and studying where to find them in school. Above all, I wish to wake up and remember being taught how to harness my majick.

There are so many things that I would like to know, to see, to do.

But alas, what should I choose? Thinking back to what I've seen in the days spent here, one thing sticks out in my mind.

"A coral reef," I scream in reply.

"Good choice! Follow me!" We dash and dart in many directions, Korah at one with her environment. The open space in front of us has nothing to indicate what direction we need to travel, but her searching eyes spot where we need to go. I wish to look into a space filled with nothing and know the precise path.

Korah may be envious of the bond formed between Astryx and I, but I am envious of her life. Her childhood. Her world. I wouldn't trade the way I grew up or the parents I had for anything this grand planet could give me, but it doesn't stop me from imagining what life would've been like if I had grown up in the sea—the world that should've been my own.

I would give anything to know the invisible signs of where I've been and where I've yet to go.

It's difficult to understand.

I didn't leave my home because I was simply curious. Every day, I felt a hole inside me—a hole that no happiness, love, gifts, friends, or hobbies could fill.

A hole that was patched for the first time when my body erupted with power in these very waters.

Whoever did this to me, whoever *cursed* me and put this forever gaping hole in my soul, I despise you. No medicine or therapy could fix it, and trust me when I say I tried.

All I can hope for is the chance that whatever I find along this journey will make me feel whole for the first time.

For that, I will do *whatever* it takes.

12

VENOM

.*⭐ VERA ⭐*.

The reef on the outskirts of Shari is more marvelous than any I've seen before as it erupts with life and color. It's more vibrant than when I was a human, as if my perception of colors has been amplified. The elkhorn coral makes up most of the reef with its green blooming structure, providing a home for a great number of spiny lobsters skittering and stumbling off each ledge.

Pectinia coral grows in curving clusters, glowing neon shades of oranges, yellows, and pinks. Tiny fish swim in and out of its flower petal edges. It's impossible to both memorize and recognize each type of unique plant growing from the reef, but that does little to stop my amazement at its beauty.

Korah holds her hand out for a blue tang to approach. She takes a steady breath as it nuzzles into her, bathing in her warmth. Slowly, a small piece of seaweed grows from her palm. The bright blue, black, and fluorescent yellow fish eats it eagerly before swimming away.

"Did you just—" I say, unable to wrap my head around how she created a plant from *nothing*. "—grow that seaweed from your hand?" I ask in awe. She opens her palms to me and focuses her energy, twisting them as needed.

From the flat surface, a plant grows millimeter by millimeter. The stem forms tiny balls that grow as she continues moving her hands. As Korah ends her spell and the plant is fully formed in her hand, she picks a few from the stem and puts them in her mouth.

"Sea grapes. Would you like some?" she asks while handing me the last two. I put one in my mouth and chew, feeling the balls pop like bursting boba with a bitter sweetness. Eating the second grape, I taste a hint of salt and revel in the interesting texture.

"The Koifinn people are blessed with the gift of growth. We can create anything that is not sentient, be it crops, minerals, jewels, and more." Korah looks at me proudly, sure of herself and her abilities. "One of the most important things in our lives is harnessing the majick each of us are born with," she says with a smile. She looks to the coral and holds her hand to a dying piece, whispering to it, and it grows fuller and explodes with revived color.

"While growing something without a start does not require words, to heal or grow a plant further is different," she explains. "I must feel its life inside of me and focus on it. While it's unnecessary to give the plant encouraging words during the spell, it can hear them, and in my experience, the health I create will stay for longer." The way she speaks about her culture, her majick, and the reef, I can't help but feel an overtaking happiness to see someone love something as small as a dying piece of coral with so much of their heart.

"The ocean birthed us before our mothers did. It is our true creator, and since it blessed my people with the ability to heal its other creations, I do just that," she says, whispering kind words to the plants around her. She lies her back against a coral ledge, allowing the fish and crustations to crawl and swim on her exposed stomach. "Once brought into the world, the ocean is no longer our mother, but she is mine. Kayiah will always be my mother. My *true* mother," she states with undeniable truth. "The fish, the plants, the crabs, the shrimp, and every other beautiful thing around us are my siblings, and one day, when the time is right, I will be returned to the waters that made me. I will meet Kayiah, the ocean's spirit, and I will live the rest of eternity watching over her creatures."

"She sounds lovely," I say, lying beside Korah and feeling the animals ticking my skin as they do the same to her.

"She is," Korah says, staring at the sky. The waves move with the sun's painted rays. I stare at her rosy cheeks, kissed with dimples and wonder what she's thinking.

Why is it that her outward persona is so overtly happy?

What is she trying to have the world think of her?

I wish I knew what part of her was the real Korah: the bubbly, hyper girl who loves everything or the calm dreamer who loves nature more than life itself. Perhaps it's a mixture of both and more.

I sit up as a small octopus creeps closer. It's adorable, with its three-inch pastel-yellow body and black dots. I cup my hand and allow it to crawl upon me, pulling it closer to my face. I trace a finger over it as gently as possible, which catches Korah's attention.

"What do you have?" she asks, moving to get a better view.

"The cutest little octopus. Look!" I push my hands to her, and she sticks out her bottom lip, softening her eyes as she looks at it. Its black eyes turn red as a stinging pain radiates from where it sat. I gasp, throwing it off me as it rushes off.

"Oh, gods! Did it bite you?" she asks, rushing to grab my hand and seeing the blood staining the water around us. My heart is pounding its way out of my chest, and I can hardly understand why. It feels like I've just drunk five cups of coffee and run a marathon, and my *head* is so…heavy.

My blinks become more forceful, and my head sags from my shoulders.

My mouth goes numb.

My throat tightens.

My chest heaves.

"Help m—" is all I can say before losing control of the bottom half of my face. Korah screams and covers her mouth before rushing me to Astryx.

"I'm right behind you, Astryx. *RUN!*" she screams as I'm thrown on the back of my hippocampus and sent soaring like a tracking missile through the ocean. With each passing minute, my arms grow weaker, and my breaths get shorter. Astryx must understand because she swims faster each time she hears me struggle for oxygen.

We're back in town in no time, unless I no longer have a concept of the passing minutes. I barely notice myself being removed from Astryx and pulled through the city, my vision reduced to clouded pinholes. I think Korah's screaming for help.

I think I hear my mother.

"What happened?" Kaileah yells.

"Get out of the way! I need a healer!" Korah retorts and pulls me faster. With each heave, my body's strength falters. Seconds after my last breath, my mind goes black.

I can't feel a thing.

KORAH

13

SACRED PROMISES

.*⭐ KORAH ⭐*.

*S*he's paralyzed and unconscious, and I don't know if she'll *wake up.* The apothecary's words replay over and over, yet I don't know how I could've prevented it. I've never heard of a *red-eyed* octopus with such aggression—much less one that causes those symptoms. The four of us gather around Vera, none knowing what will save her.

Alec grows a bed of white lilies around her body before bending to plant a delicate kiss on her hand. The apothecary fills her with oxygen and pours tonic after tonic in her mouth, to no avail.

She's dying! Don't they get it?

Her mother stares from the corner, never making a move or sound. Her face is frozen, and I wonder if she is even breathing.

Why can't I heal? I scream in my head, fighting the urge to cry.

Kayiah, please help me.

Show me how to save her.

I stare through the window of his practice and look for her

sign. I know she'll hear m*e. I feel her.* In answer, I spot a girl my age swimming back to her home and remember just who she is.

I swim as fast as possible from Herbs for Health to find her. The girl's short auburn hair hits her face as she turns. She furrows her brows before tucking her hair behind her pointed ears. Her eyes widen at her mistake, and she quickly covers them once again, but I already know what she attempts to hide.

"Hey, Korah?" she asks in confusion.

"Eclipse, I need a siren! *Please,*" I plead to her as she stares at me in horror.

"I—I don't...I've never—" she spews in a panic, instinctively putting a hand over the spot where one ear is hidden.

"I knew your father. I know what you are, and most importantly, I know what you can do." I look into her eyes and beg. "My friend is dying, and that apothecary is useless!" Her black eyes fail to meet mine, but I pray she considers helping. "Please."

"Take me to her," Eclipse whispers with a hardened expression. I nearly cry with relief as we rush back to Vera. Entering the establishment, Eclipse is met with strange looks, but she takes no time to command the room.

"Move to the far wall, all of you!" she screams. Everyone listens—everyone but Kaileah.

"Who do you think you are?" Kaileah asks with a snarl. I give her a pleading look, and she relents, never taking her eyes off Eclipse.

Eclipse places a hand above Vera's heart and mumbles incoherently. Her black irises fade to white as she continues her chanting. I see a twitch of Vera's tail and squeal in relief.

Eclipse continues, her eyes now squinting as a drop of blood falls from her tear duct. As more of Vera's body heals, the drops turn to streams as Eclipse's eyes cry bloody tears, and her nose drips the same. I try to push the clouded water away, but it only causes it to spread as Eclipse's blood doesn't stop flowing.

I worry for Vera's safety, but now also my schoolyard friend's. She stops her chant to cough up a piece of bloody tissue but, without wasting time, wipes her hand and continues again.

I need to stop her. *But you can't until she does what she needs to do.*

Vera's chest rises and falls, and her eyelids flutter as Eclipse hacks up another chunk of blood.

I can't let her continue. I can't.

I rush over and pull her face to mine, ripping her hands away to break the connection. Her white eyes fade to their natural deep brown, and she looks at her hands stained in her own blood. She looks around, horrified by how much she has clouded the water.

Eclipse moves her lips to speak, but stops as she ingests the blood flowing from her eyes and nose.

I should've stopped her sooner. What kind of person am I?

She coughs and chokes before composing herself.

"I lost myself," she mutters before dashing away, I assume far from town. I couldn't even thank her for nearly killing herself to save a stranger. A noise behind me catches my attention, and I see Vera trying to sit up with her eyes still closed.

Kaileah rushes to her side and holds her close.

"What are you saying, child?" Kaileah asks softly in response to her daughter's strange whispers. *T'eiskaeh*...I've never heard that before, but its pronunciation sounds Adleian. Vera reaches her arms forward, stretching her fingers to grab something, but fails.

"I...know...you're...there...*T'eiskaeh*," Vera says slowly before falling back into her bed of flowers. The water is still as we watch her. Too still.

The apothecary checks her over thoroughly and nods his head in approval. She's breathing on her own now, which is a good sign, but Eclipse only healed her partially before I pulled her away.

You should've never pulled her away.

What? I pulled her away before she got herself killed!

What if Vera never wakes up because you stopped Eclipse too soon?

What if Eclipse died because I didn't stop her? Listen to yourself, Korah!

If Vera stays in a coma, it's all your fault.

No, it's not! No, it's not! I'm a good person! I did all I could do!

You know how many creatures are deadly in reefs, yet you let Vera lie beside you without watching and ensuring she was safe. In what way is that all you could do? You did it on purpose, didn't you? You're not as good as you claim.

"I have to find that girl. She gave Vera the best chance of survival, and I have to make sure she's okay," I say to the group, but honestly, I only say it to drown out the thoughts. Leaving the shop, I see what feels like hundreds of staring faces, judging. They saw all of that, didn't they? In the name of our gods, Eclipse, I'm so sorry.

It's just like your mom and dad always say. You're nothing but a waste of space, Korah. A selfish, useless daughter whose only purpose is to shut up and look presentable. Is that so hard, Korah? Don't you think you can handle shutting your mouth until you're in private?

Shut up! Shut up! SHUT UP!

Selfish. Selfish. Selfish.

I find the nearest person and pull them into a conversation.

"Hi! Have you seen a girl with short brown hair and tanned skin swim through here? Her tail is mainly white with some patches of red and black, and she looked pretty disheveled," I say in a soft voice.

Talking is the only way to drown my thoughts out. Call it selfish, but I can't handle the voices. They'll eat me alive.

The man thinks to himself while rubbing his neck.

"Actually, I think I did. She went that way," he says, pointing north toward the miles of farmland surrounding Shari. I thank him with a smile and swim off.

I said I was looking for her, and I am.

Yes, but you know the real reason you want to find her. I am you, Korah. You can't lie to yourself.

I want to find her to make sure she is okay. There is no other reason.

Lies.

I just want to make sure everyone I care for is okay!

Some more than others. You would let Eclipse and Vera die if it suited you.

I swim faster to drown out those awful thoughts that are not my own. I think I know where Eclipse would have gone. Although it's wrong of me to intrude, I pivot east and head past the farmlands.

Watching the endless spans of fields nearly ready to harvest passing underneath calms me. Flipping to face the sky, I'm reminded of the world's beauty. My thoughts cannot find me when I am in nature, so I hide in its beauty. I breathe in and bask in the warm summer sun, penetrating the water and reflecting on me.

"Kayiah," I whisper. "Am I doing right by you?" I pause and listen for her response. "I know you need Vera alive. In my mortal brain, I do not understand why, but you know more than any of us. For that, I place my complete trust in you." I turn back and look down at the fields. The wheat sways delicately as I pass and create a current. "I hope you know I care the same for Eclipse as I do for Vera, but your plan, whatever it is, lies in the hands of only one of them."

I see it getting closer. Squinting my eyes, Eclipse comes into view.

White Willow Memorial Garden. A holy ground where we bury our lost souls. A cypress headboard carved with all the flowers her mother loved sits before her. Blood stains the soft deep green grass as she holds a shaky hand to her mother's name.

I can't do this.

I can't approach her in this vulnerable state.

Selfish. Selfish. Selfish.

I'm not! I don't want to hurt her to gain something. How is that selfish? How?

You're scared, so you don't want to approach her. You are only thinking of yourself.

You don't know that!

I do. I am you, Korah. The darkest part of your mind. Try all you want to push me away, but I will never leave.

I ignore the voice. As long as I live, whatever it is that makes me think those awful things will never win. The closer I get, the stronger my heart beats.

Approaching where she lies, I wait, trying to find the motivation to say something. All I want is to make sure she is safe.

She will understand.

I hope.

"Eclipse," I say slowly, noticing her body tense at the sound of my voice. She looks at me without expression, wiping away the blood and tears from her eyes.

"What do you want now?" she asks with pure hostility. She covers her mother's dedication and looks at me coldly.

"You looked like you were dying. If I wouldn't have pulled you away, I think you just might have," I answer as kindly as I can. My close presence in her sacred space is bothering her, so I move back slightly. "I needed to make sure you were okay. I want nothing more from you than what you have already done." Her shoulders relax, and she breathes in deeply.

"I am okay enough. Thank you for checking on me," Eclipse says without feeling. I know she's lying. I can see it in every strained breath and quick wipe of her nose.

"Can I sit with you?"

She looks at the carved wood and back at me before moving just enough for it to be visible. I sit on the opposite side of her, and she doesn't object.

"It must be hard without the two of them. You're stronger than I could ever be," I say, gazing at her mother and father's names, written on the same dedication.

"I don't feel very strong. It's like I'm fourteen years old again, crying at the letter from Adlei telling of my father's death," she says while never meeting my eyes. Playing with the rings on her hands, she asks, "You said you knew him?"

"I did. I used to bring him pastries and dinner leftovers when he would linger by the gates before returning to Adlei, and in return, he would tell me stories about you, his adventures, and his abilities." I see a smile tickle at her lips as she thinks about her father.

He was such a kind man. Sometimes I swim to the gate with a bag of food, waiting for him to return.

He never does.

"He must have loved you listening to his stories. I often couldn't get him to shut up long enough for me to tell my own," Eclipse says with a sharp laugh. "Thank you for treating him with kindness. I haven't spoken to anyone about him since my mother died."

"If I may ask…" I pause, and she nods her head in encouragement. "Why would you help an Adleian girl if their kingdom was the reason for…you know?" She pushes her hair behind her ear again and looks at her parents' names.

"That girl didn't kill him. There's no reason to blame her for something she knows nothing about. My father would have struck me from the grave if *that* was the reason I hesitated." She chuckles once more, but it's likely only at the memory of him. I notice a drop of blood hanging from the edge of her nose, but she wipes it quickly. She must still be hurting.

I need to make sure she's truly okay.

"Eclipse, be honest with me. What happened to you earlier?" I ask, and she tenses her core and looks back to her rings.

"I don't know. I've never healed someone so close to death. It was intoxicating, feeling whatever was leaving her body, but it was killing mine." She tries to take a deep breath but falls short and coughs. "I realized halfway through that I was giving my life to her, and there was nothing I could do to stop it. There was no one left to live for, and I could feel the kindness in her heart. At one point, I even saw her. She was human, sitting on a rock by the waves and painting the horizon. When she turned and saw me, she jumped up and ran closer, calling me a name I'd never heard before—*T'eiskaeh*, I think it was."

Eclipse heard it, too. What does it mean?

"She thanked me for healing her 'a second time' and returned to the rock, painting away. I approached her to see what was on the canvas, but I couldn't reach it before you pulled me away." Her story comes to a close, and she looks worse off than before I approached. Her skin has lost its color, and her cheeks sink in slightly.

"You need to go home and sleep. Excuse my words, but you don't look well, and you're the only siren in this clan who can cure your wounds," I plead with her, grabbing her hands and waiting for her to look at me before I let go. "If you had no one to live for, you have someone now. I care for you, and if you need a shoulder to cry on or an ear to vent to, let it be mine." She furrows her brows and can't find the words to say. That alone is enough for me, so I smile at her and leave. Eclipse stays behind and lies down again, feeling the grass between her fingers.

Making my way back to Vera, I find myself lost in all the memories of Eclipse throughout our lives. I know far more about her than she does me because my parents ensure the Fentons are well-versed in all things Shari.

There is one detail I know she would never want me to, and if I'm being honest with myself, it's the reason I knew she would save Vera. A year after her last parent died, she made a promise to her father, her mother, and herself.

She swore to never hesitate if she could save someone's life, no matter the cost. I learned this visiting my grandmother's dedication site in the memorial garden. She was in the same spot as she is today, lying beside her parents' plot and whispering the promise.

I knew it. You used her like you do everyone else. You will never be worthy of an afterlife with Kayiah.

You know nothing!

I know everything.

VERA

14

A WEAK MIND'S DECEPTION

.*⭐ VERA ⭐*.

The smell of the sea is calming. Sitting on a large rock above the waves, I reach my feet out and let the cold water tickle my outstretched toes. The stone beneath me is so very smooth. But stroking the jagged edges along its cracks reminds me I'm alive by the prickly sensation.

By my side is a canvas and paint waiting for me. The colors are placed in specific amounts as if there is something distinct I need to create. I stand and balance between the rocks, jumping and dancing as I travel over them. The black water reflects the night sky above, and the bright moon highlights the waves.

The stars are beautiful tonight. I hold out my hand to the perfectly painted sky and connect each of them until a picture is in my mind.

I walk back and sit on the stone with my paint, canvas, and brushes, rendering the photo in my heart. A streak of black. A dot of blue. I trust the process and let the brush lead the way across the canvas.

Someone's here. I should probably give them a welcome and invite them to my rock. I jump down and run over, feeling the soft wet sand caressing my feet as I skip. A masculine silhouette stands before the black abyss, not moving. He smells of rosewood and cinnamon, and his gaze is comforting, although I cannot see him.

"You're here to save me, I presume," I say to the unusually tall man in front of me. "I knew you would. You save me in all my nightmares." I look closer at him but still can't see a face. I know he's smiling. *Who wouldn't smile in a place so wonderful?* I feel the urge to frolic again, dancing with myself and the stars until he responds.

"You'll be okay. It shouldn't be much longer now." His voice is the same rich, vehement one I remember from the cave where he first saved me, even though he was half the reason I *needed* saving.

Nothing like that matters here, I think with the largest smile.

"Thank you for saving me a second time," I say, but he doesn't acknowledge my words. He instead fades away, piece by piece. While gone from my vision, I still feel him, even if only in my mind.

"I know you're there, *T'eiskaeh*," I say with the hope I'm correct. Either way, I will dream of company. I hop and spin on the spot, painting away again. The picture is almost done—a portrait of the siren that likes to hold a place in my subconscious.

It is the combination of those two paintings that flashed in my mind when I saw who I believe he truly was. He's looking off to the side with a smile. I wonder what he's smiling at, but it is my painting, so perhaps he's smiling at me.

That's a nice thought. I'll stick with that one.

The stars are beautiful tonight. I hold out my hand to the perfectly—*What's happening?*

Where am I?

What's going on?

I drop everything from my hands, the painting turning its head at an odd angle to face me directly, and the eyes turn black and drip blood. The water is red. The sand is red. The sky is bleeding. The tide rises twice as high every minute, and my rock is nearly submerged in the thick bloody water before I can even understand what the hell is happening.

I see the silhouette again, standing in the same spot as before, although now his body is covered to his knees by the rising tide. My heart pounds and threatens to crawl its way out of my chest, trying to force past my ribs.

What is that? Why is it watching me?

"Get away! Leave!" I scream at the shadow who stands there watching me, its head tilting to study me closer.

I vomit as the water touches my feet, the congealed liquid caking my skin and sucking me in. The smell is putrid, like rotting flesh and decaying metal. As I take a panicked breath, I choke while inhaling the stench.

Why am I here?

Where am I?

Mom?

Dad?

Anxious, scared tears stream down my face, and without the luxury of the ocean washing them away, I feel the burn of their heat sticking to my face.

Mother, find me, please. You found me once. Do it again. I need you, Kaileah.

I will the thoughts to find her like her words once found me.

The water has reached my shoulders now. I have only one minute left until the sludge engulfs me. I stare at the sky, wanting to die with a beautiful view in my eyes.

The stars would be beautiful tonight...if my view wasn't tinted red.

15

FOREVER DYING

.*⭐ VERA ⭐*.

I drown. Day and night, I drown. The thick, congealed water fills my lungs and suffocates me as I fight the urge to vomit.

All I can see is blood.

All I feel is blood.

All I taste is blood.

It's a never-ending cycle, and I can't understand what I have done to deserve this torment.

I don't know who started to heal me some days ago, but I want to think it was the siren from the cave. The feeling inside of me was the same. My body felt lighter and brighter, but I still do not know. I didn't get to see their face.

If this torturous mental prison has taught me anything, it is to never trust what I see. I saw Mom one day. She was swimming to grab me, and the second I extended my hand far enough to reach hers, she disappeared.

She felt and looked so real, and I was happy to finally get out of here, but I wasn't so lucky. I stopped having hope after that.

~

I've started counting how long the brightness above me lasts, assuming it means the day has reset. A week has passed—a long, excruciating week filled with dying without ever feeling the relief of death.

I've managed to hold my breath and swim to the surface, but it looks worse each time I try. The land is a wasteland of dead sea creatures. Piles of decaying fish and beached whales litter the sand, but the good news is that there is more land every day.

The tide is lowering, and I'm getting used to the smell.

The feeling of the blood in my eyes and lungs is still agonizing, but I can tolerate it. Tomorrow, I will make it to land. I will not stop until I get there.

~

My journey has begun as the brightness comes forth. I use half of my strength to pull myself to the top, and I see what I hoped for. There will be enough land to survive without endless drowning until someone can find me.

Each stroke requires a decent amount of force, so it has to be planned.

One. I count the movements.

Two.

Three.

Four.

Five. I've pulled myself a noticeable distance. If my estimations are correct, I need to do ten more strokes until I can wade the rest of the way.

Six. I used more energy than planned, and I falter and begin being pulled back under the red waves. *No. I refuse.*

Seven.

Eight. I'm struggling to keep going because I have not slept in weeks and the energy reserve I thought I had is gone.

Nine.

Ten.

Eleven.

Twelve. I can hardly keep my eyes open, and I realize now there is no way I can make it to land. I am incapable. I will have to let go and drown until morning.

Thirteen.

Fourteen. I don't know where the strength to continue has come from, but it's helping. I'm so close. Just one more, and I can make it.

Once more, Vera, stay strong.

Fifteen. I scream out in relief as I let my body drift down to touch the floor just enough to walk until I am away from the water, but I was wrong. My body is sucked into the scarlet ocean once again, and I wish I could cry, but the liquid pours into my eyes and won't allow it. Another day I will go, inhaling death.

No, I won't. I use all the adrenaline in my body and swim to the surface once again, pushing through.

Sixteen.

Seventeen.

Eighteen. I've made it to land, where I collapse, reeking of the disgusting substance caked to my skin but able to breathe. I cry until I fall unconscious and wake up the next day.

I can't remember anything from before I entered hell. The

short-term memories have begun to fade day by day as I lose my mind. All I remember is a woman named Kaileah. I do not know who she is, but I think she's important. What does she look like? *I do not know.* What does she sound like? *I do not know.*

All I remember is the name and the feeling I get when I think of her. It's a warm feeling, warm like fresh blood.

All I think about is blood.

I still remember my parents. Mom and Dad. They're in the house on the beach, or maybe they've gone home. I miss them. I miss them more than I miss my life before hell. The worst part of this place is not the torture.

The worst part is that I am losing myself, my memories, and my will to fight. I miss my friends. I miss living creatures. My only friends are the dead whales I sleep next to. They're okay. Their skin is warm and soft, and their pectoral fins make fine blankets.

I will be okay. My nose has become blind to the putrid smell of decaying flesh, and I only smell what's left of the salty air.

I still love the smell of the beach. I will always find it comforting, even if this memory stays. I wonder how much longer I must wait before I am saved.

I feel the tide turning! I see colors again! I run to a large rock by the crimson waves and climb to get a better view. The sky—the sky is blue! It has shades of pink and orange and I see a bright yellow sun coming above the horizon.

Something is changing, and I hope they're coming back for me. It has been another week since I last acknowledged the time.

I even saw a *living* fish swim past, but that was likely just my optimism.

I feel—I feel better! It's happening! They're coming for me! Something tugs at the farthest point of my peripheral vision, and I turn to see a shadow. A shadow—THE SHADOW! I remember! I run over and shake it, trying to get his attention.

"Save me, please! I've been trapped in this hellscape," I say through coughs and stutters. I haven't spoken aloud in nearly a month, and it almost seems I've lost the instinct. As I shake the shadow further, it morphs and brightens. I see features forming, and it shrinks to be slightly taller than me, not the massive height I thought.

I see eyes, a nose, a mouth, arms, legs, and everything form until a young girl stands before me. Her hair sits on her shoulders, and she grabs my arms with a sharp gasp.

"Where is this?" she screams, looking around. "This is not where I left you! It was beautiful. I should've never stopped yesterday. Gods, what have I done?" She looks around and falls to the ground seeing the week-old corpses of sea creatures washed ashore. Examining me closer, she can't meet my gaze, seeing the blood caked over my entire body, including the insides of my eyes.

"Yesterday? It's been over three weeks," my voice still stumbles as I speak. "I—I've been drowning for weeks." I fall to the ground as well, lacking energy from never sleeping, eating, or drinking. Her eyes shake as she covers her mouth.

"I don't care if it kills me. You're coming home today. I promise," she says as she dissociates from everything around us. The water turns back to blue ever so slowly, and the sand returns to a soft beige.

I feel the contents of my stomach threatening to resurface

and lack the energy to fight it. All the blood I've ingested comes out, and I realize just how much I couldn't breathe before. The animals disappear and everything is as it was before, including my skin free from the sludge.

Coming back to my reality, the girl looks at me and smiles before she fades away again.

"No! Take me with you!" I yell, as I run to where only particles remain.

My head is full of bricks, and I fall to the ground, collapsing into a deep sleep. My thoughts are black for the first time in a month, and I realize I never want to see red again.

16

PRISONER

.*⭐ VERA ⭐*.

I gasp for breath as the room's brightness blinds my eyes, along with the crowd of people surrounding me. My vision is clouded and spinning, and I can hardly focus long enough to notice who is watching me. I don't know what happened or where I am, and I look at my hands to check that I'm alive.

I try to focus on the white flowers I feel until I can calm myself. Finally, my head stops spinning. I catch my breath after what feels like half an hour, but it has likely only been a minute.

The first eyes I spot are Kaileah's, and I pull her into a hug, feeling for some reason like I need the physical comfort. She was the one person who never left my mind while I was stuck in—*I can't remember.* I search my brain for a memory to follow the beginning thought, but there's nothing. My stomach forms into knots as I know *something* happened in my mind, but I can't remember any details of it.

"K—" I try to push the word out, but my lips don't want to open. "Kaileah?" I ask with a cough, and she pulls me closer.

"What happened? I was so worried," Kaileah whispers, letting my head rest against her chest. "What happened to you?" she repeats, running a hand through my hair.

"I don't know. I can't remember anything after I went unconscious," I say in little more than a whisper. A vaguely familiar girl looks away uncomfortably in the room's corner.

She knows something.

Before I can ask her about it, Alec blocks my line of sight. He hugs me tightly, and I reciprocate as best I can. My arms are weak, and the initial burst of energy I used to hug Kaileah took most of my strength. Once he lets go, I notice Korah swimming back and forth behind him.

She bites her nails, deep in thought. I wonder if she has even realized I'm awake. Alec nudges Korah, and she rushes over with a gasp. She places a gentle hand on my forehead and sighs in relief. Korah's face drops as she feels the weakness in my hands and grabs a jar of herbs.

"Dried *deiniweed*. It helps with muscle fatigue," she says as she crushes the dry vines into a powder. The older gentleman behind a check-out desk moves to object, but Alec slips him a few *seils*.

Korah takes the *deiniweed* and puts it in my mouth, motioning for me to swallow it. I expected it to have no taste, but a light spice catches my attention.

"You'll feel better within the hour, but for now, let's worry about getting you home," she says, pulling Alec to help her move me.

Alec lifts me from the hard table I mistook for a bed and

holds me steady through my loss of balance. Now that I am upright, I see that the room is a small herb store with a table cleared off for me.

Jars, bags, and potion bottles scatter the floor, filled with various colored plants and liquids. In front is a shelved wall with the same items and multiple jars of what I know now as *deiniweed*. It grows in a curving motion, six weeds in each one, all tangled together. Some jars are packed live, others dried, and peering closer, one last group is cut into fine pieces in a one-ounce jar.

If all Koifinn people can grow crops, then why is a shop like this even needed?

I suppose some people may prefer to purchase it when needed instead of growing it themselves.

The young girl I think I recognize moves swiftly out of the shop before the rest of us, and I instinctively break away from Alec, swimming and calling for her to come back. Alec, Korah, Kaileah, and the girl reach their arms out to stop me before I realize that I'm collapsing.

"I can only heal you so much! You need to conserve your energy before you fall back into that hellscape I just pulled you from," the girl yells in a state of pure panic.

Hellscape? I was right. She knows what happened to me. I wonder if my mind is keeping me from a memory I can't handle.

"Hellscape? You said she was in a paradise," Korah states with agitation.

"Forget I said anything. I have to go."

The girl swims off, but not before Kaileah catches up with her. I can't make out their conversation, but there is hostility on both ends. I wish my mother would relax, but I can't blame her since she almost lost her only daughter…again.

Alec lifts me from the ground and pulls me to lie against his shoulder.

I lack the energy to keep my eyes open and drift into a black void of near sleep. It doesn't last long before Alec throws me out of it, shaking my face.

"You can't close your eyes. We don't know if your body has healed enough to keep you from going unconscious again," he spews in a panic. "I'm scared of what's happening to you," he continues. "This isn't normal. No octopus that looked like Korah described could've done this to you. You weren't healed through the usual means, and now I'm hearing something trapped you in a mental prison? None of this is normal. *I'm scared for you.*" The passion in his words is enough motivation to keep me from closing my eyes again, but I don't know how much longer I can hold it.

Alec's words ring through my head.

He's right.

None of this is as it should be.

Even now, there is a nauseating mental fog compressing each side of my brain. I feel like every second I stay awake, the closer I get to death.

I don't know how long the journey back to their home takes because I spend most of my time falling in and out of alertness. Everything in me begs to close my eyes, but I fight it off like medicine to a fever.

I hear Alec's whispers and force my eyes to open and understand my surroundings.

Wait, we're still in town? I thought we made it home.

"*Feina!* Kaileah—I mean *Fae Naejikōn.*" He pulls me closer, shielding me from view. "Adleian guards are at the gates. Take

Vera, and I'll deal with them," he states with a stern authority. "I don't want them knowing either of you are here."

After handing me to Kaileah, Alec rushes to the guards at the gate. She places me safely behind a tall structure and looks around, intensely contemplating her next move.

"I have to see what's going on. Stay here, please," she begs before cupping my face and rushing off to join the action. I lean past the building and see her sticking to the shadows, unseen by the Adleian patrol.

I'm too stubborn for my own good.

I swim slowly over to where my mother hides and try to listen to the conversation. To stay far enough away to remain unseen, I can hardly make out their words, but I fill in the blanks as best I can.

"My apologies, General Draik, but I haven't seen the queen. Perhaps she was traveling south or westward from where you last saw her," Alec suggests, calm and collected. Draik's cracked, wrinkled skin and old, sunken eyes are the same from my memory.

The boy is silent, not moving a muscle, as he waits for an order—just like in the *la'minōlu* forest.

Poor kid. He can't be much older than me and already seems like a hollowed shell of a mer.

"*Jōi'aen*, boy. Don't lie t'me," Draik says with a thick accent. The man grabs the silver trident from his back and holds it in silent threat. "Take me to the queen, and then I'll be leavin'. Otherwise…" He pauses, pushing the weapon's razor-sharp edge to touch Alec's neck. "I'll make a scene." A small drop of blood falls before getting washed away.

Alec didn't flinch when the trident was pointed at him. He had no reaction beyond a wince of pain when the blood fell.

This cannot end well.

I need to do something, but even with this brain fog, I know I will only make the situation worse. What can I do then?

The guards don't know I'm here from the sound of it.

Why are you protecting me, T'eiskaeh? What motive do you have to keep me a secret? I think to myself.

Kaileah tenses and moves to approach before backing away and watching again. I've noticed that she doesn't like to let others handle things. She wants to be the one to do everything and protect everyone, so I know standing by while an innocent person's life is threatened eats at her core.

"I would advise you not to threaten or *attack* the leader of a clan's eldest son when you have no reasonable cause," Alec responds, cocking his head to no longer stare down the general's blade. He trails his eyes down Draik, pushing the trident from his neck with two fingers. "Might I remind you my clan is the only reason you go to bed with a full stomach?" Alec's eyes darken, and he gazes down at the general. Draik seems beneath him, although his build is far more muscular.

"I will not hesitate to retaliate with equal force, but for your sake and the well-being of my citizens, I think it's best for you and your group to move on," Alec finishes, crossing his arms.

The power he holds through his words and mannerisms is fascinating. I feel a heat on my face, but it's hard to tell if it is from attraction, fever, or simply being proud. No matter the reason, I believe he is truthful when he promises to protect me so long as he's able.

I sense something.

Someone's close.

I look to the shadows, searching for the cause, yet I'm clueless as to why I'm certain I'll see it. Sure enough, trusting my gut pays off.

In the darkness, cast by a building three blocks down, I spot the slightest movement and see the end of a predominantly black tail. The siren. I move to follow him before stopping short.

What the hell am I thinking? The last memory I have involving him is his admission to murder, not to mention my mother's stories. If he's here, and his warning was justified, we're marked for death, but I can't help wanting to trust him.

If he hasn't told the group of soldiers about my existence, does that mean he wants to protect me? Or does he want the glory of killing or kidnapping me himself?

Kaileah paces rapidly, distraught.

"Yer kind don't scare me, boy. I never seen ya lift a Finn." Draik laughs at his pun, although everyone remains silent. His decaying teeth have rotting holes and jagged edges, his gums outlined in thick tartar. "Last chance. Where's the queen?" The trident closes the distance Alec formed, creeping closer as the seconds pass.

"She isn't here," Alec says again, his voice no longer diplomatic.

"I warned ya, boy," Draik spits, surging forward with his weapon. I hold my breath, and Kaileah can't stand it any longer, cutting through the water at record speed.

She grabs the trident before it reaches the soft flesh of Alec's neck and turns it to ash in a surge of blue power. Deep, struggling breaths and a look of pure madness in her eyes send fear through the six guards. Even the general stumbles back, but their initial shock doesn't last long before they make their next move.

"Get back. GET BACK!" she yells at the enemies before her. I can't stand by and let them fight—I can't let them get caught. I move closer with labored movements. My vision grows weaker with each push of my fin, but I persist to get closer.

"M—Mother...run," I whisper, my voice weak.

A hand grips around my hair and tugs it harshly. Another follows with the grip of my neck. I look around, panicked, searching for my assailant.

"What do we have here? The mutt herself," a man's chastising voice states with a laugh. He turns me around, holding me against a stone wall by my neck. He tastes me with his eyes, trailing them across my skin.

I can't breathe.

"I suppose I could have a little fun with a pretty mutt like you before displaying my catch," he says while trailing his knife from my neck to above my rising chest, just hard enough to cut. I gasp as I'm thrust into adrenaline-filled consciousness before falling back into the fog.

I can't think straight. My vision blurs, and I can hardly keep my head from falling to my shoulders. I force myself to focus on the man before me.

My eyes are deceiving me—his perverted smile curves too high, and his eyes grow in size each time I blink.

This is it. I'm going to die.

His hand rips the delicate straps from my collar to below my arms. The jewels pop off, and he pockets them for himself. The shells covering my chest fall forward before I can lift my arms to stop them. I shove him as hard as I can, but it doesn't move him.

"I like when they fight back." He grabs my arms and lifts them above my head, letting go of my neck to change his grip. As I gasp for oxygen, the man laughs again. Is that blood?

The red drops fall from his nose and stop his laughter.

His eyes follow, bleeding the crimson liquid as his grip on my wrists weakens. The numbness in my hands fades, and I try to blink away the encroaching black edges in my peripheral vision.

Without wasting a second, a long dagger is held at the man's throat, wielded by the siren. His deep brown eyes are almost feline in their predatory state, gazing down on his prey. The tip of *T'eiskaeh's* blade trails the guard's neck, leaving a shallow cut and staining the water red. I watch his precise movements, and he seems only to cut deep enough to cause agony.

The siren tilts his head forward, locking his gaze on the man. The guard's fear thickens as he realizes who holds his life on the line.

"I didn't want to use all my majick to end your useless existence since you almost killed her," the siren states with a deep, angelic accent like my mother. I never noticed it before. Perhaps the dire circumstance and being saved from near death make it sound intoxicatingly ethereal, or maybe it always has been. "I'll just have to kill you the personal way," he snarls with a devilish grin.

He cuts a deep gash from the man's shoulder, almost removing his arm. The cries are excruciating, but they end as quickly as they begin with the crushing of his vocal cords.

"I can't have you alerting your friends, now can I?"

The man screams more, yet no sound comes from his mouth. His panic grows tenfold, and with it, *T'eiskaeh's* look of delight. The siren houses pure bloodlust across his fair face, but I lack the energy to swim away in fear.

All I can do is sit and watch the guard be tortured.

He cuts more.

The clear blue water turns a near purple with his blood. The siren moves completely in front of the guard, blocking my view.

Staring at his back, I notice deep, healed scars from whips and slashes.

"Please, stop," I whisper and cough in shaky breaths, blood appearing in the palm of my hand. *T'eiskaeh* turns around and looks at me with tender compassion before returning his unforgiving gaze to the man.

"She begs for your mercy after you tried to kill her," he says with a sharp huff. "Thank her," he commands. No words come from the guard. The siren grabs his neck and whispers softly, and the man can speak again.

"HEL—" he tries to scream before *T'eiskaeh* slaps his mouth shut. He then inserts his knife below his heart, painfully slow.

"If you want the pain to stop, I'm going to need you to thank the woman who saved you. Let's try this again, shall we?" The siren removes his hand, and the guard rushes over. He pulls my hands to his and thanks me with tears in his eyes.

I lie against the stone wall in shock, unable to comprehend what happened in mere minutes. Looking down, seeing his hands touching mine, I want to vomit.

Metal to skin.

I feel a blade pressed against my neck.

Why? is all I can think, closing my eyes. Everything hurts. Holding on hurts.

Please let it all end.

I open my eyes to see *T'eiskaeh*'s worried face, and I feel the calloused, blood-soaked hands of the guard holding me back.

"I'll kill this mutt!" the beaten guard yells. A laugh from my siren savior catches my attention.

"I'd like to see you try," *T'eiskaeh* grits out, anger growing like gasoline thrown on a fire. "Close your eyes, *saeraih*," he whispers. "You don't want to witness what I'm capable of."

I look to where my mother and Alec stand fighting after hearing a shriek. The two of them are cuffed as they're beaten with the backs of tridents.

Make it stop. My heartbeat quickens.

Make it stop. My vision clears.

Make it stop. My chest feels hot with something—*rage.* The feeling simmers as it grows in boiling waves, infecting every nerve in its path. My body glows with power as red, burning runes carve into my skin. The cut across my chest erupts with the intoxicating brightness. I feel healthy. I'm so close to death, but I am *so very alive.*

The guard releases his grip, terrified by my radiant luminosity, and I seize the opportunity to take his knife and put it to his throat.

"You shouldn't have done that," I spit out. My voice returns, but the tone is deeper—*darker.*

Hardened arms surround me, pulling me away as whispers follow. I blink continuously as the runes fade, and the sanguine glow dulls to nothing.

"If you were to use your *maemōjik* in such a state, you would die. Wait here. He's mine," the siren says. I can hardly see with my clouded vision and thoughts, but within a second, the guard's body falls to the ground, staining the grass it touches.

T'eiskaeh approaches and tries to hold me, but I use my limited energy to back away. My eyes shake as his tall frame looms. I lift my hands up, trying to block him, but he grabs them gently.

His narrowed eyes are delicate, and the brown irises remind me of ebony wood dazzling with the sun's sparkling rays. His hair, as dark as night, flows and traces his smooth skin, and it falls below his ears, touching the nape of his neck.

His hands caress their way down my arms until he reaches my shoulders, to which I don't object. He grabs the cut strap and ties the two halves together. After, he lifts me, pulling my nearly deceased body to rest against his warm chest.

The slow beats of my heart increase in rhythm with his, no doubt from the beginning of his healing majick. As I did in the cave where we met, I bury my face into him, reveling in his body's power to restore me.

"Shhh," he whispers, running a hand through my hair. "You can sleep now." The pain that was flowing through my body, keeping me awake, ends with his soft touch and heavenly whispers.

"But my..." I stutter, forcing my eyes open. "My m—mother and Alec. They're torturing them." In trying to speak, I feel a cold wash over me. "I have to—" My voice trails off as I fight for consciousness.

"I guarantee their lives for you, my *saeraih*," he says, brushing the hair behind my ears. He's taking me. The men and women are taking my mother and Alec.

The people of the town scream in terror, completely unaware of what to do or say. It's not every day the governor's son is beaten and kidnapped without reason. While horrified, they do nothing. The people watching do *NOTHING*.

They let them take us.

The siren promised me and my friends no harm, but how can I know it's true?

Mom always knew what to do. She would pick me up when I fell and tell me to be strong. When Dad was anxious, she knew the right words to calm his mind. Mom, if you can hear my thoughts, please tell me what to do. I don't know anymore.

Even if I wanted to fight, run, or scream, I can't. I can't even open my eyes. The last sense I have is my hearing. The mumbles of Adleian spread between the guards, marking my proximity to my mother and Alec. At least I'm near.

Wait.

I move my tail and feel wood beneath me. Reaching above my head, I feel cloth. Tracing it around my body, I realize I can see. The black cloth blocks my view, and I freeze in place as a familiar whisper breaks my haze.

"Stop moving. They don't know you're here." It's *T'eiskaeh*. My breathing nearly stops, and I try to move as little as possible.

After about an hour or so of travel, I hear Alec's voice speaking up from a short distance in front of me. I'm so glad he's okay.

"Where the hell are you taking me?" he mutters with his mouth partially covered. "Are you trying to start a war between our nations? I am Sarren's son, and he will not take lightly to his firstborn being beaten and taken in the street!" he states with anger. "When I take over, your kingdom will no longer have us as their ally."

I didn't know Sarren was grooming Alec for his position.

"Enough, boy," the deep, raspy voice of the general calls out from a different cart. "We don't need ya frolickin' flower lovers for food. We got just enough meat for the lot of us." General Draik scoffs and laughs at himself. "Yer *lucky* ya get to trade with *us*."

Alec makes no response, but a thud is all I hear and the collapsing of a body.

"That'll shut him up," an unrecognizable female voice states. "I was waging the consequences of just stabbing my trident through his throat before you knocked him out. Thanks, General." Her laugh is disgustingly egotistical.

"He's out. No need ta'use Common."

My mind wanders to distant memories, and I struggle to gauge reality from fiction. The two lines blur together, colliding and breaking. I can't think or understand the words surrounding me, and all I see is black. It's hopeless trying to keep consciousness, and I quickly fall back into a thoughtless void of all color.

At least it's not red.

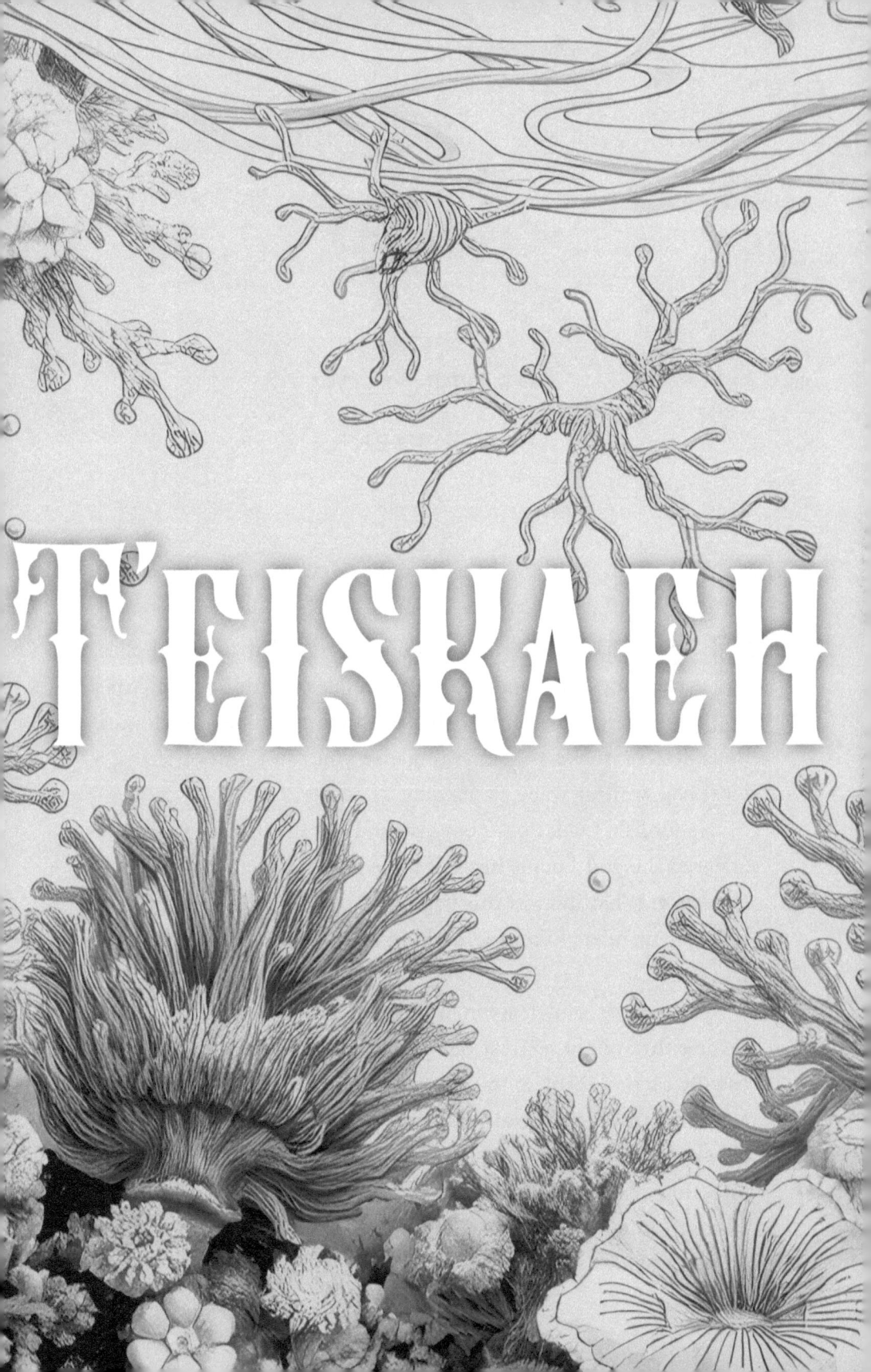

Teiskaeh

17

PROTECTION

.*⭐ T'EISKAEH ⭐*.

I stand beside the large wooden cart filled with supplies, camping gear, and other meaningless 'good luck' charms the men and women bring from their families. Necklaces, dolls, letters, rocks, and anything else you can think of sits in a large bag, waiting to be claimed by its owner.

It's foolish. Luck does not exist, and if it did, then I must have angered the god Lucius himself to be stuck in such an execrable existence. What item in this bag was from the worthless guard I killed? I wonder. Likely something as hideous as he was inside and out.

The guards and I swim on either side of our small carts, resting the weight against our shoulders as we travel. They are usually carried through the water by hippocampi and manned by a coachman on each, but no. Draik *could not wait* to capture the queen. I finally tired of his incessant whining and gave accurate directions, and the second I did, we left without gathering steeds. "I knew it," he claimed.

Idiot.

"Wait," a female sentry speaks up from a distant cart. How does a girl born in Adlei speak the language with such atrocious diction? It's not my native tongue, yet I can speak it proficiently. "What happened to Fjord? I haven't seen him since he split from us in Shari."

Hei'jaek.

As capable as I am of taking down these witches and armed men, I do not wish to start a fight. I place a hand on the tarp thrown over the princess, ensuring she hasn't escaped.

Her firm tail twitches at my touch, but it doesn't cause her to wake.

"Siren!" the woman calls. "Where's Fjord?" Her tone reeks of accusation.

How dare she assume I killed him? Even though I did, of course. Threatening the man, day in and day out, might have garnered suspicion, but to be fair, he had it coming.

"Dead," I state without emotion. "He attacked me, so I retaliated."

Each of the five guards turns to face me, halting our movement. Their emotional fluctuations distract me—their anger, confusion, sadness, and fear muddle and clog my senses. The woman who accused me stares in astounded horror.

Get a grip. It must be nice for this to be your first loss, I want to say.

"How dare you!" she yells, letting go of her cart and charging me, but not before she's halted by her intestines tearing. She shrieks in pain, and no one moves. They know one wrong step will have me doing the same to them.

"Don't even try, girl. Fjord was lookin' for trouble, and he found it," Draik responds with rolled eyes. "*Sōuriks* plus confrontation don't bode well," he adds, and after all the years I've dealt with taunting, dehumanizing words, they don't sting. "Always cravin' violence."

The girl shoots him an angry look, and he raises his eyebrows. He's surprised by her defiance, thinking her injury justifies the lack of respect.

I heal the woman—*slowly*—and after some time, she relaxes and moves to her position. The man supporting the entire cart by himself looks like he might pass out, and she doesn't seem to care.

Hours pass, and I feel each of them teetering on the edge of exhaustion. No one has mentioned it for fear of disappointing their leader, but I, for one, do not care.

"A cave system is near. It will be a perfect place to stop and rest before continuing, and we have enough sun left to set up before nightfall," I state. A wave of relief falls on the group as Draik gives a nod of approval.

Making camp goes without issue, and as I predicted, the last guard's camp is finished as the sun's rays fade to a dim twilight. When the others were distracted, I took the princess into my own cave, far enough away from the others.

She flutters her eyelashes, trying to wake.

I healed her enough to sleep, but I haven't had the time or opportunity to fully heal her ailments. Shaking her gently, she opens her eyes and jumps back, but she stays quiet after I put a hand to her mouth. Her heart is fast and strong, beating with harsh pulsating movements that try to battle their way through her chest.

That's good. She's healing.

"Where am I?" she whispers. I don't respond for a moment as I drape the tarp that covered her across the cave's opening. I pull three blue-glowing lanterns from my bag that dance their way across the space, lighting the room enough to view our surroundings.

Her knotted hair flows wildly around her head, but its imperfections make her beauty wonderfully real. Her green eyes are tinted teal, and the blue light distorts the surrounding colors. How she looks at me—trailing slowly across every part—makes it hard to breathe.

Never has a woman taken my breath away.

There's something strange about her. The connection I feel to her emotions and her pain is unlike anyone else. I can sense the feelings of others easily, a gift from my race, but I can *feel* what she feels. When she hurts, I feel the same pain. When she's angry or upset, I feel it so acutely that I almost can't distinguish it from my own emotions.

I presume that's why I haven't spoken of her existence.

Well, that's not the only reason.

While it's undeniably intriguing to feel her emotions as strongly as I do, I keep her a secret because she has never considered me anything but an equal. Even when I appeared as a monster, she saw through me, even though she had no idea there was something else to see.

The kindness...the sympathy...even after listening to her mother's horrible words and stories about my people, she sees me as something more. To her, I am an individual being beyond what society thinks of me and beyond racial stereotypes.

She only ever sees me for me.

So I suppose that's why I can't help but keep her safe because

I have never met a soul who has had not a single judgment or disgusting opinion of me. No one but my parents and sister.

"We're spending the night in a cave system until daybreak," I say, attempting to make my voice inviting. "How are you feeling?"

"I'm better. Thank you." She coughs, a forced smile prying at her lips. I move closer, and she doesn't dash away this time.

"May I?" I request. She eyes me intently, likely unsure of what I plan to do. "I want to heal you. Completely." Her face enlivens, and the apples of her cheeks protrude as a begging smile emerges. She moves closer, eagerly waiting for her body to feel like it once did many days prior.

I take her into my arms, trailing my hands down her chest and abdomen, stopping at the beginning of her tail, and repeating the motions. As I go, I whisper a song my mother would sing when my sister and I were ill.

"Through lulls and lows, I'll take the toll.
To give up control will heal your soul.
Give me your pain, the ailments in your veins,
and I will take them away."

Her eyes flutter as she drifts into a state of sleep. How exhausted her body must be to fall unconscious the second it feels relief. How long has adrenaline been her only fuel?

I feel the rhythmic beating of her heart, the blood rushing through her veins, the expanding and compressing of her lungs, the twitching of nerves, and the emotions surging around her head.

Her lips toy at the edges, twitching into a hint of a smile. With eyes still closed, she basks in my healing song. The energy it takes to heal her wounds is fatiguing, but I would never allow myself to falter. I can handle it.

"Please don't stop," she whispers, and I can't help but look at her with empathy. Poor girl. She's been fighting for so long.

I run a hand through her hair, not wavering from my concentration.

As more of her body returns to its natural state, I sense her muscles and mind relax. I feel exhaustion trying to pull me into a sleep state of my own, but I push through. I *have* to heal her. There's this purity in her, an innocence, stopping the world's corruption from destroying her. I can't help but want to give all of my life force to save her.

At least then the world will have someone who deserves a chance to live.

The suffering I feel as her body grows stronger is intoxicating. Like a vampire to blood, I devour it, siphoning the majickal energy that is killing her slowly.

This is no natural illness.

Never in a decade of healing others have I felt something like this.

Something about its aura is Adleian, but it could simply be from the princess's race and nothing more.

But I'm not so sure it is.

"How do you feel now, *saeraih*?" I ask, rocking her to wake up. She looks at me with wide eyes, her long eyelashes enhancing their beauty. She touches her skin, moving around with renewed energy.

"I feel better than ever! I had forgotten what *living* felt like after endless torment." She rushes to me, pulling me into a deep hug without warning. I push her away before realizing what I've done, too shocked by a sudden show of affection to respond without hostility.

"I'm sorry. I wasn't expecting you to be so...outwardly thankful," I reluctantly say. She thanks me verbally instead, crossing her arms over her chest. I feel her happiness dull as foreboding fear takes its place. She looks around and goes to the cave's opening, grabbing the tarp's edges and pulling them open.

"Stop!" I yell, yet still try to whisper. "This place is crawling with enemies. Are you trying to get caught? I just used most of my majick to heal you, and I don't feel like killing them the hard way." The horror I feel from her weakens me.

Gods, why does she have such an effect on me?

"Kill them?" she asks in a shaky tone. "Why would you do that?" I feel my heart softening as the disappointment radiates throughout the room.

I shouldn't have said that.

I always let the anger get the better of me.

"I would rather have a few deaths on my hands than have you seen and reported. I don't yet know what they plan to do to your mother, and I fear your punishment would be even more severe," I explain, putting a hand to my face and sighing, breaking away from her pity.

I can tell she understands. She *always* understands. It's almost as if she has an ability like mine to sense what others feel, but that's not possible. I've never seen someone so keen on reading the emotions of others without the help of majickal abilities.

I wonder if it's something she learned from living on land.

"And I'm sorry, *saeraih.* I shouldn't have said that," I add. She watches me curiously. "Forgive me. I don't have many non-hostile interactions. I may be a little rusty on conversational etiquette." She smiles and huffs a bit of air. I give a half-assed smile and fix the sheet she moved.

"You said something about my mother. Is she near? Can I speak with her?" she asks with a naive hope. That was an idiotic question for someone who seems so intelligent, but I suppose love makes us say stupid things. I nod before responding.

"She's heavily guarded. I cannot risk your safety by taking you to her."

"*T'eiskaeh, please,*" she begs. *T'eiskaeh.* I'd forgotten that's how I introduced myself to her. I hate the feeling it invokes, reminding me of the demented acts I've committed in the name of serving *His Majesty. T'eiskaeh,* he'd call me. His shadow servant. His perfect slave.

She knows no better. It was my fault that she ever learned the nickname in the first place. Why had I been trying to scare her? I had no intention of hurting her. I never have, yet I taunted her safety anyway.

I was trying to push her away because she made me feel vulnerable. She sees me in a way I haven't felt since the king stole me from my home.

Everyone I love is taken from me, so I presume my mind was shielding me. Or was it my heart?

Bruised, burned, and broken, my heart cannot take another slashing, and I fear that growing too close to this *draeōm* woman who has crossed my path will do me in. As strong as I am, I know better than to take on the mental burden of losing a love as strong as ours could be.

I feel her heart even when we're parted. It pulsates, falters, and glows; it beats inside my chest, like a second one to my own, reminding me of our connection.

Does she feel it, too? Is that why she holds me with such dignity?

I know no other explanation for her kindness and lack of fear. Hell, she watched as I tortured a man in front of her, taking his life when he threatened hers, yet she still eyes me with a merciful tenderness.

If I were not the man I am, I would've convinced myself that she was a calculating manipulator, forcing me to fall to my knees and suffer for her. But sadly, I can sense her genuineness.

I can feel the truth behind her words.

She wishes harm on no one, not even a *sōurik*.

Not even a murderer.

"The guards can see you, correct?" She places a hand on my forearm as she speaks. "Can you tell my mother that I'm okay? At least tell her I'm here." I contemplate her question for a time. As much as I would like to avoid conversing with her 'gracious' mother, I understand the importance of Kaileah knowing her child is safe.

"And the Koifinn boy?" I ask.

"Yes, tell him as well. Thank you." She smiles, and I feel her gratitude and even a hint of excitement at the prospect of the two of them knowing she's safe.

"You have my word, *saeraih*," I say, looking away from her.

For restoring a small decaying part of myself, I will tell them. I will tell them because I can't help but want to do anything I can to ease her mind.

She does something to my head, and I realize this woman will be the death of me.

HOPE

.*⭐ T'EISKAEH ⭐*.

I gave my word I would tell the queen of her daughter's safety and that I planned to do. She pleaded for me to go right away, but through *delicate* convincing, the princess agreed to wait until morning.

While I would have loved nothing more than to bring her happiness immediately, I didn't trust another sentry to keep from poking around in the other's encampments while I was out. The added chance that listening ears heavily surrounded the queen and the Koifinn boy didn't ease my worry.

I had limited sleep throughout the night, anxiety keeping me awake. Whenever I closed my eyes, I feared a guard would rip past the black canvas and see her sleeping, sending everyone to our location.

Thankfully, she slept soundly. She was as comfortable as possible in a hard, cold cave.

I had to stop myself from staring at some points. I would

grow distracted, counting her breaths to ensure she was sleeping.

Whatever majickal force was attacking her could come back, and I was going to be the first to take the pain away if it began. Her heartbeat stayed consistent throughout the night, never faltering from the correct pattern I'd memorized.

I reach the cave where the prisoners are being kept, and Intestine Girl stands, glaring at my approach.

"What do you want?" She scowls.

"Finish loading the carts. We're switching shifts," I say, looking down on her.

"*Jōi'aen!*" she yells. Once again, her pronunciation is atrocious. This time, however, it takes me out of my fluent understanding of Adleian, sounding instead like a foreign word to translate in my head. It feels like talking to a child, attempting to decode their mumbles and made-up words.

"General's orders," I push again. She angrily throws her trident down, sending it to the ocean's floor. When the weapon is nearly out of view, she relents and swims after it, leaving the position open.

I enter and see the two prisoners sitting back-to-back, tied together at their waists and shoulders. Their mouths are covered in cloth, tightly pulling their mouths shut, and each of them is cuffed at the wrists, hindering them from using majick.

At the sight of me, the Koifinn boy tenses, and Kaileah grunts with harshly furrowed brows. She shakes her head rapidly, forcing the cloth to fall to her neck to allow her to speak.

"What the hell have you done to my daughter?" she sneers with bared teeth.

"If you had let me speak, I would have told you I am here per her request," I say, already done with this conversation. The two stare at me, full attention engaged. "She's here, and she's safe. I'm keeping her hidden as we travel."

Kaileah breathes, a deep relief washing over her pale face, bringing color back to her cheeks.

"Untie us, siren. Let me go to her," she commands.

"Not happening," I say, rolling my eyes. She thrashes aggressively against the rope, cutting her arm in the process. Under her breath, she whispers a plethora of profanities and phrases I wouldn't care to repeat. "I have orders I have to follow. That being your return, and I suppose the added edition of a Koifinn captor."

The boy has made no unexpected movements. He seems exhausted by the rough thrashing movements from Kaileah, who has likely been fighting to be free all night. It honestly makes me feel a little pity for him, especially because there was no reason for him to be taken. His only crime was protecting the refugees in his clan—that bravery I admire.

"What's his deal?" I ask. The queen looks over and sees the exhausted boy she's attached to.

"Sorry, Alexander. I forgot we were connected." She winces. "Have I hurt you or kept you awake?" He nods his head slowly before dozing off and waking up again. She tries her best to apologize. He nods again, not attempting to speak past the cloth or remove it.

Alexander...he wasn't lying when he claimed to be the governor's son. Unless the Koifinn clan isn't prone to defensive retaliation, this will not end well for Adlei.

Not that I care. *I say let it burn.*

CLOSE QUARTERS

.*⭐ VERA ⭐*.

An entire day has passed since I was last in the Koifinn Clan. I'm unsure where we are, how far we've traveled, or if my mother and Alec are safe. I have spent most of the time daydreaming about my future and my past. I rarely think about the present.

T'eiskaeh has snuck me food throughout our journey, which helps to give me something to do or think about. I hope it's an extra portion of their rations and that he isn't going without food for my comfort.

From the little I've noticed about him, it seems like something he would do.

I can't peek out of the tarp to get a sense of where we are, can't have conversations, and can't even see my own hands in front of me. Occasionally, I can focus on the Adleian words spoken between the guards and pretend to understand, creating a fake scenario.

I wouldn't bet any money that I was correct, but the conversations help pass the time. At some points throughout our journey, I will catch a word or two I understand, but never enough to grasp what they're saying.

I don't know how much longer I can stare at nothing.

After a while, my body is thrown forward from an abrupt halt. I still cannot understand their words, but if I had to guess, I would assume we made it to Mōrian, the capital of Adlei. In preparation for whatever will come next, I lie stiff as a board.

Strong arms wrap around me, carrying me somewhere I do not know. I smell rosewood and cinnamon, and I can only assume the familiar scent belongs to the siren.

Once we are far enough away, he speaks in my language. Finally, *English*.

"We're heading to another cave system. Don't speak yet," he says, and the sultry, masculine voice confirms my suspicions of whose arms I lie in. The journey is relatively uneventful, and we make it to another cave for the two of us.

After removing the tarp, he nails it to the doorway as he did yesterday. As I still have yet to see anything but darkness, I wait rather impatiently for his majick lanterns.

They sway and float throughout the room, and I can't help but watch their journey, smiling broadly at both my first visual of the day and the beauty of their luminous blue glow.

The siren's face is so beautiful with the cerulean cast overlaying and softening his features. Where his usually sharp jaw and cheekbones would be is smooth skin decorated with beauty marks. A thick healed scar trails down his right eye before connecting to another gash across his nose and cheek.

His thick, groomed brows come together delicately as he analyzes me simultaneously. His neck is toned and strained, and I notice, looking closer, healed scratches and shallow scars.

Every cut across his fair skin tells a story, and I want to hear them all.

No one is the way they are without a reason. A murderer does not kill without motivation, a bully does not harm without purpose, and a king does not rule as a dictator without a story.

As horrified as I am, having watched the man before me kill another, I can't help wanting to know the reason he can and will take someone's life without a second thought. He did it to protect me, that much is certain, but why torture him first?

What does he gain through that man's suffering? He could be a sadist, feeding on the pain of others for a twisted, self-pleasing motive. He could have a history with him, having watched him do terrible things and finding justice in doing them back. He could have even believed I would be *flattered* by watching my assailant be cut to shreds before death.

No matter the reason, I will hold my judgment until I understand him, for all reasonings can be justified through the eyes of the beholder. I take pride in understanding others, even when I would not have done as they did. I find it fascinating.

One event could trigger a completely different reaction to another person. I believe it's part of what makes us human—or humanoid.

As we ready for bed, I notice the rock's opening is smaller than the last, and I can barely stay half a body's distance away from the siren before hitting the other edge. He focuses on something in his hands, and after shifting closer, I see it's a book.

Small lettering decorates each page, and the cover is intricately decorated with golden swirls like a royal frame. The front title curves and twists, spelling out a phrase.

The first letter of each word is larger than the rest, making a statement with the cursive connections and swirls surrounding them.

I hate not understanding. I wish I could sneak a glance and peer into his world, but I could not begin to understand.

Another phrase is written across the spine in the same fancy lettering. This time, I'm almost sure of its meaning.

The author's name is carved beautifully into the hard black spine. I assume the words are written and cased with gold foil because in the harsh blue light, they appear green.

"What's that?" I ask, waiting for a response like a curious child.

"This?" He gestures to the book and hides it slightly. "It's something my sister wrote. I promised to give her a detailed review the next time I saw her, so I try to dip into it when I can."

He stares back at the pages, and a sadness washes over him. His reading speed slows until he looks away from the pages and stares at the cave's wall.

"Are you worried her writing won't be respected because she's a siren?" I ask, and he jerks his head at me. Confusion is painted across his face, and I figure the same is true for me after seeing his reaction.

Opening his mouth to speak, he closes it again and shakes his head to himself.

"How did you put that together? Can you feel what I'm feeling?" he asks, running a hand through his hair.

"Um, no? Based on your mannerisms and what I know about your race, I just assumed." I try to smile, but it falls into a grimace. He analyzes me further, content with my response but still questioning.

"She's undeniably talented with beautifully vivid descriptions," he says softly, trailing his finger across the spine of the now-closed book. "It deserves to be seen by the world, not just my mother and I."

Does he not have a father?

"What's the title?" I ask, and he turns it over and reads it carefully.

"*Lē'reöan Aeḥuntūnda* or *A Love That Rivals Darkness*."

It sounds like a romance, but I will have no real idea unless I can read it.

"How did she learn to write?" I ask, reaching slowly to touch the book, and he doesn't move away. Taking it into my hands, it's heavier than it looks.

"My father used to bring her old damaged books from libraries and bookstores. I attribute most of her skill to his teaching and the Ancient Adleian writing we all read," he explains, looking over my shoulder to examine its cover with me.

The pages are as thick as cardstock yet soft and bendable. Feeling the words, they're indented like the opposite of braille. I wonder if she used a typewriter, or I suppose its underwater equivalent.

I try to sound out the words and catch *T'eiskaeh* wincing in embarrassment.

"Okay, read it to me then," I suggest with a chuckle. "In Common, of course."

He takes the book from my hands, grazing his fingers across mine, which causes my stomach to flutter. Clearing his throat, he skims the page before reading aloud.

"IF I WERE THE ONLY ONE LEFT AND HAD HIM BY MY SIDE, THEN ALL WOULD BE WELL AND RIGHT IN THE WORLD. HE AND I ARE ONE, STUCK TOGETHER BY FATE AND SEALED THROUGH DESTINY. I WAIT BEFORE THE GRAND PALACE DOORS AND KNOW THAT WHEN THEY OPEN, MY WORLD WILL CHANGE FOR BETTER OR WORSE, AND BY THE GODS, I AM READY."

The look of pride he wears reading his sister's work warms my heart. It's hard to imagine he's the same person who killed someone only a day and a half ago, but I can't quite find it in myself to care.

Does that make me horrible?

By excusing his murderous tendencies, am I just as evil?

No. He did it to protect me. By my standards, that makes him my hero, and by my morals, he did the wrong thing with the right intentions. That's all that matters.

"Her writing is beautiful. We need to get her word out! Maybe we could publish under a pseudonym so no one knows she is a siren," I blurt, and he watches me in deep thought. "You know the ins and outs of the kingdom, so we could sneak in and go to a book publishing firm. I could even pretend it was for me because I would blend in!" I say, pushing my hair back to reveal my racial ears.

He smiles and takes my hand, and heat rises from them and settles on the apples of my cheeks.

"I love the enthusiasm, but you and I would stick out like a pair of seals in a dolphin pod. Adlei isn't kind to unrepresented authors, especially young ones, so it's not just my sister's race keeping her from her dreams," he explains, and I frown at the thought.

He releases my hand shortly after, and something inside me wishes he would have kept it there a little longer.

I look away quickly, avoiding his eyes as my cheeks get brighter. Out of the corner of my eye, I catch him with a half-smile, returning to the book. As he reads, I notice the author's name again, and now that I know it's his sister...

Marsh must be his last name.

"So your last name is Marsh?" I ask. The siren tenses before nodding his head far too slowly. His name must be personal to him. I don't want to pry, but I can't help being curious about what it is. "Valerie is such a pretty name."

He closes the book and places it back in his bag, turning his full attention to me.

"My mother always loved the name. Valerie was the main

character in my mother's favorite novel growing up, and she swore she would name her daughter after her."

"What's your real name, *T'eiskaeh?*" I ask, no longer playing the waiting game.

He closes his eyes and visibly shudders.

"Stop calling me that, *please,*" he says, and my face drops.

"What else am I supposed to refer to you as? You're the one who said that's what you were called. I'm sorry if I've said something that upset you."

He sighs and looks away, aware of the validity of my words.

"I—I know. No one wants to know my name. I suppose it's become personal," he explains.

As he turns his head to the side, it reveals a large bruise across his upper back.

It looks fresh. I don't understand why they treat him the way they do.

"I understand. Just give me something you'd like to be called instead, even if it's not your name," I suggest tenderly, placing a hand on his shoulder. He flinches and grabs my wrist before quickly dropping it.

He looks ashamed but says nothing.

"*Nallac.* You can call me Nallac."

UNCONSCIOUS DESIRES

.*⭐ VERA ⭐*.

I wake up to the voices of guards packing up for the last day's travel. Light peeks below the tarp, highlighting the edges of my iridescent scales. I feel something warm beneath me, cushioning my head from the hard stone.

Turning to look at what it is, I see Nallac's chest rising and falling with the deep breaths of sleep. He hasn't noticed I'm awake.

There is no way I cuddled with him in my sleep. Embarrassment floods my face, and I am *so* glad he didn't see it first— which is surprising, considering he seems to never sleep. The exhaustion must have finally overpowered his insomnia.

I try to move away but can't, considering his arm is tightly wrapped around my waist. I can hardly think as he delicately trails his hand lower down my side. A shiver overtakes me, and I have to remind myself to breathe.

He pulls me closer, tightening his grip and mumbling something I can't understand. He throws me back onto his divinely sculpted chest, and I feel a crimson kiss spanning from cheek to cheek. It burns hot as his hand grabs me, and he pushes his head to rest between my neck and chest.

"Hey," I whisper, trying not to startle him. He opens his eyes and notices my hand on his chest and his tight grip. He jolts away and collects the blue lanterns and other small items scattered around our space without a word. "Are we going to ignore what just happened?" I ask with a hint of flirtation. He needs to feel the same embarrassment I do.

"That's exactly what I'm going to do," Nallac responds, lacking the playful energy.

"You pulled me closer when I moved," I tease.

"You're imagining things."

"*Bullsh*—" I start before he covers my mouth. I mumble the rest in spite.

I hear a man's voice approaching us, so I push myself against the wall, as far from the cave's opening as possible.

"Leavin' in five," the general states, and I hear his signature spit when he's done. "Hurry," he adds when the tarp doesn't move.

Even in the dark room, I can see the eye roll Nallac does while listening to him speak, and I can't help doing the same.

As the tarp is removed again, I notice a compact and densely furnished room, unlike the spacious guest room at the Fentons' home. I sit on a twin-sized bed, touching a wall on every side but one. A bookshelf is stacked full at the foot of the bed, and a second shelf, just as packed, is where a nightstand would be.

The floor's wooden planks are damaged—some lifted, broken, or rotting.

Across from the bed, a wooden desk and chair sit, the only decoration a bowl of flowers. There are two types: a white lily with a blue center, its veins glowing sapphire, and the second is a smaller purple hibiscus with a blooming white center, its veins a beautiful glowing violet.

The two bookshelves have those same flowers used as accents, stuck precisely between books at the ends, making the otherwise plain room cozier.

Swimming closer to the desk, I notice a short hallway leading to another closed room to the left. Filling the hallway is a piano with the same extra keys as the instrument in Taelani. It, too, has flowers placed on each corner.

The smell of wood wafts across my nose like it would on land. The colorful plants, however, have a very interesting smell, unlike any flower I've smelled before.

I lean down to sniff the bowl of flowers, and the hibiscus catches my attention first. It smells almost identical to cinnamon but sweeter. I recognize it. I've noticed it a lot recently.

I turn to see Nallac leaning against the doorframe, watching me, and I know exactly where I must be.

His room.

A banging on the door startles us both, pulling our attention to the shaking wooden frame. Nallac's pointed ears twitch in recognition. They don't have fins like Koifinn or Adleian ones—instead, his ears look like a human's, with the helix extended into a sharp point.

They remind me of elf ears from human stories.

"Siren!" a deep voice bellows from the other side of the door. "King Argyros needs to see you immediately."

"I'm sorry to leave you here without warning, but I must go for a while. Will you be okay waiting?" he says tenderly.

I nod my head, and he leaves, never looking back.

~~T'EISKAEH~~

NALLAC

21

PERSPECTIVE

.*⭐ NALLAC ⭐*.

I can hardly imagine what the king wants from me. Am I to be used as a live punching bag, again, standing still and taking the hits and slashes that I cannot heal? Or, better yet, am I to be killed on the spot like my father, deeming my service to the royal family complete?

The white golden doors before me span the distance of five grown men and are carved with detailed hieroglyphs telling the story of years and years of monarchies. The center is a mural painted by the most renowned artist in all the seas. She is rumored to be blessed by the Queen of the Gods, although some say she is Naejik's mortal reincarnation.

All of which are lies. She is like anyone else, gifted in a trade she spent years mastering. I don't doubt that she is more talented than others, but to be blessed by Naejik with a gift? Absurd.

The gods don't bless; they curse.

I, for one, can attest to that.

I force the doors open, combatting the weight of water

holding it in place. The king's guards stand on either end, making no movement to assist.

Why would they? I'm a *sōurik*, and I always will be.

He sits atop his throne, three sizes too large, to show off the Argyros family fortune while citizens on the outskirts of Mōrian starve. It's made entirely of marble and gold, the back curving into what looks like a set of wings. The sheer cost of the throne alone makes me sick to my stomach, and I wish for nothing more than to burn this entire kingdom to the ground.

Two women sit on either side of his tail, wearing only a few strings of pearls to cover their chests. They lean in and giggle, kissing his cheek and neck as he grins back. His eyes snap to me, and his face drops as if he's seen a ghost.

King Argyros shoos them away.

Disgusting disgrace of a king.

"My shadow servant! How wonderful of you to join me for a chat," he says, clasping his hands together with a face-splitting grin.

A six-year-old girl sits by his side on a miniature throne. I've seen her before—she was taken from her parents at birth to be a servant of the king. We have that much in common. The king's right-hand witch, Daevia, sensed the girl's psychic abilities and confiscated her to train her like a pet.

Psychic abilities are a beautiful gift that comes at a price. Caused by a mutation in the occipital lobe, it allows sight into someone's mind at the price of blindness. It is incredibly rare, so it is no surprise Daevia wanted her.

Her pale face houses two large clouded eyes, and she stares at the floor, rarely blinking. I can't begin to imagine what they do to that poor girl behind closed doors for her to sit without emotion day after day—for her sake, I hope it's nothing like they do to me.

She should swim with children her age, playing pretend with her innocent imagination. No child should be a slave.

No one should be.

I grit my teeth at the thought of what they did to me, of what they do to psychic children, and of what they do to the witches. I can feel my head throbbing from the start of a clenching-induced migraine, but I don't care.

Anything to keep my thoughts from that.

"Alice doesn't need pity, Siren. Alice is happy," the little girl says, lying through her teeth, but how could she know any different? I feel desolate sadness inside her, and I doubt she even knows what 'happiness' feels like.

I understand as much. Until recently, I forgot what it was to feel anything at all.

"I've heard whispers that the witches felt a majick so powerful it swept to the Earth's core, and I can't help but assume a certain banished princess has made a reappearance." He speaks clearly, staring straight into my eyes and waiting for a nervous movement. He won't see one. "You wouldn't know something about that, would you?" He leans forward, eyeing me intensely.

"I felt the majick you described, but I have seen no sign of Asherah. I assure you, my king," I respond. His eyes harden before he turns them on Alice. The king wants to know if I'm lying.

"Alice thinks Siren is telling the truth, King. Alice isn't sure. Please don't be angry with Alice." The child quivers in fear, folding in on herself and waiting for what he will do to her.

"Look again!" he screams in her direction, the words echoing across the endless chamber. Alice pulls her tail to her head and sheds silent tears. Her light ash-blonde hair falls across her face as she tries to hide.

"Yes, King," she mumbles in a shaky voice. She places her tiny hands on either side of her head, focusing her energy on looking inside mine. I want to let her in for her sake, but I can't forsake the princess's safety.

I could not care less about myself. If it weren't for Vera's fate tied to mine, I would admit I lied. If only to protect a fellow servant child.

I center my thoughts, grounding myself in the partial truth I stated and ignoring the rest while keeping my breathing and heart rate in check. The ability to sense what others feel has given me the skills I need to fool others with similar abilities.

"Siren is telling the truth, King. Alice is sure," she states with false confidence. I'm not foolish enough to believe it is to protect me. She couldn't read my thoughts and settled for the best option: telling him what he wants to hear.

The king is displeased but continues anyway.

"When we find Asherah, the witches have something special planned." All humanity leaves his eyes as he speaks. He smiles, likely imagining the terrible things he wants done to his queen's daughter. "That curse didn't last long enough, and if she doesn't want to stay away from where she doesn't belong, then she leaves me no choice." He shrugs as if believing she really is *asking* for it.

"If I may ask, Your Majesty, what did you have in mind?"

"So curious. I suppose I *could* tell you since you can't repeat what I say. Isn't that right, siren?" he asks with a smile that doesn't meet his eyes. I grit my teeth at his taunt, which refers to my binding. "I'm surprised it's still so effective, given how long I've owned you. You must be weaker than your father. What a pity," he says, leaning forward in his throne to make me seem small and pathetic.

I have to hold myself back from rushing forward—it would do nothing, even if I tried. I cannot harm the one who controls my binding. If I could, he would be the one crouched with fear, begging for mercy. I would show none as he never did.

"Siren wants to harm King," Alice whispers.

I don't mind him knowing. It's quite obvious, really.

"It's fine, Alice. He knows he can't do anything." He laughs, clearly pleased with himself. "To your question, Daevia has a curse planned that will lock Asherah in the dungeons for the next century. The witches will siphon her majick whenever necessary to power the spells I need." Gods, it's worse than I thought. "Think of it as a renewable energy source, and if she ever tries to fight back and uses some of her precious majick..." He grins, and it sends a chill down my spine.

He's dead.

The second I break this binding, *he is dead*.

He will not turn her pure heart into a battery for his demented dreams for Adlei's future—not my princess.

"And what would you like done to the queen and the Koifinn boy?" I ask, shoving down my anger to not trigger Alice's receptors. King Argyros thinks for a while.

"We need Kaileah's majick for the curse, and what better way to kill her than using her own unchecked power to cement her daughter's fate?" he asks with confidence. His laugh echoes throughout the grand throne room, bouncing off each wall and slamming into my head.

The room is longer than a full-grown blue whale and unmeasurably tall, with eight pillars growing from the ground on either side. Looking up, I see the murals on the ceiling, created by the same artist who painted the door. The space looks fit for the gods, which is precisely what the king thinks he is.

Sixteen sentries line the walls in mirrored symmetry. Their eyes are the only thing that moves. Two more guards swim back and forth behind his throne.

He could have a dozen more guards, and I could still slaughter them all before they laid a hand on me. One day, I will rip out the king's heart. The thought tugs a smile from my lips.

"As far as the Koifinn boy, Draik should have never taken him. Release the kid before I have a bigger diplomatic problem to deal with. *Imbeciles!*" he yells, and the room falls silent as the echo ends.

And the pieces begin to fall into place.

The keys for each cell are different to prevent the exact thing I plan to do: release *extra* prisoners.

I'm halted by his voice as I turn around.

"Don't repeat my words. Is that clear?" he commands, and I feel the binding reaching around my throat. I turn my head and look into his eyes.

"Loud and clear, my king."

The room reeks of rotting fish and rusting metal, and the bars lack proper care. Why would *His Majesty* care if the prisoners ward off bugs and poisonous crustaceans instead of sleeping? Why would *His Majesty* care for the quality of food they eat? I would hardly call it edible.

I have to hold my breath as I enter. The smell of feces is over-powering.

The two prisoners sit in cells side by side, with only a row of bars connecting them. Alexander looks one more day from decomposition, whereas the queen looks fine considering her circumstances. However, the extreme dark circles forming under her eyes show she isn't as tough as she seems.

Her anger fills my chest with a thick heat that's hard to swallow.

She's the first to notice my figure emerging from the shadows. She throws her body around to face me with her arms still cuffed behind her back.

Their cheeks have sunken, and I doubt either one has eaten.

"Please, sir, I haven't done anything. Let me go," Alexander pleads with a weak voice, using considerable energy.

I almost feel bad for him. He's a protective friend caught in a dictator's crossfire.

"I'm sorry, but I can't release you until tomorrow. King's orders," I explain with a shrug.

"Please, I can't live like this. I—I'm starving, cold, and can hardly breathe with the stench. I know you understand. Please, by the grace of the gods, *have mercy*," he begs, leaning his head against the bars, and I feel inclined to help.

I can't let the king know the binding is so weak. I have to obey.

I'm sorry, Alexander. I have to do this…for her.

"I have a plan. Try to remain patient," I say, looking from Alexander to the queen. Her stare burns through me, and I *almost* feel intimidated before leaving her line of sight.

I gain some respect for her after having such an effect on me. A mother's love is nothing to toy with—especially not hers.

～

It doesn't take long to make it back. Slave quarters are only a short swim away from the only place worse: the dungeons. If it weren't for my ability to stick to the shadows, the room would still have a mold-growing, bug-infested interior with nothing more than a bed and desk.

The piano was the most challenging item to steal and bring back discreetly. Steal is a strong word—I found it near a large trash deposit, waiting to be crushed and sent to the ocean's floor for no reason beyond being old and tattered.

Old is beautiful.

Old is unique, holding stories from years of wear on the keys.

You can place your hands in the position most worn away and follow the pattern, playing a song someone loved throughout their life. Music is the window to the soul, and instruments make us feel whatever we want to experience.

It is not linear.

It forever changes based on the listener's ears.

When I glide my hands across the keys, I find peace in song, experiencing and expressing everything I've held back. It allows me to escape as I am transported to a world away from reality.

The louder I play, the more it drowns everything else out.

Music is language, the one universal way of communicating with anyone across the vast seas. It has no bounds, barriers, or misunderstandings. It holds our culture, our teaching, and our souls. Music breathes life, celebrates death, makes us remember, and gives us revenge. Music runs through our veins, connecting each being in the delicate weave of chords strung together note by note.

I unlock the door and see the princess holding a small box and a photograph given to me by my mother. *Why would she go through my things?*

"What the hell are you doing? Put that down!" I yell, slamming the door and ripping it from her grasp. Holding her wrist tight, I throw the box across the room.

My attention is pulled back to see her eyes full of fear and *pain*. Releasing my grip on her wrist, I see a bright white handprint she covers and winces.

Hei'jaek...What have I done?

"I'm sorry. I didn't know it was personal," she mumbles, backing into a wall and pulling her arms across her chest. The understanding and sympathetic thoughts are gone.

She's terrified of me. She should be.

I drop my offensive position and stare at my hands, forcing them to stay still as they threaten to shake. Why would I have ever believed I'm more than a monster? They're right about me. The only thing I'm good for is harming others.

"Vera, I shouldn't have—"

"You're right, so why was that your instinct?" She interrupts my apology, barely meeting my eyes. "I don't know what has happened to you, but you have to understand that I will never hurt you. Not physically or emotionally." She looks into my eyes while dropping her arms to her sides. She is making herself vulnerable, giving me access to any part of her, but why? She sees what I will do—what I'm capable of.

She moves closer, and I swim back, anticipating something I can't pinpoint.

She grabs my forearms, and I jolt. Yet she doesn't let go. She stares into my eyes, forcing me to find comfort in being touched by another person. Slowly, my fight-or-flight calms to a light buzz of adrenaline.

"I will not hurt you. Not today, not tomorrow, and not the

next," she states softly, moving her hands across my scarred flesh.

"How can you treat me with kindness? Look what I did to you!" I yell, gently taking her wrist and analyzing the still white marks. It baffles me that even now, she doesn't flinch from my touch. "I did this! *I hurt you.*"

"You thought you were defending yourself like you've always had to," she tenderly suggests, turning my face to meet her eyes. "You've healed me. You've saved me. You've risked your life to protect me."

Her eyes are a dazzling green, like a forest begging me to explore what lies behind the first line of trees. Flecks of gold scatter like the sun's rays, painting the edges of each leaf.

I never knew the color green could be so beautiful.

I hold her hand between mine and whisper my siren song. Focusing on her injury, I feel the muscles relax, and the blood flows strong again, preventing the beginning bruise.

She gasps at the feeling of intense relief, and her heart rate slows.

My touch lingers longer than it should—I know it does. I healed her from my mistake, yet I can't let go. I don't *want* to let go. I want to pull her to me, wrapping myself around her in a tight embrace, but I can't.

Her skin touching my own weakens and forces past a boundary I don't remember creating. I don't know why I allow myself to feel defenseless in her grasp. I don't why it doesn't cause me to drop her hands instantly.

She pulls back, leaving only her fingers touching mine and drawing me closer. My heart skips a beat as her captivating gaze trails up my arm to my chest and finally finds a resting place on my lips.

"It's getting late. You can take my bed, and I'll sleep on the floor," I say, returning to an expressionless face as I drop her hands. She furrows her brows, likely displeased by how I avoid the conversations that scare me. The way she makes me feel *scares me.*

I, the siren who looks upon his torturer without fear as they beat him to unconsciousness, *fear* how a sweet, pure-hearted girl makes me feel. The happiness she brings through nothing more than her smile and presence is terrifying because I don't know what I will do if they find her.

If the king carries out his egregious plan, I don't think I can take it. The white scales that linger amongst the black of my tail will become pure abyssal darkness, and I will be left without my soul and anything to live for.

I would have my mother and sister, but each month, I think they will be better without me. For the longest time, they were the only things keeping me from shutting off every part of my humanity and falling into the darkness's alluring grip.

For months, I have found opportunities to see them, but I have convinced myself they would be better off alone. I have to protect them even if it means leaving them behind.

When I go there, it threatens the safety of our home, and as observant as I am during my travels, I fear that one day I will miss something. I could not live with myself if I led danger to their door, so I stay away. It's better.

You would feel no pain, no suffering, no torment. You would be free, the darkness claims as another ivory scale falls to the floor. I would also feel no love, no comfort, no happiness. I would be a shell of myself, existing only to please the one who controls me.

My master. His Majesty. His *Naejikōn.*

I would go through another hundred years of torture fighting against the king's control if it meant he didn't have access to an emotionless siren with my power. And so my mind is made. If the princess is ever found, I will never stop fighting.

"I will not take your bed. It's your room, and you've been traveling all day without breaks. You deserve to rest comfortably," she states while sitting at my desk. "Besides..." She trails off while looking at the wood, gathering her thoughts. "I don't think I can sleep tonight."

Her stomach turns, and she hides her face from me, but it does little to hide her feelings. Her sadness is strong enough to taste.

I only wish I knew more about her to understand what caused it.

Peering further into her heart, I feel a longing sensation similar to what I feel for my sister. It's the feeling of always wanting your loved ones near while being unable to go to them...I understand completely.

I place a hand on her shoulder, and she jumps back. Her eyes are bloodshot and welling with tears.

"You miss your parents on land, don't you? You want to run back and forget everything, but you know you can't because there is too much you want to know," I declare, and she stares in silent thought.

"How—" she mumbles, staring at me with unblinking, concentrated eyes. She shakes her head and looks away. "I need to be alone—to breathe."

She swims to the locked door and tries to open it. When it doesn't budge, she tugs again before undoing the lock.

I reach for her arm but stop myself before reacting again with hostility.

Breathe.

"Vera," I say softly, pulling my hand back. I know they're shaking, but I control it—*not now.*

She looks at me with *those eyes.* Those large, emotional eyes that pull the strings of my heart. All I know is that I've never loved a color more.

"I can't protect you if you go out there," I add.

"I can protect myself. I assure you," she says, but she doesn't understand.

"You don't know these waters, this kingdom, the guards, or the citizens. You don't know where the shadows lie at what time of day or what storekeepers will keep your existence secret. You don't know the customs, how to talk, blend in, or act Adleian. My *saeraih,* I'm trying to keep you safe. Please let me keep you safe," I beg.

I fall to the ground for her—to show how much I need her understanding. She gets to my level and grabs my head, tilting it up to look into her eyes again.

"You will never bow to me," she commands, and for the first time, I can see the crown atop her head. "I didn't understand the extent of the dangers for me here," she adds.

Reluctantly, the princess locks the door and sits, staring at the bowl of *cunjitōllies* and *daendidukes,* which are decorating the area with their vibrant petals.

"As a gentleman, I wouldn't feel comfortable taking the only bed when a princess is staying with me. So until you're ready for sleep, my *saeraih,* I will play a song for you," I state with a polite dip of my shoulders before sitting at the antique piano.

I prefer music that screams into the distance, but for today, I choose a softer melody. Dancing my fingers from key to key, I revel in the soft tones.

I see the story I tell without words: two lovers, hand in hand, dancing through an abandoned city as the waters churn in swirling circles. Their tails twist and connect, pulling them closer and deeper into their dance as the water grows in intensity. It tries to pull them away.

One grabs at the other, holding each other close as the world tries to tear them apart. Their grip stays strong as a light bursts between them, calming the water and reviving the city.

They turn and see the ecstatic faces of civilians grateful for their saviors. One lover bows to the citizens, and the other stands tall, proud of everything she did, as a tiny smirk twitches at the corner of her lips.

"Nallac, I—" Vera's voice breaks my trance. "That was so— *you're incredible.*"

My chest is warm, and her happiness becomes my own. I allow a small smile to enlarge my cheeks, turning my face away until I can compose myself. The feeling of a smile is foreign, and it hurts.

"I could continue if you'd like. Perhaps you'd enjoy a different tone?" I ask. Her cheeks rise high, causing her eyes to squint as she quickly nods her head. There's a brightness stronger than any other, but deeper down, I sense something that dims her light.

I feel the darkness, too.

I place my hands on a lower set of keys, each movement aggressive yet deliberate. A slow *dun dun dun* cascading into a more profound and faster *duh duh duh* that reverberates off the cracked stone walls and rattles the water in small vibrational ripples.

The story it tells is a far different one: a young girl searches the dark waters as arrows and tridents fly in all directions. She tastes the blood of wounded soldiers clouding the water around her as her eyes sting from tears. She can't find someone; they are lost in the chaos as screams from all directions pull at her attention.

The rate of my chords slows as they rise in pitch.

The girl looks around and sees the one she is searching for. She grabs their limp body, and her screaming shakes them both.

The notes I play increase in speed once more, filling us both with anxiety until the final *boom* sends the song into a spiraling decline.

I feel the girl's screams sending the hair up on my back until she quiets. The notes become eerily soft and delicate. Not long after, the chords explode in intensity as she rushes into battle, a heat rising to her chest, which controls all her actions.

I stop the song abruptly as a stupid mistake resounds and mocks me, echoing off each wall. I always forget the ending.

Vera's face sends another cold chill over my exposed skin as she stares, her eyes sunken.

"Is something wrong? You look a little pale," I ask, trying to gauge her thoughts but gaining nothing.

"Could you play the last part one more time?" The way the question leaves her lips is not in admiration but from unease.

"Of course," I respond, replaying the climax once more, her intense dread washing over me.

"The way you play it gives me this feeling in my chest like a rising, almost nauseating heat," she explains and places an unmoving hand across her heart. "I've only felt it once when that guard attacked me in Shari."

Ah, her *maemōjik.*

The emotion that triggered her body's instinct was rage in its purest form.

Sweet Kayiah, she will be unstoppable if something ever triggers it again. An emotion as unpredictable as rage could destroy an entire army, much less one enemy.

It will kill her if someone does not break her from it, for her bloodline cannot regulate its power. She will explode with energy, and the second it ends, she will die a violent death as her skin tears away from the muscles and the muscles from the bone. And if she is not graced with death, the consequences will be far more severe.

I remember the tales of the first sorceress's power and the myths of that majick's consequences.

I play the first song again and whisper my healing melody, focusing on her mind. I want her to feel nothing but comfort. After the last few days, she deserves it.

A siren's majick cannot heal mental disease as it is not a tangible wound, but it can relax the mind. My mother used to sing her song when I'd awake from night terrors after the death of my father.

Before the end of the last song, she fell fast asleep. I undress her without glancing at her naked form for all of a second. I resist even though I'd love nothing more than to memorize every bit of her skin. Once she's in something more comfortable, I tuck her underneath the covers to keep her warm as the water chills without the sun's heat.

I realize as I gaze down upon her that she looks absolutely beautiful in my clothes.

VERA

22

PASSIONS

.*⭐ VERA ⭐*.

arkness surrounds me as I jolt awake. A soft blanket, a firm pillow, and a cold stone wall are at the end of each swift movement of my arms and tail. I don't remember falling asleep.

It's so dark.

I spring myself upward, feeling my heartbeat raging against my ribs as I search for someone or for any idea of where I am.

"Hey," Nallac whispers, placing a hand on my shoulder. "I could feel your panic. What's wrong, *saeraih*?" he asks while moving his hand in soothing circles. My eyes finally adjust, and I can faintly see with my dark vision.

"I've never had an issue with the dark, but when I'm here—" My voice trails off as a shiver snakes its way across my skin. "I'd be lying if I said it didn't terrify me."

Lay beside me, my mind begs in his direction.

Why did I? Why do I want to...My cheeks grow red as my

thoughts jumble into an incoherent string of half-finished questions.

A small chuckle sounds beside me, and I feel his hand trail slightly lower down my arm, sending an intense heat to my otherwise chilled skin. His touch lasts longer than necessary, and I sense he doesn't quite want to stop.

"Is there anything I can do to fix that for you?" he asks. Yes, there is.

"I'm not sure," I answer, ignoring that thought before I stumble over my words.

"Perhaps turning on a light would help?" he suggests, and I shake my head.

"No! I don't want to keep you up. Speaking of, am I in your bed? Where have you been sleeping?" I ask, speaking quickly as my heart beats faster. I push myself out of bed before the siren catches me around the waist and hoists me back in.

"*Nallac!*" I gasp. His grip is gentler than ever, and I can tell he is trying to control himself as best he can.

"Calm down, *saeraih*. I prefer to sleep on the floor, anyway. It helps with my back pain," he claims with a shrug. I stare at him blankly.

"Considering your sheets smell like they were freshly washed in your scent, I don't believe that for a second," I state with rolled eyes. He stifles a laugh and moves to return to the floor before I catch his wrist. "See how *you* like it," I mumble before tugging him to me.

It sends us both flying back into the bed. His heavy body presses firmly against me, pinning me down. We breathe heavily while staring at each other with wide eyes.

"What was *that*?" he asks in a quickened tone, holding himself above me. The weight of his tail continues to press against mine as he regains traction. "You can let go of me now," he says.

That catches my attention, and I notice my firm grip on his wrist and his veins throbbing against the constriction. I can feel his pulse, and it's faster than mine.

"Why should I?" I ask with a smirk. What the *hell* am I saying right now? I need to go back to sleep before I say something I'll regret.

"I—*Vera*." His words become shaky after he swallows the lump in his throat. His gaze trails from my eyes to my lips before continuing farther down past my neck. I wish that's how he always said my name—like a delicate caress.

The breathless, uncontrolled tone and actions...it's intoxicating.

I want him forever unraveled.

"Enough of this," he states before tugging his arms away, quickly forcing my grip open and releasing himself. Without another second's delay, he pins me to the bed, pulling my hands above my head with only one of his. "Now, *sleep*," he nearly growls with the deepness of his tone.

I, in fact, do not sleep.

23

A HAPPY ACCIDENT

.*⭐ VERA ⭐*.

Nallac brushes his dark waves in his small bathroom mirror. His flowing shoulder-length hair makes him appear softer than usual, a stark difference from his hardened exterior. It doesn't last long as he pulls half of his hair into a messy bun at the back of his head, with a short area left at the base of his neck.

My watching comes to a close as he walks out.

I look down and notice that I'm wearing his shirt for the first time, and an intense flush covers my face. He notices and seems almost embarrassed.

"I didn't look. You have my word," he explains, understanding my thoughts as he always seems to do. Not a doubt crosses my mind of the truth in his words, and I hope that is just a sign of my good judgment.

"Thank you," I respond, and I swear I catch his eyes trailing down my frame before he snaps back into his closed-off mask.

"I have to do the king's bidding," he says, giving me a partial smile. "See you soon."

"Take me with you," I remark with a quickness I didn't expect.

"Absolutely not! Have you not learned?" He glares. "Look, Vera, if anyone sees you, that's it. We would both be done and so would your mother and the Koifinn boy."

"It's Alexander," I correct.

"Okay? The point still stands."

"What am I supposed to do while I wait? You don't have anything in here," I say, slightly agitated.

"You were saying?" he says, opening a drawer to reveal a notebook bound with paper, a glass of ink, and three different-sized quills. "Have at it. I know you like to draw."

I mouth a thank you, although I am unsure how he knows that.

"If I'm not back by the morning—" he begins before I cut him off.

"No, Nallac, don't talk like that."

"Listen to me. If I'm not back by the morning, I need you to find a way out and meet your mother at Taelani. She'll be waiting there for you. I can ensure that much." He rubs the back of his neck while looking away.

"You said it yourself! I don't know how to walk, talk, or act Adleian. How will I even know how to get there from here? I've never even seen the palace!"

"Vera, calm down. *You'll know.* I promise," he says, and I take a deep breath and focus on the look in his eyes: one of truth and sincerity.

"Okay," I say reluctantly, watching him leave for the day—*or longer.*

~

The hours drag by as I go through page after page of his sketchbook, drawing what I've seen throughout my travels. I draw the la'minōlu forest, the first dinner I was served, Astryx's eyes, and the reef Korah took me to. My lack of skill ruins the first few, splattering a large ink stain on the center of two sheets.

The pages differ from anything I've experienced. They're thick and firm yet soft and flexible. It's thin enough that I can rip it by choice, but not by accident. The color is tinted greenish yellow with flecks of white and darker shades, showing that it is handmade.

I haven't heard a sound outside the halls ever since Nallac left. It has to be safe by now. Unlocking the door, I open it slowly to avoid any sound and succeed. I whip around the corner while scanning the area from all angles.

My heart pounds as adrenaline surges through me, fueling my exploration.

The halls are dark, and the densely packed stone cracks farther as I run my hand along it. A brighter light leads me right, and I follow the halls until they transition to a marble floor and white stone walls.

It's beautiful.

The marble is placed in large rectangular tiles, leading me further down the hall. With the bright lighting above, I see the stone glittering as if it were made with flecks of silver.

I hear something.

I swim quickly behind a decorative table and wait for the cause of the sound to reveal itself. It doesn't take long as I'm tackled to the ground by a strong man's grip.

"Oh, sh—" I let out as my face slams into the cold tile.

"Commander Laurence, I got a girl round here!" the man screams in Common. Why would an Adleian guard speak my language? I thrash against his arms to no avail.

From the direction I thought the previous noise came from, I see a man with a grey tail swimming at a hastened speed. I can't explain why, but something about him makes me feel almost safe.

Yeah...I'm too trusting.

Looking up at him, I silently beg him to help me. Through his facial expressions alone, he doesn't seem to care and makes no movement to help. The guard who holds me back pulls my arms together in a swift movement, causing me to cry out in pain.

"Enough!" the man before me yells as he shoves the guard away, allowing me to upright myself. When I regain stability, he grabs my arm to keep me from escaping.

"Commander Laurence, what are you doing? She's not supposed to be here! I need to report her to His Majesty."

"Silence! Remember your place, *Raekaih*. You have no authority to command your superior officer," Laurence commands in a firm tone. His deep and assertive voice sends a chill up my arms.

"You're right, Commander. I apologize. What would you have me do?"

"Leave. Go back to the training grounds and wait for me there."

"But Commander Laur—" he objects before Laurence silences him.

"*I*," he annunciates, "will deal with her. Don't even think about saying anything to the king, or I'll hunt you down and kill you myself. *GO!*"

The man backs away and disappears without another word.

"Thanks for helping me. I'll be on my way," I say as I pull away from his grip, not getting far before I realize he's not letting go.

"Not so fast, love," he says with a slight smirk playing at the corner of his full lips. My face drops, and I meet his eyes for the first time.

His left eye is a piercing blue that stares straight through me, reading me like an open book, and the right is a deep brown that seems to hold all his secrets. The heterochromia makes it nearly impossible to look away and just as difficult to keep our gazes locked.

I notice a scar on the edge of his jaw and another across his eyebrow. His browbone is prominent and structured, and a golden eyebrow piercing shines above his strikingly blue eye. He swallows, and as he does, I can see his strong jawline tightening, as well as the muscles in his neck.

This man is undeniably gorgeous in a ruggedly handsome way.

"I'm sorry, but I really need to go," I plead. I grab his arm and imagine his skin tightening and convulsing, focusing on causing him pain. For my first attempt at Adleian majick without any coaching, I do remarkably well, as he lets go with a gasp.

It gives me precious seconds to flee.

What I don't do well is find an effective exit. Instead, I swim into a dead end with nothing to conceal my path. I turn around and lack the energy to fight against my third capture. There's nothing I can do to avoid it now.

"Look, *girl*, as the Supreme Commander of the Adleian Regiment, I have the right to know what you're doing in the palace of all places," he states, clearly angry.

He throws back his hair, which had fallen onto his shoulder, showcasing it in its long, luscious black form. Half of it is neatly tied in a ponytail, with only a few stray strands falling out and framing his masculine face.

"Look, *Laurence*, I'm not telling you why I'm here. You're just going to tell Dorian, which, in turn, will get me killed," I explain in defeat.

"Dorian?" he asks with a confused look before shaking it away and returning to one of authority. "First of all," he states firmly, "that's Supreme Commander to you."

"Sorry, and I meant the king."

"You know the king's first name?" he asks with another look of confusion, but this time it's mixed with apprehension.

"Don't you?" I ask, and he laughs hard for a moment.

"Well, I do now," he says sternly. "What I don't understand is how *you* know when the only people who do are his wife and his right-hand witch."

My eyes widen as I back into the wall, where he looms over me. Kaileah didn't tell me that.

"Love, I gave you the courtesy of a second chance to get out of a dungeon stay, but you are quickly rising in suspicion. I will consider you an enemy of the crown if you continue to dodge my questions."

"Well, I can't trust you!" I yell in desperation.

"Then I have no other choice than to report you and lock you up with the other prisoners. Come with me." He shrugs and drags me down the white hall.

"Fine! I'm Princess Asherah Dlari," I quickly spit out.

"Try another excuse. The princess is long gone."

He doesn't bat an eye and keeps moving us closer to the dungeons.

"I was cursed with the same majick as my mother. You know my mother's curse was broken, so you must realize mine broke too. Right?" I explain, and clearly, I've finally gotten through. He whips his head to face mine, a look of shock painted across his tanned skin.

"How did you get in here then?" he asks.

"Uh, majick?" It was the first thing I could think of, and it was a horrific excuse.

"Last chance." He gives me a look that reads *my patience is wearing thin*, and I don't intend to test whether that is true.

"Nallac snuck me in," I mumble in defeat.

"Hah! I'm surprised you're still alive!" he laughs before his flirtatious grin returns. He likely sees the horror on my face because he soon continues. "Ah, don't worry. Nallac is harmless. I mean, except that one time he killed Ol' One Eye. Oh, and the time he killed that blonde boy, and then there was that group of three in the stables. I can't forget the other six when they—"

"Okay, that's quite enough," I cut him off, unable to hide the shiver that crawls down my back.

"The point I was trying to make is that if he risked his tail for your safety, he won't hurt *you*." He rubs his jaw and eyes me intensely. "Count yourself lucky, Asherah. Even someone as insanely strong and handsome as me would be wary of getting on his bad side. Sirens are no joke, especially that one."

I don't know if that should comfort me or not.

He stops our movement and lets me go, but I feel that attempting another escape would be a stupid idea.

"I'll take you back to his quarters. Follow me," he says, and I obey without hesitation. I'm quickly growing to trust the man who holds my life in his hands. "You know, the point of the guards communicating in Common is to catch our enemies by surprise. It defeats the purpose when it's your native tongue, human girl." He grins.

"I'm not a human. Not anymore, at least," I respond, looking away.

"I'm sure that's difficult to process. Hell, if I woke up tomorrow as a Koifinnian, I wouldn't know what to do, and that's not even close," he places a reassuring hand on my shoulder.

"A Koifinnian? Can't say that I've heard that term before." I chuckle.

"Unofficial term. I think the proper term is 'Koifinn person,' but who cares? We don't call ourselves Adlei people. We say Adleians."

"They do call themselves Koifinns, though. Don't they?" I correct.

"I don't know, honestly. I think it's different because it's a clan, not a kingdom. But hell, I don't care. If they want to be complicated, so be it. I'll continue calling them Koifinnians," he explains, ending the conversation.

As we arrive at the door to Nallac's room, I'm hesitant to enter. The conversation during the swim back was nice, and I don't want it to end so soon.

"Your secret is safe with me, Your Highness. Let me know if any other guards bother you during your stay," he whispers, with a slight bow and a flirtatious wink. "Since you've been honest with me thus far, and I serve my nobility, I think you deserve to move to a first-name basis."

He kisses my hand and goes to leave before I can ask him to keep me company for a while longer. I find myself unable to respond as I stare at where his lips touched.

"I have important work to attend, love. Don't miss me too much. I have a feeling I'll see you all too soon." He pauses. "Next time, you will call me Flynn." With that, he's gone, disappearing into the dark stone corridor.

24

LEADER OF A REVOLUTION

.*⭐ VERA ⭐*.

I wake up with a jolt, startled by breaking glass outside the room. The room is still dark, and the beautiful flower-shaped lamps are yet to be turned on. I hadn't noticed them until he turned the lights on yesterday morning. Afterward, I analyzed the ceiling.

"*Yune*," I whisper, and the petals curl open and light up the room. That's when it hits me—Nallac never came back.

I can't do this. I'm not ready.

Think, Vera. You're on your own now, so think.

I scan the room in a desperate attempt to find anything useful before I depart. My eyes fall to a book lying on Nallac's desk in front of me. The title running across its spine is in English: *Dictionary & Translations*.

Without hesitation, I grab the book and flip through the pages in a frenzy as I realize what this is: a dictionary complete with Adleian words translated into the one thing I understand.

The pages are old and weathered, and I wonder if Nallac left it here for me to find. Of course he did. It wasn't here before he left, and why would he be reading a book on a language he understands?

I spend *hours* practicing and reciting phrases I might use to escape, and I don't put the book down until I'm confident about my plan. If only I had something to store it in—he has to have a bag or satchel somewhere.

Searching through every drawer in his desk and bathroom, I find nothing and choose to waste no more time, shoving the book in the area between my hip and the translucent fabric that hugs my waist. While I love the elaborate outfit Korah had made for me, I miss the soft touch of Nallac's shirts.

I open the door and dart from wall to wall, following the same path as yesterday. The hall brightens with daylight— exactly what I need.

I take a breath and prepare myself.

You belong. You belong, I assure myself.

I nod at passing guards, and they pay me no attention.

"Excuse me?" I ask in Adleian, and one of the guards whips around and eyes me intensely. "Where can I find Supreme Commander Laurence?" I continue.

"Why?" he asks. Thankfully, I predicted this response.

"I need to speak with him." He raises a brow, and I quickly follow up with his promise to help me.

"Follow me, *draeōm* girl," he says with an odd look. I haven't read that last word, so I pull out the book and flip to the page with all phrases and words beginning with 'd.'

A way to say that someone is strange or peculiar, the book reads. Great, I've blown any attempt at blending in. I stuff the book away again and follow close behind them, making sure to commit each landmark we pass to memory in case they are not taking me where I asked.

I hear them mumbling under their breaths while glancing back every so often. We make it to another hallway, this one lined with a maroon carpet. Each door is labeled with a different phrase, which I assume is a military title, given that the Adleian word for Commander is above one of the doors.

The farthest end of the hallway has a door larger than all the rest, with golden encrusted edges and five large stones molded into the wall.

The guard turns before it, pointing to the door to its right.

This one is slightly smaller, with the same ornate edges, but there are only four stones instead of five.

"This is his office," the guard says in Common. "I don't know your business with him, but you better hope it's good. You're dead if I hear one word that you were not invited. I'll be waiting."

He stares as if I'm nothing but a stone blocking his path.

"Th—thank you," is all I can manage before making two shaky knocks on the door. A young girl pokes her head out and locks eyes with me before opening it the rest of the way.

"Come in!" she calls out in Common. "Anything I can help you with?" she asks the guard behind me.

"No, thank you. Watch her."

"Of course, sir," she says with a slight bow and closes the door. "What can I do for you, miss?"

"I need to speak with Flynn. Is he here?" I ask, losing hope.

"Flynn, you say? He rarely gives someone permission to call him by his first name."

"He told me to find him if I was in trouble. I'm taking him up on that offer."

"I see. I will get him right away. Make yourself comfortable," she says with a soft smile. I sit on one of the two armchairs along the wall.

The room is clean and proper, with a deep red carpet with golden designs on top of the light brown wooden floor. In the center, a candle chandelier lights the room, and the fire almost dances in the water as if it's enchanted by majick. On the wall farthest from me is an oversized couch in the same auburn color as the one I'm on, and I can see the indentations of wear from many visitors over the years.

"Asherah?" Flynn asks, and I turn my head to see a familiar face. His tanned skin and soft grin remind me of the sun rising above the darkened clouds, signaling the end of a storm. Thank the heavens I found him before someone found me.

"Flynn," I respond with relief.

"*Asherah?*" The young girl yells as she slams the door shut. "Your Highness, I apologize for my lack of manners when we spoke previously. I was unaware of your return to Mōrian." She bows, staring at the floor while waiting for my response.

I feel my stomach drop from the change in how she is treating me.

"It's fine, really," I respond quickly.

She lifts her head and nods before swaying her hand like Kaileah did in the cave, revealing an opening in the stone.

"I will leave the two of you to discuss your affairs privately. Do let me know if there is anything I can assist you with, *saeraih*, as well as you, Supreme Commander."

With a final hand movement, the wall rearranges itself to appear as if it had never been opened.

"I knew I'd see you all too soon, although I was *not* expecting it in less than a day. How can I be of service, Your Highness?" he asks with a slight chuckle as he walks toward a second door and unlocks it with a brass key. "Let's speak in my office."

Walking in, I see a table to my right full of weathered books thrown and piled on top of each other. Every wall is covered with shelves stacked tightly with books of various stages, some old, some new, and some covered in a thick layer of rot and muck as if the slightest touch could turn them to dust.

In the center of the room is a large wooden desk, the legs carved into serpentine shapes that end with the head of a dragonlike creature connecting them to the top. A large map with hundreds of dots, flags, and other markings is laid across the table with notes in the margins in a foreign language.

It does not resemble Common or my little knowledge of Kefian and Adleian.

"Sit," he says as he motions to a maroon couch similar to the one in the lobby. I do as he asks before he sits in the elegant chair on the opposite end, crosses his arms, and waits.

"What language is that writing in? The one in your notes?" I ask to break the growing silence.

"A dead one." He sits back and rolls his shoulders, relaxing his posture. "So, what had you leaving the safety of the siren's care to find me?"

"Something is wrong. He didn't return to his room last night, and he told me that if he wasn't there by morning, I should leave and find my mother." It all feels wrong. "Something has to have happened to him, and while I'm inclined to search for him myself, I'm self-aware enough to realize I would not know where to begin and would likely find myself in a situation worse than his."

"Did he expect you to go to the dungeon to get your mother?" he asks with tense concern.

"No. He told me to go to Taelani. It's supposed to be a place of safety she created for majickals." I sigh in defeat. "He said I would know where to find it, but I'm not so certain. Even if I could, there's no way I'm leaving the city unnoticed. He made that very clear."

"How exactly would your mother be at this 'Taelani'?" he asks with a raised brow.

"Nallac had a plan for her escape," I say before my stomach drops, realizing the depths of what he's done: being caught disobeying direct orders and releasing a prisoner as valuable as the queen.

If he didn't return...Flynn seems to follow my thought process, springing from his seat and running a hand across his pulled-back hair.

"Listen to me very carefully, Asherah. I will find a way for you to leave this kingdom and do my best to lead you to your mother. The only thing I ask is for your word."

"My word for what?" I ask.

"That you will under *no circumstance* return here."

"I can't promise th—" I begin, but the power in his gaze stops me mid-sentence.

"You will. You will go with your mother, and you will not return. Not unless Nallac or I are with you. Do you give me your word?" he asks, his look the closest thing I've seen to him begging.

"I can't. What if you don't come back either? I won't leave anyone who has risked their life for me behind," I try to explain. He only sighs and stares at his map.

"Fine. Give me your word you will not return for three days. If you have not seen or heard from us, you may return and search until your heart is content. Deal?"

Three days.

Can I promise to not protect someone who has killed for me when I know they are in danger? I don't know what I'm thinking.

I'll only make things worse by being here.

"Three days. You have my word," I respond before I think of a million reasons to stop me from making the promise. I will not break my word.

Nothing is more sacred than a promise.

"We leave now. Follow me, and do not look at, speak to, or acknowledge anyone unless I tell you to. Understand?" The previously funny and almost flirtatious man who brought me back to Nallac's room has been replaced by the Supreme Commander who interrogated me yesterday.

It's hard to imagine that they are the same, but for someone to have climbed to a rank and gained as much respect at a seemingly young age likely requires donning a different face.

We leave his office in silence.

The first word is from Flynn as a startled guard blocks our path.

"Return to your sector and leave my sight *immediately*. I will inform sector five's *Raekaih* of your utter disregard for military regulations." Flynn barely gives him a moment of attention before turning away, not checking to see if the guard is following his orders, seemingly certain there is no way someone would disobey him.

Sneaking a glance over my shoulder, I see the guard, now pale in the face, rushing back from where he came.

"What did I tell you?" he whispers through clenched teeth. "Do not acknowledge anyone without my direct permission," he finishes, following my line of sight.

"Is that any way to speak to your princess?" I try to joke, although part of me feels insulted by his orders. To my surprise, he huffs a quick laugh.

"You're no princess, *Asherah*," he answers with a taunting smirk.

"That's 'Your Highness' to you, *Flynn*." I grin.

"Yeah, yeah. Now, try to stay out of sight behind me. We're about to exit the military headquarters." I do as he asks, but only because he's stopped barking at me like one of his subordinates and speaks to me as an equal.

I can see the city for the first time, which is *breathtaking*. I stop following him, in awe of the buildings, the architecture, the hundreds of Adleians, the shops, the fish, the pets, the words being spoken, the bioluminescence covering every surface, the transport, the food, the—

"For the love of Naejik, follow me, woman!" he snaps back at me.

"But..." I plead. "You can't possibly expect me not to be completely enthralled by this—" I stop, gesturing around me. "I am—*was*—a human. I've never seen anything like this!" I move to grab his arm. "From the people to the shops and the buildings, I'm in a new world." I notice everything from the purple grass growing in a plant bed to the delicate pink coral growing on the edges of roofs.

His eyes soften as he places a hand over mine on his arm. He looks around before leading us to a stand with happy Adleians eating what the shopkeeper hands out through the opening.

The walls are a soft blue with paintings of fields of growing crops, flowers, fish, and other meat items that look hand-painted with random smudges and shaky lines. Looking closer at the paint, it looks like it protrudes as if it was painted too thick or had multiple coats. Unless Adleian paint is a naturally thick consistency; if so, I want to experience its unique texture as soon as possible.

Flynn walks up to the opening and smiles at the man who pops his head out.

"Two orders of swordfish skewers for me and the lady, please," he says, looking down at me and winking.

Does that mean I can talk, or is he trying to flirt with me?

I take my bet on the first and meet the man's gaze. He stumbles back immediately.

"You've done well for yourself, Flynn. She's gorgeous. I'd dare say she gives the queen a run for her money, although their eyes are quite similar." He narrows his gaze at me.

"It is an honor to be compared to Her Majesty," I say without thinking, trying to speak with the same inflictions Kaileah has when speaking Common. Flynn looks at me in a way I can only assume means he's impressed.

"It is, indeed. I have quite missed the queen's presence. I do wish she would come visit us again. I will never understand why she decided to remove herself from her people," he says with a frown.

I furrow my brows and begin to explain before Flynn gives me a warning glance.

"Harrison, I've told you before. King Argyros had the queen cursed so she can't leave the castle. It's not her choice," Flynn responds with what I wanted to say.

"Oh, right. I'm sorry. I fear my age is catching up with me. I'll have your *reybamicht'ka* out shortly," he says before retreating into his tiny kitchen. I take out the book tucked neatly at my hip and scan through the words starting with 'r' before I hear Flynn laughing beside me.

"And what on earth are you doing?" he asks, still laughing.

"Shh! I'm trying to focus."

"It means cooked swordfish. What is that thing?" He takes it from me, scans the cover, and laughs again. "You have an Adleian to Common translation book?" He scoffs and flips through a few pages. "Hmph. Not bad. It's pretty accurate," he says, handing it to me. I stuff it back at my hip with a huff.

"Take my things without asking again, and I'll make you regret it." I glare at him.

"That. Is. Pathetic." He flexes his bulky frame. "Have you *seen* me?"

"No, it's hard to see past your insanely inflated ego," I mumble with a scoff.

"Well, now is your chance, so take a long look, love. I'm not judging," he says with a wink. I roll my eyes before he responds. "Calm down, sweetheart, I'm just teasing. I rarely see someone trying to find a translation during a conversation. It was quite funny."

"Well, not everyone can speak two languages, smartass," I answer with a more than playful shove, although it doesn't sway his balance.

"Four," he corrects.

"Excuse me?"

"I don't speak two languages. I speak four. Well, I speak four fluently, but I know a little bit of seven." He leans in and smirks. "What? Can't relate? Was the little princess not educated properly?"

I narrow my eyes and try to slap him before realizing what I'm doing. I close my eyes and make contact with skin but open them to see Flynn with an even wider smile with his hand wrapped around mine. Now I really wish I had slapped that stupid smirk off his face.

"You'll have to be quicker than that to hit me, love."

That insufferable—

"Two swordfish skewers!" the man calls, and Flynn and I move to grab them as Harrison asks for payment.

"One *nae'yun* and two *yundijkons*, please," Harrison calls while handing me the food. Flynn reaches into a small pouch at his hip. He places two silver-looking coins on the table that are larger and thicker than a quarter with the engraving of a purple hyacinth in the center and two semi-opaque pieces of currency with a portrait of a man I can only assume is the king.

"No, Flynn, I said one *nae'yun*, not two," Harrison corrects, handing him one of the paper-like currencies. Unsurprisingly, Flynn refuses. "I'm not fighting you. Take it."

"Neither am I. You will never discount my prices. Have a good day, Harrison," Flynn says before grabbing my arm and swimming off. He finds a secluded area for us to sit and hands me one of the skewers. "Eat and get your fix of staring because this is as much interaction as you will have with anything in the kingdom. I only stopped there because Harrison is a long-time family friend of mine, and I trust him greatly. We can't risk anything more."

He proceeds to stuff the entire stick into his mouth, devouring it in one bite.

Men...

I take a smaller bite and am surprised by the difference in taste from the dinner served at the Fentons'. This one is chewier and less flaky, but the taste is heavenly. The spices mixed with the charred exterior give it a crunch, and I find the vegetables between each piece of meat to be just as delicious and well-seasoned.

It reminds me of green beans with a hint of Brussels sprouts and lemon.

"Wow, that was amazing! Where has this food been all my life?" I ask with a mouthful of food.

"Right under your feet. I have something I've been wondering about your human years," Flynn asks, looking off at the city.

"What is it?"

"Let's continue. We can talk on the way," he says, leading me away as more people gather in the city. "Have you ever been over the water, like in a boat or something similar?" He watches me intently, waiting for an answer.

"Yeah, of course. My parents loved all things to do with the ocean. Now that I think about it, I feel like they were trying to tell me all along. All the vacations we'd take on the water, the annual beach trip to where I was brought to them as a baby, building a pool...It all makes sense now. Maybe they hoped I would break this curse and be free like I am now," I say with the familiar burning of tears. They always knew—this is what they wanted for me.

"You never saw anything out of the ordinary?" he asks.

"I'm not sure. Why?"

"Humans don't know of our existence because of a spell Naejik created to hide us. The only way to view our civilizations or people is to be born of our world. Therefore, you should've seen us if you've ever been above us in the water."

"Who is Naejik?" I ask, intrigued.

"She is the Queen of the Gods and the Goddess of Majick. She is who witches draw their power from. She gives all of them their limits, and she will punish those who take too much, taking their life as retribution," he explains, looking over our shoulders as he leads us farther from town.

"Is that the same source the Koifinns use for their majick?"

"No, they draw power from Kayiah, the Goddess of Land and Sea. She is what you would know as Mother Nature. While powerful in her own right, having created all the sea creatures and mer around us, she cannot give out the kind of power Adleian witches require, not to mention the Koifinnians," Flynn explains, and I huff a laugh at his name for their people.

"I can't answer any more questions about majick. As you can see, I am just a regular Adleian, not a witch. All I know is from the little I learned in childhood. After witches come of age, they attend a different school to learn their craft," he adds, clearly realizing I'd have more questions.

Before I know it, we've exited the kingdom, or Mōrian at the very least. I stick close to Flynn as we travel, often linking my arm around his to keep up with his speed.

There's something about him that draws me in. When he's next to me, I feel as safe as I can be in the heart of a kingdom that wants me dead.

"Flynn, why are you protecting me? You're a Supreme Commander. Don't you have an obligation to report me and take me to the king?"

"Sure. I also have an obligation to kill that soldier for falling out of line earlier. Would you prefer I followed my oath?" he answers coldly. "I follow my morals and do enough of the king's bidding to be in a position of power to help the little guys. My parents were assassins, and I saw the toll it took on them. I vowed to stay true to myself and my morals above all else." His tone softens, but I sense I'm dangerously close to overstepping his boundaries.

"Sorry. How are your parents now?" I ask, trying to change the conversation.

"Long dead. My mom died in the Witch Massacre of '04, and my father long before that." His face shows no emotion, staying neutral and unrelenting.

"I didn't know. I'm sorry. I'll stop talking," I mumble, slinking back slightly from the tension. He turns and looks at me, rolling his eyes and pulling on his signature grin.

"Come back, princess. I won't bite," he says with a broad smile, running a tongue along the edges of his teeth.

"See, I'm inclined not to believe that."

"No, seriously. You need to see if you remember any of the landmarks around us. I have no idea where Taelani is."

"Right," I say, looking around. Nothing looks familiar except maybe that rock. No, the entrance had a far larger stone right before the door. I close my eyes and take a breath, willing my majick to lead me where I need to go.

When I open them, I feel a phantom tug and follow it, taking his hand and swimming quickly. It pulls me like a tether, and I wonder if it's not what but *who* I feel pulling me home. Flynn seems distraught, being dragged by a girl half his size, but something is giving me the strength to do it, to keep swimming faster and faster.

I nearly squeal with excitement as I see familiar rocks and ledges. The warm embrace of my power settles as I stare at the doors carved into stone. It did exactly what I asked.

If only I knew *how* to command it...

"Asherah, calm down. What are you so excited about?" he asks, looking around. "There's nothing out here."

"What?" I whip my head around and point to the cave very clearly in front of me. "It's right there."

He shakes his head, grumbles about proving it, and swims toward the cave's wall. I wince, waiting for him to impact the stone.

"*Sweet Kayiah!*" he screams, staggering back and grabbing his head and shoulder that hit first. "You weren't lying. As I cannot see it or enter, this is where I leave you," he says with a hand on my shoulder. "I'll do what I can to find Nallac, and when I do, I will meet you here within three days."

He pulls away and cups my face.

"You asked me why I chose to protect you, and the answer isn't a simple one. I'm a part of the same revolution you and the siren wish to bring to light, but there's one more thing." He bends close and pushes a rogue hair out of my eyes. "The gods have plans for you, love."

NALLAG

25

ESCAPE

.*⭐ NALLAC ⭐*.

The familiar stench of the dungeon fills my nose as I follow the path I know all too well. Most of my time has been spent here, and the blood and rust caking the walls remind me of what I am: a monster.

There is no denying that fact. I kill for revenge and as commanded.

I used to lie, telling myself that I only did what I was forced to, but what about the countless lives I have *chosen* to take in this hallway? The guards I killed in cold blood, the citizens that insulted my family and I beat until they were unrecognizable, and the feeling of their lives being drained by the same hands that used to be so capable of good reinforces that fact. The one everyone reminds me of so often.

Perhaps I should let the king's guards kill me and save Vera the mistake of trusting me. I am a vicious killer, and she deserves to be with someone who never has to hold himself back.

Her heart is pure. I feel it inside of me, a second beat to my own.

Ever since she first transformed, when I healed her body from her surge of power, I have felt it inside me. It's more than just feeling her emotions like I do from others.

What I feel from her is a connection like no other, and I've foolishly allowed her righteous morality to trick me into believing it was my own—that I could be capable of becoming my old self again.

She's falling for me. I have tried countless times to find a justification for it, but I can't. Yet, I have taken advantage of her naivety, feeling her attraction and intensifying it. I know the feelings she keeps inside, and I have used that knowledge to tease her, to push her further into the state she tries to run from.

I am a darkness slowly pouring into her light, corrupting her, and it has to stop.

But I can't.

I fear I'm a man stumbling through a barren desert, and she's my oasis. Her presence, kindness, and open-mindedness overload me in all the best ways. She is my drug, and gods, I am addicted.

I did not know happiness again until I looked into those forest-green eyes.

I need her.

But she needs someone better.

I turn the corner and see the queen asleep on the floor, either by choice or from exhaustion finally overpowering her stubbornness. Her face is gaunt, and I see a pile of untouched food in the corner of her cell.

Is slave food not good enough for Her Majesty? Does she

expect a five-course platter that she could not possibly finish, only for it to be thrown in the trash after she's done? Pathetic.

I contemplate killing her, removing one more privileged leech from having power and rid myself of an oppressor, but I resist. Only for Vera's sake.

"Wake up," I command without care as the queen lurches, eyes snapping to mine as if her stare alone could kill me. "Wake up!" I snap, louder than before, directed at the Koifinn boy. He reluctantly opens his eyes and sits up.

I look to Kaileah and clench my teeth so hard my head throbs. I cannot believe I am risking my life for hers.

"This is going to hurt. Don't scream," I warn.

"What do you mean—" She screams for a moment before slamming her mouth shut. The only thing that shows her pain is her eyes wide with horror. I relish the pain I cause her, feeling her wrists break and fall limp.

The majick-binding cuffs fall off, allowing her full access to her power.

"Come to the bars, and I will fix your wrists," I state neutrally, and she narrows her eyes. Her anger boils inside my chest.

Always so angry.

She comes closer and throws her limp, almost jelly-like hands through the opening, and I take them in my own, whispering the song my mother taught me as I feel the fragments of her bones and muscles mending back together. A single tear streams down her cheek, but her face would give no indication of the pain I know she feels.

Once repaired, she rips back and throws her hands, bending the metal bars to either side of her cell with little effort.

"Thank you," Alexander says the second I unlock his cell.

"Anything you want to say?" I ask, looking over my shoulder

at the angry queen. Her eyes are full of her intense hatred of me and my kind. Though she has identical eyes to her daughter, they have such different effects.

"Thanks," she hisses.

"Alexander, I need you to go back to your clan and hold further action against Adlei. Do not stop on your way there," I say before turning to Kaileah. "I need you to go to Taelani. Vera will meet you there, but you need to wait until Alexander has left. I trust you know how to remain unseen?" I ask, trying to sound at least a little friendly.

"It would be wise to start discussions with your father and his council about stopping trade with Adlei. I sense war is brewing, and cutting off their food supply would help our efforts tremendously," she says, directly opposing the advice I gave. "I will do my best to create any enchantments or items needed from our kingdom in the meantime."

He nods and rushes off.

"And yes, I am well aware of how to *hide*. I spent the better half of twenty years studying the layout of the kingdom, so if anyone could escape, it would be me, *siren*." Her words remain hostile, but I feel her internal gratitude. She doesn't want to be thankful, and she sure as hell does not want to be scared or unsure. "Where is my daughter?" she asks, kinder now.

"Safe. She knows what to do should I not return," I reply.

"Thank the gods. Has she been seen by anyone else?"

"Not to my knowledge."

A significant enough time passes in silence before I clear my throat and motion for her to leave. She nods, and I feel a change brewing inside of her. Her final glance is not one of disgust but of growing respect. Interesting.

After she leaves, I feel a lingering presence that sends the hair on my skin standing to attention. I didn't notice it before, but I now know exactly who stands behind me.

I'll be dead by the end of the day.

"Well, well. It looks like someone's binding is getting weak," the emotionless voice of a woman I know all too well says, and I can almost hear her grinning. I try to spin around to fight back, but she's faster than me, cuffing me with the same majick-binding ones that fell off the queen. I am powerless as she laughs again, running her hands across my cheek and down my jaw. "It's a shame such a pretty face is going to get *so broken.*" Her piercing blue eyes match the underneath of her hair, contrasting the black of the rest.

"*Daevia,*" I grit out, lunging away from her touch but remaining in place.

"Ah, not so fast, darling." Her touch moves down my neck and trails a path across my shoulder, sending bile rising. "You know you can't hurt me." She moves closer, her lips almost touching my ear. "No matter how weak your binding is, as long as it's there, you can't lay a single *malicious* hand on me, and you know it." She grazes her lips across my neck, which threatens to expel last night's dinner. "Now, follow me."

I feel the familiar grip of the binding around my throat, commanding me to obey, and I resist. Her fake smile drops, and she meets my gaze with soulless eyes.

"Interesting." She grabs the back of my neck and rips my head down to meet her, her pupils turning to slits. "*Come,*" she growls, gripping harder with each second I hold back before my eyes cloud over, and I do as she asks. She smiles again and swims out of the dungeon with me trailing behind her.

～

I can hardly focus as I'm led to the throne room. Daevia lays out everything she witnessed. I never heard any mention of Taelani or Vera, so a small fraction of hope remains for the safety of my princess.

The king yells in my direction, but I don't take any notice. I simply wait for what I know will follow. I will be brutally killed in the same way as my father, and my family will feel it all. *My poor mother.* She felt the death of my father, as did I. Now, it will be the death of her son she will bear witness to. *I'm sorry, Mom. I'm so sorry.*

I think next about Valerie. She was too young to comprehend the emotions of others when my father passed, and I will be her first death. My baby sister.

I can no longer be her protector, and I will not be there to bear the weight of responsibility for them. I still need to tell her so many things.

I should have visited her more.

I should have been there to watch her grow into the beautiful, intelligent young woman she is now.

All my regrets run through my head as I feel the first slash of the king's trident. The searing pain and warm, flowing blood that follows give me a sense of clarity, allowing me to feel and understand every attack that follows even more acutely. He throws the trident to the side, reaching instead for a curved dagger at his hip. My arms are bound to the ceiling above me with the thick, unbreakable chain that allows me no leverage.

He takes the knife and trails it along my arms, leaving a fresh trail of blood where it touches. He reaches the soft skin of my forearm, and he stabs, forcing through the muscles and tendons and bursting my skin open to better show the gash he has created.

He smiles as my blood clouds the water around us, and his smile grows as he listens to the pure anguish in my cries. Against my will, I beg for mercy.

"Please, stop this!" I scream through grueling waves of pain that make me fight for consciousness.

"Silence, filth!" he yells back, slapping my head so hard I see double. "I'm satisfied. You!" He points to the closest guard. "Finish him off. Do me a favor and *make it hurt.*"

He smiles at me with a toothy grin. I want to rip out every single one.

The guard cuts my chest in deep gashes until my skin is covered in open wounds screaming at me to heal them.

I dissociate from my body as I'm beaten, cut, slapped, and stabbed over and over. All I can think about is Vera, my mother, my sister, and my father.

I miss him so much, but I suppose I'll be with him soon enough. I hope he put in a good word with Kayiah and she will take my undeserving soul. My mind wanders further still, remembering my family before the king took everything from us.

"Budda! Budda! Come here!" I swam to my sister and saw a baby seahorse holding on to a small stick, and I smiled at her happiness.

"Come, my little sirens. Dinner is ready. There's someone here to see you as well," my mother said with excitement. My sister and I looked at each other and each swam as fast as we could to get to our father.

I am older and faster, so I should have won. However, she got to him first as I stopped and stared at the fresh scars and bruises on his face. They'd beaten him again.

"Valerie! My sweet little girl! I've missed you so much!" my father

said in a voice of pure happiness. There was no hint of the pain I felt inside of him.

"Daddy!" She hugged him tight. Her innocence kept her from realizing the severity of the situation. I swam to my father and sang a slow song with my hand on his cheek. Within a moment, the wound was healed.

"Oh, Nallac. I wish more than anything to have gotten to watch you grow. I tried to make it back for your birthday this year, but the king, he—"

"Dad, it's okay. Just seeing you now is the best present you could've brought me," I interrupted.

"Your tail—the white is fading," he stated with concern. His eyes grew red with the sign of tears, but they were carried away by the water around us.

"All it means is that I look more like you and Mom! It's okay, really," I insisted. My mother and father looked at each other and back at me.

"We love you so much, Nallac. Never let the world change you," my father said. He made me promise, and I failed him.

I come back to realize my body has sunk to the ground, my arms lying limp on either side of me. My neck is nearly broken as it lies at an unnatural angle.

I deserve this.

My parents would have hated what I became. My father was in the same situation, and yet he stayed true to himself. He never once killed for any reason beyond absolute necessity, unlike his fallen son. All they asked was that I stayed good and never changed. Yet here I am.

A disgusting, manipulative, evil monster who hurt the

woman who showed him kindness because she found a box my mother gave me.

I hurt Vera. I hurt innocent people. I've killed children, mothers, whole families, and I did it without thinking. Yes, I was forced to obey the binding, but their blood is on my hands.

The weight of their death and the burden it brings is mine alone to bear.

A swift kick to my spine sends me forward on the floor. I hear a loud crack as my tail is paralyzed. My head pounds, and I can no longer tell if it's from an attack or the internal damage they've already done.

My eyes have clouded with blood and black spots stopping me from seeing my attacker. My mind trails again as I imagine the horrors my poor family must be feeling.

I closed my eyes, trying to block out the pain I felt. I could feel each whip, each cut, and each slap against my father's skin. I shook in bed, alone, while my mother and sister slept peacefully in the next room.

Three years without a father.

Three years without a complete family.

This beating was different than the rest. I could feel his heart slowing and his breath weakening; he was dying this time! I could taste his blood on my tongue—my father's blood.

I vomited into the bathroom sink, scrubbing my tongue until the taste was gone.

The pain ended for a moment, but when I looked up at the mirror, I saw my father's bloody face staring back at me.

I screamed.

Even closing my eyes, I could not stop what I was witnessing. I watched as the man before my father stabbed a final knife through his heart, and I heard his scream. The agonizing, desperate scream, and I went numb.

I knew what it felt like to die.

"Nallac! What's wrong?" my mother asked, entering the bathroom. She saw my body curled in a ball, shaking with sobs, and knew what had happened.

I witnessed the death of my father.

She felt it then, his heart's final beat.

She pulled my small frame into her arms and sobbed with me.

"He's gone! Mom, he's gone! His face...it was bloody...I saw him," I choked out in between grueling cries. "I watched it. I heard him scream!" I clutched her blouse and sobbed harder into her shoulder, unable to forget the sight of my father's corpse flashing through my head.

Her face was pale as she stared at me in horror.

Feeling every second of my father's death and seeing it through his eyes scared me in ways I can't express, hardening me beyond recognition. I then bore the responsibility for my family, as I still do.

I wonder who will take my place.

I wonder if Valerie will ever be safe to fall in love.

Does she have any friends?

I choose to believe she has found someone who treats her as she deserves, and that she has more friends than time in the day to spend with them all. I hope she's dreaming of publishing one of her books, and I hope she doesn't worry about me.

I hope she can't feel my pain as I can with hers.

My mother always said that there was something special about me. I could not only sense the emotions of others but feel them, and my bonded connections were like none other. Yet, I have never felt them as accurately as if they were my own until I met Vera. I've always had an issue distinguishing what others are feeling from myself, but with her, it's like her mind is merged with mine.

The only person who'd ever given me a similar feeling was my father.

Perhaps my abilities were commonplace, and Valerie and my mother were the strange ones, but since sirens are killed on sight unless kept as slaves, we have no way of learning about our people. All mentions of our kind have been destroyed in text-books—everything but the lies spread by the Argyros family.

I remember something my mother said when I last saw her.

"If this is the last time I see you, I need you to know that no matter what you've done in the past, you will always be my son. I will always love you the same as when I held you in my arms for the first time. You are not a monster, and you are not beyond repair."

I smile at her words. Maybe she was right, and I am still good. Maybe there is a small part of my tarnished soul that is pure like she believes.

Maybe the white scales left on my tail are real indications of that truth.

I am more than what the king says.

I am more than what they believe I am.

I am more than I believe I am.

"Alright, I think he's close enough to death for now. Frankly, I'm surprised he still has a heartbeat, much less the ability to hold himself up." I hear Daevia's muffled voice through my shattered eardrums. An intense ringing drowns out any response, and I lack the ability to hold on to consciousness any longer.

My mind finally blacks out as the world around me grows silent.

VERA

26

MAJICK

.*✫ VERA ✫*.

"Absolutely not!" Kaileah yells at my suggestion. She refuses to acknowledge my concern for Nallac even after all he's done for us, even after the hours I've spent begging for her to understand.

"He saved my life *and yours*!" I yell back with increasing anger. "He is dealing with God knows what because of his *kindness*. Don't you get that?" Her look of disgust makes my stomach sink.

How could she harbor such hatred for someone who sacrificed himself for us?

"He is a siren, Vera! They are not to be trusted. They are evil creatures that thrive on the pain of others. If you let yourself care for him, he will break you. He is waiting for the day your pain will satiate his need," she says, hands splayed. She waves off my protests and packs supplies from the cave into a satchel. "I will speak no more of this matter. We leave tonight."

That's the final straw as I feel a heat rising to my skin, a burning sensation that comes from the very center of my soul and cascades over me in waves. My chest burns hot with a feeling I don't quite understand, and everything I see now has clarity.

"*LISTEN TO ME!*" I scream in a voice that rattles the stone with its hellish, unearthly tone. She turns around and pales.

"Vera, sweetheart," she says softly while inching closer. I gasp as hot runes carve themselves into my flesh, searing the skin around them as they glow a bright red. It fuels my fire, and I feel even more angry. I feel enraged. "I need you to calm down right now," she says, donning a sweetness that hasn't been present for the rest of our conversation.

"*I am calm,*" I respond as I grab the power surrounding me. It whispers to me, begging me to take it, to consume it. I inhale deeply as my eyes roll back in my head.

I laugh, the sound demonic and detached from my body. The energy rolls into me in dissociating waves—the power overwhelming every part of me.

"You do not understand your power enough to consume your *maemōjik*. If you do not calm yourself, you will burn out from the inside! Do you hear me?" she asks as she grabs my arm. She drops it as if my skin is a searing flame. "Vera, you're nearly on fire!" I look at my arms and see the dancing waves of heat and reluctantly realize she's right.

But at the same time, I can't let this much power go. I have to keep going.

I reach for another wave and pull it toward me, feeling it wrapping around my fingers like an invisible rope. I laugh again, curving my hand and giving it a sharp tug. It's almost too late, the majick inches from consumption, when a familiar gasp knocks me from my trance.

I see Korah's face plastered with pure fear, and I let go of the power. The icy water cools my skin, and I struggle to control my breathing as the runes slowly disappear with the same burning pain.

My head clouds, and I fall to the ground, my tail like a weight I haven't learned to use.

I slowly turn to Kaileah and see her looking both horrified and proud.

"What the hell was that?" Korah calls out from behind me. I shake away the thoughts of what would have happened if I had consumed that final wave. I lost control.

It can't happen again.

"We need to start training your majick immediately. You cannot have that unchecked power ravaging your body until you're prepared to embrace it. As angry as I am at you, I am still impressed beyond explanation. You are a force to be reckoned with, my child," Kaileah states, her eyes sharpened.

"Then we train for three days. I refuse to leave before I know the two of them are safe," I say, taking a deep breath before facing Kaileah. "*I* will hear nothing else." She raises one brow at my assertive tone before releasing her crossed arms.

"Spoken like a future queen," Kaileah says, a smirk on her lips. "Very well."

I take a stance, facing the pile of stone my mother has stacked in the center of the cave. I ground myself with the walls as she taught me, imagining I am standing flat against them for support. I reach for an invisible string of power and pull it to me, stopping before I consume it and instead holding it in the palm of my hand.

The majick is all around me, I feel it grazing past, whispering in the distance. All I have to do is reach out my hand, and I can feel myself touching it like a living organism.

Maybe Naejik allows us to hold her hand while using her energy.

"Just like that! Hold it until I say to let go," Kaileah encourages with a smile.

I take a deep breath and imagine myself running through a meadow full of flowers like Korah suggested, but it does little to help. I access my energy reserves and steady myself until I find something that works for me.

"Now, I want you to use your other hand to grab the majick without letting it go," Kaileah instructs. I adjust my grip on the majick, nearly letting it go before I regain my former control. Barely.

It sends a vibration through my arm, and I grit my teeth together to keep from losing it.

"I can't..." I pause with a ragged breath. "...hold it...much longer."

I reach into my mind for a place I feel comforted, and it hits me. I see myself in a dimly lit music hall, the sound of violins and pianos surrounding me. I hear the songs Nallac played to me before I fell asleep. It helps, but my grip falters faster, and the majick fights against my control.

I need to find something that will truly ground me.

"Now, I want you to imagine what you want to do. Think about that string of majick going into the center stone and sending them flying to the walls."

I change the image in my mind once more, and this time, I

see myself sitting on a large rock with the ocean lightly touching my toes. The most beautiful sunset is before me, and when I look down, I see a canvas with a perfect-sized stand to hold it. All of my paints are there, with a few Adleian additions.

I take the brush and hold it in my hand, and I feel the control on my majick strengthen tenfold.

I'm about to release it when Kaileah adds, "And don't release it all at once. Send it out in a stream until you're ready for the force, and then give it everything."

I do as she says, sending out a small stream of majick before throwing it all and sending the rocks slamming against each wall. The explosion is louder and stronger than the example Kaileah gave, and I hear Korah shriek and duck in the corner as a rogue stone comes straight at her face.

"I'm sorry!" I yell, trying to catch the stone and failing. A small crater appears exactly where her head would have been. She looks at it and carefully controls her face to not show fear. She doesn't do a very good job.

"We'll keep working on control," my mother states, placing the stones back in the center.

"I held it until you said to let go. How was I not in control?"

"Sweetheart, you almost killed your friend," Kaileah says with a huff while gesturing to the hole. Korah nods far too quickly in agreement.

"I—Okay, yeah, you're right. What do I need to do instead?" I ask, rolling my shoulders at the increasing pain.

"We've been practicing for hours, and you need to rest before we continue lessons. I see you're running out of energy," she says with sympathy. I message an area of my arm that is causing me exceptional pain.

"You said witches pass out when they use too much energy. I

don't feel close to that, just a little muscle pain, is all," I say. It's a lie; my whole body is throbbing, but I must master this.

"You're not a witch, Vera. You're a sorceress. We must be in tune with our bodies because we have no clear limitations. We will go mad with power if we push past our maximum," Kaileah explains. She removes a book from the shelf and hands it to me as she hums. I see the pages shift from Adleian letters to Common.

"I want you to read about your abilities while I make our dinner for tonight. Korah, would you like to join me?" my mother asks. Her ears perk up in excitement when she nods.

"I would love to!" she says, swimming into the next room as my mother follows.

The section I'm supposed to read is titled 'A Witch's Maemōjik.'

A MAEMŌJIK IS AN EMOTION THAT AN ADLEIAN WITCH FEELS THE LEAST. THIS IS NOT SOMETHING THAT CAN BE CONTROLLED OR MANIPULATED. MUCH LIKE THE COLOR OF AN ADLEIAN'S TAIL, THEIR MAEMŌJIK IS DETERMINED BY THEIR SUBCONSCIOUS.

THIS EMOTION ALLOWS A WITCH TO NOT LOSE ENERGY FOR A STRETCH OF TIME. IN BASIC TERMS, WHEN A WITCH EXPERIENCES THEIR MAEMŌJIK, THEIR ENERGY HAS NO LIMITS, AND THEY CAN CONSUME MAJICK PAST ANY NATURAL BOUNDARY UNTIL THEIR EMOTION ENDS.

My maemōjik must be triggered when I get angry, and now that I think about it, I have rarely felt such rage as I have since I've gained access to my majick. Another point of the book jumps out at me.

A MAEMŌJIK CAN BE VERY DANGEROUS DEPENDING ON WHAT EMOTION THE BODY CHOOSES BECAUSE WHILE IT IS TRIGGERED, THE FEELING WILL INCREASE ITS INTENSITY UNTIL IT IS ALL THE WITCH CAN FEEL. ANGER, FOR EXAMPLE, WILL CLOUD A WITCH'S JUDGMENT, SENDING THEM INTO AN UNCONTROLLED FRENZY OF UNRESTRICTED POWER.

THE MORE A WITCH INDULGES AND TAKES FROM THE POWER, THE STRONGER THE EMOTION WILL BECOME.

This is bad.

No wonder Kaileah has been harping on me to gain control.

If I trigger that emotion again, I could do something I'll regret to the people I care for. If Korah hadn't broken me from the trance, I could've killed her or Kaileah. The guilt of that moment alone would have eaten me alive, much less if I did something worse while in that rage.

I can never let myself feel that way again. I need to learn how to stop it.

WHEN A WITCH IS USING THEIR MAEMŌJIK TO PUSH PAST THEIR MAXIMUM BOUNDARIES FOR AN EXTENDED PERIOD, DEPENDING ON HOW HARD AND FOR HOW LONG, THEY WILL EITHER COLLAPSE UNCONSCIOUS, AGE UNTIL THEIR DEATH, OR BLOW THEIR BODY TO PIECES. THE THREE CONSEQUENCES ARE IN ORDER FROM HOW SEVERELY THEY ABUSE THE ENERGY. NO OTHERS HAVE YET BEEN OBSERVED.

I can't comprehend the pain of such exertion on the body, and I can't say I want to test how true those consequences are. I look up from the book and walk to the kitchen to watch without Korah and Kaileah noticing.

"First, you have to put the vegetables in the pan and sauté them, and then add the meat," Korah explains delicately. I soon notice one pan thrown to the side with a thick burnt layer on the bottom.

I suppose a queen doesn't have much reason to cook for herself.

Kaileah places the cut vegetables in the pan and watches them closely.

"Now, stir them around," Korah adds, and Kaileah mixes with something like a wire masher. I see Korah trying her best to stay patient, likely fighting the urge to rip the tools away and cook it herself.

"They look perfect," Kaileah states with certainty, and Korah shakes her head slowly. "What could possibly make them better?" she asks pompously.

"They're still raw. I mean, Your Majesty!" she adds quickly, her ears flattening like a scared puppy. Kaileah gives her a side-eye glance before stirring more and grumbling to herself. "Try to mix it by pushing it around and less like—" Kaileah snaps at her in Adleian, and Korah sinks back more.

My mother sighs and stirs the way she's been told, ranting to herself in her native tongue. I shake my head with a smile and return to the book. Skimming through the rest of the page, I stop at the mention of my bloodline.

A SORCERESS HAS EVEN MORE SEVERE CONSEQUENCES FOR THE OVERUSE OF MAJICK. SINCE THEY HAVE THE ABILITY TO PUSH PAST THEIR MAXIMUM WITH OR WITHOUT USING THEIR *MAEMŌJIK*, THEY NOT ONLY HAVE A HIGHER RISK, BUT INSTEAD OF FALLING

UNCONSCIOUS, THEY WILL START TO GO MAD WITH POWER. IF A
SORCERESS LOSES THEIR EMPATHY, THEY BECOME NEARLY
IMPOSSIBLE TO STOP WITH NOTHING TO CHECK THEM.

I can't tell if that is a better or worse alternative to the consequences for a witch. Is that what my mother is so afraid of happening if I push myself too far? I have to believe there is a way to get someone back from madness without losing them altogether. I refuse to accept that could be my, or my mother's, end.

"Dinner is served!" Kaileah states with a thick layer of confidence. "Korah grew some greens for us and brought them over in her travels." She smiles at Korah which Korah returns while sliding to my side. Thankfully, they finished just as I read the last of what I needed.

"Your mother is very intense. Terrifying, even. I think I'm going to throw up," Korah whispers. I hold in a laugh.

"She has a way of making people fear her. It's quite impressive, honestly," I respond, smoothing her hair. "I heard you attempting to give her directions."

"Oh, did you? Heh…" She trails off. "I was ready for it to be over. Please remind me not to teach royalty how to do a simple task again. That was a disaster!" She ends her sentence slightly too loud, and Kaileah turns her head. Korah stops talking, her eyes widening like a rabbit staring at a wolf.

"Well, I'm starving, so let's eat!" I change the subject. I take the first bite and am not surprised it is relatively bland and overcooked. My hunger drowns out the taste, and I scarf my portion down.

"See, Korah, I told you it was perfect," Kaileah huffs. "You young mer always think you know best," she scoffs and takes another elegant bite. Her pride keeps any hint of disgust from showing.

Reading the front cover of what I initially assumed was a textbook, I now understand its colloquial writing—*A Witch's Guide to Majick* by Ali Janki.

The rest of my night is spent reading the freshly translated book to learn everything I can about controlling this majick that begs release. As my vision blurs and I struggle to stay awake for a moment longer, I prepare myself for bed.

I stare at the ceiling of the carved-out rock cave, thinking about the nights I shared with Nallac in similar caves. All I can do is hope he's okay.

TO BE COMPLETE

.*⭐ VERA ⭐*.

Three days have passed without a word from the men I've grown to care for. Kaileah never stops reminding me of her opinion on our delayed departure, constantly informing me of everything Nallac plans to do to me. One thing her misguided views have taught me is how to keep my *maemōjik* in control.

I refuse to indulge in my majick until I am beyond confident I can control the uncontrollable. There is no power worth the cost.

I'm awake before everyone else and take that precious moment to myself.

It's been over two weeks since I left my parents, and each day that passes feels like a knife being pushed deeper into my heart. I can't help feeling that I've betrayed them by growing to love my birth mother, along with everything this world has to offer.

I know they'd want that, but it doesn't lessen the guilt.

On land, I never felt I belonged. I never knew why, but there was this hole no happiness could fill. I had a life anyone could dream of.

I had two loving parents who gave me everything they had, friends who cared for me without asking for anything in return, and a school where I could learn about almost any subject.

Yet, I found it difficult to pull myself out of bed in the mornings. I found it difficult to brush my teeth, to wash my hair, to put on my clothes, and on the worst days, I'd barely eat. No doctor could understand what was wrong with me, and many of them suggested therapy, but it never helped. Trust me when I say I tried.

I turned to lying to those around me and myself. They gave me everything I could ever dream of. I had it all, but most of the time, it felt like I had nothing.

It was perfect.

My last birthday was the first time it felt like the gaping hole that nothing could fill began to repair itself. I felt whole and complete, and then it went away like a flame put out by a burst of wind.

It wasn't until I transformed a few months later that I felt the same fullness, and it wasn't until I arrived in Shari that I felt truly happy. It ended soon after when the guilt of being away from them set in.

I miss them more than anything.

I hope they tell my friends what I am and why I have to follow this path, because nothing is worth them thinking I abandoned them. Have I abandoned them?

I sit outside the cave, watching the small groups of fish that enter and exit, and let the cold water that freezes my skin distract me from these thoughts.

I mean, what more could I want? I'm a princess. I'm the heir to the throne of the largest and most powerful kingdom in all the oceans.

I have a mother who would kill for me. My friends would do anything to protect me even though they barely know me—even one who *has* killed for me and likely sacrificed himself for my safety with no ulterior motives.

Hell, I have the potential to be more powerful than any witch.

What more could I want?

"WHY DO I WANT MORE?" I scream, feeling the hot sting of tears developing in my eyes before I swipe them away. "Why is it not enough? Why is it never enough?" I sob as my voice cracks. My wall crumbles without anyone to see me break.

I have no reason to mask it anymore.

Mom would tell me to stay strong. She would tell me that everything is happening as it should for me to find myself. She would want me to continue.

Dad would tell me that he wanted me to come home but that I couldn't. He would tell me that I was the strongest person he'd met. He would tell me I must protect those who cannot protect themselves.

They would tell me they missed me and hoped I was okay.

I need to find a way to let them know I'm safe and have found such incredible people. I can't continue until I hear the words from their own mouths instead of just my imagination.

"Are you going to be able to see the cave, or are you not a majickal creature?" a faint man's voice asks from near the cave's entrance. I freeze and push myself hard against the wall as I inch closer, trying to gauge who the voice belongs to.

"You just watched me mend my own broken bones. What about that is not majickal?" another man's voice answers, even fainter. The rich, sultry tone I know all too well assures me of who waits beyond the entrance.

I rush out with a relieved smile, tackling the familiar siren to the stone beneath us. I bury my head between his neck and shoulder as his surprise lessens, and he places a reluctant hand around me. His warmth calms me and proves he's really here.

He whispers something under his breath before engulfing me in a hug so tight it's hard to breathe.

"You're okay," I whisper, trying to convince myself.

"I'm okay," he reassures me, releasing his grip just enough to catch my breath. I forget about everything as I realize he's alive. "What did I tell you about leaving my room? This Adleian guard isn't someone I remember introducing you to," he jests, but it reminds me of the other cause of my relief.

As I pull back, I find myself lost in his eyes, staring for longer than necessary as he does the same.

I reluctantly let go of Nallac and hug Flynn just as hard, although he is prepared and doesn't falter. He smooths my hair and embraces me strongly, allowing me this moment I desperately needed, even if he didn't.

"Your worry is flattering, love, but considering I'm the youngest Supreme Commander ever appointed, it's completely unnecessary," he says loud enough for Nallac to hear. His signature cocky attitude is in full force, and I can't help but smile bigger, knowing that means he's okay, too. "I know you needed an embrace from a real man." He grins at Nallac.

"I can send you into heart failure without laying a hand on you. You'd do well to watch your tongue," Nallac warns with a glare.

"It only took a touch of *her* hand to knock you over," Flynn retorts. I slap his arm, but he only laughs. Nallac takes a deep breath and turns his head away from Flynn.

"I'm going to pretend you didn't just say that," he states, remaining neutral.

"Pretend all you want. At least I didn't fall when a girl hugged —" I throw a hand across Flynn's mouth to stop him from baiting Nallac further, sensing the siren's control on his emotions faltering.

Nallac rolls his neck and stretches his shoulders before grunting and rubbing his arm. It's covered in a fabric densely stained red. Oh God, how did I not notice he was hurt?

"Nallac, what happened?" I ask reluctantly, unsure I can handle the truth. I desperately search the rest of his body for more signs of injury. I notice a fresh scar across his chest with three evenly spaced slashes, the center one almost twice as deep as the others. He was cut and stabbed with a trident...a large one at that.

The rest of him seems fine from the surface, but I can't help but feel like it's only the beginning. He looks away, unable to meet my eyes.

"I'm alive. That's all that matters," he says. His face turns a ghostly white. "Besides, I'd rather not relive it."

I place a delicate hand on his chest, trying to avoid the fresh wound. He flinches but doesn't push me away. I back up slightly to give him space, but his eyes beg me to return. He shakes his head and lowers his gaze.

I wish to peer into his mind and know his thoughts like he does mine.

I want to help him but don't know what he needs.

"Nallac," I start before he looks up at me. "Tell me what you need." He seems confused, like I have said something he's never heard before. He begins to speak and stops with the hardened face he wears returning. The face that drives fear into everyone —everyone but me.

"I see you, Nallac. I see what you don't let others see," I say, moving closer. His jaw ticks from nerves. "I want to understand you. All you have to do is let me in."

He finally looks at me again, and I can't help losing myself in those silver-specked, onyx eyes.

"I'll ruin you, Vera."

"Then ruin me."

He closes his eyes and takes a deep, steadying breath to calm his slightly shaking arms. He removes the cloth bond around his arm and reveals a grotesque sight.

The skin is split open, and I can nearly see the bones of his arm underneath the destroyed muscle. I watch his veins tense with the beat of his heart through the gaping chasm of his arm.

Flynn eyes the wound with sorrow and something like guilt across his tanned face.

"Who—" I begin to ask before Nallac cuts me off.

"The king. I was caught. They do what they do to those who disobey their binding. I won't say more," he explains, devoid of emotion.

"What do you need me to do?" I ask, placing a hand on his uninjured arm. "Wait, why can't you heal it?"

"I cannot heal any wound made by the one who controls my binding. It's why I've collected so many scars over the years," he explains while attempting to hide his facial scars.

"I think they make you beautiful," I say, lightly touching the one that makes a path across his cheek and nose.

This instantly brings color back to his face.

"Hey, I have scars too. Are you drooling over mine as well?"

Flynn asks with a slackened smile. I throw him a side-eyed glare. "Don't be shy, princess. We can take it slow if you're nervous," Flynn says, his voice a dangerous lure.

I roll my eyes and huff a laugh, earning me a wink.

Glancing over my shoulder, I notice Nallac's menacing gaze locked on Flynn.

Is that jealousy?

"Don't worry. I'm not going to steal your girl," Flynn states with a smirk encompassing his whole face. "Even though I easily could if I wanted to."

He looks Nallac up and down in appraisal.

"I am no one's to steal!" I snap at him.

"That look on your boy toy's face tells a different story," Flynn fires back.

"The only reason you're still alive is because I would rather not upset Vera by killing you," Nallac responds, and I notice the slightest hint of a smile on his lips.

"Oh, yeah? Does my saving you from imminent death not give me a pass as well?" Flynn adds, feigning heartbreak. I can see steam coming from Nallac's pointed ears.

"Fine. Two reasons," Nallac grumbles.

"Also, what's with the 'Vera' nickname? Is there a V I'm missing in your name?" Flynn asks, turning his attention back to me.

"My human parents call me Vera. I only recently learned about my birth name," I explain. Flynn crosses his arms.

"It would have taken two seconds to inform me of that."

"Honestly, I hardly noticed it."

"Yeah, like how I 'hardly' notice when people call me Laurence instead of my first name," Flynn argues, displeased and seeing through my white lie.

I shrug, and it's his turn to roll his eyes.

My moment of normalcy is over as the reality of Nallac's situation sinks in. He gasps in pain while trying to wrap the gaping hole of flesh once again.

I rush over and take it from him, wrapping it gently.

"Sorry, I should have asked first, but I knew a far less painful way," I say with a smile that he doesn't return, although I can feel his thankfulness. He grips my arm harshly, and I hide any reaction to give him an outlet for his pain.

I clench my jaw from his firm grip, but a part of me finds comfort in it. From the short time I've known him, he seems to avoid physical touch, so seeking me in his vulnerability...it's sweet.

"Thank you," he whispers under his breath.

I hate to see him hurting because I know it's because of me. How else would the king have found out his binding had weakened if not for ensuring my safety?

Why? I want to ask him.

Why save me? Why heal me? Why do any of it?

I am barely more than a stranger to him, yet he has continuously put his life on the line for mine. I feel an undeniable pull to him without any idea of a cause. There is this need to be close.

It's unlike anything I've ever felt. He's like a novel with twists and turns as I learn more about him and how he thinks, and I don't think I can put it down. Not that I have any intention of doing so.

28

WHAT COULD BE

.*⭒ VERA ⭒*.

"Oh, hello there!" Korah's kind voice calls out as she exits the cave. "You must be the two men Vera was waiting on! I'm Korah Fenton, Governor Sarren's daughter from Shari. You may or may not know him, but we do most of the resource trading with Adlei. I'm sure his name has come up during—"

"Yes, I'm aware of your father," Flynn states, cutting off her excited rambling. "Supreme Commander Laurence of the Adleian Regiment." He sticks out his hand sternly. "It's a pleasure to meet you, Miss Fenton."

Her smile droops as she takes his hand.

"I'm thankful Vera was able to garner the support of someone in power within Adlei. It will help our cause greatly, I'm sure." Her previous childish joy falls, and the governor's daughter is the one who remains. "Is there a shorter title I can refer to you as?"

"I suppose Laurence will suffice."

"Really, Flynn?" I ask, irritated by his formality with my friend. "She's not some subordinate."

"Everyone is my subordinate," he jests arrogantly.

"Not me or my mother," I correct.

"There are a handful of exceptions." I roll my eyes, although this time, it's not playful. Kaileah exits the entrance to the cave soon after and gasps at the sight of Nallac and Flynn.

"You brought an Adleian commander here?" She yells the question. "I built this place specifically so that they would never find it! Hardly any other race is considered non-majickal." She seethes as she turns the full brunt of her anger to me. "How can you be so naive?"

"*Fae Naejikōn*, I can assure you that I mean no harm. I serve the royal family, and considering you are the Queen of Adlei, I would not jeopardize your well-being," he explains with a bow. "That is why I am also willing to protect your daughter."

She looks at him in assessment and seems to believe what he says. If not, she doesn't show it.

"Who are *you* to call *me* naive?" I ask, returning the same look of anger. "I'm not the one who believes the actions of a few sirens means that every single one of them is a horrible person! If it isn't naivety, then it's being horrifically close-minded."

"You watch your tongue!" she snarls back.

"I will say whatever the hell I want to! You may be my mother, but that does not mean you dictate my actions. You are not the one who raised me," I spit without thinking, but I'm instantly struck with guilt. The anger on Kaileah's face falls, and her hurt is more prominent than anything.

"I'm sorry. I didn't mean to—" I start before she cuts my sentence short.

"No. You're right. I wasn't there to raise you, and I've spent every single day since your birth wanting nothing more than for that to have been different. Not even for my sake, but for yours. It is not natural to separate merfolk from our world, which has undoubtedly left a lifelong impact on you." She keeps her gaze locked on mine as she speaks, and I feel myself wanting to grow smaller and smaller with the weight of shame.

"I've never cared about myself. Not before you were born, and sure as hell not after. Besides your father, you are the only thing I've ever loved," she says, finally looking away. "You can love your adoptive parents more than me. You can wish they were here instead of me. You can even wish you had never met me. I won't care. All I ever wanted was for you to be safe, happy, and cared for," she says, the weight of her words resting deep within me.

I see a tear develop at the corner of her eye before she slaps it away.

"I may be a horrible mother, but I'm trying my hardest to be what you need. That's all I can do," she mumbles before darting back inside.

I can't shake the horror, guilt, and, above all, shame painted so clearly across my face.

Worst of all, she's right. Even though I try to suppress it, a part of me wants my parents here instead of her. After all, she's nearly a stranger. Then there is that small, dark part of me that wishes for the last thing as well—that I never knew she existed because my life would not have fallen apart.

I stand alone, holding a hand to my mouth and trying to calm my unsteady heart.

"It's okay to feel the way you do. Anyone would feel the same. I promise," Nallac whispers in my ear. I don't understand how he miraculously knows precisely what I'm thinking or how he knows what I need.

I don't understand how every subtle action he does makes my heart grow fonder for him and convinces me more of Kaileah's wrongful assumption.

I may be overly trusting with my life, but I haven't been wrong yet.

Flynn is the reason I made it out of Adlei. Nallac is the reason I avoided capture on numerous occasions, and he has continuously shown his care for me, even if his actions and words do not always align.

"How?" I ask, and he knows what I mean. By now, everyone has moved inside to either give me privacy or perhaps to comfort my mother.

I pity the soul who attempts that.

"It's complicated," he says reluctantly, pausing momentarily. "It's something sirens can do. We sense what someone feels, but it's different for me. I can feel the feelings of others beyond sensing them. I can feel their hurt, love, anger, and sadness, but that also allows me to understand how best to comfort someone...or how best to hurt them." He sighs and moves away. "I shouldn't have said that. I'm sorry."

"I'd much prefer your honesty than telling me what I want to hear. If you use the feelings of others to determine the best way to hurt them, I want to know. I want to know everything you'll allow me to. Yes, it may be worrying. Yes, I may be upset that you exploit people's unspoken weaknesses, but at the same time, I understand your need to protect yourself when no one else will," I reassure him with a comforting smile.

Nallac stares at me, deep in thought.

"You're special, Vera. Don't ever lose that."

~

Entering the cave, I see Flynn sitting on the tattered couch with a book in hand. It's one of the many Adleian tomes Kaileah has acquired. He doesn't spare me a glance as he turns the page, focusing all his attention on the words before him.

To his right, I see Korah sitting as far away as possible on the same couch. She sways her hands to and fro, and I can see a flower bud growing from the palm of her hand.

I watch her for a time, and the small bud turns into a beautiful heart-shaped flower in perfect bloom. Only then does she look up and smile at my presence, seemingly fixated on her previous task.

"A bleeding heart," Korah says, "for you." She hands the collection of flowers to Flynn, which he reluctantly takes.

"How did you know this was my favorite flower?" he asks interrogatively.

"It's my thing. I just know, I guess," she says with a shrug and begins to make another.

This time, however, it's a black flower with hints of bloody crimson. It expands and grows in her hand, adding more and more petals as its size doubles, then triples.

"This one is for you," Korah says, handing it to Nallac. "A black dahlia. When I look at you, that is the flower I feel, but they often aren't connected to happy things. Are you okay?" she asks as he takes it from her and appreciates its beauty.

"Yeah, I'm fine," he says. Rarely has a more untrue phrase been said. "What other plants can you make?"

"Anything, really. Although, I have to have seen it before," she explains while beginning on a third.

"I often decorate with *cunjitōllies* and *daendidukes*, but they're hard to find around Adlei. When they die, it takes weeks before I can find more," he says while she listens intently, pleased someone is making an effort.

Their casual conversation is drowned out as I feel a fresh wave of guilt over my words.

Kaileah had every right to respond with equal hostility but didn't. I'd be lying if I said that didn't make it hurt so much worse.

I don't know how long I've been zoned out, but when I clear my head, Flynn and Nallac seem to be waiting.

"Great! Now that you've joined us, we need to go over the plan," Flynn states with mild agitation. "For some ungodsly reason, Homicide over here wants us to return to Adlei."

"Uh, Homicide?" I ask, pinching the center of my brows.

"Yeah, inside joke. You would know if you didn't space out for ten minutes at a time," Flynn teases and nudges Nallac to continue.

"I want you to meet the resistance against King Argyros. You need to meet the people we're fighting for and see how the lower-class citizens live under his rule. From what Flynn has told me—"

"That's Laurence to you," Flynn corrects with a raised brow.

"Laurence," Nallac grumbles with a glare, "told me you were fascinated by the city but were unable to experience it or its people. I know a safe community in Kaerious where we can take you." I nod in agreement before realizing Korah is nowhere to be seen.

"Where did Korah go?"

"She's sending word to her brother about where she is and our plan. She left Shari a few days ago without informing anyone," Nallac explains. If my son had been kidnapped for multiple days and then my daughter disappeared as well, I would have people searching every inch of the ocean for them.

What is wrong with her parents?

"Is she coming with us?" I ask.

"No, she'll likely await his response before the three of you move on. She should be ready to begin your trip to Royan, the capital of the Jellean Kingdom, after we return," Flynn states.

"Uh, Jellean Kingdom?" I respond, aware of my lack of knowledge.

"For the love of Naejik, have you not heard a word we've said?" Flynn sighs deeply with a hand to his face. "The Jellean Kingdom is a safe place for you and your mother to stay while rallying them to our cause. They have the means to protect you, unlike the Koifinn Clan, and they are powerful enough to make a *very* strong ally."

"I'm supposed to convince these people to fight in a war I'm not sure I want to be a part of?" I ask, and the anxiety that has been at bay begins rising again, sending me into a near panic attack at the thought of leading thousands of people I've never met with no experience.

"Yes, you are," he says without sugarcoating the truth.

"You have time to find your strength, Vera, but this is what must be done," Nallac says, reassuring me. I run my hands through my hair as I stare at the fin of my tail, thinking of what this means for my future.

I knew being the Crown Princess of Adlei would mean I had responsibilities if I chose to stay, but I never truly understood all it entailed.

I need to speak to my parents.

I need them to tell me what to do because I'm scared and can't do this without their support.

I feel someone's hand graze across my own before their fingers interlock with mine. Looking up, Nallac avoids meeting my eyes, but his touch calms me in ways I can't express.

I want to hug him and feel his arms around me like a compression that takes me away from it all—his touch that always seems to remove my anxiety—but I can't.

Not when he seems to recoil at large amounts of affection.

I reluctantly let go of his grasp and move to the door I assume my mother went into, raising my hand to twist the knob but stopping short. My hand shakes, and I try to calm myself, taking a deep breath before twisting it open.

Kaileah sits on the bed and stares at the opposite wall.

"Are you coming with us?" I ask, trying to break down the wall between us.

"To Royan? Yes. To Kaerious? No. You can return when you are ready to leave." The loving tone she used to have is nowhere to be found.

"I'm sorry. I wasn't thinking when I spoke earlier."

"Be safe," is all she says before she lies back on the bed, facing away from me. I feel a tear forming in my eye, but I don't let it fall.

I shut the door.

"Let's go," I say, no trace of happiness in my voice.

Flynn eyes me carefully, but he doesn't make any movements to come closer. We swim to the opening and leave. I don't spot Korah as we exit, but I can't find it in myself to look harder than a simple glance in either direction.

As we move farther from the source of my pain, the lingering dark releases, and I find myself chuckling at the banter of the two men who act like rivals stuck together for a group project.

Nallac stops us, looking around, likely ensuring we have not been seen or followed.

"I have something I need to do. I will meet you there," Nallac says before looking to Flynn. "You know how to get to Kaerious, correct?" Flynn nods, and with that, Nallac is gone, disappearing into the open water like a shadow cast by the waves above.

"Do you find it creepy how he just disappears like that?" Flynn asks, staring intensely at the area where he was last seen. "I mean, there is nothing to conceal him. Not even a rock or anything, and *poof.*" He makes a motion of an explosion. "He's gone." I chuckle and nod in agreement.

We continue, but I can't help staring off into the darkness around us, hoping he will return any moment. I can't help but worry he won't, and the thought fills me with a dread I can't quite explain—for my safety or his, I don't know.

29

FROM THE SHADOWS

.*✦ VERA ✦*.

A presence overloads my senses and sends me gasping for air. I writhe as I fight for a way to keep my lungs from completely closing. Flynn swings an arm out, shoving me behind and whispering to stay very still.

"Reveal yourself!" he yells out to nothing. The water calms, and the overwhelming presence lessens, but a strong scent of burnt ash remains.

Come out, little one, a voice says, and I look to Flynn to see if he heard it, but he doesn't react.

It's in my head.

That's right, clever girl. Now, come out before I get angry. The voice grows in volume and intensity, and the sound isn't human. It's bestial and violent but, at the same time, angelic.

"Flynn," I whisper.

"Don't speak. Stay behind me," he says, gripping me harder.

You have five seconds. Five. Four. Three. Two. Before it can count any lower, I push away from Flynn and move a few feet to his left. All the air is sucked from my lungs as I stare at what is before me.

A white serpentine head stares at me with deep chasms filled only with spheres of glowing blue light for its eyes. It appears out of nowhere as if it has materialized before my very eyes.

The head is four times my size, and I can hardly take in the full scope of its ice-white form as I struggle to think of anything beyond fear. My heart rate increases with each passing second, and I fear I may be a few moments away from a heart attack.

Flynn has not moved from his position, just as shocked by the sight in front of us, although a look of recognition flashes across his face.

Look into my eyes, child. I do as it asks, not wanting to risk the retaliation this creature would no doubt inflict if I chose to disobey. Staring into the blue orbs of glowing energy, I feel my power lessen.

"Vera, look away! They can siphon a witch's majick!" Flynn yells, and I do as he says. I rip my eyes away from the creature and feel my energy—my power—return.

Clever once again. I have half a mind to be threatened by you. It does what I can only interpret as a laugh but sounds like a guttural growl.

"Why would I threaten you?" I ask, attempting to steady my voice, but it comes out as a stutter.

"What are you talking about?" Flynn asks, not removing his eyes from the creature.

"It's in my head," I explain, risking a glance at Flynn. He grabs at a trident attached to his back.

I wouldn't let him do that if I were you, the serpent warns, turning its gaze to Flynn. I motion for him to stop, and he listens and removes his hand from the weapon.

Silly land girl, you know nothing, it hisses, and I feel it vibrating throughout my entire body.

Do you even know what I am, Asherah? My spine stiffens at the mention of my name. It makes the same growling laugh, the hair on my arms now standing on end.

"No, I—I don't know what you are," I answer.

Do you know the only thing that can kill a Letiferna? It moves closer, and I brace myself for a sudden death. Its breath feels like hot steam on my face, and I clench even harder.

"Letiferna are the deadliest creatures in the ocean," Flynn warns, and I see an emotion written across his face that I have yet to see in the Adleian commander.

Fear.

He's right, but no, he's not. I'll ask again. Do you know the only thing that can kill a Letiferna? Its voice vibrates through me, rattling every bone in my body and threatening to shatter them.

All I can manage is to shake my head, and it grumbles something I can't understand.

An Adleian sorceress, it answers, opening its mouth and running a tongue across its teeth that are nearly five feet long and an almost clear white.

"I don't have that kind of power," I state in a voice stronger than I feel. "I could never kill something like you. Not that I want to," I add quickly, hoping I haven't said the wrong thing.

Oh, but you could, little witch. You can kill me, but only if you can see me. For a split second, it vanishes into nothing before reappearing in the same spot.

I'd kill you right here while your power is weak, but you're spoken for. I don't mess with the gods' will. It growls again before moving a few feet from me.

Go on now, child. You have business to attend, and with that, it disappears for a final time. The presence vanishes, and I can catch my breath for the first time since I felt it. I hug Flynn tightly, not wanting to think about what happened for a moment longer.

"Shh," he says, wrapping his strong arms around me. "It's okay. It's gone now."

I take another deep breath and another before I've calmed down enough to continue. I explain everything it said to me as we continue our travels, but I never release my hold from his arm.

30

WEIGHT OF THE WORLD

.*⭐ VERA ⭐*.

The settlement before us vastly differs from Shari or my small look at Mōrian. It's small and cozy, with Adleians conversing in the streets, trading goods, and inviting friends into their homes. The lodgings look like large pieces of coral with circular windows.

Their homes seem smaller than necessary for the number of people who enter or exit, and I realize they must be enchanted.

I look to Flynn, and he nods, seemingly understanding my request to explore.

I move to a building and touch its exterior, feeling the smooth yet prickly walls of varying colors, from neutrals to bright blues, oranges, and pinks. The buildings I assume to be shops are similarly shaped to the houses, although many of them still resemble the ones on land with a wooden, rectangular exterior.

I spin in circles, trying to take in every piece of Kaerious. I wave to those who pass us, I smell the beautiful vibrant flowers, I trace my hands along the walls, and I admire every mural and painted surface.

One building catches my attention more than any of the others. It has a large open archway for an entrance, and the walls are lined with stained glass and swirling ivy. The inside is full of round tables with chairs, food, drinks, and happy Adleians conversing.

The large arch, plus the open wooden-beamed roof, allows fish and other small sea creatures to swim in and out as they please. Along the far wall is a bar bustling with business. This must be a tavern.

"Can we wait there until Nallac gets back?" I ask, childishly giddy at the prospect.

"Are you trying to get me drunk, love? I didn't take you for that kind of girl," Flynn teases with a flirtatious smirk. "I mean, if you're asking."

"Flynn!"

"I'm just messing with you. Yes, come on."

He grabs me by the arm and leads me, but a group of gawking women stops us before we can get through the door. They push me off and grab at Flynn wherever they can.

"Ladies, ladies!" He laughs, looking at a few with a devilish grin that sends them swooning. The perfect curve of his full lips and the strong gaze cast by his blue eye have an effect unlike any other. The women feel it greatly.

His golden eyebrow piercing shines with the dancing sun's rays above, matching the golden rings and studs across his ears. "There's *plenty* of me to go around," he growls, taking one of the more beautiful women and kissing her hand.

She smiles coyly in response.

Her hair is a soft blonde, and as she looks at me, I notice her amber eyes with streaks of hazel. I stand back, crossing my arms at the inconvenience.

"I'm still here," I say, swimming closer. The blonde girl glares at my approach.

"I'm sorry, but my attention is needed elsewhere," he tells the women. "This little lady wants to get me drunk." He winks at me, and I can't help but sigh and throw my head back. The blonde woman whispers something in Flynn's ear and swims past me.

"Laurence is mine," she whispers in my ear like a serpent's hiss.

"I doubt that, considering you don't know his real name," I remark with a raised brow. "Besides, I'm not the one you should worry about. I don't have any interest in him."

She grumbles under her breath and leaves.

"Do you know her?" I ask, looking over my shoulder to ensure she's left. "Also, do you often have multiple women drooling over you?"

"No clue who she is, and yeah, that's pretty normal." He laughs. "Sometimes, if I'm bored, I'll—"

"I don't want to know," I interrupt, faking a gag as he rolls his eyes. I'm fascinated as we swim inside, seeing fish of all shapes and sizes coming close and tickling my cheek before hurrying past. We sit at a circular table in the corner.

"I'll get us something to drink and send a letter. What would you like?"

"I'm guessing lemonade doesn't exist here?" I ask with little hope of the answer being yes. It's been too long since I've had food that reminds me of home.

"Of course we have that. Is that what you want?" he asks, and I nod.

Even though it's only a drink, I'm so glad to have a piece of my previous life.

He returns with a blue drink with a lemon wedge on the side of the tall glass. I eye it carefully, unsure if he got the right thing. After a slow sip, I spit it out from the intensely bitter taste.

It has a citrus undertone but lacks the sweetness I'm used to.

"This isn't lemonade," I say, studying the contents of the glass again.

"It's one part lemon juice, one part *daendiduke*, and a shot or so of some alcohol I don't fully remember. Is that not what lemonade is?" he asks, looking at me like *I'm* the strange one.

"No." I sigh. Of course there wouldn't be anything I'm used to here. "It's just water, lemon juice, and sugar."

I take another sip and can barely swallow the strange liquid.

On my next, I gain a slight appreciation for the drink. It's not *as* repulsive as before. I now taste a hint of vanilla, adding a slight sweetness like I craved.

To my left, Flynn is drinking a dark amber liquid in a short glass with intricate detailing and carvings along the edges. He drinks it in one long gulp before slamming it down and doing one slow blink.

"Someone's in a rush," I snort as I take another sip. He smirks before the glass refills itself to the same amount.

"How did—"

"Majick, love," he explains, downing it once again. This time, it stays empty.

"I've been meaning to ask you something, and now that we're alone, it seems like a good time," I say, and he raises his brows.

"Are you about to break up with me?"

I slap Flynn's arm at his stupidity.

"You're a feisty little thing," he jests. "Always slapping and punching me."

"Anyway," I begin with a side eye. "What happened when you saved Nallac?"

His smile falls, and he motions to the bartender, who comes by and fills his glass once again. He drinks half and begins to speak before stopping and finishing the rest.

"I heard that the king learned about Nallac's weakened binding and *knew* he was dead. No siren survives it—they make sure of that." He shudders at the thought. "But the weird thing was that his name was nowhere on the army death roll. Anyone who serves the king, by choice or force, will be listed when they die, so I knew something was off," he explains before taking a moment to himself. I see his glass refill, and he wastes no time taking it in one gulp. This time, he slowly raises his eyebrows and shakes his head. "That stuff is *strong*. It usually takes six before I feel it."

"Maybe you should slow down," I suggest, subtly moving the glass away from him.

"I'm fine. After I didn't see his name, I started searching prison records. It took a day to find what dungeon they held him in. Of course, it was one of the few maximum-security ones in the kingdom," he says with a sigh and traces the rim of his glass.

"I told the dungeon guard that I was doing a routine check, and I was let through without an escort. It pays to have a title." He attempts a smirk, but it doesn't reach his eyes. "I finally found him. Prisoner 0120. He was unconscious, and I wasn't even sure he had a heartbeat. Patches of his skin were split open, caked in day-old blood, and he had been beaten beyond recognition."

I put a hand over my mouth at that, disgusted beyond belief at what the king and his guards would do to someone who broke past forced servitude. Flynn rubs a comforting hand on my forearm. With each new sentence, I feel his composure falling.

It must have been a truly terrible sight.

"His unconscious body was chained at the wrists to the wall, hanging like an animal waiting to be slaughtered. He had another chain around his neck to avoid falling to the floor. I told the guard I would need an interrogation with the siren per the king's request. They were to send word to my office when he awoke."

He stares at his glass again, perhaps contemplating buying one more round.

"The next day, he showed signs of consciousness but could barely open his eyes. I took him out of the chains, brought him to the nearest interrogation chamber, and locked the door. He didn't even try to fight back. It's like he was ready to die," Flynn says, his voice distant and mournful.

I can't imagine it. I can't even begin to fathom the amount of trauma that moment has caused and how many similar situations Nallac has dealt with before.

How could these people do something so beyond evil?

Flynn is holding back information, but I can't push him.

He might not tell me anything more if I do.

"It took a while to convince him I was his ally, not his enemy, but I finally did. He was pretty angry when he found out I knew you, though." He exhales through his nose. "Seems like *someone* didn't obey their orders to remain in his room." He levels a disappointed look in my direction with a small smile. "It took everything in me to leave him there another night, but I had to find a logical way to remove him without incriminating myself in the process. I sent word to the dungeon that prisoner 0120 would be moved to a holding facility on the other side of the castle in a forged king's decree."

"Did they hurt him again?" I ask, unsure if I want the truth.

"I'm not sure. I hope they didn't, but I..." He pauses. "I wouldn't put it past them." I curl in on myself, waiting for him to continue. A staggering dread washes over me and lands in a pit in my stomach.

"I came to retrieve him the next morning, and as per the plan, he killed the two dungeon guards who grabbed him, only using his wrists," he says with a proud grin. "I've never seen anyone so strong while only seconds away from unconsciousness. No one but myself, of course," he adds quietly. "He didn't even use his majick, just pure willpower and force." I shouldn't find that as attractive as I do—I am too far gone. I cover my face to cover the flush of heat I feel. "You okay, love?" he asks in a teasing tone.

"Yep," I say through my pressed hands. He laughs and pushes me with a force I don't expect, knocking my hands from my face.

"You think that's hot, don't you?" he asks. My eyes widen, and when I don't respond, he laughs a little too hard. "I don't blame you. I think it's hot, too," he says, biting his bottom lip.

"Oh?" I ask, furrowing my brows at the thought of Flynn and Nallac.

"I'm very comfortable in my sexuality."

"So you like men?"

"Nope, but I meeeean..." He draws out the word with a nefarious look. "I'd try anything once." He winks, and I nearly fall back in my chair with laughter.

I know there is still more that he has not told me, but I sense that his serious manner has gone, and he no longer wants to speak about it. We sit in silence for a while longer, and the sound of me finishing my drink and Flynn's occasional laughter at nothing in particular is all that fills the emptiness.

I find myself staring at the opening, waiting for Nallac to arrive, and with each passing minute, my worry grows.

"Looking for me?"

I whip around and grip the back of my chair as I take in Nallac's form, healed of all his previous wounds—arm, chest, and all. He answers the question rolling off my lips.

"My sister healed them. That's why I had to make a stop before meeting you here." He rubs the place that used to be an open hole of flesh, bone, muscle, tendon, vein, and— "Vera, look at me," he says softly, his words cutting off my quickened thoughts.

I turn to him, and he studies me.

"It's healed," he reassures, touching the spot again.

All I can see is the wound, not the skin I know to be healed. My breath catches in my throat, and I bite my lip to calm down.

"Vera."

I hear the words, but I can't stop staring now I know what he went through.

He's alive.

He's healed.

I repeat the phrase as my breath calms, and I finally meet his eyes again. His face is a mask of concern that stares straight through me.

"I'm just glad you're okay," I whisper.

"What happened when I left you?" he asks. He always knows. I'll never understand.

"I saw a creature. I'm still a little shaken up. That's all," I mumble again, not wanting to remember that paralyzing fear.

"A Letiferna," Flynn says in a grave tone, and Nallac's pale skin grows white as snow. "It threatened her. It *spoke* to her. I don't know why it let us go, truthfully."

I space out as I remember that moment all too clearly. It could have killed me, but it didn't.

"Something about the gods' will," I explain, unsure if it means anything. Flynn is still in his seat and takes another sip of his drink, which I hadn't noticed had refilled itself. Nallac studies his movements and scoffs.

"Well, I'm glad to see the gods are participating with their creations again. I guess that means my ceaseless torture as a child was a part of their plan, too?" He fakes a laugh and moves to the end of our table. I feel the color drain from my face. "The gods only care about those with titles and political power. It's always been that way."

He quickly glances at me, and it's enough to tell me *exactly* what he thinks. I feel the familiar heat of anger but push it down, not letting it gain a single foot on the staircase.

"What are you trying to say, Nallac?" I ask, attempting to conceal the accusation from my voice. He huffs a breath and doesn't respond. "Don't you channel Naejik's majick?"

"I do. It doesn't change the fact that she only cares for the whims of nobility. But don't worry, Vera, I'm sure she'll answer any time you pray." I shove off the anger once more and move so he has to look straight at me.

"You may have only known me as a princess, but as far as I am concerned, I am on the same level as you. I do not appreciate your sudden hostility to the title I did not choose to have," I state. Perhaps the mention of the gods triggers something in him.

He puts a hand to his face and sits down, seemingly contemplating what he wants to say. I hope it's an apology.

"Trouble in paradise?" Flynn asks with a sarcastic chuckle.

"Alright, children." He leans forward. "Let's use our big boy words and discuss our issues."

"I don't have any issues," I scoff, aware I sound just like my mother.

"Okay...and what about you, Homicide?" He laughs to himself at the mention of the nickname. He's undoubtedly tipsy.

"I do not have an issue," Nallac grumbles. "I was simply stating my opinion of the gods."

"Yeah, by insulting me." I glare in his direction.

"I didn't *intend* for it to insult you."

"You basically said, 'The gods would rather let me die than listen to anything I have to say, but oh, Vera, don't worry! They'll listen and respond to you! Because you're so much better than me, and I can't stand it!'" I mock, almost yelling. "'Because you're different than me. You're not broken like me. I won't let you in because I don't want to hurt you, but I'll insult something you can't control in front of others.' Did I miss anything?" I keep my eyes locked on him and see him shift in his seat.

"I didn't say that."

"Yeah, but you meant it."

He doesn't move to deny it, and it sends a stake through my heart. For all the kind things I've done—for everything I have tried to do to help and understand him—that's how he sees me? Like I'm no better than the king?

Flynn sits farther back, attempting to avoid the argument he's accidentally started.

"I'm sorry," Nallac says under his breath, refusing to meet my gaze. "I temporarily saw you as your title and nothing more, and for that, I apologize. It is never my intention to hurt you, but I seem to fail time and time again." He finally turns to look at me, and I feel him reading my thoughts and emotions. "You are too good for me in more ways than one."

The anger I felt falls, and I want nothing more than to understand the siren before me.

"I don't deserve you. I don't deserve your care after I have treated you like that. You can't just let me push you around. Don't let me hurt you," he says.

"I told you I would take whatever damage being your friend would cause, and I meant it. You have dealt with several lifetimes' worth of pain, so taking a fraction of it is the least I can do." I give him a soft, comforting look, yet he seems taken aback. "I forgive you."

"Homicide," Flynn says, grabbing Nallac's shoulder, which causes him to jolt. "I think you need a drink. Or a couple. Maybe four?" Nallac shakes his head, and Flynn pouts while sipping from an empty glass.

"I prefer to feel my pain at all times. I fear that one taste of a life without it would lead me down a path I won't return from," he mumbles. If that's how he sees life, he is worse off than I thought. To be in constant, never-ending misery...I couldn't possibly imagine.

"Yeah, that sucks. Can't relate. I should get another. V, you want one?" Flynn asks without waiting for an answer. He attempts to swim to the bar but stumbles on Nallac instead. "Hey, handsome, come here often?" he asks with a too-large smirk, looking up from Nallac's arms.

Nallac shoves him off with a disgusted scoff.

"I'm going to get a remedial drink to stop whatever *that* is," Nallac says, gesturing to a now completely drunk Flynn. "I can barely stand him as is, much less without control." He rolls his shoulders and moves away with the careful grace I'm so fond of.

For a while, I'm stuck with a wholly wasted man that could easily snap a lesser enemy in two but is now a laughing, joking mess. I can't help joining him with his stupid, absurd jokes and hilariously dramatic, flirtatious comments.

"What do you call a well-balanced hippocampus?" Flynn asks with anticipation.

"What?" I ask with a harshly furrowed brow, unsure what his next joke will be.

"Stable! Ha!" He bursts into laughter, and I do, too, even though it isn't nearly as funny as he thinks. Seeing a man who can be so protective and ruthless become this is more than I can take. I try to breathe as my laughing becomes silent.

"Okay, okay! But what do you call a mer that walks into a tavern bar?" he asks, barely able to get the question out through his laughter.

Nallac returns before he finishes his joke and shoves a silver liquid down Flynn's throat. Flynn shudders as he swallows, and a few seconds later, he has returned to his previous self.

This is miraculous.

"Yeah, I had a few too many," Flynn admits, fixing his hair and dusting off his armor.

Looking closer, I notice the thick black titanium with detailed curves and edges enhancing the natural lines of his chest and shoulders. It shines as if freshly cleaned, making him look nothing short of a warrior.

The two pieces come together at the center, where they are molded into a military crest that reads S.C.A.R.

"Supreme Commander of the Adleian Regiment. I see you staring at my title."

"How high do you rank?" I ask, unsure of his true power within Adlei.

"High enough to have direct counsels with the king." He grins and moves to the door. "There are very few above me. Now, let's go."

As we reach the open doorway, a small creature appears in front of Flynn.

Its skin is a translucent blue that glows like bioluminescence, its shape resembling a jellyfish but with eight legs like an octopus.

The adorable thing has two antennas that look like fins atop its head. The eyes are large and black with long glowing blue eyelashes that give it an even cuter appearance.

It tilts its head as it stares at Flynn, making purring clicks as he pets it.

"Squish! Perfect timing," he says, grabbing the creature and cuddling it like a puppy. "Vera, this is my pettiel." I stare at the tiny creature that is no bigger than Flynn's hand and reach to pet it.

It pushes its head into my hand and makes a series of high-pitched clicks as it rolls around.

"Is it a pet?" I ask, rubbing the pettiel's belly.

"Yes, and it delivers letters to whomever I wish. They can teleport a few feet at a time, making communication very fast. I sent word to my assistant for Squish to come along on our journey," Flynn explains. He ruffles its antennas, and it purrs even more.

"Hi, Squish!" I say, pulling the pettiel into my hands. "Aren't you just the cutest little thing!" It coos and pushes behind my hair like a rabbit hiding in tall grass.

"Okay, little guy, come back," he says, holding his hands out, and the creature burrows farther into my hair. "Really? I've had you for three years, and you betray me for a girl you just met? I'm hurt."

Flynn crosses his arms and shrugs.

~

I follow behind the two men and stare at the elegant architecture of each building, the carvings along the support pillars telling stories of their age, and the flowers and plants that decorate every surface.

Flynn leads me as I can't tear my eyes away from the beautiful sights around me. They finally take me to a large fountain pouring silver fluid that defies all laws of physics, flowing as it would on land.

Mer children play with the silver liquid, scooping it with their hands and throwing it at each other as they laugh and scream.

I lift my hands and imagine myself on the rock above the waves. My hands are covered with paint as I pick up one of the many brushes. I use it to focus my majick and reach for the strings of power.

Holding it while humming a low tune, I release one finger at a time and send it into the fountain in a slow stream that sends the liquid flying, drenching the two children in a wave of metallic fluid.

They look at each other and then at me, to which I grimace and mouth 'sorry.'

They pause momentarily before laughing harder and rubbing their hands along my skin and covering me in the substance. It feels like a luxury oil paint, and I soon wish I could use something as exquisite in my paintings.

I laugh with them, picking up a scoop and dumping it over the elder child's head. She can't be much older than thirteen.

She wipes her eyes and jumps into the fountain, flapping her tail and sending a wave over me that drenches every last bit of skin and hair. I spit out what landed in my mouth, which tastes mildly of iron.

Flynn and Nallac aren't safe either, as I pull them both against their will. The two children and I cover them as well. Nallac seems the most displeased.

"*Fraeda, my nōmani Xaeda. Tejs?*" the older girl asks with a smile.

"Sorry, I don't speak Adleian," I respond while wiping the oil from my face.

"Oh, that's fine! My name is Xaeda, and this is Kerron. What's yours?" Xaeda translates to English.

"I'm Vera," I say. I notice the little boy's confusion.

"*Kileōa daemōre?*" Kerron asks, and his sister explains in his language.

"My brother doesn't speak Common. He's a little..." She trails off. "Anyway, can I ask why you don't know Adleian? Your ears and tail are very much, you know, Adleian."

I look to Flynn, and he nods in approval.

"Do you know the stories of Princess Asherah?" I ask, and her eyes go wide as she nods. "That's me," I whisper with a finger over my lips.

Her jaw falls to the floor, and she grabs my arm and squeezes. Perhaps she wants to check that I'm not a part of her imagination.

"I thought she was a myth! Are you serious?" she asks with wonder. I nod, and she squeals in excitement. "Are you going to save us like the elders say? They say your return will end King Argyros's rule and free us of his tyranny."

My smile drops, and I don't respond. I can't promise to end her suffering.

I can't promise to start a war, and I'm unsure I can lead.

She waits for a response I fear will never come before Flynn saves me and explains.

"We are in the process of gathering allies from other nations." He smiles as he moves to her level. "I will do whatever I can to ensure this ends. I promise you." He speaks to her as an equal, giving her a hope I don't think she's had for years.

She smiles tightly and takes her brother's hand.

"Thank you, princess. Our lives depend on it. Mother and Father don't think we'll make it through another year," she says before swimming off.

I feel a weight in my chest that wasn't there before, and I find it hard to think straight.

My heart quickens.

All these people are placing their final hopes of escaping on *me*. I am the only one who can do this, but *can* I do this?

The beats are stronger and faster, and I try to calm myself to no avail.

I'm too young for this, too young for the fate of a civilization, and too young to carry the burden of their lives. I close my eyes as hard as I can until I see stars. I hope when I open them this will all be a misunderstanding.

I hope I'll realize I'm not the lost heir.

Instead, when I open my eyes to the blinding light of day, I see the truth behind this beautiful city.

I see bone-thin children hiding in alleys. I see adults begging for food and owners reluctantly denying them. I see the effects the king has had on these people. And as I look closer, I don't see a single witch.

"Why are there no witches here?" I ask.

"The king has begun taking them as slaves," Nallac whispers and my heart sinks. All those families without daughters and mothers. All those families without sons and fathers. I take a breath and look at Nallac.

I will do as he said, even if I must change myself to do it—for them.

For Xaeda, Kerron, Nallac, and every single mer that has ever felt the effects of poverty and oppression. For anyone who that monster has ever slighted...For my mother.

I will take it one step at a time, and I will not back down.

NALLAC

31

POTENTIAL

.*✦ NALLAC ✦*.

Vera looks like a statue cast in white gold from the liquid silver that flows from the central fountain. Some of the oily substance covers my skin, and if any other person had done such a thing, they would be dead. Yet, I almost feel like smiling with its disgustingly slick and sticky texture that clings to every part of my skin, seeping into the pores.

This woman clouds my better judgment to the point where all I think about is her. Be it her safety, her feelings, or her interests—all I want is *her*.

She stares into the distance, looking at the people of Kaerious who need our help. She is flooded with anxiety, worry, and guilt. I want to take it all away.

"Flynn, what do I do? I don't understand any of this. You're the *Supreme Commander*, so why aren't you uniting them?" Vera asks in desperation. He looks at her with a rare softness that few ever experience. A month ago, I would have said he was just another worthless leech set on taking everything from the impoverished citizens, but now, seeing him with Vera, I fear my judgments have been wrong.

I've watched him kill guards who disobeyed orders in front of their friends, and I've seen him not shed a tear when a comrade was murdered before him.

Heartless.

It's what they called him, and I did, too, even if it was only in my head.

A memory flashes by like a glacier that has finally come crashing down.

I was fourteen, kidnapped, and beaten for the first time. I cried in front of the king. I *sobbed* in front of that wretched creature, giving that sadist what he craved. When he left, a guard picked me up and brought me to my slave quarters—the room I later made a home.

He placed me on the bed and began tending to my wounds with the few supplies he had. He sighed, knowing the gashes across my face would never heal, unlike the others. He knew I could not heal any wound caused by the king, and he cursed himself for being unable to stop it. He hugged me while I cried, and he stayed like that for what felt like an hour, not letting me go until I was ready.

The heartless man who climbed the ranks faster than any other was the same man who cared for a servant child when he had no one else. It was Flynn.

The revelation hits me as everything I thought I knew spins. This was not the first time he'd saved me, and something tells me it won't be the last.

I don't think my mind will ever let me properly thank him due to my years of resentment. That memory, the day my servitude was set in stone, was shoved so far down that I haven't relived it until now—until I looked at the true face he hides so well.

He knew I suppressed that moment. He knew I needed someone to place resentment on. He let me believe he had never met me and didn't care. He did it to *protect* me.

Everything I know changes, and I wonder how many people I unjustly hate.

Before I know it, we have reached a clothing shop.

One of the workers casts a spell to rid us of the disgusting sludge that seems to cling to me stronger with each passing moment. I feel reborn after it's cleansed from my skin.

Unfortunately, Vera's attire is not cleaned through the spell, and I fear it may be destroyed altogether.

"Korah is going to be so upset," she says, trying to wipe the caked liquid that doesn't budge. I see Flynn turn and whisper to the shopkeeper out of Vera's range.

"I'll buy anything she likes, so convince her to try some things," he murmurs. The woman nods in acknowledgment and casually approaches the princess.

"Excuse me, miss. I can't help but notice that your beautiful clothes are ruined. Would you like to try on something else?"

"I can't. I don't have any money to pay for it. Thank you, though," Vera says with a polite smile that causes my stomach to twist in knots. It feels like a swarm of insects struggling to escape. What is this feeling?

"Nonsense! I would love to see you in some of our wares. Are you sure you can't indulge me by just trying them on?" the lady asks.

"Alright, fine," she relents with a happy grin. She's adorably clueless.

They swim off to a nearby dressing room, and I wait with Flynn for her return.

"Thank you," I say without thinking, instantly regretting the words when they escape my lips. He stares with confused apprehension.

"For what?"

"For saving me," I add on. He nods and pats me on the shoulder.

"You would've done the same. You don't have to thank me," he says, reassuring me. He doesn't realize *what* saving I'm referring to, and it kills me to think he's pretended none of it happened for my sake.

"I wouldn't have. That's why I need to thank you," I respond honestly. He doesn't react, as if he already knew that was the truth when he said it.

"I know," he says quietly.

Something about the look in his eyes—he isn't talking about the dungeons.

He talks as if he had nursed my wounds a day prior and not five long years ago. There's no doubt why he holds the rank he does. Few match his intelligence and strategic thinking, and I can now attest to his insight.

"I forgot about that day. Most of the first three years are a blur. I suppose it was my mind's way of dealing with it," I explain, the most I've shared with anyone in a long time. He doesn't respond and only listens. "All those years I spent hating you and blaming you as part of the problem when you were always on my side."

"I know it was easier that way. I let you hate me when you forgot and never reminded you. I mean, hell, you were just a kid, Nallac. I couldn't be the reason you relived that torture." He sighs with a weak smile. "Your past could make most people's worst memories feel like a daydream."

I can't find any words to respond, and he nods in understanding.

Vera walks out in her first outfit, a deep blue cloth that drapes across her chest and shoulder, wrapping around her waist and coming together with a golden belt at the center.

"How is it?" she asks as she spins around. I try to tell her how beautiful she is and how the color brings out her eyes, but nothing comes out like my mouth has been sealed shut.

"Eh, the shape isn't very flattering," Flynn says. She tries to move the cloth around with a frown.

"Yeah, I thought the same," she agrees.

The shopkeeper takes her back into the room to try another, and then another, and each time, I feel my tongue caught behind my teeth. I want to tell her so many things, but I just can't. Thankfully, Flynn gives his opinion each time.

She steps out once more, and this time, she looks more insecure than the previous options, holding her arms across her stomach and looking away with a fire in her face. I have to stop myself from gaping as I stare at the utter divinity before me.

Her chest is highlighted with a top that shows off every perfect piece of her. It's an iridescent material of pinks, purples, and hints of blue. The hue changes with each slight movement she makes, and it's mesmerizing.

Gold detailing surrounds the edges of the top in delicate curves and swirls that create a point at either end. Inside each area, a small golden filament is woven to create a rose, engulfing the entirety of each of her breasts.

The golden curves come together in the center and underneath to give support, almost forming the shape of a butterfly.

Strings of pearls hang across various points with a gem dangling from each edge.

It is held up by a string of white stones on her shoulders, similar to her previous outfit.

She looks nothing short of a princess, and I can't stop staring, taking in every intoxicatingly beautiful part of her. Although it isn't until she turns around that I truly lose my breath. Her back is completely open with rows and rows of pearls holding it together.

Gods, she's perfect.

"Vera, you look—" My voice catches, and I have to clear my throat. "You're mesmerizing. I can barely put it into words." Her eyes jump to mine and the raging crimson across her cheeks grows brighter.

I'm drowning in it, in the best way.

Her fire fuels my own, and I have to remember we're not alone.

"You think?" she asks with a soft smile, and I feel the insecurity slowly fade. "I thought it was a little too revealing." I quickly shake my head with wide eyes, unable to take them from her. "You're confirming what I just said, you know." She laughs with a smile that creases her eyes and nose.

Flynn looks to the shopkeeper and nods with a wink, likely telling her this is the one.

"Perfect! It's yours," the worker says. Vera refuses quickly, restating that she has no way to pay for it before Flynn speaks up.

"I already paid for it, love. It's yours." He grins with that hungry look in his eyes which would make me jealous if I could not sense him joking.

"Flynn! You can't just buy this! It's—" She looks down at the price tag and gasps. "It's sixty-five *nae'yuns*! That's almost four hundred dollars in my world!"

"You humor me. That's nothing, so just look pretty and follow me, will you?" Flynn asks, reaching out an arm. She shuts her mouth with wide eyes, and I can't quite understand what she's feeling. It's a jumbled mix of too many feelings that change quicker than I can analyze.

As we swim outside, we're swept into the *Moōndaen* celebration. Mer of all ages pull us into dance at the center of town now that the sun has set and the moon is in full view. Vera is full of an overwhelming happiness as flower necklaces are thrown over her head.

She dances with them without even knowing what it's for, and in that moment, I understand that this is where she's meant to be. She may not realize it, but this is her home.

There is not a single doubt in my mind that when she has to step up and lead, she will. Even if she doesn't think she can, I see something in her. I see a fire beyond her *maemōjik*. I see a fire to rule, lead, and save these people.

For eighty years, Adlei has suffered under King Argyros's rule, and it will only take one woman to destroy it all. A woman raised on land, unaware of our preconceptions about races, who will unite the clans and kingdoms.

She doesn't even realize her own power.

A Letiferna, the deadliest creature on our planet, is scared of her. She can shatter stone like it's a simple spell.

Vera is twirled from hand to hand as dance partners shift until finally landing in mine. I spin her and dip, letting myself smile for the first time in a while as she laughs, her joy filling me and taking over my own emotions.

"What's happening?" she asks with the biggest grin across her face.

"It's *Moōndaen*. We celebrate every full moon because it's when witches are their most powerful, and the gods are willing to hear our prayers. The dancing, drinks, and food just came about as the years went on," I say as I spin her again, not yet wanting to let her go into another man's arms.

"This is amazing, Nallac. I wish I could stay this happy forever. Promise to dance the night away with me every *Moōndaen*." She moves her arms from my shoulders to my neck as our movements slow. I take a risk and move my own from her upper back to her lower waist. Her skin is unnaturally soft against mine.

"I promise, my *saeraih*." And with that, I spin her to another, and the night continues in a blur. None of the women I dance with after hold a space in my memory; the only moment that stays is the smile on her perfect face and the way my name sounded when it left her lips.

I move away from the crowd unnoticed and find a secluded spot on the outskirts of the bustling city. I look up to the sky, the moon staring back at me, and for the first time in my life, I pray to the gods.

VERA

A LONG WAY AHEAD

.*⭐ VERA ⭐*.

Once we're back at Taelani, I'm forced to part with them. All I can think about is the possibility their treason will be discovered and there will be no one to save them. I first hug Flynn, and he engulfs me in an embrace I will crave in his absence.

I've grown fond of him, and I can't imagine how I would feel if either of these men were to die on my behalf.

"I'm stronger than I look, love. I'll be alright," Flynn says to comfort me, but it's not just his safety I worry for. I still haven't learned to control my majick, and I don't have any hand-to-hand fighting experience if I were to be cornered again.

"Are you sure you can't come?" I ask, fighting back tears. He nods.

"I'm very important in keeping the military running," he says with his signature arrogance. "They would not only greatly notice my absence, but it would be incredibly suspicious." I hug him tighter, and he reciprocates. "I'll be okay. I promise."

I let go and stop myself from hugging Nallac the same.

"Can I hug you, too?" I ask. He doesn't answer and instead embraces me so strongly and passionately I feel tears finally fall. I nuzzle my head into his shoulder, finding a comfort I can't get anywhere else. I breathe in the rosewood and cinnamon I have grown so accustomed to before I feel him let go.

"Please be safe," I whisper so quietly I'm unsure he heard it at all. I use all the willpower I have to pull away.

"Always," Nallac says, grazing a hand along my cheek before jerking back. "I can feel you in my heart, Vera. I will be there in an instant if you're hurt." I don't know how such a thing could be possible, but if this world has taught me anything, it's that impossible doesn't exist.

Korah and Kaileah wait for me inside as I give them my farewells. I glance behind to Taelani. This is where I first learned of what I was, and now, it feels like another home.

The moon is still out, only barely lighting our faces.

Nallac looks divine, with his fair features so graceful and feline. His black hair is tied neatly behind his head, with some left out to touch his neck and the front of his head.

I wonder if he has grown more comfortable with the deep scars across his face.

I'm unable to tell how long we've all spent in silence, but at some point, I say my farewells. They leave soon after, and loneliness settles deep within my chest.

I feel completely and utterly alone without them. I don't know them well enough to warrant grieving their absence, but I do all the same.

They said it would take us three days by carriage and five if we swam on our own. Thankfully, Korah had Alec send a few more hippocampi to carry us along the way, and they arrived by the next morning.

Kaileah hasn't spoken to me unless unavoidable, such as when making sure I grabbed enough provisions, any book I might want to occupy myself, and the classic motherly checklist of things to bring on a trip.

It had felt almost normal, listening to her worry about Korah and me possibly forgetting something we needed, and I began imagining what being her daughter would have been like.

I shake away the thought, instantly feeling guilty about my human parents. I remember Flynn mentioning his pettiel would be nearby to send word with updates on our plan, and the thought calms me for now.

Our plan. The words feel so wrong but somehow right.

As the first day of travel ends, we're all fatigued. Kaileah spots a nearby *la'minōlu* forest that agrees to hide us, animals and all. I feel content within the forest—the soft touch of the glowing kelp is like an otherworldly blanket wrapped around us all.

I can tell the days we spent in caves have taken a toll on Kaileah. That and her days as a prisoner. She seems tired at all times, day or night. Being used to sleeping on the finest mattresses with the softest duvets money can buy, this must be the most uncomfortable time of her life.

For once, I'm not the first to wake as I hear Korah speaking to someone. Comfort floods me, so I stay engulfed in an almost-sleep for a while longer, only conscious enough to hear her voice.

"How long do you want me to wait? She's terrified of the

prospect of starting a war. How can you be certain she'll step up without knowing the full truth?" Korah asks. After a moment, I hear her sigh before growing silent.

Is she talking about me?

I try to stay as still as possible, faking sleep as I slowly open one eye. If I didn't know better, I'd say she was talking to *herself*. Kaileah is fast asleep, tossing and turning, and she curls further in on herself.

"I know your plan is beyond my comprehension, and I am still beyond grateful for you choosing me," Korah continues. She bows her head and clasps her hands together. "I will not question you again. You have my humblest apologies, Kayiah."

I remember the Goddess of Land and Sea from Flynn's explanations of majick.

She speaks of a plan the goddess has—for me, I assume. Flynn's strange words as he left me in the cave four days ago come to mind. Mention of the gods wanting something of me, and then I remember the Letiferna claiming the same.

What are they keeping from me?

How many people in my life are keeping secrets? Perhaps Kaileah was right, and I do trust too quickly. I always thought I could spot the right people like a sixth sense, but maybe even she is one of the ones I'm not meant to trust.

I begin to overthink every moment from the last few weeks, trying to pick apart every word said to me and wondering which of them were lies.

I'm done dancing around confrontation like an iced-over lake waiting to shatter, so I plunge my foot through by force instead. If they do not respect me and show me their honesty, then why should I respect them?

"Korah, who were you just speaking to?" I ask. She turns with horror on her face. Stumbling over various excuses and transparent lies, she puts her hands to her face.

"I—How much did you hear?" she asks in a quiet squeak.

"Enough to know if you're lying to me if you don't tell me exactly who you were talking to."

Her eyes widen even further, and she looks around for something.

"I was just praying. To my deity! Kayiah. That's all." She blurts out each word with quick and abrupt halts.

"Right," I mumble with apprehension. "And who are you worried won't step up without the truth?" I ask with a raised brow. She whispers a string of Kefian phrases before covering her mouth in exasperation.

"I'm sorry! I don't know what came over me to speak such profanities!" she apologizes with a bright red face.

"Korah, I don't speak Kefian. I literally have no idea what you said, so there's no need to apologize."

"Oh, good! Wait, how did you know what I was saying then?" she asks, the redness in her face dimming as she contemplates something. "Everything I said was in my native language. There is no way you would have known I said that unless..." She trails off before gasping. "I should've known!"

"Known what exactly?" I ask, growing more curious by the minute.

"She wanted you to hear me. That's why I woke up before you, and why you must have felt an urge to stay asleep for longer. I can't tell you any more than what you heard, not unless my goddess allows me to. I hope you understand."

I can't find the words to respond, and I'm caught in my thoughts about this new information.

Korah's goddess, Kayiah, wanted me to know she has a plan

for which I'm the main pawn. Flynn claimed the same, but he never mentioned the god or goddess for which he spoke. The Letiferna didn't either.

As of now, I know of Kayiah's involvement, but how deep does it go?

"How many gods are there?"

"Well, there are the Majick Three, including Naejik, Kayiah, and Adnitis. All of them are capable of channeling their power. Then there are the lesser gods and goddesses, mostly in charge of concepts and ideas, such as luck and karma. Why?" Korah asks with a blank expression.

"How often do these gods communicate with mortals?"

"Rarely. The gods don't often bless us with their communication," Korah responds but seems to grow more uneasy with each question.

"And what does it mean if someone has had contact with one of them?" I ask, finally getting somewhere.

"Heh—I mean. Uh," she stutters, likely trying to avoid my question. "There's no proper name for it, but I would call them their chosen."

"You're Kayiah's chosen?" I ask, trying to soften my tone.

"I mean, she's never *said* that, but I—I mean...maybe so." She fidgets with her hair, and I stop questioning. I don't want to push our relationship too far.

While I may not trust her as much as I did before, I don't want to sever the connection we've made altogether.

"Thank you for telling me what you have. I'm sorry if my questions upset you," I say comfortingly before packing. Kaileah reluctantly wakes up, helping gather the last items. It doesn't take long to load the hippocampi after.

I've ridden Astryx since she arrived to take us on our journey, and I've sensed something in her that I haven't yet figured out. Her mind goes deeper than an animal's; I know it. She houses so many memories, loves, stories, and scars.

Beyond that, something about her makes me feel safe and understood.

~

Another few hours have passed, and there has been little talking from anyone.

It's all my fault. I pushed Korah too far and said such horrible things to Kaileah.

Nallac is wrong about me. Perfect is the last word I'd use to describe myself. If anything, I am a plague to the people I love.

I pretend to be what they see me as.

I pretend to be perfect, without faults, and always see the best in people. The truth is that dark thoughts often cloud my judgment, and I have to push them away to bring out who I want to be. I *work* for who I am.

And sometimes, I'm too kind for my own good when I let people walk over me.

I put myself in situations I shouldn't, knowing they will hurt me in the end.

I don't know how to fix the problems I create, and it kills me. It hurts to see the people I care about in pain, especially when I'm the cause.

If I choose to fight in this war, I will be prepared to lay down my life if the need arises, and that's what I am so terrified of. I know beyond a shadow of a doubt that I will because I could not imagine letting someone give their life for me when I could very well do the same.

How can I possibly start a war knowing the lives I'll risk?

How can I start something that could harm those I love? I would never let myself live it down.

"Kaileah?" I ask, trying to test the waters.

"Hmm?" she responds in a soft tone.

"I was wondering about your marriage to the king." It's impossible to know how much she is willing to say before I push her too far. My only hope is that she will stop me before I ruin things between us further.

"Ask me anything," she prompts. Here goes nothing.

"What led to you being with him? Why would your parents let it happen? I couldn't imagine," I say with sorrow in my voice. She lets out a sharp exhale, yet I can tell she's not really laughing.

I truly feel for her. She has to be one of the strongest women I've ever met.

"My wonderful parents are the reason it happened. They were always members of the nobility, having plenty of power and wealth, but they were greedy for more. My mother and father were getting old and had nothing to offer that the higher ranks didn't already own, so they had a few children and sold me to the highest bidder." She forced out a small smile before moving on.

"They never wanted children and only had me and my siblings when they realized it would benefit them. Dorian already had his fair share of women, but what king would ever have an heir with a *commoner*?" She rolls her eyes at the idea. "And there I was. A beautiful, naive girl who came from royal blood. A fourteen-year-old child who wouldn't know what rights she had," she says, her fake smile falling. "A child who wouldn't know she could fight back," she grits out and shudders at the memories I'm sure it invokes.

"That's horrible," I say, covering my mouth.

"Which part?" She stifles a laugh. "I would've thought Naejik would have protected me since I'm of her blood, but I guess she thought I needed that pain to make me stronger." She must have noticed my shock. "The sorceress bloodline—we're her descendants."

My mouth hangs even wider, and I see her start to really smile, no longer faking it.

"Like demigods?" I ask, still dumbfounded by this information.

"Let me start from the beginning." She chuckles and clears her throat. "Many millennia ago, Naejik created the barrier between the mer and human realms to protect each of us from the other. She saw the evils of man and thought the best way to protect us both was to allow mer to venture into the human world without allowing them the same luxury."

"Why?" I ask, intrigued.

"The humans tried to conquer us, venturing into our seas and taking our materials, land, and people. She forced them out, wiped their memories, and made the barrier after that. The only stipulation was that we could not retaliate. So far, we have stayed true to that promise," Kaileah explains like a teacher.

"Back to what I was saying. After Naejik protected our people, she gained a substantial following, allowing her to become Queen of the Gods. One worshiper would spend every day giving her new offerings and praying for *her* happiness. She grew fond of the man, intrigued by his nature, and began to converse with him directly." She runs a hand through her hair. "Needless to say, he grew a following as a direct messenger to our supreme goddess."

"Their relationship eventually developed into something

deeper and more passionate," Kaileah continues after a slight pause. "I doubt Naejik ever planned to fall in love with a mortal, but she did. That's when the first demigod, as you called them, was born. She was perfect in every way. Gifted beyond explanation at Adleian majick, unbelievably smart, and divinely beautiful, she was both envied and adored."

"What was her name?" I ask.

"Elvira," Korah answers with a sad smile.

"She grew to hunger for more power than her mother could give her, and it drove her mad. There was nothing to stop her from siphoning every last bit of Naejik's power, so our goddess killed her," Kaileah says, her tone growing somber.

I gasp at the realization. I understand what she did. Adleians and sirens losing majick and the death of the Queen of the Gods would have unfathomable consequences. As terrible as it sounds to kill your child, there was truly no other choice.

"Before she died, Elvira had a daughter of her own, and while she was not as powerful as her mother, the child held a much greater potential than other witches. Thus, our bloodline was born," Kaileah explains proudly. I can see her pride in what she is —of what I am.

"And only a firstborn female can show the gene. I remember that from the day we met," I say, sharing her look. She glows with a blue radiance. "I have another question."

"Ask me anything, darling," she answers.

"What is your *maemōjik?*"

Her smile lowers slightly before she straightens.

"Love," Kaileah says as I realize it's the same blue glow as the day we met, when Alec was captured, and now it all makes sense. She always seemed more majickal and *powerful* when I noticed the aura of color.

But for love to be the emotion she feels least…oh, my poor mother.

"Love and rage. Dangerous apart, irreparable together," I say with a smile, and she huffs a quick breath. "You never seem overtaken by your *maemōjik* like I am when it happens. Why is that?"

"Like it said in that book I gave you, some emotions will have different effects. Love, for example, does not cloud my judgment. If anything, I feel that I can think clearer than usual," she explains while letting the glow dance across her skin, not inhaling its power like I am drawn to do. "I'm also twice your age, my child. I have had many years to learn how to control it," Kaileah says with a kind grin, and I wonder if things are alright between us after all.

"Weird question, but would that make Naejik our great, great, great, et cetera, grandmother?" I ask, and Kaileah raises her eyebrows with a strange grin.

"I suppose so, but I doubt she'd appreciate such a title," my mother remarks with a chuckle. Korah has remained unusually quiet throughout our journey, so I decide to give her time.

Days of travel blend as we make the final hours of our journey to a new kingdom, and I have to fight myself to not run away. It's not like me to run when things get scary or difficult, but I have this urge to go while I still can—before I promise to protect a civilization.

I will not back down.

I take a deep breath and remember the promise I made to myself.

33

A PLAN IN MOTION

.*✩ VERA ✩*.

The gate of Royan comes into view, with its swirls of coral growing like vines over the lightly yellowed marble. The vibrancy contrasts with the stone and metal of the archway, which is decorated with three-inch metal curves in patterns floating in place, not quite touching yet somehow molded together.

A mer could easily swim over or pass beside the gate, so it stands no purpose unless the rest is bound by majick. So many of these backward rules seem to defy logic and still leave me baffled.

My mother speaks to one of the many guards outside in what I assume to be Saanien, the language of the Jelleans, and they bow and let her in shortly after. I shove away the pang of inadequacy always lingering as I watch my mother communicate with grace and dignity.

After the guard allows us passage, I see the crowded kingdom is full of smiles and laughter. I look for anyone who could be struggling or starving, and I see nothing of the sort, unlike Kaerious. That wasn't even the worst of it, Nallac had told me. Kaerious is a wealthier city than many on the outskirts of Adlei, where food is rationed and scarce.

I wish they could have shown me so I could help those poor mer. But it was too dangerous. The three of us could only be seen in Kaerious because it is the heart of the rebellion.

The Jelleans look so genuinely happy, and I wonder what it is that the king and queen do so differently here.

Jellean people of all colors swim free with their purses and children in hand. Their shape is unlike the sirens, Koifinns, or Adleians. They appear humanoid with an opaque jellyfish shape of varying sizes and colors below their waists. They swim like they're gliding back and forth, their extremities barely moving yet pushing them in their chosen direction.

Graceful and elegant are the only words I can think of to describe it.

Vulpanis and dolphins glide around the kingdom along with various fish varieties I can no longer identify because my mer sight makes the world sing. Everything is enhanced like the world has been put through a vibrant filter. The things I once knew are now foreign—the dolphins are a soft blue instead of gray, fish are neon, and every plant is a burst of color.

The occasional guard rides on the back of a hippocampus, each with a different coloration from ours. Astryx and the others throw back their heads and neigh as the few creatures pass. They respond in recognition.

Korah is more awed than me, staring with her mouth agape at the sights. She told me along the way that she could not stand to be stuck in her clan any longer, and that she wanted nothing more than to explore and see the world like her brother and father often did.

Her brother is being groomed for their father's position without much thought for Korah's abilities, and I see how it hurts her. She wants to help her people but is brushed off because she's a daughter.

As Korah told me, Alec is the eldest son, giving him authority over his siblings. While this world may be something out of a fairytale, it does not fall short of its flaws.

I will change that. I will change it all.

Riding farther through the kingdom, many young Jelleans gape and wave at us, surprised when I return the same appreciation. They scream and swim off, and my cheeks burn from my wide smile.

This is what I want to be a part of.

I want to live in a kingdom where I can roam freely and am never afraid for my safety or that of others. I want to feel proud to be a princess and not feel my title is taking resources away from the lower class.

We reach the pearly entrance of the Jellean palace, where we're greeted by two large men with emerald tendrils and large tridents. Massive Corinthian columns line the entrance, decorated by the brightest coral and ivy, perfectly placed to highlight their full beauty.

The architecture is so detailed I would need months to examine it properly.

The metal before me gleams with the setting sun, but my appreciation is cut short as the guards' booming voices wrap around us like chains and shackles.

"State your business," one of the two demands in a low growl.

"I'm Princess Asherah, and my mother is Queen Kaileah Dlari

of the Adleian Kingdom. We're here to speak with Queen Delmaris," I state with a royal tone, having practiced my short speech in the last few minutes before our arrival. Kaileah wanted to ensure I was prepared to speak for myself when needed.

"Princess Asherah was lost long ago," he says disapprovingly.

"The fact that I am here is proof that our joint curse has been broken," Kaileah corrects, and the guards stumble back after recognizing my mother.

"Oh, Your Majesty, I apologize. I hadn't realized you were here. Come in."

Both men give us deep smiles and a bow as they shut the gate behind us.

"I hope you understand the confusion, Your Highness," the guard says to me.

"Of course. I would be hesitant to believe it myself," I respond politely.

Kaileah expertly leads us to what she describes as the queen's meeting room, and I am surprised by her knowledge of this castle. The thought is discarded as I gaze at the beautiful halls with royal-blue walls and extraordinary artwork hung everywhere.

The paintings are more complex and colorful than any I've seen, and I yearn to use the colors that only exist here. I want them all from the purples so rich they seem blue to the pinks that glow white at certain angles.

I imagine how the paint might feel. It would be grainy until mixed, and then it would become the softest satin, gliding like oil above water.

The floors are lined with hundreds of blue and gold marble tiles hand-carved into perfect rectangles. Small details shine through as I bend to see their depth.

The hallway is dimly lit only by the fixtures on the wall, lacking natural light that would make this space even more entrancing.

As we arrive, I see a large doorway surrounded by more sentries blocking the entrance. They allow us through after my mother steps in front, and I stop in my tracks as I see who I can only assume is the queen.

She's magnificent in every sense of the word.

Her hair is styled into a gorgeous curly afro, and she wears golden eyeshadow to enhance her dark skin. Within her hair, a golden crown is nestled neatly inside, showing just enough that I am enthralled by its intricate detail and hidden enough for me to want a better look.

Her cheekbones are high, and her features are sharp and refined.

She looks up from her stack of papers, and those beautifully dark eyes widen as though she's seen a ghost. All color flushes from her ebony face, and she gasps.

"Oh my gods—you're here?" Her voice is rich and silky, flowing like a river as it lightly echoes off the walls. She swims to Kaileah and cups her cheeks, tears welling in her eyes. "It's really you? My sweet baby, I've missed you so much!"

The queen, whose name I remember to be Abeda, pulls her into a tight hug, and my mother's eyes fill with tears as an over-joyed smile spreads across the plains of her elegant face.

A true smile. One I have come to know as rare. The sight of it has my heart tightening in my chest.

"My sweet girl, you made it out of there. Tell me everything," she says and wipes at her eyes before looking at a girl reading in the corner. "Lex, fetch us some tea, will you?" she asks kindly, unlike how I imagined royalty would command their staff.

"Of course, Your Majesty." Lex nods and places her book on the auburn armchair before leaving the room.

"There's so much to tell you, but first, I want you to meet my daughter, Asherah," Kaileah says with that same euphoric smile plastered on her face. Abeda turns and gasps once more. Without a second thought, the queen pulls me into a hug as loving as the first one I shared with Kaileah.

I return it, feeling overwhelming comfort in her embrace.

"Oh, my apologies. I've known your mother since she was born," she explains as she lets go. "It feels like I'm meeting my granddaughter for the first time." She smiles, wipes a tear, and continues. "I've heard so much about you, Asherah. Your mother loves you with every piece of her heart."

Before I can think of a response, a young girl similar to the queen swims in from the same rose-stained cypress archway Lex left through. The girl's hair is a deep black with tight curls cascading down her shoulders and lower back.

Her sepia-brown skin glows with the lights around, and the majestic beauty I see in Abeda is transferred tenfold on the girl I can only assume is one of her daughters.

I see Korah growing weak, stumbling into my arms, where I catch her.

"Korah, what's going on?" I ask, deeply concerned.

"She's—She's so..." Korah blinks slowly before almost fainting in my arms. "I've never felt like this before. This feels like my heart is being filled with every good thing the world has ever known. It's as if my mind has been swarmed with millions of plankton, keeping me from forming a complete thought," she whispers almost incoherently, and I push her upright, smiling at her clear captivation by the princess.

And truthfully, I can see why.

Her eyes are a rich black with flakes of gold and brown, and her lips are full, painted with a deep red gloss. She swims with an elegance that undeniably shows she's of royal blood. Her large, flowing Jellean bottom glows a rich cerulean, contrasting beautifully with her dark skin.

"Mother, who's this?" Her voice is flowing and calm, sharing the ethereal quality I love about my mother's. Abeda turns and pulls her daughter closer.

"Kaileah, I know it's been so long since you've seen her, but this is Zuira. She's all grown up," the queen says. Kaileah carefully swims to Zuira, placing a gentle hand on her face as she often does to mine.

"Zuira," my mother draws out. Her voice is tender and deep, and her eyes trail all over the princess's face. She removes her hand from her cheek before pulling her into a hug. "You've grown to be such a beautiful young woman."

"Auntie Lei?" she asks, now examining my mother in the same way. Kaileah nods, and she buries her head in my mother's shoulder. "I never thought I'd see you again."

I hear the pain in her voice, and I'm struck by the overwhelming love radiating from their reunion. Perhaps these people are my mother's real family.

It's clear because her *maemōjik* dances across her skin like a fawn in tall grass.

"Does that make you my cousin?" I ask, eager to immerse myself in a family who mean so much to my mother.

"Oh my gods! *Asherah? O cuann kelfia yirenka aleveih!*" Zuira pulls me into a hug so quickly it sweeps us both off balance. "Oh my, I'm so sorry. Your mother spoke of you so much in her letters, and it's almost like I knew you in a past life. I can't believe you're here!"

"That's quite alright," I reassure her with a laugh. "I go by Vera if you wouldn't mind." She nods with a smile that shows off her deep dimples.

"Vera...that's a truly beautiful name. Your human parents did a lovely job." I smile at her words, the kindness filling me. "And hello there, Miss—?" Zuira asks, turning to Korah, whose face is a bright red.

"Me? Oh, Korah! Hi!" she says, rushing over to shake Zuira's hand. She returns it politely, not nearly matching the ecstatic reaction Korah is so clearly displaying. I wonder if she knows how obvious her infatuation is. "You're, um, really beautiful," Korah says with a breathless voice.

Zuira raises her brows and looks at me.

"Thank you, Korah," Zuira responds with a small curtsy.

Lex returns shortly after with the tea, placing it on a small table, then brings out an extra chair for a fifth person. We all sit, and Abeda begins to pour a small cup for each of us.

It tastes like a raspberry zinger, and the temperature is perfect.

"Sugar?" the queen asks, holding out a small bowl full of white grains. I nod, and she stirs in a spoonful. The taste intensifies, and I suppress the urge to down it all.

I collect the details of the room, only partially aware of the conversation between Kaileah and Abeda. Their love is so apparent, like a mother and her daughter.

As I examine the patterns on the walls, she tells the story of her escape and our journey thus far. Focusing on her words is hard as I can only think about the views within this small part of the castle.

The entire room is pristinely clean.

As I stare at the ground, I notice the golden rays and streaks of rainbow light painted across the floor like lightning. They move as if each burst of color has a mind of its own.

The ceiling of Abeda's meeting room is a dome that comes to a center point, built entirely of multicolored stained-glass shards like a cathedral. From it hangs a chandelier of hundreds of crystal shards that shine like diamonds, the sun's rays catching every curved edge.

The walls are lined with tall, slender windows, partially covered by the golden curtains that sway with the moving water. Each slight movement gives the room a new decoration of light. At the top of each window, shells, jewels, and stars hang and clink together in a calming song.

Last, I notice a painting of an ivory-white serpentine creature that seems to come off the canvas, staring at me—its glowing blue eyes moving with me.

I blink, and it's right before me.

Instant paralyzing fear pins me to my seat.

The Letiferna glares at me, licking its teeth the same size as me. It taunts me like easy prey, and I close my eyes so tight I feel like I'll be filled with complete darkness forever. No creature is before me when I open them, and my companions don't acknowledge the beast that plagued my mind.

It's all in my head.

It's all in my head.

Or is it? that bestial, fiendish voice brands into my skull. Is that my imagination? Am I on the path of going completely mad?

The questions swirl and overtake me, and I fight the urge to bolt to where I know Astryx will be waiting. I can pretend that none of this happened—that it was an elaborate dream brought on by exhaustion from lying in the sun all day at my family's beach house.

The beach. The place where I stayed with my parents year after year since the day I was born.

The day I was taken from my birth mother.

The day I was cast out as a way to torture her further.

I want to run from the contradictions. I want someone to tell me exactly what it is I want without having to siphon through my thoughts for the truth. I want to know for once what it is I need to be complete.

"And Vera, what do you make of your new world?" Abeda asks with the love of someone who has known me for years.

"Oh, it's wonderful. It's beyond anything I could ever imagine." I flash her a soft smile, trying to forget the memory or perhaps nightmare of that beast. "Your kingdom is beautiful, and your people seem so happy," I remark.

Abeda gives a knowing nod.

"Our subjects are our priority. The King of Adlei does not have such morals, so his people suffer. I feel strongly for them, which is part of the reason I took your mother in as my own," Abeda explains. Kaileah smiles, but it doesn't meet her eyes, and I wonder what she's thinking. "I've known her since she was a little girl. Her parents often visited to negotiate trade for their territory and Adlei as a whole," Adeba continues.

"She's been like a mother to me ever since," Kaileah responds, and Abeda gives her a loving grin. "It broke my heart to be kept from you all those years."

"As it did my own. I still cannot believe that wretched king would not allow you to be with me in private when I visited. He will pay for what he has taken from you." The queen's tone grows in intensity, and I see that motherly rage.

"We want to wage war on Adlei," I blurt, and it garners everyone's attention. "Your kingdom is a close second in numbers, and your race's ability to poison those you touch will be more than useful to us. I hope you will consider."

She places her tea down and watches me, intent on listening.

"We will rid Adlei of its king, the plague on those lands, and the world of tyranny. I implore you to stand with us. I fear we will not stand a chance without many allies," I speak from the heart, keeping my voice steady and unrelenting. I don't know what has come over me as I spew the words of a warrior ready for battle, not a terrified teenage girl. "Be the change our world so desperately needs."

She raises her eyebrows before taking a slow sip of her drink, setting it down, and smoothing her dress.

"Spoken like a future queen," she says, reminding me of my mother's phrase. "My kingdom stands with you, and I will aid you however I can. I have waited for his day longer than you know, my girl. You say fight, and I'll ask when."

A weight releases from my chest, and I breathe fully for the first time since arriving at the palace.

"The priestesses predicted this moment," Zuira says, breaking her silence. "A girl unaware of the quarrels between kingdoms, clans, and races will be the one to unite them all. She who will step up not for her gain but for the betterment of the world will return our people as one." She recites the phrases as if they are a common poem taught in school. "Our savior has returned," she claims with a knowing grin.

"That she has," Abeda agrees.

Night has fallen, and I can't sleep. I can barely close my eyes, even in the remarkably soft bed that hugs me in all the right places.

The walls are a vibrant mauve with streaks of lighter swirls that curve across the doorway, the windows, and my bedframe. As I stare at them, I almost feel like painting. I imagine how beautiful roses, lilies, and leaves would be painted along each arch.

Marble tiles of rose gold line the floor, and the voile curtains flow as the water pushes them, revealing the intricate lace detailing on all the edges.

My bed, however, is the most beautiful.

A king-sized circular mattress sits upon a plum-colored velveteen frame with a large shell strung above. From it, lights of various colors hang, reminding me of the night sky.

As if done by majick, the covers follow me as I sit up, keeping me fully engulfed in the warm cocoon until I push them off and enter the attached bathing room. A large white granite tub sits in the center, along with a mirror spanning the length of the wall.

I climb into the tub, unsure why they have one underwater. The warm water I sink into clears away all those questions. I'll add that to the list of things I don't understand.

An Adleian enchanted object that allows the water inside to be warmed to a perfect temperature takes a lot of willpower to pull yourself from. I hoped it would calm me enough to sleep, but as I exit its warm embrace, all my worries come flooding back.

I need to speak to someone who will listen without judgment.

Making my way down the elaborate spiral staircase, I try to remember where we left our hippocampi when we arrived. The dark hallways are dimly lit by wall fixtures that glow in pinks and purples.

While unfamiliar with the castle in the daytime, I know even less without proper light. Consequentially, I run headfirst into a collum I hadn't noticed until it was too late.

Another hall comes into view, lined with paintings hanging from almost every open space. Some are portraits of previous kings and queens, others of animals, events, and places. I can barely tear my eyes away as I continue through the next hall, turn left, go through two doors, and finally make it outside the palace.

No guards are watching the gate as I swim past.

Perhaps I caught them in the middle of a shift change. Either way, I find my way to the stables, where Astryx is alert and waiting as if she knew I was coming.

Hello, child, a voice rings inside my head, and I realize that all this time, those words in my head I believed were my own were her speaking to me.

"It was you," I say, and she nods. "You know why I'm here, don't you?"

You wish to escape to the land from which you came, but you know you mustn't. You want to be heard without judgment, so you came to me. I stare at that scared white eye and wonder how it is possible to communicate with such a creature.

"I love my parents. I love them more than anything, and I feel like a part of me breaks each day I stay here. I don't think I can do what Kaileah, Flynn, Nallac, Zuira, and every other person wishes me to," I say, the words pouring out without me thinking.

I can't lead an army.

I can't combine the clans and kingdoms.

I know nothing of this world or its people.

"I don't even think I convinced Queen Delmaris with my words! I think my mother let me give that speech to convince me I could do it." I stop as my breath catches in my throat, and I choke out a sob.

Astryx doesn't respond.

"I don't know what to do! I don't feel like myself...like every new weight placed on my shoulders is sending me sinking farther and farther down, and I'm scared of what will happen when I finally hit the bottom," I continue, the words mixed with sobs.

I will do it.

I have no choice, but what of my own sanity?

What will happen if I give everything I have to everyone else?

I lose my breath, my cries growing silent as I feel my words. Clutching my chest, I try to keep from falling to the ground.

You will be ready when the time comes, child. You are stronger than you have yet realized—both in your majick and your person. Astryx turns her head to a dark corner of the stables, and I can't see what she clearly can. *The priestesses are correct in their assumptions, and they are correct that it is you. You will be the savior of Wynderan.*

"Wynderan?" I ask, wiping the tears from my eyes.

Long ago, each clan and kingdom were one, united under a single name. It represents a time of peace and prosperity, but no clan or kingdom would ever use it now. You will return us to that state. Returning all mer and creatures as Wynderans. She turns her head again and nods to the shadow, and I stumble back as a person exits—the princess.

"How long have you been watching me?" I ask with more malice in my tone than I expected.

"I heard you leave your room and went to check on you, but you seemed to be on a mission. I didn't want to interrupt you, so

I just followed." She tucks a strand of thick curls behind her ear, revealing a flowing fin with three tendrils matching her skin, holding each translucent dark blue fin in place.

As she moves into the moonlight, I can see the color removed from her face, a dark brown ash all that remains.

"I can hear them, too," she says with a tear of her own.

"That's not normal?" I ask kindly, as I realize she meant no harm in eavesdropping. She shakes her head slowly, unable to speak. "Please, whatever it is, just tell me. I'm tired of being kept in the dark."

She takes a deep breath and looks me in the eyes.

"There's only one reason we can hear them, and it's nothing good." She stumbles on her words. "Someone we love will die in this war. That's why we can hear them." My hand covers my mouth, and my eyes swell with tears once again. "They are pure creatures that know things we could not begin to understand. They know who will die and how it will affect us. They know the outcome of the war and everything that will be lost." Her voice is raw and broken, and I believe every word.

"Astryx," I say, gazing at the creature before me. "Who wins this war?"

She stares at me, and my mind is silent. I begin to ask again before she stops me with narrowed eyes.

You may wish to know that information, but you do not realize that the outcome would change by telling you. The fabric of the universe is thin, and it is the duty of my kind to ensure its balance. I am sorry about who you will lose, and I am sorry that I cannot answer any questions regarding these matters. I remain stunned as I think about everything she said. The way she speaks with such insight...How old is she?

I have been alive since the beginning. I have seen kingdoms rise and fall, and I have been the confidant of many. I have seen war and blood-shed unlike anything you could believe, and I have experienced death far beyond what a mortal could fathom. She has to be thousands of years old.

The things she must know.

I wish I could peer inside her head and understand it all. She almost laughs at that thought.

You would go insane the second you saw all that I know. I know every outcome of every situation from years past and centuries in the future. I know who I will grow to love and care for and how they will die, and I feel the love and pain at all times as if it is happening in the present and not years in the future. There is a reason it is my kind that is tasked with this burden, and it is why only a few of us are truly enlightened to it all.

Knowing everything that has, is, and will happen must be suffocating, and she is right, I do not think I really wish to know. But she said only a few of her kind will ever truly understand.

"If you've lived so many valiant lives, why do you allow your-self to be kept as a simple steed?" I ask, worried my traitorous mouth may offend her.

I do not enjoy hunting for my next meal, and while it may seem demeaning to a mer to be owned, Korah is a kind soul. She feeds me in a timely manner and gives me what I need to be content. You grow fond of stability when you have lived as many lives as I have. She turns to Zuira, holding her soft gaze until Astryx returns to me.

Many in your life hold secrets. I nod, and she sighs as if searching her mind for an answer. *All will be revealed in time.*

"Who holds these secrets?" I ask, hoping that *this* is something she will allow me to know. She shakes her head and retreats into a corner of her stall. She curls her long mer-like tail under her before lying down.

"Are you immortal?" I ask, and she makes no motion to stand.

Yes, in a way, but I am unlike others. An average hippocampus will live two centuries at the longest, but I have taken on a burden to protect the rest of them from what I know. Innocence is bliss, child. Remember that. She gives a neigh of annoyance that I can only assume is her asking me to let her rest.

I oblige, quickly leaving the stable with Zuira, who motions for me to follow.

"I know you won't be able to sleep tonight, and I don't believe I can either. Would you like to join me in my room until the sun rises?" she asks, her eyes wide and innocent, still full of tears from the revelation of our future.

"I'd like that," I say with a soft smile, but it's not me who responds. The real Vera is tucked away in a deep, darkened corner of my mind, allowing every horrible feeling and worried thought for the safety of those I love to overtake me. I don't care about the meaning of my ability to speak to those creatures.

I will not let someone I love die. I will put myself in the direct line of fire, and it will be me who perishes.

Not them.

Never them.

34

REVELATIONS

.*⭐ VERA ⭐*.

"**M**y mother has been planning for this day for quite some time, but I have always had my reservations," Zuira admits as she brushes and braids sections of her hair. Her vanity is larger than most people's bathroom mirrors, with lights carved into the glass. "I suppose her finally saying it aloud set the events in place. If the hippocampi speak to us, then the death of someone we love is set in stone."

She sets down the brush and stares off with unseeing eyes.

"You're sure there is no way to stop it?" I ask with little hope.

"I wish," she answers, giving me an attempt at a comforting smile. "I will keep my heart open nonetheless because I would rather feel that love and deal with the pain than forsake it all. Feeling is what makes life worth living."

A small creature appears before me, and I recognize him instantly.

"Hi, Squish," I say as he rolls into my outstretched palms. He has a folded letter attached to his belly, so I remove it.

Vera Dtari,

Flynn Laurence

There have been some developments with our plan, and I will be joining you within the next two weeks to discuss it in full. The king has grown outraged at hallac's escape along with the queen's, so I will be dealing with it for a time. As of now, the king is unaware of you or your mother's location.

Wait for my word before continuing further.

— Supreme Commander of the Adleian Regiments

His note lacks the playful flirtation I've grown to crave to draw me out of my thoughts, but I understand he must be overwhelmed trying to calm the king. I pet Squish before looking for something to use to write my response.

"Oh, here," Zuira says as she pulls out a sheet of elegant stationery and an equally ornate pen.

"Take this to Flynn Laurence," I say, and Squish coos in agreement before disappearing as quickly as he appeared. I curse myself, wishing I would've added something else, but the creature is gone before I can call him back.

"Is this Flynn perhaps a lover?" she asks with tasteful curiosity. I laugh and shake my head.

"No, just a friend," I respond with a smile, staring at my hands. I've never had a 'lover,' and I wonder if I'll know the difference between being in love and my love for a friend.

"That little grin tells me you have someone in mind, though," she says, sitting with me on the bed. "Do tell. I could use a distraction."

Zuira waits patiently for me to continue as she takes a few strands of my hair and braids them. I think of who I've possibly felt something more than friendship for.

"I can't deny that Korah's brother, Alexander, is rather handsome—someone I'm sure any girl would fall for, and with good reason. From the little time I have known him, he seems very kind and protective," I answer, and she huffs a breath, nudging me to continue.

"But I suppose I don't feel much more than friendly attraction to him. There is someone else, although I promised to be his friend," I say, imagining his onyx eyes and dark hair. Those scars that curve across his beautiful face, his eyes and jaw sharp enough to cut, and his masculine, almost sensual voice...It's hard to pretend that it's only friendship I crave.

"Well, now I'm intrigued. Continue!" She laughs as she braids more of my hair.

"He's a siren."

Her smile falls slightly, not from disgust as many others would, but from confusion.

"A siren?" she asks. I respond with a simple nod and feel color spreading over my cheeks. "I thought their species had escaped to land, living among humans."

"Adlei keeps them as slaves," I correct. This statement garners a harsh gasp from the princess. "It's horrible. So unbelievably horrible. All I know of the rest is that they stick to hiding to avoid being caught or killed by Adleian hunters," I say with a shaking voice. She grabs my hand, and I look into her wide eyes, full of compassion and sympathy.

"I pray to Naejik you will be able to keep him free from such atrocities. He is welcome here, even if my parents or people would be hesitant. Any friend of yours is a friend of mine."

"I appreciate that. I will be sure to let him know he is safe here."

She removes her hand and swims to a large window covered by thick black curtains. Peering past, she notes, "It's about an hour until daybreak."

We watch the sunrise in silence, resting our heads on each other. She pulls me into a loving hug as the sun reaches its peak.

"Come to me if you're in pain, Vera. I did not mean to listen to your confession, but I heard it nonetheless. I understand and do not fault you at all. I will be here," she says softly before letting go. "You are family in all ways that count—a sister or cousin or whatever you wish to call it," she says with a quiet laugh. Those words break past something in me, and I fight away the tears that swell in my eyes—a sister.

I've always wanted a sister.

"Thank you, Zuira," I respond as I remove myself from her arms. "I hope you will come to me too. This will be a hard burden to bear, but I know it will be easier to face it with a sister," I say with a smile so full of happiness that I forget, if only for a moment, about the horrors to come.

The Delmaris family decide a tour of Royan is in order for Korah and I. Kaileah is more than excited to see the lands she loved so much as a child, so we leave soon after first light.

The smiling faces of the citizens we pass along our tour of the kingdom do little to stop the dark hold Astryx and Zuira's words have on me. Everything feels like a blur as if my body is not my own. I watch from afar, waiting to be alone to process it all.

My mother seems happy, a nice change from the harsh edges she leaves unsmoothed to protect herself.

For her, I will pretend to enjoy her family's company because I owe her at least that much. I don't mind them, of course. Abeda is a kind-hearted queen who loves her people, and her children are the same. But I can only think about who I could lose and how it will change me.

At dinner the next day, blackened shrimp on a bed of pasta sits before me on gold and white china, but I don't have the appetite to eat it. I push it around the bowl with my fork to look like I've eaten something. I don't want to alarm anyone or have to discuss why I'm not eating.

The queen, Abeda, and the king, Wyndham, are at the table's head on either end. The king's hair is cut short with the sides fading down. He shares the same deep bronze skin as all their children and has rich brown eyes. Along the row of seats in front of me are the eldest children in order of their ages, Alabaster and Avalon, the twins who share the same handsome face with soft features. Their hair is wild and untamed, with loose curls that fall across their faces as their perfectly straight teeth shine through their smiles.

Next, Zuira's oldest sister, Saylaid, sits with perfect, refined elegance, unlike her elder brothers. She looks the most similar to her mother, their only child to have Abeda's deep blue eyes.

Her hair is kept neatly slicked back in a ponytail that explodes in volume, showing off her chestnut-highlighted curls.

In front of her face, she has two braids of hair decorated with cuffs and jewels. Hanging from her ears are two large golden hoops, and her makeup matches them with gold glitter placed on her inner corner.

To her side is the next brother, Fendrenan. His skin is brighter than the others, holding a golden shine. He keeps his jet-black hair slicked back with gel. After straightening his lapels, he takes another bite of food.

He is by far the most beautiful of the brothers.

Next is Zuira, sitting as elegant as Saylaid but smiling and conversing, in contrast to her sister's graceful silence. Zuira keeps her hair down, her beautiful curls falling across her shoulders and back, and small braids with beads, jewels, and golden rings scattered throughout. Other than the playful banter of Alabaster and Avalon, she leads the table-wide conversations, and I can tell she has the potential to take her mother's place due to her undeniable charisma and grace.

Finally, the youngest fraternal twin girls, Gardenya and Serena, are last. While not identical, their faces are noticeably similar. Gardenya has her hair in a large bun with curls taken out to fall across her face, and Serena keeps her hair tight, with coiled twists like vines falling across her shoulders and flowers placed throughout.

"Hey, Saylaid," Avalon says, nudging his twin with a wink.

"What?" she asks without interest.

"You gonna finish that?" he asks, and before she can say no, he begins devouring her food without having finished his own. She breaks her composure and slaps him before shoving his face into his bowl as punishment.

"*Saunniazun!*" Saylaid screams before composing herself. She then takes a delicate bite, ignoring the complete shock plastered on everyone's faces who could understand. Even Korah seems surprised, and she can speak minimal Saanien.

Avalon and Alabaster try to keep from laughing at her response, likely having planned for that reaction. Avalon doesn't bother wiping the sauce off, which now covers his hair and face. It almost looks like he has white highlights now. I would usually find it amusing, but I just feel numb to it all. The quiet silence, the laughing, the compliments, and the kind remarks all feel like nothing.

"Do learn to control yourself, Saylaid," Fendrenan says, never breaking his neutral face. "You know they only do such things to get a reaction." Saylaid glares at her brother.

"Oh, aren't you all high and mighty, you perfect, polished little—" Saylaid begins before her father cuts her off by clearing his throat and shaking his head. Fendrenan smirks ever so slightly before continuing to eat in silence. He can claim his brothers crave her reactions, but that smirk tells me he loves it, too.

"Vera," Serena says. "Would you mind if I asked you about your life before you came here?" I nod, although I wish I could have told her no. I don't feel like socializing, much less talking about the life I miss. "What are your human parents like? Are they as animalistic as the legends say?"

I furrow my brows, unaware of the preconceptions about humans.

"They are as animalistic as you would consider yourself. My parents were as perfect as they could be," I answer, and she stares for a while longer than I'd like.

"Oh, okay. I mean, they have to be pretty terrible for Naejik to have cast them out of our world. Are you sure they aren't worse than our kind?" I take a deep breath before responding, feeling my temper rising.

"Humans are just as capable of evil as mer are. I am unaware of the full legends, but I would assume they made a mistake that any other race would have been capable of making," I say with an irritation I hope conveys that I don't wish to speak on the subject any longer.

"Humans are known as the most evil of all creatures. They are said to hunger for the pain of others," Serena pushes further, clearly not getting the hint. Her parents converse quietly on each end of the table, unaware of our discussion.

"You do realize I am a part of the people you speak of? Sirens are regarded the same, and from my experience, they are as kind as anyone else. Humans are no different than you. I assure you." My voice is strained, and I feel that familiar bubbling rise. I shove it down with the last of my energy and find myself fading out of the conversations again, only vaguely listening.

"Serena, I've told you countless times to watch your words. How would you like it if someone spoke about our race that way?" Zuira warns in a stern voice. Serena sighs.

"Sorry, Vera, I didn't mean to upset you," she apologizes, and I lack the energy to respond. I push around the food on my plate again. I suppose Zuira notices because she removes herself from her seat and speaks directly to me.

"Vera, would you like me to show you around the castle? I know we spent the day showcasing the kingdom, but I realized you've never explored where you're staying." She offers me a comforting smile before turning to her father. "May we excuse ourselves?"

Her father nods, and we head back to my room. Before we are out of earshot, I notice conversation booms in my absence.

Kaileah laughs and smiles, Saylaid rolls her eyes and speaks, the twin girls giggle to each other, and the twin boys talk to my mother like siblings. I realize it then: Avalon and Alabaster are my mother's age, so they must have grown up together.

I am not needed here.

I can't remember if I spoke to Zuira along the way, but I only find myself aware when I'm alone in my room, staring at those shining marble floors and the moonlight streaming through the windows.

Squish appears before me, and I can't even form a smile at the creature I usually love to see. I take the letter from his chest, and his eyes are filled with sympathy as he curls into my lap as I read.

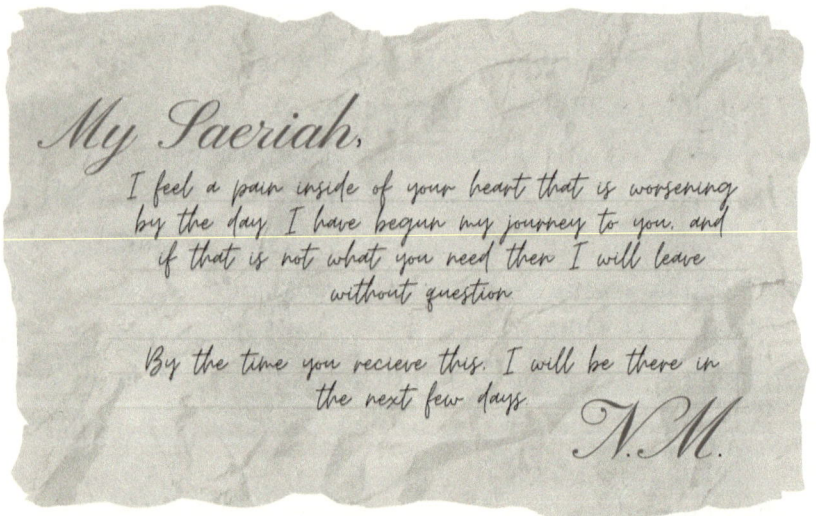

My Saeriah,

I feel a pain inside of your heart that is worsening by the day. I have begun my journey to you, and if that is not what you need then I will leave without question

By the time you recieve this, I will be there in the next few days.

N.M.

I stare at the letter and feel a slight prospect of happiness. I knew I was not wrong to trust and care for him as I have tried to do. He has no obligation to my happiness, yet he chooses to come? I don't understand it.

How can he know everything I feel all the time? How far can

he see into my head? Can he hear what I think? I don't have the energy to think about the matter any longer.

I stare at the ceiling for a while, counting the multicolored tiles.

One. Pink.

Two. Blue.

Three. Green.

The numbers and colors blend together as sleep takes me, and part of me wonders what would happen if I never woke up at all.

35

TO HAVE STRENGTH

.*⭐ VERA ⭐*.

I skipped breakfast.

Lunch did not sound appealing.

Dinner is quickly approaching, and I still feel no hunger, no motivation, and I haven't even removed myself from bed. The overwhelming comfort I found in this bed the first night has disappeared, so now it is nothing more than a place to sleep.

A knock on my door has me sitting up, the most movement I've done since yesterday. I have no energy to open it. Instead, I hope they will leave.

Unfortunately, the door opens, and my mother swims in, a hand to her mouth as she sees what I look like.

"Vera," my mother says with exasperation. "Are you okay? Are you sick?" She places the back of her hand on my forehead, and the coolness soothes me. "Well, you're not feverish. Sweetheart, what's wrong?"

"I don't know."

It's true. I don't know what is wrong with my stupid body for making me feel like this. I hate it. Every second I spend in my bed makes me feel useless for being so lazy, but I can't get up.

Useless.

That's all I've become: a worthless waste of space.

What if it's my parents who die? I can't live without them. I haven't seen them in almost a month.

What if the witches find them?

They promised to kill them if I ever found out what I was.

"When was the last time you ate?" Her voice gains an edge. I struggle to remember, but I suppose it was probably...*Oh gods, it's been that long.*

"Dinner," is all I can muster. "Two days ago."

"Vera!" she yells, grabbing my arm and leading me to the bathroom. I see myself with a sunken face, a hunger ravaging my skin. My skin is pale, and my green eyes, which used to be so full of color, are dull.

Kaileah brushes my hair and helps me change into something presentable before pulling me into the kitchen. I dissociate, watching her prepare something while shooing away the staff for privacy.

She places a dish before me, but I can't tell what it is. She sits beside me, taking a piece of bread and putting it in my mouth. She begs me to chew, and I oblige. It takes more willpower than it should to swallow it, and I instantly feel nauseous.

I clutch my mouth to keep from vomiting, and Kaileah rubs my back in a gentle, circular motion.

"Please tell me it's just my awful cooking making you nauseous," she says with a partial smile. I can't return it.

"It tastes fine," I answer. She takes my hands and pushes a piece of hair from my eyes.

"Tell me what you're thinking. Something has happened. Just let me in so I can help you," she pleads. I try to respond, but no words come out. "My baby, please."

"I can hear the hippocampus," I'm able to push out, and my mother nods in understanding. "I can't lose someone I love. I won't make it."

She pulls me into a hug that I struggle to reciprocate, but her love is enough for us both. She smooths my hair, doesn't say a word, and gives me time to myself. As a minute passes, I pull her closer and let the tears that felt so far away now escape.

"It's okay. I'm here. I'll always be here as long as you allow me to," she says. I begin to choke on my cries, pulling her even closer. She starts to sing in Adleian, and I recognize the words—the song she dedicated to me all those years ago.

The one I thought I had written when I felt compelled to play it.

"*Haenur ti'deōrin,*" she begins, and I find myself understanding. *No matter the time we go.*

"My love for you will only grow," I whisper, continuing her verse. She lets out a sharp breath and runs a hand through my hair.

"*Jaenōrjik tekōnah naehiema,*" she continues, a slight stutter developing in her voice. *You're safe with me, my dear.* My tears slow, and I feel a light growing within me. I feel her words inside my heart—a majick like no other. "*Nō'laihmi kenjaei,*" she sings, her voice breaking. *I'll keep you close for all your years.*

"*Cōur saeraih, tekōnah.*" Her words have become so mumbled only my memory of her song allows me to follow. *Come, my princess, to me now.* "*No'friunda yaeurōi.*" *You'll be safe, oh, don't you frown.* She finishes her song, and I look at her face to see her eyes red with tears.

I take another few bites of the food she made for me, and she smiles, never leaving my side. I lean on her shoulder, and she allows me to sit with her silently.

Only then do I realize how alone I was before.

As the morning sun streams through my tall windows, I hear a knock on the door. I open it to the happy faces of Korah and Zuira waiting for me.

"Vera, you *have* to come with us!" Korah exclaims as she rushes inside.

"Korah, darling, you have to tell her where we want to go," Zuira says with a playful roll of her eyes. Korah's cheeks flush a deep crimson, and I feel like I could almost laugh. Kaileah brought a small light into the shadows of my mind that had blocked me from feeling.

"I—Yes! Right!" Korah clears her throat before continuing. "Alabaster and Avalon are about to joust on the hippocampi! This is going to be absolutely hilarious." Her smile is so happy that I wish I could return it.

"For context," Zuira starts. "They have never done this before, and I foresee it being *quite* the sight. Kaileah is coming." She nudges me, and I begin to smile slightly at the visual. Her eyes plead with me, begging me to listen. She walks past and whispers so only I can hear, "You're fading. Come with me."

I stare at her in silent understanding. She feels the same pain as me, and I wish I could be as strong as she is. I wish I could let myself love knowing what will happen.

"I'll get ready," I say, and Korah nearly throws me down with an excited hug.

"Yay!" she screams, and I find myself laughing—a real laugh.

As we make our way out, I'm nearly blinded by the bright sun shining directly down on us, not obstructed by any clouds. I understand why the many men and women wear head coverings and hold parasols for shade. I feel my skin growing hot like I have laid out too long at the beach.

Zuira rubs a cream on my skin that instantly cools me.

"It's our form of sunscreen," she says with a smile as she rubs it into my back and arms. "I won't put it where you can reach." She hands me the container as all that is left is my chest, neck, and abdomen.

"I wouldn't have cared," I say with a slight laugh, and the lightest red develops on Zuira's cheeks. *Oh*, I think, as I realize why she likely did not want to touch such areas.

Korah quickly volunteers to help Zuira, perhaps a little too quickly, yet the princess does not decline.

The crowd hushes as we make our way to the front, getting a front-row seat to see the disaster of two twin princes dueling. Kaileah takes her seat beside me, and she places a knowing hand on my tail. I reassure her, letting her know I will be okay in time.

"Did you eat breakfast?" she asks quietly. I nod my head, and she sighs in relief. "Good," she says, kissing my forehead. "Now, get ready to laugh. These boys will be the death of me. I'm glad my daughter has some sense about her, at least." She squeezes my arm slightly. At that moment, it feels real, like I've grown up with Kaileah as my mother for all these years.

Alabaster lines up on the right-hand side, readying his deep-emerald hippocampus with iridescent scales. His chest plate matches his steed, and he taunts his brother on the other end. Avalon has a light blue band of metal across his shoulders and chest that matches the hippocampus he rides.

They ready themselves and rush forward, yelling at each other in their native language before crashing their poles into the other. They're both flung off their creatures and sent uncontrollably spinning before hitting a nearby stone wall. I put a hand to my mouth as Kaileah bursts into laughter.

They try again, and before they can start, Kaileah screams, "You suck, Avie!" Avalon glares at her, flipping her off before readying himself again. "Bassy, you're just as uncoordinated as you ever were!" She laughs again as Alabaster gives her a similar glare and gesture.

I find it strange that my mother would have nicknames for these men, but considering they grew up at the same time, they probably feel like her brothers. Oh gods, that means they could be my father's age. I look to my mother's pale skin and then to my tanned skin, a possible combination of the two.

My birth father is dead. What am I thinking?

The princes are sent flying again, but they don't remount their hippocampi this time and instead take the battle hand-to-hand. They throw deflected punch after punch, and I share in my mother's laughter.

"This is what you get for kissing my girl!" Avalon yells as he lands a punch that does minor damage. Alabaster laughs with a wicked smirk.

"It's not my fault I have the same face." He bellows a laugh as he dodges another hit. "Either way, she knew it was me. Clearly, she's not loyal enough!" He keeps laughing, and Avalon grows even more angry.

"They're not all they're cracked up to be. That being said, I *was* fourteen—" I shoot Kaileah a glance as she keeps talking, my eyes widening.

"Do you mean you—with them? Did...do I even want to know?" I say, and Kaileah gives me a nefarious look.

"You know how teenagers are. It was bound to happen at some point in my time here." She gives me a look, implying I've done the same. "She probably wanted to see if the other one was just as bad!" Kaileah jests with the two boys again, and they both turn to her and start yelling back.

"You take that back!" Avalon starts before his brother continues for him.

"That's not—How would you even know that?" He glares at his brother, and Kaileah responds with a wink. "Really, dude?" Alabaster asks as he shoves his twin. Avalon shrugs and asks his brother if their fighting is done. They swim back to the palace with their arms slung around each other like they didn't just brawl.

"What was that?" I ask with a chuckle.

"They have this thing where almost every girl they've ever been with has also been with the other. It's pretty funny, honestly," Kaileah responds, adjusting her outfit and removing herself from her seat. "I'll see you later. Spend some time with your friends," she says with a smile that I return. "I'm going to check on those two."

"Probably for the best," I respond as she leaves.

The town quiets, and my happiness has grown dim once again. I want to retreat into my room and forget about it all.

I've used up my energy for the day, so I begin swimming back before I spot something in the shadows of the kingdom. It's someone I could never forget: my siren.

"Vera?" he asks as I enter the darkest part of the building's shadow. I pull him into enough light to see the beautiful features that I've grown to memorize. The curve of his nose is like a mountain falling into a glacier spring. His deep, abyssal brown eyes, so sharp and slender, always calm my raging thoughts.

"Vera." He says my name like a plea, begging me to explain.

I can't.

I can barely hold his unwavering gaze, much less expel everything I feel.

"Can't you just look inside my mind?" I ask, and he shakes his head.

"I only feel what you feel. I don't know the cause," he says, running the back of his hand along my cheek. "You have to let me know." I fight the urge to pull him to me, to tell him everything I feel for him.

"Nallac, I—" My voice catches as I stare at his full, soft lips and how he watches me with a kindness I've never seen.

Just kiss me.

He swallows deeply before waiting again for me to explain.

"Someone I love will die. I don't know who. I don't know when. I don't know what to do." I say the last words in a whisper.

"Look at me, Vera," he pleads, and I obey. "You will get through this. You are stronger than you know, and you will survive. Yes, someone you love will die, but do you know what else it means when the hippocampus speaks to you?" he asks, and I'm shocked at how he knew. "It means that you will make it through. It means that through that pain, you will become someone greater." He takes my hands, and I furrow my brows.

I look down at our interlocked hands and feel warmth running into my chest and through my veins.

"But how?" I ask. "I'm scared, Nallac." He moves his hands to my arms, moving higher as he keeps my line of sight.

"I know," is all he says, but it's enough. I believe he knows. I believe that his experiences are worse than mine will ever be, and he is here. He's okay.

I can be okay.

I will stay strong.

"We leave tomorrow morning," Nallac announces, glancing over my shoulder at the passing Jelleans. "To see your parents. I sent them word to return to where you left them." I gasped, not able to believe such a thing could be possible.

"How?" is all I can manage, with a million thoughts running through my head.

"That doesn't matter. Just pack your things and inform anyone you wish. I don't care what they say. We're going," he speaks with authority, but there's a caring soul unlike anyone else beneath it. Still holding my hands, he looks around, almost worried, and I try to understand why.

"Zuira said you're safe here. You don't need to hide in the shadows any longer."

The mental wall he keeps stacked high enough to reach from the bottom of the ocean to the top of a wave's crest cracks, and I catch a glimpse of who he is.

I see the softened man who loves so strongly that it hurts him.

I see the pain of being cast out of society.

I see the burden of caring for his family as a child.

And above it all, I see the way he looks at me. I see the fire in his eyes—the mirror to my own.

"Thank you, my *saeraih*." He bows to me, and I stop him.

"No. You will never bow to me," I say as I lower myself to him, just like the first time I uttered that phrase. "You are my equal in every way. I will forever be in your debt for saving me countless times." He lifts my chin and brings me back to his level before embracing me.

"I don't deserve you," he whispers under his breath, the heat tickling the shell of my ear. It sends a chill down my spine that I try to hide.

"You do, Nallac. You deserve everything." I kiss his cheek before turning, sure I would have made him uncomfortable. I curse myself for being so foolish.

His hand grips my arm, pulling me closer as he grabs my face and devours me with his eyes. He takes in every piece of me before pressing his lips to mine in a kiss that sends my vision spinning. The soft touch of his lips, the way his large, smooth hands run through the back of my hair before grabbing at the back of my neck, and how his other trails a line down my back to rest on my waist.

"*Nallac—*" I breathe as I throw my arms around him, desperate to deepen it.

He obliges, pushing me against the wall and taking my mouth with his own. He knows exactly what I want, *exactly what I need.* One arm is laid above me to brace himself, and the other cradles my head to keep from hitting stone. The way his tongue trails along mine sends me deeper into an overwhelming ecstasy.

My heart explodes with a light that brightens my darkest parts, filling the hole like liquid gold. A wave of power shreds away the darkness of the building's shadow, and I don't care. I don't care who sees, who watches, who knows. All I want is him in this moment for the rest of my life.

"Vera, gods, you're *perfect,*" he says in between kisses, moaning into my mouth as he pulls me closer. I can't help but do the same.

He finally breaks to move to my neck, and I gasp as the intensity sends me nearly unconscious. His mouth betrays him as the sounds of his enjoyment overshadow my own, and I pull him back to me.

"Don't you ever stop," I say, and he looks at me with the grin of a predator ready to devour its kill.

"I wouldn't dream of it, princess," he says with a voice that caresses every inch of me. I can't think. The only thing in my head is him, his smell, his skin, his lips, his *taste*. It feels like this moment has lasted an eternity and only a second all at once.

"Vera?" a voice calls, breaking me from my trance. I peer around the corner and see Korah looking for me.

"It's probably for the best that we stopped," Nallac says, coming from behind me and kissing the shell of my ear. "I don't know how much longer I could have resisted…" He trails a delicate finger across my shoulder, and I melt beneath him. "…doing something more."

"You don't know what the sound of your voice does to me," I say over my shoulder with a grin.

"I think I do." He smiles, and my cheeks flush a deep red as I realize he knows *everything* I feel. He kisses my cheek before continuing. "Don't be embarrassed. There's a reason I sounded the way I did just now. Everything you felt doubled my own desires."

My embarrassment falls away, and I can't help but wish I could have experienced the same. To feel every desire he had for me—I don't think I would have contained myself.

36

THE THINGS WE KEEP INSIDE

.*⭑ NALLAC ⭑*.

S itting at a round table in the sunroom, nursing a cup of hot black coffee, I wonder, *What the living hell did I do yesterday?* I pulled her to me. I kissed her. I didn't even ask. Then I teased her. What is *wrong* with me?

I mean, I'd be an absolute idiot to deny that she enjoyed it. She practically begged me to keep going, but I can't help feeling guilty. My hands shake on my mug as I worry about the next time I'm alone with her.

I won't take advantage of her.

I won't let that happen again. She needs to stay as far away from me as possible.

I'm a plague in her life—a disease.

Her mother and friends insisted they spend this last day with her to help her pack and say their goodbyes. It's a bit dramatic if you ask me. She's not going to die in my care—*that* I am certain of. Although it has, fortunately or unfortunately, kept us from talking about the situation at hand.

I haven't seen her since that moment, and I couldn't sleep last night, replaying it over and over.

Her taste was heavenly, like warm vanilla and sugar. It was everything sweet and delicate and divine. I can still feel her tongue against mine, the tender push of her lips, the way she bit mine without realizing it. It sends me into another world, and I want to stay there, with her, for the rest of time.

I want to inhale her delicious scent and feel the way her hair brushes across my chest. I want those soft, full lips to run across every inch of my skin. I want her to touch me anywhere she desires, to claim me as hers, but I can't take away the memory that touch brings.

The guards' relentless torture, the king's assaults, and all the times Daevia would bring me to her room and—

I don't want to remember it.

I can't taint the memory of Vera's touch with thoughts of that vile woman.

As my coffee grows cold, I hear the familiar sound of my princess's voice.

"I'll be okay. I promise," she reassures someone as they continue to fawn over her, entering the sunroom.

She looks absolutely ravishing. Half of her hair is braided into a crown decorated with sapphires and rubies, along with silver cuffs and hoops. The other half of her black curls are down and full of small braids decorated in a similar fashion, and atop her head is a white-gold tiara placed perfectly within her hair to hold it in place.

It looks as if it was made for only her to wear. From the stones and the carvings to the details and pearls, it would over-shadow the appearance of a lesser woman. Luckily for her, Vera is far from it.

Her eyes are painted with a purple shadow and shimmer that makes her glisten as if her very skin is made of stars. Her lips are a deep red, and I have to stop myself from removing every bit of the paint, but I am incapable of resisting the urge to stare at the way it makes them look even more delicious than before, like a perfect apple waiting for me to sink my teeth into it.

"Vera, you look simply stunning," I say so only she can hear. I see that blush I love so much run across her cheeks, and it sends my stomach turning. "If I can ask without offending anyone," I start before Zuira raises her eyebrows in a silent warning. "Why are you so dressed up for a day's travel?"

She sighs with a look at Kaileah and Korah.

"We just thought that Vera's parents would like to see how she looks as a princess, *and,*" Korah says, pointing an accusing finger at Vera. "Vera agreed. She even suggested wearing the tiara!" A partial smile tugs at my lips as Vera side-eyes her friend.

"I said it would be *pretty*. I did not say 'yes, please, put this in my hair for my journey,'" Vera corrects with feigned annoyance. Korah flaps her hands as Vera talks, mouthing a *blah blah blah* before Vera playfully shoves her. "But yes, I did agree. I would love for my parents to see this part of me. I want them to see the woman I'm becoming."

She smiles at me, and that change I sensed in her remains.

Her darkness is at bay for now, and I will do anything for that to stay true.

"Nallac," Kaileah says in a strained voice, clearly struggling to stay cordial. "I'd like to talk to you for a moment. *Alone.*" I feel in her heart that beneath the malice she always holds for me is a different emotion—a mother's love.

"Mother," Vera warns, giving Kaileah a stern look. Kaileah rolls her eyes with a smile.

"I won't bite," she responds, and Vera simply narrows her eyes as the two of us move away. "Without a good reason," she adds in a whisper. "If she dies, I will skin you alive and make any torture the king and his lackeys have ever subjected you to look like child's play. Do you understand?" Kaileah asks with an intensity that would send any other man shrinking in fear.

"I would sooner skin myself before letting any harm befall her. If she dies, it will be because I was already killed trying to protect her." I bow to her even as my pride pushes against it. She stares in silent examination, and I wait for her sigh before returning from my bow.

"Take care of her," she says with kindness, placing a hand on my arm that I fight like hell not to rip off. "I can't lose her again." Vera gives me a look that reads, *Well, how did that go?* I nod, and a wave of relief washes over her.

"Good luck, sister. I hope you find the answers you need," Zuira says with a knowing smile in Vera's direction. The sincerity of her words hits me like a rogue wave. Vera pulls her into a quick hug and whispers something I can't hear.

The kingdom is full of so much color. I find it almost overstimulating, with the bright sun blasting down on me like a spotlight, and I can barely see as we make our way to the exit. My mind was too overshadowed by the worry of being seen to have truly looked before—to have seen its true beauty.

I can't remember the last time I was...safe. I can't remember the last time I didn't watch my surroundings at every moment, sticking to the shadows, waiting for darkness.

It's beautiful.

The streets, the shops, the way the sun dances across the buildings and our skin, it's nothing like the darkness I am used to.

But at the same time, there's something so serene about the night sky. The way the stars are reflected by the waves makes the ocean floor look as though it's made of glittering stardust. The way the moon sends beams of silver light that bend and break, reflecting and refracting like a path meant to be followed.

The sun is beautiful, and the day brings undeniable happiness.

But the night is home.

The night is a blanket of protection—a veil that allows us to be who we want to be without fear of what the next day will bring. The night is full of dreams, memories, and hope for the future. For change. For growth.

As we exit the kingdom, I find that blissful daydream quickly ends as I take up my watchful eye. I try to focus on our surroundings, but all I can think about is the way Vera's eyes sparkle as she blinks, the way her lips touch and part as she speaks, and the way she fiddles with the rings that now adorn her fingers.

Her hands are long and slender, delicately bending and curving like the statue of a goddess reaching out for a mortal's gift.

Every movement she makes takes all of my attention, from the way she adjusts her curls falling across her shoulders to the way she pulls at the dress that hugs her full figure in all the right places.

The deep, rich blue perfectly contrasts with her golden skin like the sand of a beach at sunset, and the silver embroidered swirls and curves and flowers make her look ethereal.

She is meant for our world. In every way, she is meant for it.

Riding on the back of two hippocampi, I notice the watchful silver eye of Vera's. I remember her name being Astryx, her coat a nearly pure white with iridescent scales that shift their colors depending on the way the sun hits her.

Mine is a light blue male that does little to set his personality apart from the average, but Vera's is nothing like I've seen before. She looks at me like she can read every thought I've ever had, and I feel myself growing uneasy.

"Astryx said to stop staring at her. She said it makes it easier to see your past and future," Vera says, more nonchalantly than she should at such a statement. At least she seems to have accepted the fact that they can speak to her.

"Oh, right," I reply, removing my gaze from the creature and returning it to Vera. The hippocampus exhales a breath and shakes its head. "I'm sorry, but did you just say she can see my future?"

"She's not like the others. She knows things beyond our comprehension. I mean, that's what she said, at least." Vera leans down and rubs Astryx's neck, and the creature seems to relax slightly. "She said sorry. That you have a very sad life but that it will get better," Vera says with a half-hearted smile. I see beneath it.

She feels a developing pain, not from herself but from the implication of what it means for a creature of such knowledge to reveal that information.

"I am perfectly fine, *saeraih*. There is nothing to worry your heart about," I respond to her with my best attempt at a comforting smile, but I worry it falls short. I forget what it means to smile. Astryx exhales again in a fashion that I can only interpret as a laugh. "Are you laughing at me?" I ask, directing my line of questioning at the creature.

She looks at me and neighs. *Yes, I am,* a voice says in my head, and my heart sinks.

"Astryx!" Vera says with exasperation. "Why would you do that? I never knew you to be cruel." The princess turns her soft gaze to me before clarifying. "She just wanted to scare you by responding in your head. She said you will not hold my same fate and that there is nothing to worry about."

The hippocampus nods in agreement before returning to her path, and I feel for her. A creature that holds so much knowledge and pain must feel as if there is no escape. Perhaps it was her attempt at a joke to alleviate that pain, and we retaliated too quickly.

If only I could tell her that I could not care less for my pain.

I understand the feeling of exclusion, and I wonder if those scars across her face and body are something that she, too, wishes to undo. Memories of the past that mark us as victims of the world's twisted games.

Astryx stares at me again, this time in confusion, and I wonder how something all-knowing could be at a loss.

I apologize for scaring you earlier and for speaking to you now. I meant what Vera translated. You are not like her and the others. In this war, you will not lose someone you love, but I needed to tell you something. The creature's voice is like the caress of a lullaby. It dances through my head like soundwaves, wishing to be heard in every fractured corner of my mind.

You have understood me in a way that none have in quite some time, and you remind me of someone I lost so very long ago. For that, I had to thank you in my own words. She blinks slowly, and I feel her, the sadness, the regret, the loss, the love...I feel the pain she holds for the person she speaks of.

I wish I could have met the person who holds such a strong place in her heart, as I feel it breaks at her memory.

Her name was Elvira. Elvira, I recognize it, but no. That would be impossible. Surely, it is another with the same name. *Your first thought is correct, Broken One.*

Naejik's daughter from millennia ago. When Vera said she was not like the others of her kind, she meant it. This creature's immortality is the only explanation for such a thing being possible.

My mother always taught me that a hippocampus is not able to speak to a mer unless they are to lose someone they love in the near future. They are bound by majick, and they are bound to never lie. Withholding the truth, yes, but never to lie. How, I wonder, is she able to speak to me then?

I am indeed unlike others of my kind, and if I deem it necessary to speak to a mortal without following the rules, then I can. Before you ask, I followed the rules when speaking to your princess. A small hope that began simmering like a small flame is doused before it has the chance to grow beyond a spark.

For the next hour, Astryx is silent, and I find myself almost missing the soft embrace of the creature's voice. I felt like I wasn't alone—like someone else was shifting through the broken shards of glass in my mind and heart.

"Nallac," Vera says, and the sound of my name rolling off her tongue sends an intense wave through me. I want to beg her to say it over and over for the rest of our lives. Gone are the days I wished to hide it, like a small part of who I really was safely hidden.

"Yes?"

"Are you feeling tired?" she asks. She twirls her hair and avoids eye contact, so I sense she won't ask to rest unless I say I'm feeling the same. Her arms must be sore from gripping Astryx's mane for so long.

"Yeah, I am," I answer and see her let out a breath of relief. I make little work of spotting a cave with a small enough entrance to only fit one of us at a time, but the inside is large enough for two. It will keep us hidden from anyone who might be tracking our movements.

I lay out two sleeping sacks, and she wastes no time jumping into hers. She turns to the side and shivers as a cold wave washes in.

I can't do this anymore.

"Vera, come here."

She jerks her head to see me lying with my bag opened for her. She doesn't decline, and our bodies are pressed so close I can feel her heartbeat mimicking my own, growing steadily faster.

I see how she stares at me with a hunger for more than just warmth. It takes everything in my power to keep my hands to myself.

I will not take advantage of her.

She deserves more than I can give her.

She searches my eyes, and disappointment floods her before she lays her head on my chest and falls fast asleep. I stay awake longer, my body growing hotter as I imagine the places those lips had been last night and where they are now. I can feel every spot where her hands and skin touch me, and I cannot breathe.

A WALL BREAKS

.*✯ NALLAC ✯*.

The morning sun streams through the cave's opening and jolts me awake. Vera is sound asleep against my chest, her arm draped across my shoulder, as my heart races. Her hair is messy, but somehow, it makes her even more beautiful. How her mouth parts as she sleeps and how she nuzzles her head closer with each wave sends my head spinning.

I gently pry us apart and make breakfast, taking out the portable stove and a can of vegetable and fish stew. I stir until it bubbles before turning off the heat and allowing it to simmer for a while longer.

The hippocampi are likely starving, so I bring them fruit, vegetables, and grains Korah pre-portioned for each. They enjoy their meal, and I reach out a hand to the majestic ivory beast.

She stares, reading me more than I can fathom before she lowers her head and closes her eyes. Aside from the various indentions and abrasions from her many scars, her skin is remarkably smooth.

I sense the princess rising, so I return and see her rubbing her eyes and yawning.

Gods above, she's adorable.

She smiles before adjusting her dress and hair as best she can without a mirror.

"Here," I say before moving behind her and taking apart the braided crown. "I learned how to braid hair long ago because Valerie refused to go more than an hour without having hers out of her face. She would throw a fit if she had a single strand touching her."

I laugh. I actually laugh, and Vera notices, smiling broader than I have seen in some time.

I rebraid it, adding the crystals, jewels, cuffs, and gems as I go until the plaited crown looks the same as it did yesterday—perhaps even better.

"You miss her a lot, don't you?" she asks with a soft hand on my tail. I don't pull away. Instead, I continue to style her hair like muscle memory.

"Yes. More than I could ever explain." I remember my sister's laugh, jokes, and thoughts. I remember how I kept her innocence for so long, but all I can think about is that black that began forming on her tail the last time I saw her.

She is beautiful. So beyond beautiful, and I wish more than anything that I could've seen her grow into the woman she is now. I should have been there.

"I'd like to meet her one day. If you'll allow me, of course," Vera says, keeping her eyes on me, analyzing and watching for anything she can uncover. I wish I could convince myself it was for a nefarious purpose, trying to find a weakness she can use to break me, but I know it's not true. "Perhaps I can bring her characters to life with my art, and speaking of it, do you still have that book of hers? *Lē'reöan Aełuntūnda*, I think it was."

I nod. I never go anywhere without it. Her pronunciation was better than expected, but it could use a little work. Nonetheless, hearing her speak my native tongue fills my heart in ways I can't explain.

"Would you like me to read it to you?" I ask, sensing her question.

"That's incredible," she says with an impressed shake of her head. "I wonder if it will ever not shock me how you always know. But yes, I would love that."

I take the book from my bag, and the golden edges and title come to life. A piece of my sister's creation. A piece of her I'll always keep close to my heart.

"How about this," I start, moving to pour a healthy serving of the stew into her bowl and the rest in mine. "You eat, and I'll read while you do."

"I'd like that."

I devour the meal before me, the most I've had in days, before taking the book and opening to the first page.

"There is something so strange about death, the way it consumes and devours our being until not even a soul remains." I pause, not fully remembering how this story began, and I wonder if my sister was trying to push past her own trauma from our father.

Vera sits, completely intrigued, waiting for me to continue.

I read for a while longer, the two of us forgetting about everything except my sister's words. I didn't realize when Vera had finished her meal, but she moved to sit at my side at some point. She skims the words and symbols before me even though she could not begin to understand them.

"How you can read and translate so quickly baffles me," she says, touching the indented letters. "I mean, Adleian is so different from Common. I'm surprised you can flip between the two so easily."

"This isn't Adleian," I correct, and it catches her attention. "It's Ƚi'Drēv'ön, the lost language of the sirens." She takes the book from me, analyzing the letters and words with newfound vigor, searching for something.

"This is the same language Flynn writes his notes in."

This time, it's my turn to look surprised.

"He *what?*" I ask, and she nods her head, still confused. "How could he have possibly learned such a thing? It's been banned from all libraries, schools, texts..." My voice trails off as I try to remember Flynn's features, from the color of his tail to his ears. He's smart, he sees things...is he part siren?

That's impossible because he could not enter Taelani until Kaileah lifted the barrier.

Unless he lied to lead me astray.

Perhaps Vera is mistaken, but Ƚi'Drēv'ön is so unique there is no way she could have connected the two unless it *was* the same. That being said, she at first believed it was Adleian, but I suppose at first glance it can look the same without analyzing it, but—

"Nallac?" Vera breaks me from my trance. "You okay?"

"Sorry. I was lost in thought," I respond, moving to pack up our things. "Are you sure?"

"About Flynn? Yeah, I'm pretty sure. Unless there's another dead language that resembles Ƚi'Drēv'ön." She shrugs and helps gather the last of our items, shoving them into the large bag I brought. "And how many languages can *you* speak?" she asks, almost worried.

"Well, Ƚi'Drēv'ön is my native, then Common, of course, then Adleian, and I found the Celestian language quite fascinating, so

I learned it. Other than that, just bits and pieces that I've picked up from various conversations."

Her face drops.

"I'm so jealous," she whines, letting herself flop to the floor and spread out her arms. "Is that the norm here?" she asks. "To be fluent in everything?" I stifle a smirk before responding.

"I wouldn't say it's inherently *normal*, but it's not uncommon to at least know two languages. One's native and then Common." She gives me a squinted look with tight-pressed lips.

"And you and Flynn have to be all special with a fluency in four languages. ONE OF THEM BEING A DEAD ONE," she yells with flailed arms. "I'm over here with a single language. Not two, not three, and sure as hell not four. Just Common. I mean, listen to its name. Common...like it's so normal to speak it! Urgh!"

She pushes her face on top of our bag of supplies to muffle her sounds.

"Hey, I may speak many languages, but I'm not the direct descendant of a goddess," I say with a short laugh, and she turns to glare at me. "I'm not an all-powerful sorceress that can bend the world to her will if she so chooses."

"Yeah, but you're the most powerful siren to ever exist," she remarks, and I'm taken aback. "My mother told me. You are the only one of your kind that can heal someone on the brink of death. You're the only one who can *feel* exactly what others do. *And*," she says, now having moved to be in front of me with a pointed finger, "you can deal an ungodly amount of pain and damage without so much as a single touch. Talk to me again about how my power is greater than that," she finishes, and I feel a sense of pride that I've never connected to my power before.

I never put together the scope of my distinction. While I

always knew there was something inherently different about me, I never knew I was greater than my counterparts. Perhaps that's why I could break the binding, and my father never could.

"Anyway." She rolls her eyes with a smile. "I'm just glad I'm on the good side of that power."

I take her hand and kiss it while slowly looking up, which sends her smile falling and a redness to her cheeks.

"You are the safest person alive from that power," I say with a curve of my lips, barely more than a straight line. "Now, anyone who harms you, on the other hand." The curve turns wicked. "They would be killed before they could even scream for mercy."

She blushes and laughs. I stare at that beautiful crimson that paints across her face and listen to her delicate laugh.

I find it hard to breathe.

The look of her, the sound of her, the way she doesn't fear me...I don't understand it. It's unlike me to not understand. I see and analyze everything, yet she baffles me time and time again like my own personal puzzle.

We continue our journey, and I notice her fidgeting with her many rings and bracelets. I've learned it's her way to gain the courage to ask me something.

"Was there something you wanted to ask?" I break the silence, and she jerks slightly.

"Oh, I mean, I was just wondering something," she starts before looking off. "That day I met you in the cave, you didn't look like yourself."

"A siren can take three forms: siren, human, and monster. I apologize you had to witness the latter."

"And why haven't you used it since?"

"Feeling how I do now, I would rather you never saw it in the first place. Forgive me for not wanting to show the true scope of what I am," I answer plainly, and she huffs an annoyed breath.

"Bold of you to think I would be so shallow and judge you on your appearance," she clarifies, and I glance in her direction to see her crossing her arms. Adorable.

"I know you wouldn't. I felt it that day when you saw me. You weren't scared of me even before you knew what I was—it's like you could see right through me. You brought out the person I thought was long gone." I pause and see her watching with interest, as if anything I reveal to her will be the most interesting thing. "I think something changed in me that day. Without a single word, you convinced me there was a part of myself worth fighting for, that I was more than just the king's assassin. You made me believe there was something good left, someone capable of doing good," I say, finally letting her in.

"Nallac," she says, and I take a breath. "You are full of good. You are whoever you want to be, and through whatever path you choose, I will be right by your side," she says with a kindness and understanding I remember so clearly from the cave when we met.

"I've struggled with who I was since the day the king forced me into servitude. I can barely remember life before it. It's like his control took away everything about my past, forcing me to forget." I shudder, not yet able to meet my princess's eyes. "I sometimes wonder if that boy locked deep inside was never there at all, and what the king made me into is the real me—that I am nothing more than a monster."

Vera smiles softly, and I can hear exactly what she thinks.

You are no monster. You are perfect, like a bolt of lightning in a thunderstorm. You brighten my world, taking me away from my shadows. The words are too clear to be my interpretation, and I look down to meet Astryx's eyes, realizing she had told me Vera's thoughts. She nods, only enough for me to notice it, and I wonder what the world gains from us being together.

I'm unsure if Astryx told her what she did because Vera leans down and hugs her neck.

"There's one other thing I've been meaning to bring up," she says, dancing over the topic I know she wants to discuss—*the kiss.* "We, you know. Two days ago." I keep a neutral face, yet internally, I fight the urge to laugh at how she avoids saying the word.

It's cute.

"Yeah. I kissed you," I say, and she hides her face. "If I overstepped, I apologize. I won't do it again."

"What? No!" she yells out without thinking. With a sharp turn of her head, the scarlet she was hiding comes into full view. "I mean, that won't be necessary," she says, clearing her throat.

"It's for the best I keep my distance from you. Nothing good will come of you falling for me. I mean, you'll one day be the Queen of Adlei. You deserve a man who can spoil you and has a status that would be fit to rule beside you. Plus, the world would rue the day a siren held the throne," I say with a neutral voice, fighting back the jealousy at such a possibility. "Someone like Flynn or Alexander would be a good match for you, as much as I would otherwise despise them."

I nearly vomit as the lies leave my tongue.

"I don't want Flynn, and I don't feel the same about Alec that I do about you," she says with a level tone. "I will fall for whoever I choose, and if my subjects reject them, then they will see a different side of their beloved future queen," she states, and I feel a fire in her words, likely her *maemōjik* rising.

Some time passes with various small talk to keep her from giving in to that anger that begs to be released.

I will never let her use that power—the consequences would be too great.

"You know," Vera says between mouthfuls of a sandwich I'd prepared for us. "My dad loves to cook. He absolutely loves it, but he's also very sensitive. He was never very good, so my mom and I often put food in our mouths before going to the bathroom and spitting it out. Those were my favorite nights because we'd order pizza and eat it together while my dad was in the shower." She takes another bite before shoving back a laugh to keep the food in her mouth. "Sometimes, I'd throw my serving on the floor for our dog to eat when my dad would turn away." She laughs harder now at the memory.

"Are you implying I can't cook?" I ask with the smallest grin before she furrows her brows and mumbles, "You're great" through a mouthful of food. After laughing at the memory of her father for a moment longer, her face falls, and a tear develops in the corner of her eye.

I lean over and wipe it. Her big green eyes stare up at me, so full of passion that it's hard to look away. I cup her head in my hand for longer than I should.

"I used to play hide-and-seek with Valerie when we were young, but Naejik bless her, she could not hide to save her life. To be fair, our home had no more than three small rooms, only big enough for our family. Anyway, I often pretended I couldn't see her for *hours*, and she would laugh hysterically, thinking she was fooling me. If I couldn't see her little white tail, I would've found her from her laughter."

Vera smiles at that, the piece of my past I revealed to her.

"You really love her."

"With my whole heart," I respond. "I would've done anything to keep her innocent forever, but I failed. The white began to fade within the last few years. It was my fault."

"Hey," she says sternly. "It is not your fault. It's that disgusting king who did this to you—to your family. What has he taken from you?" she asks, finally working up the nerve to ask me what I've wanted to tell her.

"He killed my father. He was a slave before me, and as I can feel your heart like a second beat to my own, it was the same with his. I felt him be tortured and killed, felt his heart stop, and I saw it too. I saw his face. I saw the light leave his eyes and heard his final scream. The king has taken everything from me, and I will be the one who ends his life in this war."

My breathing has turned heavy, and I try to calm myself. Every part of my body screams at me to stop, to say it was all a lie now that I've brought her this close.

But I can't resist.

This presence she holds makes me all but fall to the ground before her.

"I had no idea," she says between breaths. "I'm so sorry." She touches a hand to my face, and I don't flinch. It feels…nice.

38

TO START A WAR

.*⭑ NALLAC ⭑*.

Valerie's story keeps us entertained in the last few hours of our journey. At the middle of the novel, through countless plot twists, Vera's eyes glaze over as she listens intently. I take a breath, pausing for a second to prepare my translations before continuing.

Vera darts her eyes to mine in a wild manner as if broken from a trance.

"Don't stop," she says, moving Astryx to ride closer. *"Wait."* She draws out the word with a narrowing of her eyes. "Is that the guy she ends up with?" Her excitement pours out of her, and I only huff a breath in response.

"I guess you'll have to wait and see," is all I say before she lets out a grunt of annoyance. After another chapter, I put a small black piece of hardened parchment inside the book and close it, much to the disappointment of my princess.

"I have so many questions for when I meet her!" Vera

exclaims with a large grin, and it warms my heart that she is already starting to love the sister I cherish so dearly.

"We'll be arriving soon. Are you ready?" I ask, and she takes a deep, steadying breath.

"I don't know why I'm so nervous. They have raised me from birth, but at the same time, so much has changed in the last month. I don't know if they'll like who they see." She sighs and slowly runs a hand through her hair. I wish I could explain just how much I understand that worry. The worry that you have become someone unrecognizable...

"You are still the same kind and intelligent person you were when you first came to our world, Vera, and you are still their daughter. Nothing you could do will ever change that," I say, hoping she heeds my words.

She is pure, moral, and innocent of the horrors our world can bring. Who she is, and the little that has changed, is nothing she should ever be ashamed of.

"You're so sweet to me, Nallac. I find it hard to believe I've done enough to deserve such treatment," she says with a slight blush. "You amaze me with the kindness you hide."

"It's hard to show that side of myself to those who'd rather see my kind slaughtered," I explain.

"You are so much more than they have led you to believe. So much more."

She smiles with a curve of her brows that shows the sadness she hides beneath.

You don't need to put up a front, princess. I know how you feel.

Try as you might, your heart betrays you. It tells me of what you do not wish to be said. Is my ability an intrusion? Is it wrong to allow myself to feel her thoughts and emotions?

We stop as we see the waves crash against the shore and unload from the hippocampi.

"Would you mind touching up my hair?" Vera asks, and I ensure her hair is as perfect as I can make it, securing the jewels and cuffs along with the tiara at the front. She takes out a small shell mirror and looks at her makeup, finding it still in perfect condition. "I will never stop loving how makeup works here. I mean, it's still on my face! Not even smeared," she says, touching and moving her face to get a better look. "The real question is how am I supposed to take it off?"

"You just have to use a special wipe. My sister never had an issue getting it off with them," I say, brushing through the curls left unbraided. "Your hair is remarkable." She turns around with a confused smile on her face. "It's like a river of pure obsidian."

"That's probably because it's been completely untouched for my entire life since I only just now gained access to this form. Speaking of..." She sighs. "I just realized my hair will return to how it was when I was a human the second I transform. This was all for nothing." She begins to reach for a braid to undo before I stop her.

"My *saeraih*, I will ask your parents to come to the water if they are not already to see what you look like in this form." I kiss her forehead delicately before looking at the crashing waves.

Here goes nothing.

The water hits me like a pound of bricks as I crest the water's surface. I gasp at my first taste of the land's bitter air. A fire comes crashing into my throat like the gates of hell blasted open, traveling quickly to my chest and lungs.

The last time I transformed, I had nothing to prepare myself for the pain. I heard tell that it would feel like every scale was being ripped off and your tail was being cut in half, breaking and reforming into something new.

The rumors are all true; I watch as my fish-like body flakes away to reveal a set of human legs attached to my hips. The pain is almost unbearable, but I endure, keeping my screaming internal to not alarm my princess.

I pull myself from the waves, thankful for my strength against the harsh gravity of land. The blood on my legs is washed away as I take the last step out of the water before collapsing to my knees.

Having only walked on land once, the feeling of holding myself up by muscles that are never used in such a way is still strange. I dart my eyes to Vera as I hear her scream and cover her eyes.

Looking down, I notice the human appendage that is likely not meant to be seen. I take off the shirt I had worn the previous day and tie it around my waist to not alarm her further.

"You can look," I say, and she slowly removes her hand and takes a breath.

"I didn't see anything," she claims, and I raise an eyebrow in disbelief. "I swear. I looked away the second I realized you'd be... unclothed."

"I don't care. You know our kind likes to show skin," I say with a smirk, moving closer. Her face grows bright red, and she tries to avoid eye contact. "Now sit there and look pretty, *saeraih*. I'll grab your parents."

She nods, and I suspect she didn't fully listen to anything I said. Nonetheless, I attempt to walk to the oddly large building on the beach, which I assume is where they live. Why do humans make their buildings so *square*?

It's an odd shape to live in.

For a room, sure, but the whole house?

I shrug and continue, forcing my legs to move one step at a time, focusing on the tightening of my core to keep from falling in any direction. I've realized the key is to pretend to fall but to catch yourself just before losing your balance and doing the same thing again.

If this is like learning to swim as a mer for the first time, I have a new appreciation for Vera's resilience. It feels like I have to remind myself to breathe with every step I take.

As I reach the door of her home, the same color as the sea, I move to knock before dropping my hand. It shakes as I try once more to no avail.

What will they think of me?

Will they curse me out, aware their daughter deserves better? I wonder if my mother would even think I deserved the love Vera wants to give me.

Before I can try once more, the door swings open to two faces that radiate the same nervousness I feel.

No, I had felt *their* nerves. That's why I couldn't knock.

After all these years, I still can't always determine what feelings are my own. They go to speak, yet no words come out as they scan me and look all around, searching for their daughter.

"She's waiting in the water. She—" I pause as relief washes over them. "She wanted to show you how she looks before returning to her human self. I said I would retrieve you," I finish with a bow. They frown at me, and I wonder what I have done.

"You don't need to bow to us, son," the man I assume to be her father says with a hand on my shoulder. I jerk back slightly, and he releases it.

"Sorry. I'm not accustomed to…human traditions."

"No worries," her mom says with a bright smile. "May we see

our daughter now?" she asks, and I notice I have been blocking the doorway.

"Yes, of course. I apologize," I say, leading them back to Vera. They sprint the last stretch to reach her.

"Vera!" they scream, pulling her into a hug. The three of them spill enough tears to fill a tub. The droplets stay stuck to their faces, not being washed away.

It's an interesting sight.

"You look—" her mom begins, taking in the sight of the Adleian princess. "Vera, you look absolutely beautiful."

Her mother touches every part of her attire, from the tiara to the detailing on her dress to the stones braided throughout her hair.

"My little girl," her father says, looking her over in the same way. "You have become what you were always meant to be. This is you, Vera. I have never seen you so radiant. Everything about you is heightened and bright." He places a kiss on her head, and Vera cries with them.

She lifts herself farther from the water, beginning her transformation, and I'm almost jealous at the utter grace in which hers takes place. Starting from her hair, I watch the deep, black roots turn a soft lilac, taking the former's place as if growing in for the first time. Slightly past her shoulders, the hair stops, and the leftover black fades away like a mirage. Her tail is converted to legs with such elegance I find it hard to believe it ever truly happened.

Her parents seem to think the same, watching her as if she were a fallen star that has gained consciousness. An uncontained brightness radiates off her skin.

I feel as though I'm seeing her for the first time—her beauty is almost too much for this world.

I want nothing more than to stare at her for the rest of eternity.

Her body is a masterpiece of beautiful curves that I plan to memorize. I want to know every part of her, every freckle, every mole, every tiny scar, every imperfection.

She wears a fabric on her hips that must cover whatever the female equivalent of my appendage is. Is it odd of me to find her human parts so utterly beautiful? Her legs and hips are full, and her skin looks so *soft*.

As she stands before me, staring up, I realize how short she is. Well, compared to whatever height I am, I suppose.

"Oh my gods, you're tall!" Vera yells, looking me up and down. The top of her head comes to my collarbone, but I thought as much would be inferred, considering her length from head to tail is significantly shorter than mine. "What are you, seven foot?" she asks with shock plastered across her face.

"Is that a lot?" I ask neutrally, and I hear her father choke out a laugh.

"Yes, son, that's a lot," he remarks with a smile. Is it also a human thing to call a random stranger 'son'? "But I would say you're probably around six foot three if I had to guess."

"Nate, you can't be serious." Her mother laughs. "He's six foot six or seven."

Vera blinks dramatically before shaking her head.

"And here I thought I was taller than most," Vera says with a smile, and I feel something budding within her. A feeling I haven't experienced with such intensity since we—

My face heats as I realize what it is she's feeling.

She notices because embarrassment takes its place.

We make our way inside, and while she and her parents continue to talk about what has happened thus far in Vera's exploration of our world, I find myself sticking to the far wall, not quite comfortable enough to use any of the sitting furniture. I'm shocked the inside of this house is the same as the outside. I suppose the house was not as large as I thought, considering that most interiors are almost twice the size of the exteriors in Adlei.

"Come with me and we'll get you some clothes," Vera says as she walks over. "My dad gave me an old pair of pants he thinks will fit you, and I have a few baggy shirts that should as well." She takes my hand and leads me to what I assume is her bedroom.

She points out a section of her closet with shirts hung in various colors.

"That one," I say, pointing to a black item that reminds me of most of my clothes. She takes it out, and the front reads *My Chemical Romance*.

What the hell does that mean?

"What is a *chemical* romance?" I ask, staring at the strange text and writing. The design is so...odd. I've worn a shirt before, but this is unlike the clothes in my world. "I mean, I guess love is a chemical reaction in the brain." Vera raises her brows and holds back a laugh.

"Sorry, I forgot that you're the one that doesn't understand this world. It's a band my dad listened to when he was younger. It's one of his old shirts." I put it on, and it fits nicely, just loose enough that I don't feel suffocated. I see Vera staring at my body until the shirt covers what I'm sure she enjoyed seeing.

I take the pants she handed me, made of thick, black material with many pockets along the legs for storage. Thankfully, they also fit nicely, and I don't mind their look either. Neither does Vera, judging by how she's staring.

"See something you like?" I ask nonchalantly, and to my surprise, she isn't embarrassed.

"Yes, they look really nice on you," she says with a smile. "Come on, I want you to meet my parents." She walks me out, and I see a grin on her father's face.

"I looked just like you when I was your age," he says, and her mother rolls her eyes.

"No, you didn't," she counters.

"Well, I *thought* I looked like him when I was his age," he corrects with a playful glare. "Wait, how old are you?"

"One hundred and twenty-four."

"Wait, what?" Vera and her parents exclaim at the same time.

"I'm only joking. I'm nineteen," I say and feel each of them relax. Perhaps I should not joke again…clearly, I do not know when it is appropriate.

"I just realized we've never introduced ourselves! This is Nathaniel, and I'm Emilia," her mother says.

"Nallac," I respond with a slight bow before remembering that's not what humans do.

"So, how did you two meet?" Emilia asks, and Vera goes pale.

"We crossed paths when she was with her birth mother," I answer and feel Vera's thankfulness for the lack of *other* details of our first interaction.

"What's her name? Your birth mother?" she asks Vera, who smiles at the thought of sharing both parts of her with her family.

"Kaileah Dlari. She's the queen of the Kingdom of Adlei, and I found out that I'm the direct descendant of a goddess through her line. I was taken from her when I was born as a way to torture her, and afterward, they locked her in that kingdom for seventeen years." I hear a slight catch in her voice, and I put a hand on her thigh.

"A goddess's descendant?" Nathaniel yells. "Here, I thought the strangest thing about you was that you weren't human." He laughs, and the sadness inside my princess dims slightly. "I want to know everything."

"Well, we might be here a while," she says with a kind look at me. "For starters, Nallac is the most powerful siren in our world," she says, not with fear but pride.

"A siren?" Emilia asks, and for once, I can't read the implication. "Those aren't myths?" I feel the fear then. Both her parents emit it at the same time.

I knew I would not be accepted.

Why should I be? I'm an assassin, sitting here and lying to their faces about the real way I met their daughter.

I was there to take her mother back to her prison cell, and when I saw her, I contemplated taking her, too. I genuinely considered it.

I thought, maybe, just maybe, I would gain the king's favor and be released.

I *am* a monster.

"The myths are not true, I assure you," Vera says with a level tone. I can't help but stay silent.

"Are you a siren as well?" Nathaniel asks, and Vera shakes her head.

"I'm an Adleian."

"Oh, is there a difference?" the mother asks, looking between us, likely trying to spot characteristic differences.

"Well, it's just two different races. When we're not human, the racial differences are clearer," she says.

My stomach drops, and I feel an overwhelming need to check

the house's perimeter. Something isn't right, and I must put the princess's safety above all else, regardless of the social implications.

I remove myself from the kitchen table.

"Excuse me, but I need to check something outside," I say before leaving without waiting for questions. I see my gut feeling was correct.

"What the hell do you want?" I grit out between clenched teeth.

Daevia.

"Oh, nothing from you, my little pet," she answers, running a hand along my arm. A violent nausea spreads through me. "But I wouldn't mind you joining me in my room again. You always did listen *so well.*" Her nearly gray eyes narrow with the taunt. She knows what those memories invoke in me and wants me distracted.

She wants me to be vulnerable.

I shake off the thought and step closer, pushing her to step back.

"I will ask one last time before I shred this binding and murder you right here. What. Do. You. *Want,*" I nearly growl out the words as I push closer after each one.

"*Tsk,*" she says with a click of her tongue. "I just wanted to see the people my witches brought her to all those years ago. Nothing *nefarious,*" she says with a snake's smile. "Just coming to say hello is all." I see the God of War in that smile, that endless, unsatiable need for violence.

"I know Adnitis wants his war, but you can tell him that if he allows the death of anyone she loves, I will make sure it never comes." Daevia smiles again, pressing herself to me so I feel every part of her.

"Aw, where's the fun in that? But don't worry, siren, he hears your words. He said he'll be patient…so long as you keep her on that path." She turns to the water and looks back with those disgusting pale eyes. "I'll be back soon. Don't worry," she says before disappearing into the waves.

This will not end well for Vera.

What have we started?

39

CHANGE

.*⭐ VERA ⭐*.

"I'm scared, Mom," I say, finally ready to speak on what has been eating me alive. "I must build an army and start a war to save my people. Please tell me what to do."

"I know you want to hear that this shouldn't be on your shoulders and that you should run away from it all, but this is who you were meant to be," Mom says, taking my hand. "We don't always like the cards we're dealt, but it's our responsibility to use them to the best of our ability. We must help those who can't help themselves."

"These creatures speak to me, which means someone I love will die. I don't know who, but I can't imagine life without any of them—any of you. I can't start a war knowing what it will cost," I say, knowing no judgment will come from them. "What if this is the last time I ever see you two?"

"Vera," Dad starts with a sniffle. "Any day could be our last. We have no idea what the next day will hold, so we have to live each one like our last. If this is the last day I see you, I will be happy knowing you are cared for, loved, and protected. I will die happy knowing I got to see my beautiful girl one last time." Tears begin to fall, and I wipe them away before I start again.

I knew I had to hear it from them.

I needed their encouragement—their love—to know I'm making the right decision. It will be hard, it might just kill me, but I will be making a difference. I will take a step toward changing the fate of all the struggling Adleians, the witches taken from their families, and the sirens outcasted from society.

I will change the world.

I will make a difference.

"I see it in your eyes that you've made a decision," Mom says with a smile. "You always were so unique, Vera. It was something that went beyond being more than human. You have a heart that is far bigger than most. You love things most people wouldn't and care for people you've never met. You are the daughter of a queen and a goddess and will shake the Earth's very core. I know it."

SECRETS

.*⭐ VERA ⭐*.

*W*hat *has gotten into him?* I think as I move to the nearest window. Perhaps Nallac felt overwhelmed, or maybe my parents were asking too many ques-tions. Regardless of the reason, I want to make sure he's okay.

As I get closer to the door, I hear him speaking to someone... no, *yelling*.

The sounds are too muffled for me to understand, but I see someone whose body is mainly covered by trees. From the looks of it, it's a woman, and the interaction is anything but friendly as he towers over her, pushing her back with each loud word he speaks. She gets far too close for my liking, and I feel something foreign.

Jealousy.

Who is this woman to touch him in such a way?

Why don't I go out there and stake my claim before her? But

did he invite her here? What is a girl of his world doing on land and *here* of all places?

She leaves before I can formulate an answer, and I'm left wondering what has gotten into me. He is not mine to claim, nor am I his, yet I can't help but want him to myself.

I feel the fire spreading over my skin, begging to come out. Each time, it shows itself as a crimson blush across my face, even just at the thought of him. I know I should not allow it to have any more control over me.

Pushing down my anger has only made it show itself in other forms.

It's as if my *maemōjik* has a mind of its own and is punishing me when I won't let it out.

I have felt that my desire has grown since I began repressing it. How do I tell if he is the source of my body's inability to function or if it is the power that wishes to be the one in control?

I wonder if it would be easier to let it overtake me.

Maybe then it wouldn't have such a hold since it would be satisfied, but I know better. The book Kaileah gave me warns of such.

I can't imagine the repercussions, and part of me wishes that a sorceress could die to prevent the alternative. What is to stop me from killing Naejik if I grow too angry in my state? Her daughter nearly did...maybe I will share her same twisted fate.

To be struck down because I grew to hunger for too much—I can't help but feel sorry for the goddess. To make that choice, to have to choose to save yourself when saving your child likely meant so much more. All because it would leave the world vulnerable and weak against the enemy.

By saving her people, she doomed herself. I hope she believes as much, as twisted a thought it may be. To imagine the gods as human in nature is the only way I can justify doing their bidding.

Korah doesn't have to tell me that for me to know it's my purpose: to be the gods' special pawn, destined to start a war to bring Wynderan together once more. I don't understand the part I play in all of this, but I know enough to see that the gods need me for their plan.

I return to my spot on the table, waiting with a large smile as Nallac enters. I may not be able to read emotions like he can, but I can tell that anger is burning under his cool exterior. I will leave it for now, but before the night ends, I will find out who that woman was outside my home.

"I apologize for my abrupt exit," he says, sitting down with an awkward adjustment. "I just needed some fresh air." My parents buy his lie, but I see the truth.

"So, this kingdom that my daughter is the heir to," Dad begins, his words full of thought. "Where do you fit into it? I guess what I'm asking is what's your title or job?"

"I am but a humble servant to the royal family. A protector, if you will," Nallac says without hinting at the horrors his 'job' entails. I understand the need for lies regarding this, but I find myself questioning if he does the same to me. The way the false words leave his mouth, the way I can hardly find a tell...it's concerning.

"Well, I'm glad to know my daughter will be safe with you," Dad continues. "Make sure she's happy there. I can tell you have that ability within you," he says with a knowing tone.

"I appreciate your faith in me, sir," Nallac responds with a nod of his head. "She is in good hands in our world. Be it with her mother, the Adleian commander, the Jellean royal family and—"

My brain turns his words into a simple buzz.

Do that many people truly care about me? I am taken aback by the sheer number of people I have met and care for in such a short time.

Astryx's words strike their target as I remember the possibilities for my future. There are so many people I find myself loving, so many people I could grow to love too strongly for my own good, and so many possibilities for death. I can never protect them all.

Nallac will fight in the war.

Flynn will lead our armies.

Kaileah will never stay behind with her power to change the tides in our favor.

Zuira doesn't seem like the type to let her people die without tending to the injured and wounded. How many will die until my fate is finished?

She never specified how many I would lose as a consequence of this war, and maybe a better question is, who will be left?

"Nallac, would you mind if we talked for a little longer while Vera showers?" Mom asks as I leave the table. I suppose the last hour of interrogation wasn't enough to satisfy their curiosities.

I, for one, can't wait to get him alone to find out about his visitor.

"Of course," he responds, only briefly watching me leave. I catch his eyes and feel like we share a dozen thoughts, but I shake them away and continue into the bathroom.

As steam fills the room, I can barely think past the intense heat. I realize how much I missed the feel of the water falling from my skin, how it collides and pours, and a burden is washed away with each droplet.

I try to listen to the conversation between Nallac and my parents, and I find that my hearing has changed along with everything else. I can even hear past the rushing water.

"Do you love her?" Mom asks bluntly, and my stomach is washed down the drain along with everything else. After a silence that echoes longer than I would like, I hear that rich voice I've been waiting for.

"I do not deserve to love her, I'm afraid."

"Why do you say that?"

"She deserves so much more than what I can give her. My only hope is that she can find exactly what she needs," Nallac says with sorrow.

And what if the only thing I need is right before me?

"You saying that tells me you are the opposite of what you claim," Mom says, and I smile at her words. She never backs away from an opportunity to heal another's wounds, stranger or family. "My daughter may be too caring or naive for her own good, but I would never question her judge of character. If she deems you worthy, then you are. She does not love lightly, and when she does, you will feel it in every part of your being. Treasure that gift."

I feel a tear threaten to escape at her words, at the idea that I ever left them to begin with—that I could possibly leave again.

I hear a scrape of a chair as someone takes their exit.

"She's never had a boyfriend. She's never even expressed an interest in anyone in such a way, but there's something different in how she looks at you." Dad continues my mother's thoughts, and I find myself cringing at that part of my past being revealed.

"If what I suspect is true, then all I can hope is that she is not wrong about who you are."

"I pray I never disappoint her, then," Nallac says, and I swear I feel my heart break slightly at the truth in his words. How can he not see himself the way I can?

"She has this sense about her. She always has," Mom says, her voice growing louder as she walks to her room. "She knows things about others—sees things most people wouldn't. If she senses something in you that you don't believe is there, it's because it's waiting for her to bring it out of you."

With that, a door closes, and silence replaces their chatter. I sink to the floor, letting the water pour down my face until I can't see, hugging my knees as I fight the feelings I had been harboring.

She does not love lightly. Mom's words ring out. *There's something different about the way she looks at you*, I hear in Dad's voice.

When I think of Nallac, I see those perfectly sculpted eyes devouring every inch of me, and I can hardly breathe.

I can't think.

He turns off every logical thought, and I can't get enough.

They're right. I've never felt that way about any man until Nallac. I guess that's why part of me hoped he would say yes to my mother's question, even though I don't know if I could have said the same just yet.

I turn off the water before I burn my skin, roughly drying myself before returning to my room and finding it empty. I don't know why I expected Nallac to be waiting for me, but I suppose it's for the best as I drop the towel to change.

Adleians like to show skin. How about I test how true that is?

I put on a lacy maroon underwear set, in shock at how I own

something so revealing, and touch the door's handle before the last of my confidence dies down.

I throw on a large shirt that falls to my knees to cover it… Maybe next time.

I find Nallac sitting at the kitchen table, either waiting for me or simply too nervous to go anywhere he isn't invited.

"Come outside with me," I say, and he follows as we exit, greeted by the beginning of a crisp fall breeze. I try to cover my exposed arms to hide from the chill, but it does little to help. "How come I barely react to cold water temperatures, but the second the air on land cools, I feel like I need a thick jacket?"

Nallac huffs a breath as he watches me, clearly not having the same reaction to the air around us.

"Your body is adapted to handle sudden drops in water temperature. It doesn't account for air." He stares off at the swaying palm trees and breathes in the fresh, salty air. As the sun sets, its rays paint a perfect picture across the grains of sand, the horizon casting the most beautiful of colors along the crest of each wave.

"And how are you fine then?"

"I've had to deal with worse things than a cold breeze, *saeraih*," he says with the slightest smirk. It's gone so quickly I wonder if it was ever there. I glare and roll my eyes before sitting on a rocking chair by the window. He follows suit.

"Why did you come out here earlier?" I ask, first wanting to see how far his lie will stretch.

"Ask the hard questions, Vera. I know you took me out here to question what or *who* you saw from the window."

How did he—

"No, I didn't see you. I just know you well enough to assume you'd want to make sure I was okay, and in doing so, you would've seen a part of the full story," Nallac says with a deep breath before staring into the distance, his mind seemingly working through a hundred scenarios.

"Fine. Who was that girl, and how do you know her?"

"Daevia Phoenix," he says through clenched teeth, and I notice a shiver that crawls across his skin. The way he says her name, I feel like I should recognize it, but I don't. "Right-hand witch to the king. Better known as the one who cursed you and your mother." My stomach drops at the words—at the name and face replacing a blank slate in my mind.

"And *what* was she doing *here*?" I ask, sharing the same anger-riddled tone as the man beside me.

"I think it's better I don't say," he mumbles, and I see something in him turning off, like he's shutting down a memory he wishes to push away.

"Nallac, this is my family. Do not keep this from me."

"She didn't say her intentions, but I felt them. As best as I tried to hide it, I knew better than to think our presence here was unknown or unexpected. She knows things no one should and is always six steps ahead." He takes a deep breath before picking at the sand caked under his nails. "She wants something that involves your parents."

"What is she capable of?" I ask with widened eyes.

"She channels her power directly from Adnitis, giving up any humanity she used to have as payment. With unrestricted power from the God of War, there is no telling what havoc she would unleash." He runs a hand through his hair, the movement catching my eye as his neck strains with the tilt of his head. "I will have Flynn send as many as he can to watch this location after we leave. I will do everything to ensure nothing happens to them. I promise you," Nallac says, meeting my eyes for the first time since our discussion began.

I find myself finally letting go of a breath I had been holding, but it does little to calm the fear for my parents' safety.

"How can Flynn adequately protect this area without alerting the king of our plans?" I ask, and Nallac nods slightly, likely questioning the same thing.

"I thought as much before I realized the spies he has. They're soldiers trained, as I have been, to be undetectable when necessary and to kill before you know they're there. They answer to him, not the king, and I have no doubts about their loyalty from how they were chosen."

I believe him, and I trust Flynn's militaristic judgment.

"When can you send word?"

"Flynn's pettiel should arrive by the morning with an update or to check for any needed correspondence. I will then send out a detailed explanation."

"Would it be safer if my parents returned home or stayed here?" I ask, and Nallac thinks for a long moment before responding.

"They need to leave as soon as we do. My only hope is that Daevia hasn't tracked the same route I did to find them, but the farther they are away from our world, the better."

"I'll tell them to leave in the morning," I suggest reluctantly. "They can't be gone much longer from work without raising suspicion. Thank you again for everything," I say with a hand on his arm.

"You don't need to thank me."

"Nallac—"

"You should get back inside. I need to tend to the animals, and then I will shower and turn in for the night. Your parents showed me the guest room." I try to object, but he walks into the waves, diving into the abyss with his beautiful black and white tail.

I sigh and do as he says, returning to my bed to wait for sleep to take me.

It never comes.

Even as I hear the opening and closing of the front door, the sound of the shower starting and stopping, the rustling of sheets, and the click of a light.

I knock once and nudge the guest room door open with a creak.

"Is it okay for me to come in?"

I can hardly see him in the dark room, but I hear the sheets rustle as he adjusts.

"What's wrong?" Nallac asks in a groggy voice.

"I couldn't sleep. I keep thinking I can hear someone outside, and every time I close my eyes, I see Daevia standing above me. I'm sorry if I woke you, but I just couldn't be alone any longer," I explain, moving closer with a flick of the light.

His hair is disheveled and messy, falling in lazy strands across his face and neck, making him look effortlessly beautiful. His eyes, like a river made of the night sky, watch me. As the cover around him falls, I notice the lines of his chest are carved like a sculpture of the gods.

I wonder if Naejik crafted him herself, hand-picking every feature to make him exquisite without even trying.

He has to be the most beautiful man I've ever seen.

"Sit with me," he says with authority, and I do just that, moving onto the bed. "I have to say I miss my world already. It took me five minutes to figure out how to turn off a light source on land. Majick is the solution to everything down there, as I'm sure you've realized." I smile at his attempt to change the subject, but it only works for a moment before I remember why I came here.

"I can't do this, Nallac. If my family is involved, I—"

"Hey," he says, moving my face to look at his piercing gaze. He runs a delicate hand down my cheek and says, "You can, and you will. This is not what breaks you." I lean into his touch—the warmth from his hands making me pine for more.

"All my life, they've been the ones to protect me, and now I feel it's my job to do the same. How can I be certain that witch will not target them?" I ask with a catch in my voice that forces me to pause. "I won't be able to live with myself if something happens to them because of me. Because of what I am."

I run a desperate hand through my short hair, and he grabs my wrist to pull it down to his level.

"Vera," he says, and I can't meet his eyes. They see too far, too deep, and I can't let myself see how much he truly understands— how much he *feels* my pain. "No matter what happens, it is *not* your fault. You did not choose to be born of our world, and you did not make yourself chosen by fate to save it. You are not and will never be responsible for the actions of those who have no heart," he says with a voice that caresses my very soul.

"Thank you," is all I can say as I stare out the window at the endless night. The darkness is not a cover for evil but a cloud of freedom…a blanket of protection. I remember the same thought from the day this spell was broken.

I remember the first time I found myself completely consumed by a void of all light and realize something.

It is not darkness that is our enemy but those who use it for their own twisted motivations. Perhaps that's why the darkness in Nallac doesn't scare me, how the black of his tail does not make me want to run, how his eyes don't cause me to panic, how his dark thoughts don't push me away.

Perhaps it's because I've always wanted someone to see my own darkness that way, to see the bad parts of myself as beautiful. I see it in him.

Those demons that tell him he's evil are wrong, and if I am the only one who sees it, then so be it. I will be there to encourage him to be whoever he wishes to be, never anything more and never anything less.

"Can I stay with you tonight?" I ask as a spark of color appears on his face.

"And what will you tell your parents if they find you in my bed?" he asks with a raised brow, and my face burns at the implication.

"I'll tell them the truth," I respond with a smirk that sends Nallac, ever the reader of thoughts, into a mess of questions.

"Which would be?" he asks with furrowed brows.

"That I'm falling in love with you."

NALLAC

A NEW WORLD

.*✧ NALLAC ✧*.

My heart pounds against my ribs with striking force, and I can't remember when I took my last breath. She can't be serious. *She can't.* Yet, I feel it in her, that potential love, that fire.

All I have done to distance myself.

All I have done to keep her safe.

Yet, somehow, she believes she is beginning to fall for me. If only she knew the way I felt. The way I can't get her out of my head, the way every speck of my being is wrapped around her finger. She sends every part of my soul into a place of pure bliss.

"You don't know what you do to me," I say in a near growl, pulling her in by the back of her head and kissing those lips I've craved every moment since the first time I tasted them. She pushes deeper, shoving me back as I pull her frame onto me.

I open my eyes for a moment to gaze upon her form, and I notice her full curves arching into me. I nearly fall back as I take in the way her baggy shirt rises with the touch of my hand. The skin of her lower back and stomach is exposed, showing off a lacy set of underwear begging to be removed.

"Did you wear these just for me?" I ask, devouring her with a hungry grin. She looks down at what I see, and her eyes widen as she pulls her shirt down. "Oh, don't be shy, princess," I say, taking her hand to prevent her from removing them from my sight. "Don't wear something so enticing if you don't want me to look."

"I—" She stumbles over her words as I kiss her neck. I move my hand slowly across her back until I reach her neck and pull her closer. She emits a sound that lets me know just how much she enjoys it. "I don't know what I was thinking when I put this on," she says, nearly out of breath before she pulls my mouth to hers again.

I don't stop her as I devour every part I have access to, and with each passing second, I feel my ecstasy only growing stronger, and I wonder if I can go much longer before I have to stop this.

I can't take this to where I wish it would lead—not until I feel we're both ready to make that choice. For now, I enjoy every crumb she gives me.

I pull her deeper into me, grabbing her thigh and pulling it higher so even more of her beautiful tanned skin is exposed. I want to run my lips across every part, to claim everything as mine. I don't want anyone else to touch her or to look at her the way I can.

Mine.

That's what she is.

She moans again, and I bury my head into her neck once more, biting and kissing the spot I know sends her into complete euphoria. I *feel* her euphoria, and it makes it hard to keep from ripping her shirt and leaving it in shreds at the edge of my bed. I want to see the matching top to that red lace. I want to see her beautiful, exposed chest because, by the gods, I have never seen someone so perfect.

Every. Single. Bit. Is *perfect*.

"We should stop," I say into her skin, and she runs her hands through my hair, causing me to roll my eyes back in pleasure. That sweet vanilla wafts past my nose, and I want to taste that delicate, delicious scent that envelops her skin.

"No," she whispers, and I find it difficult not to adhere to her request. "Don't," she breathes out harshly, "stop." I grin at her before pinning her beneath me in one swift movement. I hold her hands above her head, taking my claim of her mouth and her neck.

She bucks her hips under me, and I lean down to whisper in her ear, "Ah, not so fast, princess." I kiss her cheek, moving closer. "I'm in control now, and I say we stop before either of us does something we'll regret."

She tries to pull her arms from my grip but can't move them at all. She stops fighting and gives me a devilish grin before I feel her skin growing hot. After another second, I have to let go as her skin becomes molten lava. She laughs.

"In control, you say?" she grins again, pulling my face to hers. "You forget I'm the daughter of a god."

I open my eyes to see her curled on top of my chest, and the feel of her skin wrapped around my own is almost too much to bear. Peering out the window, I see the sun has barely begun to rise, and I know her parents will wake up soon.

Hei'jaek.

I need to get her back to her room before they notice. The last thing I need is for them to think I seduced their daughter.

I run a hand through her hair, and she mumbles incoherently as she pulls me closer, and it takes everything in me to not stay here and hold her forever. She does unspeakable things to me, and I don't even care.

I don't care that I've lost all control of my thoughts because she has brought out a light I believed had died with my father. A light that died when I was taken, when I was beaten, and when I thought my life was over.

"I am so lucky to have you," I whisper, knowing she can't hear me.

I pick her up, bring her to her room, and tuck her into bed. I place a soft kiss on her forehead before moving for the door.

With a final look back at her sleeping, I can't help feeling something I never have before. It fills me with these endorphins that have never been apparent.

It sends my stomach spinning, and I grip the doorway to keep from falling. She's too good for me, far too good, and I worry that I will ruin her. I worry that I will not be able to become what she needs, and her need to heal me will turn her into someone unrecognizable.

But if that happens, I will spend every breath bringing her back to who she is meant to be—my pure-hearted princess.

Perhaps I am not a punishment for her, but she is a gift to me —a gift for all the torment the gods have allowed to plague my life. And perhaps I am meant to be her protector, a gift that will forever keep her safe.

Maybe, just maybe, we are gifted to each other, and maybe I am the only one who can guide her to her destiny.

~

Her parents left not long ago, their words bittersweet, and I wonder if they may be the last words they ever speak to each other. I can't tell her, but I don't know if they will be safe from Daevia.

No one could stop her will if they tried.

I doubt even the God of War could stop her.

No matter who stays to protect them, no matter who watches their every move, if Daevia wants them found, they will be. She channels the god known for his strategic thinking, known for determining every possible angle.

I should tell her. I *really* should, but I can't. I won't.

I want her happy. I want her to believe they will be safe, but they will always have a target on their back. The only person who has ever thought one step ahead of Daevia is the person who can all but read her thoughts: *me*. But that's exactly what she wants. Daevia wants me to forsake Vera's safety to protect her parents, and even though it kills me to have to choose, I will.

As much as I wish I could keep the people Vera loves safe, I will never sacrifice her safety for it. I know she'd understand. She'd do the same.

I will be there to heal her wounds.

I gathered Daevia's plan as clearly as I could through her emotions. She plans to kill Vera's parents. I'm almost sure of it. She's *jealous* of her, of her ability to control me without the use of majick and the fact that she is the most powerful majickal being in this world.

She will do *anything* to break her, but she doesn't know that I've thought of it all.

I knew Vera could hear my conversation with her parents, so

I instructed them to speak normally while our true conversation was held through notes in between.

You will die at the hands of the witches that brought her to you, I wrote to them. They looked at each other like they had known this for a long time.

We've known since the day she transformed. We've planned for it, and everything is in order. We have written dozens of letters for her birthdays and special events, and we have gathered things we know will make our death easier. I nodded at them, thankful for their love.

I will keep her safe, and I will be there to heal her wounds. I promise you. They nodded back and took my hands. I fought every instinct to pull away.

You have our permission when the day comes, her mother, Emilia, wrote to me. I knew what she meant, and I took that last note and kept it close, knowing that I would one day show it to Vera.

Give her this when you think she's ready, her father wrote, and Emilia handed me a folded piece of parchment.

I see how the weight of knowing someone she loves will die affects her, and I can't let her know her parents' fate. As terrible as it is, as horrible as it may make me, I will do what I believe is best for her. They made me promise.

She leads me to a small town nearby, as she insists on showing me what the human world has to offer. It is strange to see this quantity of humans wandering about, but I can't help looking at her old world and feeling...bored. The lack of majick, life, and color is sad.

"Isn't it great?" she asks, grabbing my hand and dragging me to the center of the commotion.

"It's...bland," I respond, and she rolls her eyes.

As we continue, she leads me to a building with many tall windows. Inside are several rows of tables, and in front of us is a podium with a friendly-looking human woman.

"How many?" she asks, and I turn to Vera, confused.

"Just two," Vera says, following the woman to a table in the back. I sit on one side before she joins at the opposite end.

"Your server will be with you shortly," the woman says before returning to the podium.

"Have you never eaten at a restaurant before?" Vera asks.

"No, I have not. This is new to me," I say, and she smiles and places a hand on mine. I try to remove it without upsetting her, but as her smile falls, she moves her hands to sit in her lap instead.

I shouldn't have done that.

"What do you do with your free time? Do you have any hobbies beyond music?"

"I often gravitate to music, both composing and playing songs I've heard before, but beyond that, I enjoy reading. As of recently, that means reading my sister's novel." Vera sits with her head propped up on her hands, listening intently, and I don't think she notices the woman coming back to drop off two glasses of water.

"So why did you have a sketchbook in your room?"

"I've tried to explore other creative outlets. There is a reason those pages are all blank," I say, taking a sip of the drink brought to me. I fight the urge to spit it out from the strange taste. "What is *this*?"

"It's water?" Vera says unsurely.

"This is *not* water."

"Well, it's purified freshwater. It's what we humans drink," she says with a chuckle. She takes a drink, only to be taken aback, just as I was.

"I haven't had water in a few months," she says, moving the clear liquid around her glass. "I will admit it feels wrong now." She takes another sip and swallows it with a strained gulp. Her third seems to be less of a struggle.

A new human comes over with a notebook and pen in hand.

"Are you two ready to order?"

Vera grabs a sheet of thick paper, reading through it quickly before pointing something out.

"How would you like the steak cooked?" the human asks.

"Medium, and I want double vegetables—lots of broccoli," Vera says enthusiastically. The waitress then turns to me expectantly.

"He'll get a double bacon cheeseburger with fries," she says, and the waitress nods before leaving. "Sorry, I should've probably warned you about the whole ordering thing. I want you to try something I doubt you can find in Adlei," she says, biting her bottom lip.

"And what exactly is that thing you ordered?"

"Do you know what a cow is?"

I think about the land animals my mother and father taught me about through the small number of school textbooks we acquired. I remember it being a larger animal that was often sourced for various food products.

"Vaguely."

"Well, the patty is meat from a cow, plus cheese, and the bacon is meat from a pig," she explains, and I raise my brows.

"Sounds strange, but I suppose most things here would be," I say, looking off through those tall, expansive windows at the many humans wandering and talking.

So many legs.

I notice a woman in the crowd, seemingly distressed as a larger man approaches her. He grabs the bag she holds, and she pulls away before he grips her arm harshly. She tries to run but can't counter his strength.

A wave of anger develops from seeing him take advantage of someone who cannot defend themselves, so I crack my neck and send a wave of power into him. It weaves through the innocent bystanders until it hits the target.

He falls over, clutching his chest and gasping for air. A smile pulls at my lips at the sight of someone capable of evil being put in their place, and I push a little more of my killing power into him. He frantically grabs at his throat as if that will bring back the precious oxygen he craves, unaware I hold his lungs in a grip of majick that won't allow them to expand.

"Nallac," Vera warns, but I don't break the connection on him, watching how he squirms. *Weak.*

The woman he harassed ran at the first break in his grip, and now this pain he feels is for me. For all those like me who have been brutalized by those in power—those who can hold something over us.

I imagine him as the king, as Daevia, as those soldiers who beat and tortured me day and night.

"*Nallac,*" Vera warns again, this time louder. I look back at her, and she eyes me with concern. I know exactly what she is saying through her eyes. *Don't do this.* I look back at the man, now blue in the face, and release my majick's grip one finger at a time. "You would have regretted it," she states with conviction, and I wonder if that's true.

Staring at the man, I notice him pause, looking around frantically before screaming like a frightened child. Turning back to Vera, I see a glimmer of majick in her eyes.

"What did you do?" I ask, and she smiles with a wicked look.

"Oh, nothing. I just sent a whisper," she says before sending that same voice to me. A demonic sound seems to come from every direction, filling every fiber of my being as it says: *Touch another woman, and next time, I won't stop.* The voice ends in a laugh that sends the hair on my arm standing as I admire the power of the woman before me.

If only she knew I've never met another witch capable of such a thing.

The more I see of her, the more I understand the talk of her being the one to change our world. Even untrained, she could rival the power of her mother, let alone a lesser enemy. If I didn't know any better, I'd question if she was more than just a distant descendant of a goddess like her mother, but instead something more.

The food arrives shortly after, and a cloud of steam wafts off each plate as they are set before us. Mine is a sandwich of sorts, piled high with meats and partially melted cheese, along with some land vegetables that I cannot remember the names of.

Vera has a slab of dark brown meat with a salad and other vegetables on the side of her plate. She takes a fork and knife and begins to cut frantically as if she hasn't eaten in weeks.

She stuffs the first bite into her mouth and melts in her seat at the taste.

"Oh my gods," she says with a mouthful of food before quickly covering her mouth. "Sorry, I missed steak *so much.*" She barely finishes swallowing before shoving another two bites in her mouth.

"You seem to be enjoying yourself," I say, my grin filling half my face. She tries not to laugh as she piles more steak into her mouth. "Don't forget to breathe," I suggest, feeling the urge to laugh. *Laugh*. It's been so long since that feeling has ever crossed my mind, and now, in this moment, I feel like I might just burst into a fit of laughter.

All because a princess from Adlei can't help but stuff her face with food she adores.

"Nallac!" she says with exasperation, pointing to my untouched plate. "Try it!"

I look down and remember that I have my own food.

Someone brought this to me. Someone served me a portion. This food was made *for me*. It wasn't someone's unwanted leftovers, wasn't a rotten bit of meat that needed to be disposed of, wasn't something I stole...It was made for me to enjoy.

I pick it up and take a bite, enjoying every second. The flavors are intense and trigger every part of my tongue. The vegetables are refreshing, the cow dissolves in my mouth, and the pig is perfectly crunchy. It combines to be the perfect bite, and the seasonings are something I've never had the privilege of trying.

"It's really good," I say after swallowing. "Thank you for showing this to me." I take another bite and feel Vera's happiness at an all-time high at my own enjoyment. I smile and take another bite as she beats me with two of her own.

"Can I try it?" she asks with large, hopeful eyes. I extend the food to her, and she happily takes a bite, then another, and pushes her plate closer to me. I try a piece of her steak and am surprised at how delicious it is, too.

I then wait for her to return the burger to me, and she frowns as she hands it back. She does not spare the poor food before her, devouring it with newfound vigor.

That does it.

I laugh, food coming out of my mouth before quickly covering it. I feel my stomach clench with the foreign feeling, trying to catch my breath as I laugh uncontrollably.

Vera joins me, and I ignore the obvious stares we receive, choosing instead to have this moment—this single moment—to be happy. How have I possibly been lucky enough to have her? How could I possibly deserve this beacon of pure light?

She is like the sun. Her radiance is unmatched, and she brightens everywhere she goes. I feel the happiness of anyone she speaks to grows.

She is a gift to both our worlds—a gift to us all.

And she's mine.

We laugh the whole way back to her home, we laugh as we pack our things, and we laugh as we transform and find our hippocampi waiting for us. I help her onto Astryx and finish loading all of our supplies before returning to the Jellean Kingdom.

I stop holding back.

As we sleep in caves, I hold her close.

As we wake up to the early morning sun, I kiss her beautiful tired face.

As we travel, I ride closer, often grazing past her.

The days blend together, the two of us sharing decades of memories from our childhoods, our interests, and our passions. We talk about what we want out of our future, what we'd do if we won the war, and everything we'd do together. We talk about our fears, worries, and next steps.

We talk until midnight, then until daybreak. We hardly sleep

as we both ride the high of being with each other. I am infatu-
ated. I want to know every detail of her life, every like and
dislike, every love and loss she's ever been through.

She wants the same, but even as I try to let myself be open, I
cannot bring up certain memories. Some things I don't think I
have fully accepted are part of my past. Some things I cannot
remember.

"I used to dress up my dog in pretty dresses and bows and
have him sit on a stool while I painted a portrait of him. That
was one of my first experiences with painting, and oh, he was
such a good sport, but now that I think about it, I feel bad for
that poor dog. He passed away a couple of years ago, but he was
my best friend in those years I had him!"

I share a memory of my own after.

"On *Moōndaen*, Valerie and I would pretend to be at a ball.
We'd make paper masks and pretend to be someone we weren't,
and we'd introduce ourselves and play the part. I've been a duke,
a peasant, a thief, a guard, you name it. She was almost always a
princess, though," I say, a genuine smile on my face.

But despite my inability to remember certain things, she is
happy with what I can give her. I feel she'd be satisfied even if I
could not tell her anything, which sends me into a world of my
own—a world that only exists for me and my princess.

There is no world for me without her in it. It would be none
worth saving or living in because she has become my world.

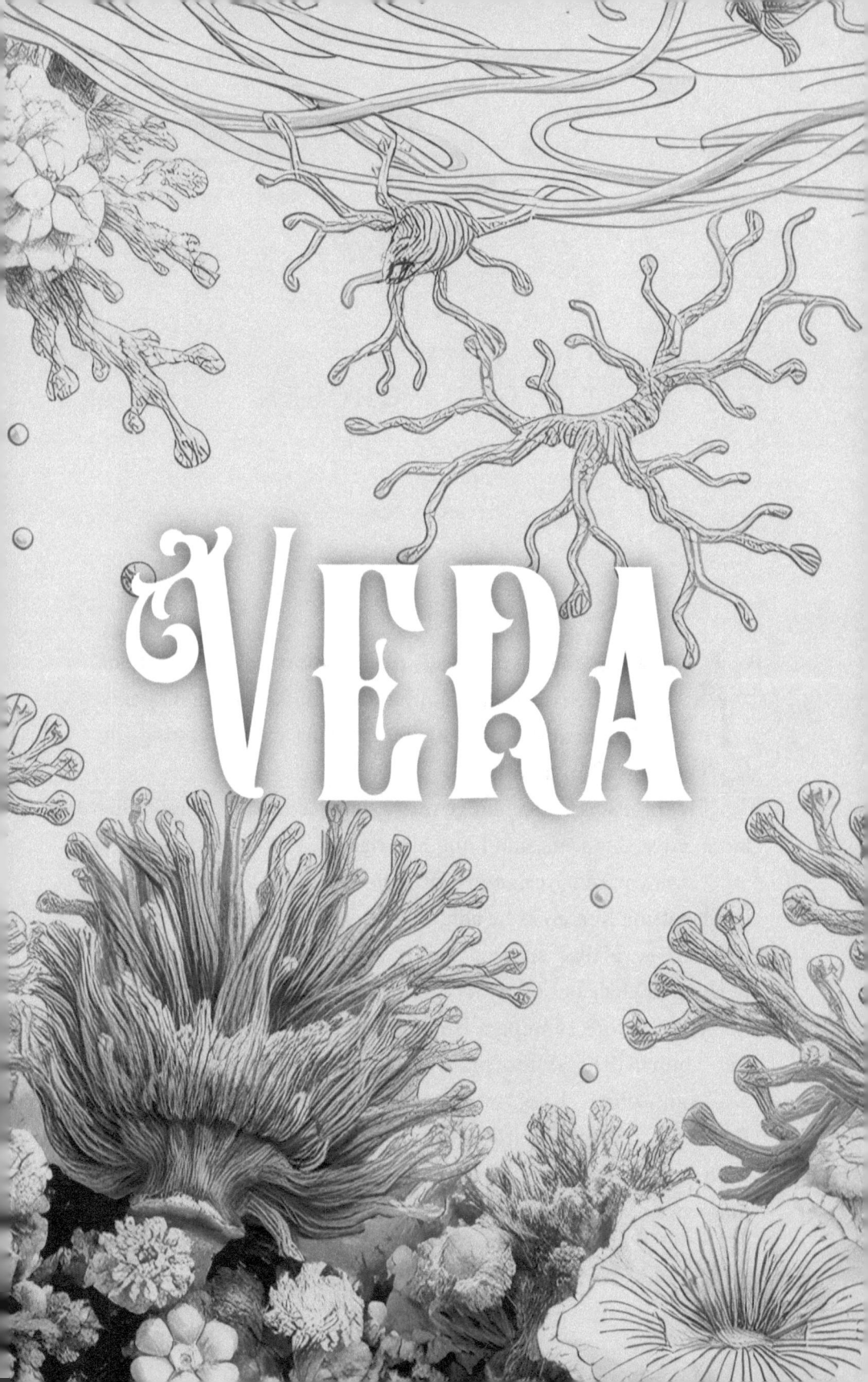

THE GODS' CHOSEN

.*⭐ VERA ⭐*.

"Miss me?" a man calls from behind as I take a bite of the fruit salad Zuira's staff made for me. Quickly turning to see his face, I can't help dropping the bowl with an open mouth.

"Flynn!" I scream as I lunge into a hug. He cradles me with his large, muscular arms, and I hug him tighter.

"Love, you're covering my gills," he says with a forced smile. I laugh, letting him go as he adjusts from my sudden outburst. "I'm glad to see Nallac succeeded in raising your spirits," he says, pushing the hair out of my face. "Now, as much as I'd love to talk," he begins before running a hand through his hair, loosely pulled into a bun in the middle of his head, "we need to gather people *now*."

"Wait, what?" I say, moving to collect the fruit and lettuce floating in the water around us. "My mother is about to leave with Queen Delmaris to rally the Kingdom of Octavia. What happened?"

"King Argyros is outraged, and he knows you and your mother are here. I convinced him that waging war on Royan would not end well because of their close ties with the Koifinn Clan and Octavia, but to keep my involvement out of question, I had to convince him to begin rallying a bigger army. We are disgustingly outmatched, even with you and your mother fighting with us." He paces as he seemingly runs through countless outcomes.

"At the moment, five million soldiers are enlisted. Over half of them have completed their training and are skilled warriors. For half of *those*, I personally instructed their *raekaihs* on how to train them most effectively." He takes his hair down, likely needing something else to focus on. It falls across his face in the slightest waves, not stopping until it reaches his chest. "Jelle only has two million soldiers, and a large quantity of those are likely getting too old to fight. If the king decides to go against my warnings, we are absolutely screwed."

"And what about the witches?" I ask, remembering that the king controls many of them through Daevia. "How many does he have?" His hair is now disheveled as he runs another hand through it.

"He has three hundred thousand under his control. He's been…gathering more lately. I worry for all of those capable of majick in the kingdom. He might not stop until every single one of them, even children and elders, are under his control in this battle," he says with sorrow. He takes my face in his hands and leans his head against mine.

"We have to find a way to save them before this battle. I refuse to allow innocents under his control to be killed," I say, staring up at him with a soft frown.

"I think it's time we asked the Angelik Clan for aid," Flynn states.

"They haven't allowed trade or communication for a century," Zuira says, having just entered the sunroom. "They only care about their people. They won't help us."

"They're our best chance in terms of numbers. I've studied past wars and censuses; they have the soldiers and the majick we need. Not to mention they're the only civilization known to have correspondence with the Letiferna," Flynn says, retying his hair in the same fashion.

"Those beasts?" I ask, and he nods in response.

"It's unheard of for them to communicate in Common or any language other than Le'tieh like it did with you. It's nearly impossible to understand because it has no written form and can only be learned from the creature itself or someone fluent," Flynn explains.

"A *Letiferna* spoke to you in *Common?*" Zuira asks with shock. "You are special."

"Thanks," I say with a grimace. "I don't have a good feeling about it. Especially when it mentioned knowing of the gods' plans for me," I say. Flynn seems slightly uneasy before clearing his throat.

"About that," he begins, slicking back his hair in one swift motion. "I think it's time we had a talk."

I feel my nerves at an all-time high as I sit before Kaileah, Korah, Flynn, and Zuira on the opposite side of the elaborately carved meeting hall. Thankfully, Nallac sits beside me with a hand on my tail, keeping the anxiety at bay before they begin.

The room is a deep royal blue, with edges laid with gold. The windows line every wall, allowing a clear view of the world outside. Fish of all shapes and colors and the occasional octopus and squid swim about. A pod of dolphins even appears with a mother-daughter pairing spinning circles around each other with adorable echolocation clicks.

"Vera, you need to focus," Nallac whispers in my ear, and I come back to see the four of them waiting for my attention. I take a bite of the biscuit before me as I gaze past each of them.

"There is no other way to put this than to say it in its full, unbridled truth," my mother says with a look to Flynn and Korah that reads: *speak.* She rolls her eyes and rises, staring at me with authority. "I am Naejik's chosen. I can communicate with her whenever I feel necessary, and I know of her plan for you, child," Kaileah says, and I lack the look of shock I know they all expect. Betrayal is what I feel.

She's been lying to me—deliberately keeping this information from me.

They've all been *using* me.

Flynn rises up next and clears his throat.

"I am Adnitis's chosen, and I know his plan for you," he says with a saddened look. "I've wanted to tell you for some time, but I haven't found the right moment. I'm sorry." I can't help but understand his reasoning. He's had the least amount of time to reveal that information to me, and still, he was the one who decided it was time for me to know. On the other hand, my mother should have told me long before now.

Before someone else forced her hand.

Korah moves next, and I feel her unease and worry more than any other. She looks almost terrified.

"I—" she stutters. "I suppose I could be considered Kayiah's chosen, but you knew that," she says, sitting without meeting my eyes. The other two remain upright, and the silence between us becomes deafening.

"Adnitis is not one to side with whom he deems has the moral cause, and I can say with certainty that he cares very little for the betterment of the world. However, as the god of all bloodshed and carnage, he craves a war—one that will bring about a wave of death. He knows that by supporting our efforts, we will wage a war that will decimate millions," Flynn continues. "That being said, he couldn't care less about our safety, so he will not stop giving Daevia information and allowing her to draw unchecked power from him." Flynn speaks like a general rallying his army.

I'm suddenly even more glad to have his brain and brawn on our side in this war.

I feel Nallac gripping my hand tighter. A tick of anger shows through his clenched jaw at Flynn's words, and I can't stop him fast enough before he speaks.

"You're *working* with that monster?" he grits out, and I have to let go of his hand as he grips me harder than I can take. "That *monster* who has allowed Daevia to curse me, my family, Vera, Kaileah, and thousands of witches?" he says, now upright and grabbing the edge of the deep brown table. I feel it vibrate and threaten to break as Flynn shows the slightest bit of guilt through his hardened exterior.

"I can assure you that our 'relationship' is nothing more than mutually beneficial. He teaches me new ways of strategic planning, and I ensure that his war stays on track. Do I need to remind you that we will not win this war through simple numbers or power? We have to be smart and carefully plan our attacks to have a chance of defeating King Argyros." Flynn takes a deep breath before continuing. "I need to learn his skills, and I'm sorry. I can only be one step ahead by indulging him."

Nallac sits back in his chair, keeping back the lingering insults, questions, understanding, pain, and guilt I see across his face. For someone who often speaks so few words, his face can tell me thousands.

Kaileah crosses her arms and sighs.

"As I was saying," she says with arrogance. "Naejik wants the return of balance and order to our world. Adlei used to be led by her—*our*—bloodline, and she believes the Argyros line has gone on long enough, and it has caused over a century's worth of trauma, pain, and detrimental impacts to our ecosystem. He has insisted on no fishing regulation, often allowing thousands of them to be caught and rot in his storage chambers so he can gorge himself on far more food than he could or *should* ever be able to eat." She sits down and takes a deep breath.

"He has no care for the starving folk on the edges of our kingdom. He would rather see thousands of sea life become inedible waste than send it to impoverished areas, allowing them to fill their stomachs for the first time. I know you understand how true that is, Nallac," Kaileah says, looking at him with sympathy for the first time. Nallac nods, only once, and that slight acknowledgment of each other as not enemies, but allies, sends my heart soaring.

It only lasts a moment, though, as the sting of betrayal fills my heart again at what she has kept from me.

"Even living within the palace, I cannot remember a time when I could eat something fresh without having to steal or catch it myself. My old hunting grounds have become barren, and many Adleians have found similar struggles. What I don't understand," he says, his kind tone becoming accusatory, "is how our queen has done nothing to fix these issues. That majickal marriage binding was supposed to allow you full authority over the decisions made in the kingdom in the same manner as the king, wasn't it?" he asks. I hadn't thought of it like that.

"Don't speak on things which you do not understand," she responds through bared teeth before seeing the look of sorrow on my face as well. I don't understand why, if she had that power, she wouldn't make a change.

"But if you both must know, I had the legal authority to make decisions. That being said, if I were to defy the king, he would have his way with me for as long as he decided was adequate punishment, and because of the curse, I could not fight back. If I were spared from *that* fate, he would pick a child from a nearby village with black hair and emerald-green eyes to remind me of you. He would stab them in the heart before slitting their throats, leaving their lifeless bodies in my room as a memory of my defiance."

Though her voice shows no sign of pain, I see it in her eyes, like the perfect mirror of mine.

"I'm so sorry, I—" I begin before she cuts me off by raising her hand.

"After enough of these punishments, you decide to stop fighting. I carry the weight of those poor children with me, their deaths made in vain to a heartless king. You didn't know, child. I don't fault you for wondering," she says with a loving look. She then turns to Nallac. "*You*, however, know of his usual punishments, so I have no sympathy for your outburst and doubting my character," she huffs.

"I truly had no idea. I'm sorry," he says, no hint of animosity in his voice, and I realize that all this time, he has hated her for something out of her control. Even through my mother's hardened mind, I see the harshness in her brows cease as she realizes it, too.

She realizes the number of people who believe her just as evil as the king even though she, too, is a victim of his reign.

She covers her mouth as that revelation dawns on her even more, and I see her again as that scared girl she let slip out in the cave the day we met. That girl slumped to the floor, unable to handle the pain of her past: no longer the hardened queen but the fourteen-year-old taken as a child bride to the king.

"They see me that way, don't they?" she asks, and Nallac understands her question, nodding with reluctance as he knows how it feels to hear this. "Oh gods, they think I'm just like him... they think I'm just as horrid," she says, a tremor becoming apparent in her voice. I don't care about how she's hurt me anymore. None of it matters—not when she's in this much pain.

I rush over and climb into her lap, pulling her into a hug that she reciprocates without hesitation. "You shouldn't see me this way," she whispers into my hair as she clutches me, a silent sob clawing its way out of her. "I'm your mother. I should be the one comforting you."

"No, you have done enough. You have been a better mother than most could ever have the privilege of experiencing, and I'm thankful for you. You need me now, just as I've needed you," I say, and she pulls me closer before her breathing slows and her grip loosens.

Astryx said that the future's paths are everchanging and fragile, so I have to believe my mother would have never kept this from me unless she believed there was no other choice but to wait. I know she wouldn't have.

"I'm sorry for that, everyone." She wipes her face and fixes her outfit and hair. "We shall continue. Korah," Kaileah says, and the freckled girl jumps at the mention of her name. "I believe you have something to say."

"Right, of course," Korah says before clearing her throat. "Kayiah wants the same thing as Naejik—the return of order to our world. She is a righteous goddess, unlike Adnitis, and she wants good to prevail. She chose me because I hold her values close to my heart, always appreciating nature as the gift it is and helping anyone I can." She smiles now, more at ease with finally revealing this.

"We have told you that the gods have a plan for you, and they do. You are the only mortal capable of catalyzing everything they want. Adnitis knows you will be the one to rally the nations together, leading to his bloodshed, as Flynn said. Naejik wants your line to lead again, and through her bloodline, you will be the heir to the throne after the king's death. And finally, Kayiah knows of your power and can see the pureness in your heart. She does not doubt that your moral standing aligns with her own," Korah explains, the words flowing freely.

"It has to be you for it all to fall into place. Not to mention, she would like the return of a kind ruler to the most powerful kingdom in our realm," Korah says with a smile, her words full of truth and passion.

"*Moōndaen* passed during your and Nallac's travels, so we must wait until the next one for our final steps. We need to be ready when it comes," Flynn says with unwavering authority.

It must be me, only me, who leads this war to completion. I understand that now.

I know what I must do. I understand the reason the prophecies have decided I am the one to change their fates, and I am ready.

I am ready to accept my fate—as the gods' chosen.

43

MEMORIES RESURFACED

.*⭐ VERA ⭐*.

My mother and the queen left not long after our conversation ended, but there was little time to worry about their safety as I scrambled to pack what I needed for my own journey. It's not easy to store enough food to last us the two weeks it would take to arrive at the Angelik Clan and the return, especially when feeding Flynn is included.

I used to think *I* had an appetite, but Flynn eats the portions of three grown men combined, making this pack incredibly hard to carry. I insisted on making it myself, ushering the staff off to not burden them with such a task as they needed to prepare for the meeting between King Wyndham and local lords and ladies to discuss our upcoming conflict.

They reluctantly agreed, returning to the kitchen to continue preparing food, as I was instructed to take any amount I needed. After tasting one, I may have snuck a few pounds of assorted sweets as they were the most fantastic dessert I'd ever had, but that seems to be a regular occurrence here.

I slowly drag the sack to the sunroom, our unofficial meeting spot, and see Nallac and Flynn waiting with bags twice as small as mine. Nallac rushes over, taking the sack from me and insisting he will be the one to carry it, as well as my bag of clothing and his own.

"Trust me, *saeraih*, I can handle it," Nallac assures me, throwing all three bags over his shoulder and rushing off to load our carriage, kissing my cheek as he passes. A hot blush comes across my face the second I feel his lips on me.

"You've got a gentleman," Flynn says after he leaves, and I roll my eyes with a laugh. "Also, what the hell happened over the past few weeks? I see how you two look at each other now. I don't particularly enjoy seeing you undressing each other with your eyes," he says with a raised brow.

"I have no interest in you or anyone else if that's what you're asking," I taunt with a smirk.

"Does that mean I can't tease you anymore?" he asks with a fake pout.

"As long as you don't *actually* try to seduce me, go right ahead, perv," I respond with a big smile, and he pretends as though I've shot him with an arrow.

"You wound me, love."

"Walk it off," I say as I swim to join Nallac, and I hear the loud, hearty laugh of the man behind me. I let out a quiet one of my own, covering my mouth to not disturb the staff I pass. They smile, and I can hardly contain myself. I don't even know why I can't stop laughing. I guess I've just been so *happy* lately.

I feel as though I've found my people. It all feels so right, like

I've been holding out for my real home all my life, and I'm finally back. I'm home.

These people are my family, and I think I finally have the strength to protect them.

Three hippocampi lead us. The two closest are identical dark blue males with purple iridescence, and at the front is Astryx. She insisted she join us, even though I told her it would be best to rest from our previous journey. She even allowed them to put a harness on her, something she said hadn't been done in decades.

I lean against Nallac, and he wraps his arms around my waist, pulling me closer.

It sends my stomach spinning, the touch of his hands never failing to make my heart skip a beat. Flynn seems to notice as he smiles and winks before returning to the pile of tattered books he brought. Each one looks older than the last, and the titles become increasingly unreadable.

"*The Tactical Advantages of Being There First,*" Nallac says, reading the ancient cover of the deep merlot book Flynn holds open. Flynn grins and raises one brow at Nallac.

"I shouldn't be surprised you speak Łi'Drēv'ön as well," he says, turning the next page and skimming its contents, "considering it is your race's native tongue. I guess you're probably wondering how I know it."

"It's a banned language. I would think *you*, of all people, wouldn't be able to acquire such writing," Nallac says indifferently, but I notice his grip tighten ever so slightly.

"My position is precisely what allows me such a privilege.

There's a reason its secondary name is Ancient Adleian, you know," Flynn retorts. "All of our kingdom's oldest battle strategies and histories are written in it. How do you think I climbed the ranks so fast? I'll give you a hint. It wasn't my incredibly handsome physique." Flynn flexes his muscles before grinning at me, and Nallac straightens.

"Can you only read and write it?" Nallac asks, now curious at how far Flynn's stream of knowledge goes.

"I haven't had the opportunity to speak it with someone else, so I'm unsure. But yes, I can read and write it quite fluently." He clears his throat before saying, *"Reładraön'dē pēnfutren?"*

Nallac smiles with a scoff, and I dare say it looks genuine.

"Cū'nerön ħ'undra'sëndrōn? Cū'nerön undra'sëndrōi rēyustruōn?" he asks with a hint of excitement before Flynn smiles back.

"I can," he says before shutting the book and picking up another one. "Now, let's stop before our guest feels left out," Flynn says in my direction. I stick out my tongue and grab a sketchbook and various travel paints that Zuira found for me.

I hadn't even asked her for them, but she said she could tell I would like them by how I lingered on each painting I passed. She said my stories told her I was an artist in my soul.

I was shocked at her keen eye, but she said that she likes to observe people and how they interact with their environment. She'd make an excellent psychologist if she were not obligated to train for the crown.

I take out a beautiful set of muted paints and create whatever draws me in. I've felt the itching need to paint Nallac how I see him, a portrait of that beauty I see so clearly and others do not. I start on his eyes, one of my favorite parts, perfecting each dark speck and flurry of light within them.

Next, I make his face, with his nose and lips, before painting those scars that adorn his face. They make him who he is, as they are both a memory of his trauma and a symbol of his perseverance.

I add flowers and streaks of dazzling light, and the painting comes to life with each stroke of hair and beauty mark that kisses his skin. I paint his shoulders and his neck and—

I try to continue, but my hand freezes, dropping the brush and the painting in my lap. My chest heaves, and I don't understand why. But as I look at the face I have painted, I see its eyes dripping red.

"Vera," Nallac says in a distant voice as I feel myself fading away from this world. All I can see are those eyes, bleeding, *relentlessly bleeding.* "Vera, tell me what you're seeing." He shakes me, but I can't react, my body a shell, out of my control.

I remember.

I remember that place.

I'm being taken there again.

I can't stop it.

"Vera, listen to me. Follow my voice," someone says. I can barely make out the words as my mind fades, and I see that shoreline. I see those same rocks, the paint and canvas waiting for me, and I see the sky.

The world is already tinted red, but the water hasn't yet risen.

A new voice, this one much clearer, comes from behind me.

"*Tsk,*" a woman says, and I turn to see the witch that plagues me in my nightmares. "It's about time you finally painted. Just when I thought my little curse would never work and you'd given up the hobby." She laughs, her tone sarcastic, and the demonic sound floods me. "Although, I wasn't quite ready for us to meet. Always a shame when people don't follow the script, hmm?" Daevia says, moving to twirl my hair.

"What the hell do you want from me? Why did you bring me here?" I ask, shoving her away, and she raises her brows in shock.

"Feisty little thing, aren't you? You *are* your mother's daughter, after all." She laughs with that same lifeless tone. "I guess Kaileah's spawn wouldn't fall too far from the tree, but what a shame you didn't have her same *maemōjik*. It always did make me laugh how she felt such little love. Ha!"

"Keep my mother's name out of your mouth," I warn through clenched teeth. The fire of my power claws its way up my spine like a beast with razor-sharp claws. I let it come, just enough to hold in my hand without letting it consume me, and throw it at her. Red tendrils of majick cleave out of me like homing daggers, and she dodges them...*all but one.*

It cuts the side of her face, leaving a deep gash of living flame in its wake. She touches it, sees the blood that now coats her fingers, and smiles, showing far too many teeth.

"*How?*" she asks, moving closer with a strained tone. "How did *you,*" she spits out, "an untrained little witch, draw blood from *me* in *my realm?*" I see her hands morphing into animalistic versions of themselves, and her pupils turn to slits. I back up as she pushes closer, keeping an eye on my approach to those red waves that drowned me day and night.

"You made this place?" I yell back at her, no longer stepping behind but shoving her away from me. She growls at me, *actually growls*, as I'm able to push her, even if it is just a few inches.

"Of course I did! You stupid girl. You've been here for months, and yet you still don't understand anything, do you? Thanks to Adnitis, they call me the mother of curses," she says with a too-large grin.

"So what?" I ask, feeling my majick's hold on me, begging me to free it. "Do you think this is some game? That you get to find all the ways to torture me? First, you come after Kaileah, then you come after me, and now, you involve my parents?" I let out another wave of red power, and this time, it takes the form of molten lava flowing from me like an active volcano, ready to explode.

She stumbles back a step to avoid it, and I can tell from the look on her face that she underestimates what I'm capable of. *Good.*

"ENOUGH!" she yells, and my lava cools into solid stone. I try to melt it again, but I feel as if the power in my veins has cooled, the fire doused. "I have neither the time nor the energy to deal with you. Be gone," she says, turning around and walking into the distance.

"I say when we are done," I whisper under my breath, digging deep within me to fling the one grain of power I have left. She turns, and right as she meets my eyes and sees the spear of fire coming straight for her chest, she doesn't move. Not a flinch, not a blink; she stands there waiting as it hits an invisible barrier.

I push it farther, and the barrier begins to burn, and as well as an invisible substance could melt, it does. Like molten glass, it pours down around her, but my spear falls as the last of it dissolves. She stares at me with bared teeth, and I feel her anger as clearly as my own as she screams.

"LEAVE!"

In a second, I am awoken to find Nallac and Flynn looking over me. I rub my eyes and sit up, trying to gauge my surroundings.

I'm in the carriage.

Nallac is at my left.

Flynn is at my right.

The bags are where I left them.

And the painting is right in front of me, free of blood. The perfect painted version of him stares at me, free of the horrors of the place where it was first created. That's why I felt drawn to paint it...because I already had before.

"Vera, are you okay?" Nallac asks with a hand to my heart.

"I remember everything," I say, the words feeling dull as they leave my mouth. I felt like something was missing in my memory, a lapse of time, and there it was. "Daevia cursed me once more so that if I ever painted again, I'd be brought back to the hell she kept me in for months. She was there this time, and I drew blood," I say, remembering the look of utter shock she had when she touched her cheek.

"You drew blood in a world of her creation and left without a scratch?" Flynn asks. "Either you are more powerful than I thought, or she wants you alive."

"Or both," Nallac says, still watching me closely. "As powerful as Vera is, Daevia wouldn't have let her leave without a proper fight if she didn't want her alive," he says as he places a hand on either side of my head, beginning to hum a song I remember him singing once before.

I feel myself calming, and my thoughts slow to a natural speed so I can finally exhale. I try to push away the memories of that place that have resurfaced, choosing to pretend it does not exist, and look at the paints before me with longing.

I throw them at the wall, although not hard enough to shatter the jars.

"I hate her!" I scream at no one, throwing the brushes next. "She has ruined *everything*! She has taken away the last thing I had to feel at ease—to take myself away from the responsibilities. Gone!" Nallac grabs my shoulders and pulls me to him, hugging me in a way that takes it all away.

I don't understand the effect he has on me, but it removes every ounce of pain, anxiety, or worry as long when his large, soft hands are holding me.

"It's okay," he whispers, running a hand through my hair and throwing his majick around me like a healing blanket. "She'll get what she deserves." I nod and look in his eyes, seeing the distance within them, and wonder what she's done to him.

How much has she hurt all the people I've grown to care for so deeply?

The next few days pass without issues besides Nallac and Flynn's constant bickering. They fight like teenage brothers, never able to agree on anything, even something as trivial as bread.

"Sourdough is the best kind of bread," Flynn states with authority. "Perfect for toast, sandwiches, and frankly, to just eat alone."

"I prefer the classic soft white loaf. It goes well with everything, plus it's sweet and fluffy. It's clearly superior," Nallac says, not even looking in Flynn's direction. "You probably like blue cheese, too. Don't you, freak?"

"It's an acquired taste you're not mature enough to understand, Homicide," Flynn retorts with his signature arrogance. Nallac sighs and looks at me, expecting me to take his side and end their debate.

"I have already said that I am not getting involved in your catfights," I say, popping the tenth piece of chocolate into my mouth from the heaping bag in my lap.

"Love, just because you're sleeping with him doesn't mean

you can't take my side. I know that wonderful palate of yours would agree with me."

"We are not—" I begin as I see Nallac quickly turn away with a red face.

"Yeah, I don't actually care what you do. *Anyway*, just agree with me and let the correct party be the majority," Flynn says, taking his third helping of sourdough bread with avocado and various seasonings on top.

"First of all," I say, "they're all delicious in different ways. I literally have no preference when it comes to food. I will eat everything. Second of all," I say, taking the rest of the loaf away from Flynn, "I brought a lot of food, but not enough for you to eat for three people at *every* meal." I glare at Flynn, and he shrugs.

"A man's got to eat, love. How else do you think I keep these massive biceps?" he says, flexing his muscles in three different positions.

"I don't know how you can even see your 'biceps' from that big head of yours," I deadpan. Nallac snorts, quickly covering his mouth before taking another bite of his sandwich. "And for someone who claims to be so desirable, where's your girlfriend?" I ask with a shove, and Flynn takes another bite of his toast with a glare in my direction.

"That's because I don't settle for the first person I see like you do," he says with a quick smile. My mouth drops, and I slap his arm.

"I did not *settle!*"

"I will admit he has a very pretty face. Look at that baby-smooth complexion!" he says, running a hand down the siren's cheek before Nallac grabs his wrist.

"Do not touch me if you want to keep your hand," Nallac says without emotion, and Flynn rolls his eyes, unafraid of the truth in his threat.

"You are a pair of children," I say, and they look at each other before looking back at me.

"Love, I'm twenty-seven. The only child here is you," Flynn says with a girly hand movement.

"And yet, I act more mature than you."

"That's a matter of personal opinion."

"It's a blatant fact."

"I beg to differ."

"Enough, you win," I say with a dramatic sigh, eating the last chocolate I can before I will throw up. I put the rest of our food away, and Flynn grunts as I take away his snacks, acting like a child being denied dessert by his mother. "Exactly my point," I say, and he flips me off.

"This is going to be a long trip," Nallac says into his hand as he palms his face.

44

THE FAMILY WE FIND

.*☆ VERA ☆*.

As the sun sets on our fourth day of travel, a perfect painting fills my mind. With strokes of blues, pinks, and purples, I imagine how the sun looks as it begins to hide behind the horizon. I look at the brush at my side and fight the urge to shed more than a handful of tears.

Never again will I be able to paint.

Never again will I touch another canvas.

The image of that painting fades, aware that it will never be born. I place the thick wood with soft bristles back in its box.

Maybe one day.

Maybe once I win this war and take back my throne…one day when Daevia is a forgotten name.

We find a nearby city called Geynival. It's one of the countless mixed-breed cities that sought to establish themselves after many were cast out of their clans and kingdoms. I make a mental note of my first act as queen: to create laws prohibiting discrimination based on bloodline or status. Oh, how this world will shake with a mixed-breed queen.

Astryx asked us to take a full day's break for her and her fellow steed, and I could not have agreed quicker. Although the carriage is spacious and comfortable, I desperately need to stretch my tail.

Nallac and Flynn make quick work of undoing their harnesses and bridles.

"You three can go wherever you'd like until tomorrow evening. We will leave food out if you want to return sooner," I tell the creatures, and they nod.

Thank you, one of the two blue males says to me, his voice low and raspy.

Vera. The feminine voice I know so clearly comes into my head. *I won't be far. Call if you need us to return sooner. I'll understand,* Astryx says, and I grab her large head, leaning mine against hers.

"Rest, Astryx. You've done more than I could ask for." I kiss her head, and she wraps her neck around me.

I sense her in you. She had that same kind heart with a fire in her soul. She sighs, the sound both human and beast. *Elvira, Naejik's daughter,* she clarifies.

"You knew her well, didn't you?"

I was born when she was, and we were inseparable. I can feel her smile. *She made me promise to live even if she couldn't, so I did. I lived for decades, centuries, millennia, and now, I am the only living thing that can remember her. I'm the only one left who knows of her pure heart. But then there's you...*Her voice trails as she ponders.

"What about me?" I ask, running a gentle hand over her smooth mane.

In all the years since she left our mortal plane, I have not met another like her, but I knew she would one day come. I told the priestesses of it, allowed them that piece of the future, and they created the prophecy. One day, a girl would be born, and that would reunite our world to what it once was. A princess born of royal blood, yet she would not be raised in a palace or in Wynderan at all. Her voice is a soft embrace in my mind.

"It was you?"

She nods, and I look off into the vast ocean and can't help but scoff at the idea that I could mean so much, that my existence alone served as a beacon of hope for this world—that I could truly change this place for the better.

I shoo her off not long after, insisting she take a day of proper rest to allow her never-ending thoughts to quiet. She insists such a thing is impossible, but I am not so sure. She eventually obliges and heads off to find a secluded area to make her mind go dark.

For the rest of us, tonight is a night of *fun*.

I enter the city, one arm tightly wrapped around my siren protector and the other around my Adleian commander. These two men have become my family, and even if they struggle to get along, I know they love each other, too.

This place is *beautiful*.

The city is full of color, diversity, and life. Lights decorate every shop and building, and each entrance glitters with a rainbow of different bioluminescent algae growing along the doorframes. Some buildings are shaped like living coral, as I'd seen in Kaerious. Others resemble the townhouses and western exteriors I'd seen in the rural parts of Shari.

I see homes with thatched roofs and homes made of marble.

This place is not cohesive, but it welcomes everyone uniquely. No one is excluded, and from how the people of this town came together, there is no such thing as being an outcast, for they are all strange in their own ways. Even those born into this town all understand what it means—what it feels like to not belong.

But here, in this place, they are all normal.

There is a rich mix of customs from all cultures, ranging from Adleian and Koifinn to Octavian, Jellean, and others I don't know. Some I recognize, some I realize must be from places I've never seen or heard of.

We make our way to a place named Heirin's. Flynn claims that the wording below describes it as a tavern and hotel, but I take out my Adleian translation book to see for myself.

"You snatched that from my room?" Nallac asks with a slight chuckle. "I'm not even sure where I found that, but I suppose it's good that someone is getting use out of it." He crosses his arms in quiet observation, and Flynn just rolls his eyes and laughs at the sight of me.

"I don't know whether to be offended that you didn't trust me or just laugh at how pathetic that is," Flynn scoffs. Nallac eyes him with more than distaste at his strong words.

"Watch how you speak to her, *Flynn*," Nallac says with a glare.

"He's only joking," I say, running a comforting hand over his arm.

"That's Laurence to you," he says with a smirk. I remember the first time he said that—how long ago it seems, even though barely any time has passed. Nallac rolls his eyes with a slight grin.

"I'm *starving*! If the two of you aren't done fighting, I'm going in without you!" I stick out my tongue at them and enter the doorway. Inside, the sight leaves me speechless.

The interior is dark without any windows, but hundreds of small majick lights float around the ceiling in a million different fluorescent colors, some I've never seen before and could not begin to describe. But beyond that—beyond the beautiful colors —is the most mesmerizing group of people.

To my right, a circular table is full of characters with different features from two girls with green and purple Jellean bottoms and Koifinn ears to the man beside them whose tail is white with splotches of red showing his siren and Adleian heritage. Another man baffles me as I stare at his skin, which is pure black with white markings. His bottom half has eight tendrils with suction cups along each underside.

"Orcan and Octavian," Flynn whispers into my ear, having followed my stare.

I haven't heard much about the Orcanthan Kingdom, but I now remember my mother's quick lessons before she left. She had wanted me to understand each kingdom or clan, so she sat me down and went through each one.

While I am aware of the way Orcans look, it is still strange to see. Their skin does not hold any color beyond white and black, so they are the least humanoid in appearance.

From my brief lessons, I remember they often don't interact with others due to their race's lack of majick. They believe they have no defense against our kind, so they keep away in the far southern seas.

Moving to the bar, Flynn orders his classic amber liquid, and I take out my book to translate the menu.

"I can read it to you if you'd like," Nallac offers. I tuck the book away in response.

Today, Nallac chose to wear his armor, as did Flynn.

The intricate detailing along his shoulder curves across his chest before ending under his arm. At the center of his chest, a large stone of pure white is framed with more of the light-colored Adleian steel, and with its curves and edges, it almost resembles a shell.

In all actuality, I wonder what the armor would accomplish due to the little it covers.

"We're trained to fight so that our target only hits us in the covered areas," Nallac explains, seemingly reading my mind. "It also has the added benefit of weeding out anyone who lacks the agility to wear such a covering."

I don't know how I feel about that—the idea that it's *good* for those people to die because it meant they weren't strong enough soldiers? I can't help feeling sorry for them.

Flynn eventually orders for me since I want a surprise, and I wait as a pink liquid is brought to me, swirling with a mesmerizing iridescence. On top, a thin sliver of lemon is curved into a rose. I am taken aback by the sweetness, not a hint of the alcohol lurking beneath.

My second taste offers a slight tang of sourness that compliments the other elements.

"Kayiah's Kiss," Flynn announces as he downs the second serving of his preferred beverage. "That's the name of it, for future reference."

"Well, hello there, beautiful," a woman says, approaching us from behind the bar.

Her hair is a light brown, kept in a tight ponytail at the base of her head, not a hair out of place. Her eyes, the color of molten chocolate, meet my examining stare as I take in her form. She appears Adleian in all aspects, though I suspect another race lurks beneath since she dwells here. "I know all my customers, so imagine my surprise when three new faces entered my establishment. Heirin is the name," she says with a polite dip of her head.

"Hi, Heirin, I'm Vera," I respond with the same politeness

before turning to the men at my sides. "This arrogant baby is Flynn, and the brooding stick in the mud at my other side is Nallac. We hoped to stay for the night if you'd have us." I get a smirk from Flynn and feigned annoyance from Nallac at my description.

"Why, of course, darling," she says with a beaming smile. "That is what I'm in the market for, after all." She laughs lightly. "So, what has the three of you coming through here? You don't seem like our usual type if you catch my drift."

"I do," I say, polishing the last of my drink before digging into the appetizers Flynn ordered. "I'm partially human despite my outward appearance, and the two men at my sides are pure-bloods as far as I know," I say with a chuckle. I earn a raised brow from the woman. Her face is a refined beauty.

"It's not common that one of the mixes here is with a landling," she says with curiosity. "Your mother did quite the exploring, or your father, for that matter."

"Neither, actually. My father was half-human but lived in Adlei. That makes me only a quarter, I suppose." I shrug.

"Now, I assume you'll want to know the same about me," she says, turning and motioning to her Adleian exterior with sage-green ears. "Half-Adleian and half—" She stops as a figure enters the doorway, her smile falling. "Excuse me for a moment," she says as she swims around the bar, moving to meet the light-haired man at the entrance.

I notice the clear difference in Heirin's appearance that sets her apart from other Adleians and likely even from these people in her establishment. Two legs connect at her hips, no tail in sight. No one else here has such a form, every single one of them a mix of other races with new and strange colored bottoms and markings—everyone but her.

"What the hell do you want?" she asks the man, who shoves her back without looking in her direction. He looks Adleian, besides the pointed ears. Flynn downs his third helping and slams the glass on the table.

"I think she asked you a question," Flynn says, his voice a deadly taunt. The man turns his gaze to Flynn, still sitting at the bar, and shrinks at the power the Supreme Commander of the Adleian Regiment holds—that power that lies waiting to be unleashed, no majick needed.

"What I *want* is the money this wench was supposed to pay me *three hours ago*," the man says with the stench of alcohol and venom in his voice. He still does not look at Heirin, who is small compared to them. She moves back slightly, a scared look spreading across her previously happy face.

"I won't have it until the end of the night, Graysen," she pleads, her voice barely more than a whisper. He looks her up and down with nothing short of disgust.

"Every hour that it's late, I'm adding one hundred *nae'yuns*," he says with a look that makes the knuckles of Flynn's clenched fist turn white. He cracks his neck, moving closer to the man, and I see his eyes holding back deadly rage.

"What exactly is she paying you for?" Flynn asks in that same horrifying tone. The man looks back at Flynn with annoyance at his insistence on putting himself into the situation.

"For the rent on this building, for the rent in that disgusting home she lives in, for whatever the hell I want if she wants to keep a roof over her worthless son's head," he says, his voice lacking all humanity. Glancing back at Nallac, I notice a similar anger in him; he keeps quiet, but I can see that look in his eye— that need to help anyone who can't help themselves. I find I don't care about shielding Graysen from it.

"And how much, exactly, does she owe you?" I ask, and he doesn't deign to look at me, hearing the feminine voice.

"Six hundred *nae'yuns* for the month," he says, not breaking eye contact with Flynn. The warrior takes out a large wad of money, more than I've ever seen at one time, and drops it in the man's hand.

"That should last her the next *couple* months. I suggest you leave quickly and don't come back or else my mouth won't be what greets you," Flynn says with a glare that makes the hair on my arms stand.

"Of course, you let another person pay your debts as always, little calf," the man bellows. "Next time, I doubt he'll be here to protect you. Maybe I'll take your boy as interest."

That does it for them both. As I see Flynn rearing back to punch the man in a way that would surely knock him out cold, a wave of power crashes into Graysen that sends all the blood inside his body pouring out his mouth and eyes. I gasp at the sight, gagging at the way the water around him darkens with the stain of his blood, and see a feral look on Nallac's face.

"Nallac, what did you do?" I ask, horror gripping me at my core, begging me to pull away from him. To *run* from him.

"I didn't kill him," he says, his expression conveying regret at that fact. "I knew you wouldn't want that." He turns to face the back wall, away from the doorway, which is now crowding with people rushing out.

He stares down at his hands, now shaking, and I can see the horror in his eyes.

Monster. I hear the thought that rings inside his head, and I don't feel scared like I did for that split second. I don't feel anything except understanding and care. I let those thoughts pour off me, letting him feel every wave of them.

He refuses to meet my eyes or look at what he knows will meet him. Everyone in this tavern will look at him and think that word. The fear that he created fills the room like an enclosing cage, suffocating him with regret and sorrow. I can see it painted across his ashen face.

I take him by the hand and lead him to a quiet place away from those thoughts.

He doesn't notice our leaving, doesn't notice me speaking to him or calling his name. His eyes are clouded as if he isn't there at all.

I do not expect him to be perfect.

I see him as he is: a broken man who needs someone to put the pieces back together. I understand that he has lived a life no one should have to, and through that, he will be hardened in ways I don't yet know.

None of that matters.

He can hurt me, push me away, and refuse to accept my care, but I won't give up on him. Especially when no one else will give him the chance I know he deserves.

I feel a connection to him unlike anything else. Perhaps it's driven by pity for his situation, but no matter the cause, something is drawing me in. I can't pull away—not that I have any plans to.

I give him a comforting smile, unsure if he sees it.

"I meant what I said, you know."

He looks at me, confused. "What are you talking about?"

"I don't care if you think you'll ruin me. I know what I'm signing up for. You're damaged, and you can't be perfect. I am willing to take the consequences because you are so much more than what you and everyone else think. I can tell that you are someone worth loving, and I will be the one to show you that," I say.

He cups my face in his hand and eyes me with a hunger I haven't seen, not one of lust but of pure relief. The weight of what he is washes away, and the guilt that I know eats him alive at every quiet moment fades away with it. I can see it all so clearly.

"Vera, you are the greatest thing that has ever happened to me. I swear you were sent by the heavens because there is no mortal world where I am worthy of someone like you." If I couldn't see the undeniable truth in every word he spoke, I would think he was being sarcastic like Alec and Flynn, but his eyes are so beyond serious in every word he speaks. "You are my sun." I can't help but smile like a little girl being told she's beautiful for the first time. "You are my light."

"Nallac, I'm not all you think I am. I'm not always kind, and I am not sent from the heavens. I am like everyone else. I hope you do not think of me as having no faults because I will soon disappoint you," I say, sinking into his hand that holds my cheek as he slides another into my hair. "I wish I was not the first to treat you this way."

"I prefer how it is. I want to savor every moment of your kindness to me because you are my drug, and I have no intention to quit you," he says, staring like a dying man. I can't hide how my eyebrows raise and my eyes widen. An intense heat builds its way into my cheeks as silent seconds pass. "What I have lived through has allowed me to appreciate every second I spend in your presence, and for that gift, I wouldn't change a thing." He brushes his hand across my neck, and my body erupts in heat.

"Say one more word, and I may very well pass out," I say, although I'm unsure how it came out because every thought in my head twists together in an incomprehensible heap. He laughs slightly, not relinquishing his touch.

"What was that, *saeraih*?" he teases with an ever-so-slight smirk that reminds me of Flynn.

"Oh, yep, that does it," I say as I let my body float in the water around us, not attempting to control my movements.

"What are you—?" he asks, with a furrow in his brows and a smile. "Vera, *what* are you doing?" I let myself keep floating, sinking, and being pushed by the slight current, and I hear an almost-laugh come from Nallac. His smile looks like it isn't supposed to be there, but I love to see it all the same.

Seeing that happiness on his face, knowing how much I've brought him in the last few weeks, I feel like the dark hole inside me has one more piece to fill it.

After some time of just existing together, head to head, mind to mind, I convince him to return to Heirin's. I tell him that anyone who dares say a word will have me to answer to, so he finally caves and reenters the tavern. Anyone who looks up to see us averts their gazes quickly. Nallac may assume it is because of what he did, but it is the expression on my own face.

I glare at every single one of them. Each look I send their way is more hateful than the last, and they all get the message: they are not to utter a word or even let themselves feel anything rude or fearful. They likely know enough about sirens to be wary of their internal thoughts.

Returning to our seats, I notice my glass of Kayiah's Kiss has been refilled.

Thank the gods.

I begin nursing it, trying to ignore the stares branding their way into my back and deflect the rising tension in Nallac. I don't have to try for long, as Heirin promptly returns when she spots us sitting again.

"I already thanked your friend Flynn here until I was blue in the face for the rent he paid, but I didn't get the chance to thank *you* as well," she says with a pointed stare at Nallac. He blinks in surprise. "While the sissies left in here may be acting horrified, every single person in this town thanks you for that. For having the guts to stand up to the bastard that has been terrorizing this town with his overpriced rent and disgusting interest rates. He is able to get away with it because he's one of the few who have the money to lend such large sums. He intends to keep the poor poor, so it stays that way." She takes Nallac's hands and kisses them, and to my surprise, he doesn't pull away.

Frankly, I think he is in far too much shock to react to his environment, even forgetting the proper *you're welcome* he should be saying in return.

"I—my pleasure?" he says in a quiet, uncomfortable voice, removing his hands from hers as he sends a confused glance my way. I shrug as I feel a slight loopiness taking over me. It feels as if the adrenaline has turned off, and the consequences of my two drinks finally take hold.

"Hey," I say, touching his nose and making a *boop* sound. "Have I ever told you how pretty you are? Like, ooooh my godssss," I say, dragging out my words and squishing his cheeks together. "*So cute*," I say with pursed lips as I hold his face together. He furrows his brows, removes my hands, and places them in my lap.

Flynn bellows a deep, long laugh at my side.

"Look what you've done to her," Nallac grumbles. I start

laughing again as I reach for his face before he grabs my wrists to stop me. He glares at both me and Flynn.

"You know, Grumpy, you'd find it pretty funny if you loosened up," Flynn says, taking his time on his fourth glass.

"I am not grumpy, and I've already told you why I do not partake in such *activities*," Nallac says with annoyance and crossed arms. Flynn laughs hard at that.

"'I'm so depressed. I'm so traumatized. I can't have a drink because I'll become an alcoholic,'" Flynn says in a high-pitched mocking tone. Nallac stares at him unblinking, and I hold my breath to see his response.

"At least only one of my parents is dead, orphan," Nallac responds with a smile pulling at the corners of his lips. Flynn stares back at him with a grim look before bursting into laughter, and I join instantly. Nallac, too, allows himself to laugh with us.

"At last, Homicide tells a joke," Flynn says, clapping Nallac on his back before he rolls his eyes. I kiss Nallac's cheek, and he lets himself smile, rolling his eyes again as he tickles my sides. I scream and pull away as I laugh and laugh and laugh.

I can't remember most of the night, not from the drinks but from the happiness that takes hold. From how Nallac lights up to how Flynn knows precisely how to mess with him to take it to the next level, I am in a world of my own—one of complete bliss.

Nallac might not realize, as he doesn't often notice when someone's intentions are kind, that Flynn only creates petty arguments to get him to talk—to get him out of his own head. To place a piece of anger on another person, to give him that escape. It makes me love Flynn even more, love him like a friend I've known my whole life, and I hope I will.

Flynn cares about Nallac in a deep, brotherly way, and I hope that one day, Nallac will see that. I hope he will see Flynn as I do, a kind soul that desperately wants to see those suffering be happy. I can tell that any smile on Nallac's face makes it all worth it.

I wonder if the two of them ever crossed paths in the castle and if Flynn had done the same then. I wonder if Nallac had come to realize it—that everything Flynn did was calculated, only this time it was not to outsmart his enemy, but to help a friend.

FLYNN

45

STRONG MINDS

.*⭐ FLYNN ⭐*.

I wait until they have settled into their respective rooms before entering my own. The silence is a refreshing change from listening to their haggard breathing all night. But as the silence settles after I close the harsh creaking door, I feel the loneliness come in behind me.

It settles there, watching me from behind the black velvet curtains.

I nod at its presence, unafraid, because it is a common guest.

I turn on a light at the small wooden desk in the farthest corner of the room and take out one of the many war books to study like it will do any good. I throw it to the floor, unaware or uncaring of what sound it will make and rake a heavy hand through my hair.

Someone's angry, hmm? A deep, unearthly masculine voice fills my head. Like an endless pouring stream, it fills every part of me. I shake away the chill at having him in my head, *working* side by side with such a person. Not person—*god.*

"What do you want, Adnitis?" I ask the void, aware of how the water has turned ice-cold. A laugh vibrates through my spine, rattling my bones so hard they threaten to shatter.

Mind your manners, boy, he says, sending a shock of pain through my head. *I hold your little, insignificant skull in the palm of my immortal hand. You are nothing. You are as small and weak as a grain of sand on an endless beach. You. Are. Nothing.* The last word sends the hair on my arms standing and my heart pounding.

I will show no fear. He cannot read my thoughts as many creatures can. I tested that theory repeatedly, and never once did he react to any taunt. All he knows is what he can see and hear, and I show him none of it.

Cool indifference is how I appear—completely unfazed.

Hide behind that arrogant facade all you want, boy. I know it's all a careful lie. The metaphysical hands lessen their grip on my head, allowing me to think clearer, no longer clouded by pain.

"You know nothing," I say, removing my armor as I ready for sleep to claim me.

I know everything.

His presence in my mind vanishes as quickly as it came, and I sigh with a hand to my sweat-soaked brow. *Hei'jaek.*

"Five million soldiers. *Five million*, not including the witches he gathers, likely reaching close to half a million at this point," I say, ranting to that lonely presence that watches me, ever curious about my actions.

I should've used Adnitis's unexpected appearance to my advantage and asked him for advice, but instead, I insulted the God of War.

~

The day passes without a hitch. Vera is in awe as we explore the city of Geynival, her mouth never straying from its wide-open position. It is beautiful, not wholly different from other mixed-breed colonies, but still unique in some ways. Nallac has kept to himself for most of it, and I occasionally attempt jokes to lighten his mood.

It rarely works, as he seems particularly fond of staying inside his head today.

Our exploring ends rather abruptly, as Vera hears Astryx asking to be ready for travel. The three animals sense some danger in the nearby waters, and so we leave at first light the next morning.

I haven't heard the brooding siren say anything since we retired to our rooms after a night of laughter. While he occasionally says a few short phrases to our princess, that is all. There is no hint of the man I'd seen laughing along with us and insulting my circumstances.

I don't feel hurt in the slightest.

If anything, his remark made me laugh more than any joke has in a long time. I hope it isn't guilt or shame keeping him from speaking to me, but as I stare at him, I can only see that little boy's wounds I tended to all those years ago.

I know he barely remembers any of those moments, and it doesn't bother me. I am perfectly fine allowing him to hate me and place any residual destain on my fellow soldiers for the trauma they caused him.

I had to lie to the king on many occasions when he'd ordered me to be the one to beat him for fighting back against the binding. Be it needing to train soldiers, having a plethora of meetings to attend, or simply needing to beat someone else, I made up any excuse to be spared from hurting that poor, enslaved child.

The final two days of travel are uneventful. Vera stares long-ingly at her art supplies, and Nallac does his best to comfort her. I often distract her with flirtatious taunts, which works fairly well, although it only angers Nallac further.

We reach the area on my map that marks the beginning barriers of the Angelik Clan, and I feel a dread wash over me.

None of us or any soldier I've met has ever been in contact with these people, and I doubt they wish to change that. We stop our steeds, unload only the necessary supplies, and reach an area cast in a dim light.

The entrance is unmistakable. A large stone and steel gate begins at the unforeseen depths below and continues as high as the mouth of the cave before us. Every edge of my vision is filled with rock as we navigate passage after passage.

Some areas are cramped for three, requiring us to follow behind each other, but now the space has opened immensely. Crystals of all sizes and colors glitter deep within the rock, casting the area in a purple and blue light that leaves me nearly speechless. Never before has a sight done such a thing, but this place is unlike any cave system I've seen.

It is as if the stone holds *life*—like it is physically breathing and watching us, waiting for our next move. As if realizing this fact, Vera swims to the gate and reaches out a hand.

"Wait!" Nallac yells, rushing to her side to stop her from making a mistake. He's too late, as she grips the black metal. It thrums to life, glowing so bright we shield our eyes from the exploding sight. A deep rattling begins, and I don't have time to react as I see an opening in the cave where the stone meets steel.

"Hello?" Vera asks, and silence follows—an encompassing silence that would likely send one into insanity before a feminine voice speaks.

"*Sa'i nōe man 'nej?*" she asks, the tone echoing through the cave's hollows as if reverberating off every surface. Vera shudders at the way it lingers in ever quieting echoes.

She begins to speak once more before Nallac lightly moves her away.

"*Nōe lys mau'di se lea'ja,*" Nallac says without a second thought to the hole, and it quiets once more.

"You speak Celestian?" I ask.

"Don't act so surprised. It's not very hard," Nallac remarks with a taunting shrug. *Trying to target my ego, nice one,* I think to myself with a laugh. He's getting better.

The gate opens with a loud creak as if it hasn't been moved in years.

Before us, we can only see darkness, but I know if we venture forth, that darkness will part to reveal the true civilization.

"What did you say?" Vera whispers.

"She asked what business we had coming here, and I said we wished to speak to the leader," Nallac responds just as quietly, taking the first movement to enter the passageway. I follow right beside him, and Vera trails our rear.

As I suspected, the gate snaps shut behind us, and the darkness fades. Thirty women appear before us, clad in various armor and wielding weapons. Each one has a variation of blue hair, the natural color of their race, and all but one at the center have their faces covered with metallic masks across their eyes.

She comes forward, lacking any weapon, and looks us each up and down, lingering the longest on me. Her hair falls like navy waves across her shoulders and chest, the color beautifully vibrant with two strands around her face that are a pale blue like the sky—those match her eyes.

She throws it all behind her shoulders as she analyzes us further, and I'm ashamed to say I can't help staring at one feature in particular: her breasts. A woman is not often blessed with such…large amenities, so it catches my attention for longer than it should.

I'm confirmed of this fact by the way she scoffs, my eyes meeting hers to see her scowl.

"Disgusting man," she growls, her accent thick and ancient. She turns her gaze to Vera at the center of us and bows her head slightly in acknowledgment of the crown she wears. "Princess of Adlei?" the woman asks, both a statement and a question.

"Indeed. You may call me Vera," she says with a returning bow. The woman watches her every movement, arms tightly crossed. "And you are?" she asks politely.

"Lyra Neredras." She pauses. "I am the one you asked to speak to," she responds, each sentence short and choppy. She likely hasn't spoken Common in a very long time.

"Thank you so much for allowing us in here," Vera says, moving to shake the woman's hand. Every warrior behind Lyra moves forward, weapons raised in warning. "My apologies," Vera says, putting her hands back at her sides. "Is this where you would like to speak?" She gestures to the cool darkness surrounding us, only allowing us to see each other and the soldiers before us.

"No," Lyra says in a neutral tone. "Follow me."

The women turn and move into the darkness as we trail, and it all clears, allowing us to see the civilization in full. Little can be seen from the water, as most of their world is *outside* of it.

Lyra's soldiers pull themselves from the water, and from

what I can tell, they are instantly dry the moment they leave it, likely from the Celestians' water manipulation abilities. They watch us closely still, as Lyra is the last of them to exit.

"You can shapeshift?" Lyra asks Nallac, but yet again, it's more of a statement than anything. He nods before she pivots to look at Vera. "You are Adleian witch, yes?"

"I'm a sorceress if that's what you mean," Vera responds, and Lyra ignores her.

"Join me on land, and we will begin our discussion," she says, beginning to pull herself up.

"Wait, Flynn can't breathe air," Vera says, looking back at me.

"Then I suggest you use your majick, witch," Lyra snaps in annoyance before turning and hauling herself out.

"You heard the woman, love," I say with a laugh, and Vera only glares at me.

"I don't know what she expects me to do."

"Unlike most witches, a sorceress's majick can take many forms, so I believe you could try to...reshape his manner of breathing," Nallac says confidently, and Vera considers it.

This could end badly.

She takes a deep breath and hums, focusing her majick, and I see a spark in her eyes. I can feel my gills shrinking, and it is now hard to breathe, but I endure.

She continues, and I can't stop staring at her eyes...

They seem to glow, not red like her *maemōjik*, but silver. The closer I look, the more I can almost *see* the majick in her soul—as if she is majick incarnate.

I'm struggling for breath, and Nallac pulls me above the surface. The sensation is foreign, like knives in my lungs, but I can *breathe.*

She did it.

Looking down, I notice I still have the large gray tail attached to my hips, but as her hums continue, I see the scales falling away. It begins to split apart at the fin, traveling up my legs until the two halves fully break apart.

Vera quickly swims up with a force that allows her to jump out of the water, transforming in midair. The black of her hair fades into a soft purple, and brightness travels across her entire form as she becomes pure light.

She touches the ground with her legs, stumbling slightly as she regains her balance, and I can feel my brows rising and my smile widening at the sight. She is like a star being brought to life.

I know Nallac realizes it, too. As I turn to look at him, I see pure adoration in his eyes. Never have I ever seen a man so entranced by someone as Nallac is right now. She is undeniably beautiful in a way that not many are, but to look at her like *that*. I laugh at the thought. To look at her like that—like her every move is a perfect dance—he has to be completely and utterly in love with her.

Nallac pulls himself from the water next. His transformation is less spectacular than Vera's since his looks painful. But in true Nallac fashion, he doesn't have any outward reaction. I notice how Nallac miraculously has clothing on his legs, and I wonder where the hell those were hiding while he had a tail.

As the last of us exits, I pull myself out before Vera rushes to stop me.

"No! Not yet!" she commands in a high-pitched voice full of worry. What is she so worried about? "Lyra, do you have any pants that might fit him?" Vera asks, and Lyra smiles and emits a single hearty laugh, and I can't for the life of me understand why.

That is until I look down and see the obnoxiously large appendage below my waist.

"Love, you think I care about showing a little skin?" I prop myself up on my elbows. She blushes furiously as she shakes her head and begs me to stay in the water. Nallac covers his mouth to keep from laughing as well.

"That's what I said the first time," he whispers to me. "She was not having it."

I roll my eyes and pull myself up, not caring what Vera is trying to hide. Realizing my plan, she shrieks and turns, covering her eyes.

"Why do you two never listen to me?" she yells, not turning back, and Nallac continues stifling a laugh. Lyra, however, has stopped her ridiculing laughter and is now staring directly at it, as I did to her.

"Disgusting woman," I say with a large smirk, and she jerks her head to me before scoffing. She whispers something to one of the non-masked women at her side, who also has not stopped staring with wide eyes at my appendage, and she instantly rushes off.

The girl comes back with a large pair of black pants made of cotton, and I throw them on and yell for Vera to turn back around. Reluctantly, she does, and she sighs a breath of relief.

"Sorry about that," Vera says, walking over to Lyra. I notice that the outfit she was previously wearing now drags along the floor because of her short human legs.

Her dress has two large shells on either breast, with tan ribbing along her waist and a translucent fabric between each one. At her waist, the bodice ends in a V-shape with more shells and scales used to decorate the area trailing from her chest to her lower abdomen.

The skirt, however, is the real star, as it flows around like the fabric equivalent of waves, displaying unique shades of blue. Each piece has a mind of its own with how it moves with each step. The same fabric is draped along her arms, and with the added edition of her tiara, she looks nothing short of royalty.

Lyra notices it, too, as she seems more eager to respect our princess than the two of us who trail her. Nallac wears his signature Adleian-steel shoulder plate, and I wear my own armor, the two-shoulder-plated black titanium that curves to show my position's crest at its center.

S.C.A.R. The title I earned faster than any other Adleian soldier ever has.

Lyra leads us through the city, and all I can say is *wow*.

While unable to stop and examine every part due to her quickly leading us away, plus the added crutch of never walking with legs before, I can only take in a fraction of it.

We are inside a vast underwater cave system that leads to an opening large enough for an entire hidden civilization to thrive, and that it does. The sage-green and ivory towers shoot high into the sky, with pathways between each one on varying levels. The peaks house sharp golden spikes, like each spire's crown.

As we make our way over a bridge, I look off the edge to see a powerful waterfall that flows down into the water from which we came. The sound of its crashing is indescribable, and it beckons us all to gawk.

Before we reach the end of the curved bridge, I spy that the Angelik Clan spans farther than meets the eye. Below, another waterfall flows, higher than the one in front of me.

After stepping off, I see younger children playing in the water, reforming it into different shapes before throwing it at each other.

Lyra follows my staring and smiles at the children, sending a horse made of water to meet them. They squeal and jump on it, riding it across the river before it collapses, and the girls fall in. They swim back to the top, laughing and splashing each other.

"Welcome to Rividyun," Lyra says over her shoulder, and I make a mental note of it. Little is known of anything beyond the entrance of their clan, and few accounts have ever described it.

We continue further, and I notice dozens of girls gawking at Nallac and me. They have likely never seen men before, as their race comprises only women. Oh, how I would *love* to live here. Lyra glares at me over her shoulder as if she heard my thoughts.

"If you don't mind me asking, why did you allow us to enter?" Vera asks. "Your clan usually stays so secluded." Lyra stiffens as she continues walking.

"New leadership," is the only response she gives us as we pass by shops bustling with Celestians.

Finally, we reach a building with an ornate golden door, which she opens, gesturing for us to go inside. None of us object as we pile in. She grips the door with two hands and swings it shut.

"I'm tired of that damn door," she says in her accent, and I smile, loving the sound of it. I don't know how I didn't notice it before, but she is stunning. The way she holds herself with such confidence and poise, she might be one of the most beautiful women I've ever seen.

Beautiful isn't even the word I'd use; Lyra is a goddess.

Her lips are painted scarlet red, and her outfit threatens to send me to my knees. She wears a form-fitting pure white dress that loosens at her lower thighs with a gloriously high slit. But the front—

Tight white sleeves cover her arms before golden-swirled

edges curve around her shoulders to the middle of her breasts and back around. Her cleavage is completely exposed, and it's entrancing.

The back curves down until it meets the very bottom of her spine with the same golden edges, and along the center of her back is a tattoo of roses full of thorns and spikes. In the center is a single word: *Na'jun*.

Around that word, the spikes cling and wrap as if in protection or to destroy it.

On the edges of the tattoos, I see two scars mirrored on either side and before I can question where they're from, a pair of glorious fairy wings appear from her back. They uncurl and flare like a butterfly emerging from its cocoon, and I have to fight back an audible gasp at the sight.

The wings are blue with the edges curving to look like droplets of water. Their veins are a glowing cerulean that matches the edges, and I smile as I see them glitter in the sunlight.

How could I forget? Celestians have wings that they can unfurl at will to allow them to glide through the ocean as well as fly while on land.

"I see you staring, *Flynn*." She says my name like a taunt, and I nonchalantly trail my gaze from her form to her eyes.

"It's hard not to when you're so nice to look at, love," I say with a grin and a not-so-subtle lick of my lips. She raises her brows and lets out a huff of air before her wings disappear. She moves toward a woman behind a desk who stands at our approach but never takes her eyes off me in silent assessment.

"Rionach Zephrais," she says with an outstretched hand to anyone who will take it. Vera is the first to rush up, taking the muscular woman's hand and shaking it. Rionach looks down and towers over her.

I wonder how tall Rionach is, considering she's almost at eye level with me.

"Vera Dlari," the princess says with a sweet smile. Rionach smiles in return before shaking my and Nallac's hands afterward. Each of us introduce ourselves respectively, and I know we both feel strange giving away that personal information.

Anything to make them trust us.

She nods to us both before whispering to Lyra about something, likely regarding outsiders, specifically men, entering their clan. Luckily, Rionach doesn't instantly remove us from the premises but allows us into Lyra's meeting room.

An iron archway leads into it, where a spacious room is decorated with ornate azure tiles and a thick wooden desk carved into a serpentine shape. It reminds me a lot of my own desk; however, the entirety of this one is in the Letiferna's form, not just its legs.

The chair, likely meant for Lyra, has the head of the beast at the top, staring down at us with glowing sapphire crystals for eyes. Its arms are thick and cushioned, showing off its luxury.

At the other end are two chairs, which Vera and Nallac take up before Rionach brings out a third for me. She seats herself at what could be considered the head of the table, able to access us all.

She keeps her space pristinely organized, and all that litters the table is a map, a pile of paper for notes, ink, and a quill. The rest of the room is like any other meeting hall, full of books, globes, scrolls, and anything else she deems necessary to keep close by.

I spy one interesting item, stored far too high for anyone to ever reach without standing on another surface. It's a book bound in leather, opened to a specific page.

"I see you've spotted a prized item of ours," Rionach says, her voice not holding as strong of an accent as Lyra's.

"It did pique my interest," I admit.

"Too bad," Lyra jives with a branding stare. "Now, where were we?" She turns her gaze to Vera, once again ignoring Nallac and me.

"We need your help in the war against Adlei," Vera says, and with that, our negotiations begin.

"So, you're a girl who knows nothing about our world, yet you think you're ready to rule the largest kingdom in all the seas? And you want me to risk my sisters' lives in this battle? I respect-fully decline your offer. You may be on your way," Lyra says with indifference, shooing us off with a wave of her hand. Vera gapes at her because it is as if Lyra didn't listen to a word of what we said.

"But your people are warriors that can manipulate the ocean at will," Vera says, rising from where she was sitting. "I swear I'll do everything earthly possible to ensure few of your people die during the battle. Nallac will be healing throughout the fight, and my mother and I are working on spells to protect us all," she pleads, taking Lyra's hands. "Lyra, I'm begging you. Imagine if these were your people—being tortured and enslaved to benefit an iniquitous king." Lyra stays sitting, not making a sound as she watches Vera's every move.

"My mother, the queen, was trapped by a curse in her own kingdom. The children are starved, the witches controlled, and the sirens enslaved. Please, you have to understand." Vera's voice catches as she looks at Lyra with pure sadness. The hopefulness she held dissipates with each silent moment.

Lyra's gaze softens to an understanding look. Her eyes grow watery with the sign of tears, but they quickly diminish as if never there at all. Vera sits back down, staring at her feet as if finally giving up. We all tried. We told our stories, and yet they did nothing.

"Vera, I understand your pain, but you must also understand me. I have to think about the safety of my own before I can worry about others. I have a mother, sisters, and nieces; I can't risk not coming home to them, and I could never send my people to fight without me by their side."

Rionach clears her throat with a warning glance at her leader, and Lyra nods.

"Which of you can speak Celestian?" Lyra asks with narrowed eyes. Likely sensing a shift in her body language, Nallac doesn't hesitate to claim *me* as the one who spoke it prior. I keep my reaction internal, aware of how he thinks, and they point at the door silently for me to leave the room.

I do as I'm told, and they continue their discussion after I exit through the large golden door. Well, Lyra and Rionach do, as I see from the window into her office. I smile as I see Nallac watching them, all too aware of every word they speak.

Sneaky bastard.

The ways of the siren will always be a mystery to me, but somehow, he knows things, like he can sense their intentions. It's up to the two of them to convince them now.

VERA

46

PLANS CHANGE

.*⭐ VERA ⭐*.

I stare at Nallac, unsure of why he lied, but as the two of them begin to speak in Celestian, I understand. He motions for me to join him on the other end of the room, and I follow, where he begins translating their words in a whisper.

"I will not risk the safety of my people for a war that does not affect us," Lyra says with a tight-lipped expression.

"If this were us and we needed help from another kingdom, we would expect them to say yes, even though we have no relation," Rionach responds with a shrug.

"While that may be true, how can I willingly send our people to certain death?" Lyra asks, breaking away from her cold demeanor and becoming more frantic. "I need to discuss this with the elders before I decide, but we have to tell them no for now."

"Lyra," Rionach says, tenderly touching her arm. "This is your decision. You do not have to involve them." Lyra sighs and looks up at her confidant.

"I know," she says. "I still feel like I don't deserve this position."

"You were voted as our leader for a reason, Lyra," Rionach says, brushing her hair behind her ear. I notice their points are similar to Nallac's, although smaller and angled lower. Rionach holds her chin in her hand, pushing Lyra's head up to meet her gaze.

Rionach's eyes are a soft sage, and her hair is straight and dyed silver, with the beginnings of her dark blue roots coming from the top. Her body is heavily defined in carved muscles, and her abs are displayed with her cropped shirt.

She is like Flynn if he were a woman, and I will not lie, it's a nice sight. But even though her exterior is strong, her every move and touch is gentle, like a doe in a wolf's body.

The two women look back at us and readjust themselves before moving to speak. I cut them off before they get the chance to push us out one last time.

"Before you state your final decision, hear my words," I say, my voice of regal authority. They stare, awaiting what I have to say. "If these were your people, if this were your war, I would lay down my life for it as I will gladly do for this one. I am not asking you to send your women to the front lines to die by our side but to command the seas from our backs." I stand, moving around the edge of the desk to face them without the table between us. "I beg of you to consider this thoroughly. I beg you to think of those who cannot help themselves," I say, and as I open my mouth to continue, I find that no words come out.

Lyra and her second eye me with sympathy before Rionach places a soft hand on my shoulder.

"We understand your words, princess," Rionach says with softened brows. "If this war leaves your people without a home, you are welcome here." While not directly saying it, I know exactly what her words mean. They will not come to our aid, no matter how much they believe in our cause.

"I wish your clan all the best," I say with a disappointed smile.

"You'll always have a home here. If this war doesn't end as you plan, we'll be waiting with open arms. I promise," Lyra says in a tone of affection. "The elders may believe the best thing for our clan is to stay secluded, but I believe it's time we opened our borders, even just for a select few." She holds my arms as she peers at me. "So young, and yet you have the spirit of a lion. I wish you the best in your war."

I fight back the tears that threaten to fall, not letting them see how this breaks me. They were our only chance.

"Thank you," I say as Nallac and I leave.

Rionach whispers something to Lyra, and I look to Nallac, who whispers it.

"They'll never survive without our help."

"I know," Lyra responds, pain etching her tone, and I feel the hole that had begun to heal fade into a dark chasm once more.

I don't speak much on the way back to Royan. I have too many thoughts and worries, and I know the same is true for Nallac and Flynn. Flynn, the master of warfare, is at a loss for words, which scares me the most.

I know I need to give him time to plan an alternative solution, but all I can feel is utter hopelessness. He had been banking on the assumption that we would convince them, and now, I don't know if there is any hope, especially when I haven't learned how to harness my majick.

We still need clans and kingdoms to rally while Adlei steadily builds its army.

I have no doubt that Flynn is a powerful warrior, but even he would not be able to take on the number of soldiers needed to turn the tides in our favor. When *Moōndaen* comes, I hope the gods will allow us insight into what we need to win this.

Mom and Dad, give me strength.

I take a deep breath and imagine each of their faces. I imagine them holding my hands and giving me the strength to continue —to face this unsurvivable war with confidence.

I will not back down.

I chant the words, willing them to keep me strong.

I will not back down—not without a fight that kills me first.

47

THE BEGINNING OF THE END

.*⭐ VERA ⭐*.

As we near the Jellean Kingdom, I feel my stomach drop like I've swallowed concrete.

Danger.

My mind screams the word at me, and I feel my heart beating erratically inside my chest. I clutch the jacket around my shoulders as if that will do anything to calm its rage. Nallac grips me in an instant, staring into my eyes.

"I feel it, too," he says, pushing me behind him with a swift movement. We stop the hippocampi and remove ourselves from the carriage, searching the waters for any sign of what turns each of our stomachs. Nallac searches, his eyes darting to every possible location as we near a *la'minōlu* forest. The plants rustle as if scared of what lurks within them, not wanting to hide what or *who* but having been forced to.

I know before I see it.

I feel who will exit that forest in the marrow of my bones.

But what I don't expect, never would have expected, is who she holds in her grasp.

"Mom?" I call before noting she has Dad in her clutches as well. They both scream against the gags placed in their mouths, and the only thing that gives me a fraction of comfort is the bubble of air around each of their heads. Their legs, wrists, mouths, and even around their upper arms are tightly bound in rope.

"What the hell do you want with them—with me?" I scream, tears exploding from my eyes as my voice falters. Nallac stiffens beside me, his arms reaching instantly for the trident at his back as Flynn does the same.

"So many questions," Daevia says with a smug smile. "Turn over Nallac, Kaileah, and yourself, and I *might* let these two live." She giggles in a way that makes my skin crawl. "Probably not, though. I much prefer the long game."

"NO!" I yell, Nallac holding me back as I try to fling myself at her. "Let me go!" I cry, turning to face him. Nallac's face is grim and knowing, and my stomach drops. The daggers she holds at each of their throats...she won't waste a second before slitting them, with or without our cooperation.

Dad is the first to get the thick cloth covering out of his mouth. Daevia rolls her eyes but lets him speak.

"My baby girl," he says, tears filling his eyes. "We knew this would happen. We knew for a long time. We knew since the day we took you in, but you have been worth it. Every single second I have spent as your father has been worth it." His voice catches as he takes me in. I shake violently as I realize what he is implying.

"You knew?" I ask, nearly a shriek, while Nallac continues to hold me back with a force that will leave bruises. Mom is able to shake off the cloth next.

"Vera, darling," she says, pure love in her eyes and not a hint of fear. "I love you more than you will ever know. I love you more than a million lifetimes would allow me to express. I would have done *anything* for you, and if dying is what I must do to keep you safe, then so be it. But promise me one thing." Only a single tear falls down her face, and her every word is proud and strong. She lifts her head, exposing her neck to Daevia's blade in a way that says: *I do not fear you, and I do not fear death.* "Live for me, Vera. Promise that you'll live for me."

"I will. I love you. I love you both so much," I mumble, the words barely more than a whisper as my voice breaks on each syllable.

"That's enough. I'm growing sick of your incessant chatter," Daevia says as I freeze, my eyes unblinking.

All I can remember is the blood. The water is soaked with it, soaked in the blood of the two people I love more than anything —soaked in the blood of my parents.

My throat aches from the screaming. I cannot stop.

I see them, Dad's eyes wide with terror as his life leaves them. I see Mom never dropping her loving smile and proud eyes until the life leaves hers, too. It is all a blur.

The world moves in slow motion as Flynn flings his trident faster than I can catch a breath, and it crashes into her impenetrable shield of majick. I throw out everything I have, every ounce of power, in a wave of uncontrolled energy.

It's wild and free, and in such a state, it does nothing. It wraps around her shield like crimson vines of death, but it does nothing.

Nothing.

Nothing can stop it.

Nothing can bring them back.

Dead. Dead. Dead.

They are dead. My parents. My very soul. All dead.

I scream until I feel my mind go black, and I hope I, too, have died.

I don't know how long it has been since I woke up. It could be days, weeks, or months; I don't care what the answer is. I stare at the ceiling of the room I had grown to love, with the beautiful stained glass glittering in every color I can imagine.

This is it, I think—the moment Astryx had told me would come.

The death of someone I loved.

I don't move, not an inch, as I feel my body give way to a sob that shakes through me, rattling my bones.

I don't know if I am screaming.

I don't know if I have any voice left at all.

Dead. The word has lost all meaning. It feels like a blank word on my tongue.

Was it a threat? A promise? A gift? A punishment?

No definition sticks. It just is. It is the end—my parents' end —but it isn't mine. It isn't Nallac's, Flynn's, Kaileah's, Zuira's, Korah's, or anyone else's. It was only them—only my parents.

The thought comforts me, perhaps more than it should.

I still have them, and I realize then that Kaileah and Nallac have been wrapped around my shaking frame. The two of them never left my side as they held me in a way I needed to be held. I wish I could thank them, but as I feel my eyes nearly swollen shut and my vision hazy, I know that no sounds will come out if I try.

Their eyes are deeply sunken, with purple bags decorating each of their faces, and I know I must have been screaming, even in my sleep.

"Vera?" Nallac's voice is distant, like from a foreign land. I try to meet his eyes. Every movement is a struggle. Every muscle is sore.

I can't acknowledge him with words because I have none left.

"Your parents are being kept in a preserving space, and we waited for you to wake before doing anything. If you'd like, we'd love to give them a ceremonial Adleian burial," Kaileah says, smoothing the hair away from my face. I see how tenderly she eyes me.

As I feel her motherly love and return it, my heart is ripped to shreds. Is it wrong to love her like this? Is it wrong to see her, too, as my mother when the woman who raised me died before my eyes?

Not died. She was murdered—they both were.

All I can do is nod. I have no idea what they have in mind, but with the love I see in her eyes, I know it will be special. There is nothing left for me on land, I realize. There is nothing left to come home to, so I know having them with me, in essence, is what I want—*what I need.*

The two of them help me from the bed, where Kaileah delicately ties my hair behind my head in a bun. She helps me into a modest, form-fitting black dress of mourning. Nallac says I look beautiful, wiping a tear from my eye.

I know it is a lie, but I don't care.

We make our way to a spot with a golden glow all the way from the ocean's depths.

I can feel the Earth's heartbeat.

I feel the way the water around us seems to shake, like the world is taking deep breaths. Nallac holds my mother, and Flynn holds my father, their necks healed to shield me from the sight.

I appreciate the effort, although I can't tell Nallac. My voice still fails me.

They lower their bodies into the glow, and Kaileah speaks as Nallac takes my hand.

"We stand here to honor the death of those before us, Emilia and Nathaniel Caddel. As we return their mortal vessels to Kayiah, we ask you to take their bodies and allow their souls to roam the world, free from the burdens of mortality." Kaileah's *maemōjik* casts the area in the glow of love.

I feel my chest lighten, the weight of their deaths loosening.

"Goodbye, Mom and Dad," I whisper under my breath, the first words since their death. Nallac grips my hand tighter in his own, running his other across my arm. "Let them be at peace," Kaileah continues, and I bow my head, eyes closed. "*Malōik*. Thank you for raising and caring for my daughter better than I ever could have hoped," she finishes, and I feel my eyes welling again with tears.

I remember reading that word in my translation book and found it beautiful.

It is the most special way to say goodbye, I love you, and my mother has given it to two people she has never met, all because of me. I smile, perhaps the only time I will for a long while and realize something.

This moment is not what breaks me. This moment is not what weakens me and loses us this war. They died so that I could live. Their deaths were for *all of us* to live.

And that's exactly what I'll do.

As I watch their bodies drift into that golden glow, I smile, feeling a sense of happiness. Perhaps it is because they are now truly free of all pain and suffering or because this moment is beautiful.

But for my parents...I will fight.

But most of all, I will live.

.*☆ GLOSSARY ☆*.

PLANTS

DEINIWEED: (*DEN-E-WEED*) An herb that can be used fresh to make teas or be dried to use as a tonic. Fresh deiniweed tea helps ease anxiety and promote immune health. Dried deiniweed can be ingested by itself or used as seasoning on food to ease fatigue.

LA'MINŌLU: (*LA-MEN-OH-LU*) A sea plant that has sentient qualities. It looks like kelp with bioluminescence that gives it a slight blue glow. It can help protect and aid creatures that need to hide. It can also be cooked and eaten, and it has a naturally sweet taste.

CREATURES

HIPPOCAMPUS: (*HIP-PO-CAM-PUS*) A sea creature that is part horse. They are extremely protective of their owners and have a strong moral compass, along with being the most intelligent sea creatures. They can communicate telepathically with other hippocampi, and humans can hear the telepathic speech if they will lose a loved one's life in a tragic way. They are common but rarely found in the wild.

LETIFERNA: (LET-EH-FERN-AH) A sea creature that is extremely large but usually undetectable as it can camouflage from the naked eye and radar. They're white with bright blue glowing eyes. They resemble both dragons and snakes because of their draconic wings and serpentine body. They can manipulate water and are extremely agile. They do not listen to a master, so most kingdoms prefer to avoid them. The Celestian people are the only group that they respect and obey occasionally. They are not particularly good or evil.

PETTIEL: (PET-TEE-EL) A sea creature slightly larger than a hand. They are in charge of bringing letters back and forth to all the kingdoms, and they can travel extremely fast. They are too small to bring packages, so they are only used to send letters. Some people keep them as pets, but they're mainly used for correspondence. They understand commands, names, and locations but not everyday conversation.

VULPANIS: (VUL-PAN-IS) They're about the size of a Great Dane, and they are kept in the Koifinn Clan to assist with harvesting crops. They're very common and easy to train. They have a large, fluffy prehensile tail which allows them to pick crops with increased proficiency.

HOLIDAYS

MOŌNDAEN: (MOON-DANE) A monthly celebration during every full moon when a witch's majick is strengthened, and the gods are most likely to listen. It is most commonly celebrated in Adlei but can be found anywhere.

GODS

ADNITIS: (AD-NIE-TIS) God of War and Death. He is a god that loves to tempt his subjects to the evil ways of the world. He rewards those who give in to their immoral ways by giving them more power at the price of their humanity. He feeds on the souls of righteous citizens who fall. Adnitis and Kayiah are enemies.

ELVIRA: (EL-VEAR-AH) Demigod of Creation. She is the daughter of Naejik who perished after consuming too much power from her mother. She was the first demigod ever born.

KAYIAH: (KAI-YAY-AH) Goddess of the Land and Sea / Mother Nature. She is by far the kindest of all the gods and goddesses, and she is in charge of all life, plant, human, and mer. A soul is taken from her when they are born and returned when they die. She does not treat her subjects differently based on any superficial factors, such as status, race, or gender. She is a very moral goddess and rewards those who do good in her name or protect her creations.

LUCIUS: (LU-CEE-US) God of Luck. He is in charge of all things regarding fortune, luck, and karma. He is meant to keep the world in balance, never allowing one individual to have too much of anything without consequence. However, he is not the most attentive god and allows some to go unchecked.

NAEJIK: (NAY-J-ICK) Queen of the Gods / Goddess of Majick. She is the main goddess that is prayed to, especially when one feels their prayers have not been answered. She is in charge of balance among both the gods and mortals, and she is thought of as being wise and true. Her name is the basis of 'Your Majesty' as mortal queens and kings share a small fraction of her power and influence. It has been theorized that she only bothers with the whims of nobility due to the vast amount of prayers in her name.

PLACES

GEYNIVAL: (GEN-E-VALL) A mixed-race city on the outskirts of the Koifinn Clan. However, they are not affiliated with any kingdom or clan.

KAERIOUS: (CARE-E-US) A smaller city within the Adleian Kingdom that is the heart of the rebellion against the king.

MÓRIAN: (MORE-E-AN) The capital city of the Adleian Kingdom.

RIVIDYUN: (RIV-I-DONE) The capital city of the Angelik Clan.

ROYAN: (ROY-AN) The capital city of the Jellean Kingdom.

SHARI: (SHAR-E) The capital city of the Koifinn Clan.

TAELANI: (TAY-LAN-E) A place of safety, specifically for majickals.

WYNDERAN: (WIND-ER-AN) The old term for all civilizations combined.

ADLEIAN TRANSLATIONS

Note: All translations are in order of how they appear throughout the book.
Unlike the glossary, they are not in alphabetical order.

BEAÓN VAL LAUSIK: "Where are you?" with a sense of desperation.

KILEÓA DAEMÓRE, MÓI JI'AENRES, MÓI SIKAI, MI MEYUR: "I don't understand how you're here, how I can see you, how I can hold you."

HAENUR TI'DEÓRIN, SAENUIR MAU'JAUILÓRN. JAENÓRJIK TEKÓNAH NAEHIEMA, NÓ'LAIHMI KENJAEI. CÓUR SAERAIH, TEKÓNAH, NO'FRIUNDA YAEURÓI: A lullaby Kaileah wrote to soothe Vera. "No matter the time we go, my love for you will only grow. You're safe with me, my dear. I'll keep you close for all your years. Come, my princess, to me now. You'll be safe, oh, don't you frown."

GRÓPAETÓN: A way to describe a witch as 'practicing earth or land magic.' Adding an 'ah' to the end changes the meaning to 'living in forests and harnessing its energy.'

FAE NAEJIKÓN: "Your Majesty."

Sōurik: A slur for sirens. Taken from the term for slave, *rika*, and combined with the term for lesser species, *sōujik*.

Hei'jaek: A profanity to express surprise and discomfort.

T'eiskaeh: "Shadow servant" or 'the shadow.'

Saeraih: A way to address feminine royalty, specifically the firstborn heir to the throne. Basically 'crown princess.'

Aeyla: A form of Adleian currency equivalent to $2.00 USD. It is a large coin made of mainly gold and other materials with a carved portrait of the blood-ruler's spouse.

Frondi: A formal 'hello.' A way to greet a superior or show respect.

Joi'aen: A profanity used to imply something is a lie or stupid.

Draeōm: A way to say that someone is 'strange' or 'peculiar.' Adding an 'ah' changes the meaning to 'extremely odd.'

Cunjitōllies: A hibiscus-shaped flower that is lavender in color with a white center and smells of cinnamon but sweeter. The veins of the flower glow.

Daendidukes: A lily-shaped flower that is white with a blue center that smells of citrus and vanilla. The veins of the flower glow.

RAEKAIH: A sergeant that leads about four soldiers. The smallest element in the Adleian military.

REYBAMICHT'KA: Reybamicht is the term for swordfish and adding 'ka' implies it has been cooked and prepared in some way.

NAE'YUN: A form of Adleian currency equivalent to $5.00 USD that is a blue semi-translucent bendable plastic with the name of the current royal family, a portrait of the blood-ruler, small designs illustrating the culture, and the amount of money at the top.

YUNDIJKON: A form of Adleian currency equivalent to 50¢ USD. Ten yundijkons make up one nae'yun. The coin is larger than a quarter and made of a mixture of steel and silver with the current queen's favorite flower engraved.

YUNE: "On."

DEY: "Off."

FRAEDA: An informal 'hello.' A way to greet an acquaintance or friend.

MY NŌMANI XAEDA. TEJS?: "My name is Xaeda. What's yours?"

KILEŌA DAEMŌRE: "I don't understand."

MALŌIK: A very special way to say "goodbye, I love you." It is most commonly used by guards leaving their families for what could be their last time but can be used in many contexts.

I can feel the Earth's heartbeat.

I feel the way the water around us seems to shake, like the world is taking deep breaths. Nallac holds my mother, and Flynn holds my father, their necks healed to shield me from the sight.

I appreciate the effort, although I can't tell Nallac. My voice still fails me.

They lower their bodies into the glow, and Kaileah speaks as Nallac takes my hand.

"We stand here to honor the death of those before us, Emilia and Nathaniel Caddel. As we return their mortal vessels to Kayiah, we ask you to take their bodies and allow their souls to roam the world, free from the burdens of mortality." Kaileah's *maemōjik* casts the area in the glow of love.

I feel my chest lighten, the weight of their deaths loosening.

"Goodbye, Mom and Dad," I whisper under my breath, the first words since their death. Nallac grips my hand tighter in his own, running his other across my arm. "Let them be at peace," Kaileah continues, and I bow my head, eyes closed. "*Malōik.* Thank you for raising and caring for my daughter better than I ever could have hoped," she finishes, and I feel my eyes welling again with tears.

I remember reading that word in my translation book and found it beautiful.

It is the most special way to say goodbye, I love you, and my mother has given it to two people she has never met, all because of me. I smile, perhaps the only time I will for a long while and realize something.

This moment is not what breaks me. This moment is not what weakens me and loses us this war. They died so that I could live. Their deaths were for *all of us* to live.

And that's exactly what I'll do.

As I watch their bodies drift into that golden glow, I smile, feeling a sense of happiness. Perhaps it is because they are now truly free of all pain and suffering or because this moment is beautiful.

But for my parents...I will fight.

But most of all, I will live.

.* ⭐ GLOSSARY ⭐ *.

PLANTS

DEINIWEED: (DEN-E-WEED) An herb that can be used fresh to make teas or be dried to use as a tonic. Fresh deiniweed tea helps ease anxiety and promote immune health. Dried deiniweed can be ingested by itself or used as seasoning on food to ease fatigue.

LA'MINŌLU: (LA-MEN-OH-LU) A sea plant that has sentient qualities. It looks like kelp with bioluminescence that gives it a slight blue glow. It can help protect and aid creatures that need to hide. It can also be cooked and eaten, and it has a naturally sweet taste.

CREATURES

HIPPOCAMPUS: (HIP-PO-CAM-PUS) A sea creature that is part horse. They are extremely protective of their owners and have a strong moral compass, along with being the most intelligent sea creatures. They can communicate telepathically with other hippocampi, and humans can hear the telepathic speech if they will lose a loved one's life in a tragic way. They are common but rarely found in the wild.

LETIFERNA: (*LET-EH-FERN-AH*) A sea creature that is extremely large but usually undetectable as it can camouflage from the naked eye and radar. They're white with bright blue glowing eyes. They resemble both dragons and snakes because of their draconic wings and serpentine body. They can manipulate water and are extremely agile. They do not listen to a master, so most kingdoms prefer to avoid them. The Celestian people are the only group that they respect and obey occasionally. They are not particularly good or evil.

PETTIEL: (*PET-TEE-EL*) A sea creature slightly larger than a hand. They are in charge of bringing letters back and forth to all the kingdoms, and they can travel extremely fast. They are too small to bring packages, so they are only used to send letters. Some people keep them as pets, but they're mainly used for correspondence. They understand commands, names, and locations but not everyday conversation.

VULPANIS: (*VUL-PAN-IS*) They're about the size of a Great Dane, and they are kept in the Koifinn Clan to assist with harvesting crops. They're very common and easy to train. They have a large, fluffy prehensile tail which allows them to pick crops with increased proficiency.

HOLIDAYS

MOŌNDAEN: (*MOON-DANE*) A monthly celebration during every full moon when a witch's majick is strengthened, and the gods are most likely to listen. It is most commonly celebrated in Adlei but can be found anywhere.

GODS

ADNITIS: (*AD-NIE-TIS*) God of War and Death. He is a god that loves to tempt his subjects to the evil ways of the world. He rewards those who give in to their immoral ways by giving them more power at the price of their humanity. He feeds on the souls of righteous citizens who fall. Adnitis and Kayiah are enemies.

ELVIRA: (*EL-VEAR-AH*) Demigod of Creation. She is the daughter of Naejik who perished after consuming too much power from her mother. She was the first demigod ever born.

KAYIAH: (*KAI-YAY-AH*) Goddess of the Land and Sea / Mother Nature. She is by far the kindest of all the gods and goddesses, and she is in charge of all life, plant, human, and mer. A soul is taken from her when they are born and returned when they die. She does not treat her subjects differently based on any superficial factors, such as status, race, or gender. She is a very moral goddess and rewards those who do good in her name or protect her creations.

LUCIUS: (*LU-CEE-US*) God of Luck. He is in charge of all things regarding fortune, luck, and karma. He is meant to keep the world in balance, never allowing one individual to have too much of anything without consequence. However, he is not the most attentive god and allows some to go unchecked.

NAEJIK: (*NAY-J-ICK*) Queen of the Gods / Goddess of Majick. She is the main goddess that is prayed to, especially when one feels their prayers have not been answered. She is in charge of balance among both the gods and mortals, and she is thought of as being wise and true. Her name is the basis of 'Your Majesty' as mortal queens and kings share a small fraction of her power and influence. It has been theorized that she only bothers with the whims of nobility due to the vast amount of prayers in her name.

PLACES

GEYNIVAL: (GEN-E-VALL) A mixed-race city on the outskirts of the Koifinn Clan. However, they are not affiliated with any kingdom or clan.

KAERIOUS: (CARE-E-US) A smaller city within the Adleian Kingdom that is the heart of the rebellion against the king.

MÖRIAN: (MORE-E-AN) The capital city of the Adleian Kingdom.

RIVIDYUN: (RIV-I-DONE) The capital city of the Angelik Clan.

ROYAN: (ROY-AN) The capital city of the Jellean Kingdom.

SHARI: (SHAR-E) The capital city of the Koifinn Clan.

TAELANI: (TAY-LAN-E) A place of safety, specifically for majickals.

WYNDERAN: (WIND-ER-AN) The old term for all civilizations combined.

ADLEIAN TRANSLATIONS

**Note: All translations are in order of how they appear throughout the book.
Unlike the glossary, they are not in alphabetical order.**

BEAÕN VAL LAUSIK: "Where are you?" with a sense of desperation.

KILEÕA DAEMÕRE, MÕI JI'AENRES, MÕI SIKAI, MI MEYUR: "I don't understand how you're here, how I can see you, how I can hold you."

HAENUR TI'DEÕRIN, SAENUIR MAU'JAUILÕRN. JAENÕRJIK TEKÕNAH NAEHIEMA, NÕ'LAIHMI KENJAEI. CÕUR SAERAIH, TEKÕNAH, NO'FRIUNDA YAEURÕI: A lullaby Kaileah wrote to soothe Vera. "No matter the time we go, my love for you will only grow. You're safe with me, my dear. I'll keep you close for all your years. Come, my princess, to me now. You'll be safe, oh, don't you frown."

GRÕPAETÕN: A way to describe a witch as 'practicing earth or land magic.' Adding an 'ah' to the end changes the meaning to 'living in forests and harnessing its energy.'

FAE NAEJIKÕN: "Your Majesty."

Sōurik: A slur for sirens. Taken from the term for slave, *rika,* and combined with the term for lesser species, *sōujik.*

Hei'jaek: A profanity to express surprise and discomfort.

T'eiskaeh: "Shadow servant" or 'the shadow.'

Saeraih: A way to address feminine royalty, specifically the firstborn heir to the throne. Basically 'crown princess.'

Aeyla: A form of Adleian currency equivalent to $2.00 USD. It is a large coin made of mainly gold and other materials with a carved portrait of the blood-ruler's spouse.

Frōndi: A formal 'hello.' A way to greet a superior or show respect.

Jōi'aen: A profanity used to imply something is a lie or stupid.

Draeōm: A way to say that someone is 'strange' or 'peculiar.' Adding an 'ah' changes the meaning to 'extremely odd.'

Cunjitōllies: A hibiscus-shaped flower that is lavender in color with a white center and smells of cinnamon but sweeter. The veins of the flower glow.

Daendidukes: A lily-shaped flower that is white with a blue center that smells of citrus and vanilla. The veins of the flower glow.

RAEKAIH: A sergeant that leads about four soldiers. The smallest element in the Adleian military.

REYBAMICHT'KA: Reybamicht is the term for swordfish and adding 'ka' implies it has been cooked and prepared in some way.

NAE'YUN: A form of Adleian currency equivalent to $5.00 USD that is a blue semi-translucent bendable plastic with the name of the current royal family, a portrait of the blood-ruler, small designs illustrating the culture, and the amount of money at the top.

YUNDIJKON: A form of Adleian currency equivalent to 50¢ USD. Ten yundijkons make up one nae'yun. The coin is larger than a quarter and made of a mixture of steel and silver with the current queen's favorite flower engraved.

YUNE: "On."

DEY: "Off."

FRAEDA: An informal 'hello.' A way to greet an acquaintance or friend.

MY NŌMANI XAEDA. TEJS?: "My name is Xaeda. What's yours?"

KILEŌA DAEMŌRE: "I don't understand."

MALŌIK: A very special way to say "goodbye, I love you." It is most commonly used by guards leaving their families for what could be their last time but can be used in many contexts.

KEFIAN TRANSLATIONS

Tei, towandi e halan lu fevun?: "Hello, what can I help you find today?"

Feina: A profanity used to express shock.

Dei o thalen?: "Who is that?"

Uesi Cengleso: "Use Common."

Dei o lu, rouinala?: "Who are you, little girl?"

Tuy oi peika cengleso, mota: "They only speak Common, Mother."

O nedi trenlata?: "Or do you need me to translate?"

Landling: A slang term for humans.

E penkai'n e waun nu penka: "I have said all I wanted to say."

Espenadai: Swordfish.

Lu a beutia: "You are beautiful."

Seisa carzondies, pe'il devor: "Six carrots, please."

Quatre fesos, doucen seils: "Four fesos, twelve seils."

Teinta lu: "Thank you."

Feso: A form of Koifinn currency equivalent to $1.00 USD that is a green semi-translucent bendable plastic with a koi fish in the center, with various crops sold by the clan growing from the bottom and the amount of money listed at the top.

Seils: A form of Koifinn currency equivalent to 25¢ USD. Four *seils* make up one *feso*. The coin is the size of a quarter and is made of a mixture of copper and nickel with the national crop of wheat engraved.

SAANIEN TRANSLATIONS

ASHERAH? O CUANN KELFIA YIRENKA ALEVEIH!: "Asherah? I can't believe you're really alive!"

SAUNNIAZUN!: A string of profanities.

ŁI'DRĒV'ÖN TRANSLATIONS

LÉ'REÖAN AEŁUNTŪNDA: "A Love That Rivals Darkness"

REŁADRAÖN'DĒ PĒNFUTREN?: "How's this, pretty boy?"

CŪ'NERÖN ŁI'UNDRA'SËNDRŌN?: "Can you understand me?"

CŪ'NERÖN UNDRA'SËNDRŌI RĒYUSTRUŌN?: "Can you understand what I'm saying?"

CELESTIAN TRANSLATIONS

SA'I NŌE MAN 'NEJ: A phrase that is used to greet or attempt to scare away potential intruders. It is usually used by guards. It can mean "what do you want?", "who goes there?", or "state your business."

NŌ'E LYS MAU'DI SE LEA'JA: "We wish to speak to your leader."

NA'JUN: "I cannot be broken."

ACKNOWLEDGMENTS

It all feels so surreal to have finished my first book. Now, I'm writing my acknowledgments—how crazy! So many people in my life have helped me in ways both seen and unseen, and I am beyond happy to have a place to thank each and every one of them.

Addison Douglas, my childhood best friend, has a very special place in my heart because of her undescribable support in creating some characters, editing, being an ear to listen to me talk, thinking of witty dialogue, and designing some elements. She has been there since the beginning and has seen the highs and lows of my process, never faltering in her encouragement to push me to finish it. For that and everything else, I thank you. Even our beloved Flynn was created through a road trip to Natchitoches, where I let her create her perfect male character. This was before we read ACOTAR, and needless to say, once she met Cassian, she fell in love. Since then, I have always gone to her when I finish Flynn's dialogue to make sure it lives up to everything we wanted, and she does not hesitate to give her advice on his snarky responses.

My boyfriend, Zack Beach, helped me in many ways as well, although coming into my life toward the middle of my writing. From aiding in creating the Vulpanis and Umbra mori (to be revealed in book two), to creating Rionach and some magic weapons, he has been a huge creative help to bounce ideas off of and to speak about my story for hours to. He is why I fell in love with Dungeons and Dragons, which has also impacted my writing and creativity. I can't count how many times I have discussed the looks of the gods and goddesses and how the story unfolds without a hint of annoyance or boredom. Thank you for it all; I love you.

To my mom, I thank you for always giving me the best support you could (even though you've never been a big reader, haha). I will forever think of how much you enjoyed my work and how proud you are of me. From helping me with finances to being a physical support, you are a part of what made this book a reality. I love you.

To my almost stepdad, Joe, I thank you for all the support even though I am not your daughter and you have no idea what this story is about. Although, I'm sure my mom will make you read it eventually. I could not have moved forward with this journey without your unfaltering support, from buying Vellum and Dabble to helping me purchase countless other small necessities.

My editor, Eleanor Smith, thank you for taking on my story and helping me prepare it for publication. I always went back and forth on whether I could or could not afford an editor and if it would be worth it, but your contributions have made me have no regrets about my decision. I can't wait to work with you on my next one!

To the Bookstagram community, where I met so many new friends, thank you for supporting me throughout the process! I can't wait to share this with you all!

And finally, to my wonderful readers, thank you for giving my story a chance. I cannot thank you enough or express how happy you have seen my book and purchased a copy for yourself. All I can hope is that I have impacted you and you will continue this journey with me.

I love you all!

. ° .*. ⋆ .*. ° .
+ + + +

.* ☆ ABOUT THE AUTHOR ☆ *.

When Melina M. Givens isn't writing her latest novel or daydreaming about her other works in progress, she is probably found drinking a far too sweet coffee in a café. Melina is writing her books part-time while studying English with a concentration in Creative Writing at Louisiana State University. She has loved writing for as long as she can remember.

At five years old, she would sit at the computer in her mom's dentist's office, creating any story she could think of after teaching herself to type. Anything creative has always sparked her interest, from nails and digital art to jewelry making and painting; she has tried it all.

instagram.com/melinamgivens
tiktok.com/@melinamgivens